PLOWED FIELDS
<u>TRILOGY EDITION</u>

BOOK TWO

PLOWED FIELDS
TRILOGY EDITION

BOOK TWO

ANGELS SING, THE GARDEN, FAITH AND GRACE AND THE FIRE

JIM BARBER

Copyright © 2019 by Jim Barber

First Printing: 2019

Published by Morgan Bay Books™

Library of Congress Control Number 2019901846

ISBN 978-1-7327845-5-0

ISBN 978-1-7327845-6-7 (Ebook)

Printed in the United States of America

Cover design by Jane Hill

Cover photo by Krivosheev Vitaly

Author photo by Brandi Williams

Morgan Bay Books
432 Princeton Way
Suite 101
Lawrenceville, GA 30044
www.plowedfields.com
www.jimbarber.me

ACKNOWLEDGMENTS

I've always loved to write, but writing a novel was never one of my big goals in life. And then, on a beautiful spring day when I was traveling between two small towns in middle Georgia as a young newspaper reporter in 1985, the idea for *Plowed Fields* came fully alive to me, and I felt compelled to write the story. I wanted to preserve a time and place that had shaped my life and positioned me to achieve my dreams. So, first, I must acknowledge my family, friends and many others whose presence influenced my growing-up years.

Specifically, I credit my parents—my daddy Elmo who died in 1991 and my mama Marie who remains eternally young; my sister Caye Robinson and brother-in-law Charles Robinson, who really lived the era I wrote about; my grandmothers Flossie Lee Willis Barber and Carrie Elizabeth Weaver Baker who loved unconditionally and worked as hard as anyone I've ever known; my uncles Jake Baker and Bug Baker who managed to raise crops and earn livings—though Lord knows how—with help from a bunch of young'uns like me and my cousins, Greg, Don and Chipp Griner, and Mike and Regina Baker; my uncles Virgil Barber (a World War II hero) and LA Barber, who shared their knowledge of the old days and farming before my time; my cousin Faith Barber Noles; one of my oldest friends, Jerry Moore, with whom I shared the only real experience recorded in this book; and the best friend ever, Greg Harrell. I also must pay homage to the amazing teachers at West Berrien Elementary School and Berrien High School—particularly Wanda Vickers, Gail Danforth, Linda Davis Brooks and Calva Gill McDaniel—who gave me far more than I gave them through my efforts in the classroom. And to the late S.T. and Clarice Hamilton, who gave me my first newspaper job at *The Berrien Press*.

I populated this book with names and places near and dear to my heart, but the characters are completely fictional. The Taylor family may be villains in this story, but the real Taylors are lifelong family friends and nothing like their namesakes in this book. Not to mention some of the most amazing gospel singers God ever put on this earth!

It is no easy task to turn an idea into a book, and many people read my manuscript, offered ideas and encouragement, and helped make *Plowed Fields* a reality through their criticism, proofing and insights into the publishing industry. In alphabetical order, they were Betty Bell,

Becky Blalock, Janice Daugharty, Sam Heys, Jane Hill, Maggie Johnsen, Joey Ledford, Cindy Theiler and Emelyne Williams. In addition, I would be remiss not to mention the late Jim Kilgo and Conrad Fink, two extraordinary professors at the University of Georgia who gave me confidence to believe in my talent; and the late Duane Riner, press secretary for Georgia Governor George Busbee and an *Atlanta Journal-Constitution* editor. Duane once gave me a byline above the masthead in the AJC, but more importantly, he believed in me from the beginning and proved to be an extraordinary mentor and more. Rarely a day passes when I do not recall his influence and I hope I give back a small measure of what he gave me.

No doubt, I have overlooked someone worthy of mentioning, so to all who helped make this dream a reality, I offer my sincere thanks and gratitude.

PRAISE FOR PLOWED FIELDS

"Not since Larry McMurtry's *Lonesome Dove* have I read such a solid, unembellished, detail-rich portrayal of rural life lived out in fiction. In fact, while reading *Plowed Fields*, it seemed I was watching an intriguing TV miniseries. *Plowed Fields* is all that a family saga should be—natural, endearing, superbly written and enchanting. Add to that fresh and exact! The characters come alive under Jim Barber's control. Jim Barber is a master storyteller; so by definition, that makes *Plowed Fields* a masterpiece. Readers are in for a glad experience."

— Janice Daugharty, author of *Earl in the Yellow Shirt*, nominated for the Pulitzer Prize

"If Pat Conroy had been raised on a tobacco farm in South Georgia, this is the novel he would have written. *Plowed Fields* is a powerful story about a time in history that left more scars than we care to remember. With his rich detail of farm life, complex characters and sure sense of storytelling, Jim Barber has captured a time and place in Americana with lyrical precision and stunning beauty. Amid the darkness and evil, he has infused this story with warmth, heart and hope as promising as a newly plowed field."

— Becky Blalock, author of *Dare*

"Set in the recent past this is the perfect novel for our time of national uncertainty, cynicism and corruption of values emanating from the very top. In nine episodes, *Plowed Fields* gives us the turbulent 1960s as lived in Georgia by the Baker family. Their haunting saga of desire and responsibility—of revolution and resolution—has a great deal to say to us today. In the words of the aphorism often attributed to Mark Twain, 'History doesn't repeat itself, but it often rhymes.'"

— Alan Axelrod, author of
The Gilded Age, 1876-1912: Overture to the American Century and
How America Won World War I

PRAISE FOR PLOWED FIELDS

"*Plowed Fields* explores the hard choices we make, the love we give and the joy, sorrow and hope that shape our lives. It is a deeply moving story of "ordinary people" navigating through extraordinary times. Ultimately, *Plowed Fields* paints a portrait of faith lost and found. Joe Baker and his family will resonate with you long after the last page is read. I hope there's a sequel."

— Sam Heys, author of *The Winecoff Fire* and *Big Bets*

"Imagine a family like TV's The Waltons living and loving on a tobacco farm in South Georgia during the 1960s, and you will have a strong sense of *Plowed Fields*. The story certainly has a wholesome quality—some might even say sentimental—but it's also 'glazed with the sorrow of a devastating truth.' Jim Barber has captured a time and place with exquisite detail and superb storytelling. *Plowed Fields* will break your heart, but it's the warmth and tenderness of the people and the story that will stay with you."

— Emelyne Williams, editor of *Atlanta Women Speak*

"Jim Barber's extraordinary *Plowed Fields* is reminiscent of Laura Ingalls Wilder's masterpiece series of Little House books. Barber's canvas is hardscrabble Cookville, Georgia, of 1960 rather than Ingalls Wilder's 1870s Minnesota. And rather than focus on a daughter, *Plowed Fields* centers on Joe Baker, the oldest of Matt and Caroline Baker's six children. The family saga tracks the Bakers over a tumultuous decade in which they weather struggles with drought, fire, a family feud, loss of faith, death and the cultural changes shaking the rural South of the civil rights era. Barber is an exciting new voice who defines family and coming of age with an engaging style."

— Joey Ledford, author of *Speed Trap* and *Elkmont: The Smoky Mountain Massacre*

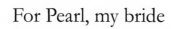

For Pearl, my bride

PLOWED FIELDS
TRILOGY EDITION

BOOK TWO

Ordinary routines dominated their lives, yet the seemingly endless repetition remained fresh, each sunrise bringing a new twist and variation to the sameness. A bucolic cadence distinguished the days, beginning with the crowing of a single rooster, seasoned by the aroma of good Southern cooking and ending with the natural light of a fading horizon. Tranquil nights followed the eventide, spent watching the phenomenon that was television or quietly engaged in a leisurely pursuit of relaxation. It was not serene. Rarely are large households where the living is enjoyed.

There existed forty-five relationships among the ten members of the household, each an enclave of private and shared moments. Each member was the other's best cheerleader and, on occasion, an archrival as well. The best and worst of their ancestors had fused and concocted rare breeds, people remarkable in every nuance of simplicity or complexity. They understood love, responsibility and thanksgiving. They were a family in the truest sense of the word, tied by blood and the struggle of enduring.

The family's life was a blend of rituals and feats of epic proportions, a mix of precious elixir and steady servings of sustaining fortitude. Rather than simply mark time, they filled the space between the tiny and seemingly insignificant points on the ruler of life with things of lasting value. Thus, the essence of the family was found in the details. But it was random moments of forced confrontation—between soul and conscience, desire and will, want and need—that made them aware of the ruler and provided a measure of the journey.

ANGELS SING

1963

CHAPTER 1

"DAMN!"

Summer was on a warpath on this last afternoon of 1962, battling the angst of youth and forced domesticity. New Year's Eve had been uneventful thus far on the Baker place, especially for Summer, who heretofore had washed windows, ironed clothes, vacuumed floors and presently was polishing furniture in her younger brothers' room. It was unfair the twelve-year-old girl had told Joe a moment ago in his room next door to John and Luke's.

"I could just scream," Summer railed even as Joe gave her a reprieve on orders from their mother to make his bed. "The men around here never have to lift a finger in this house. Y'all are doing exactly what you want to do today, and I'm stuck cleanen up after you. I'm tellen you, it ain't right."

"Do you hear me, Joe?" she yelled a moment later when he failed to acknowledge her tirade. "It ain't right."

Glancing up from his desk where he was writing an essay—a holiday homework assignment in senior English—Joe shot his sister a disinterested look. "I heard you, all right. Listen, Summer, I'm busy here, and I told you not to worry about my bed. What more do you want?"

His sister bristled, hands flying to her hips in outrage as Joe's casual dismissal of her tirade became apparent. A quick retort appeared on the edge of her tongue, then disappeared. "I could still scream," she muttered before leaving his room.

Instead of screaming, Summer apparently had decided to utter every profanity in her vocabulary. Listening to his sister's ranting, Joe smiled and sympathized with her plight. In a few years, she would learn to control these outbursts, but now the desire to vent her anger blotted out twelve years of training in good manners and responsibility.

"Damn!" Summer growled for the fourth time and loudly enough that Joe thought it wise to advise his sister against foolhardy conduct.

"Damn!" she said again, even as Joe leaned back in his chair and saw her admiring the shine on the fireplace mantle in John and Luke's room.

"WHAT did you say, young lady?" Rachel said unexpectedly, sternly.

The question rang with accusation and startled Summer. Gaping, she withered under the glaring eyes of their grandmother and started to apologize. Something stopped her though. It might have been indignation, but Joe figured it was more a mixture of stubbornness, frustration and plain stupidity.

"I said damn, Granny, and I meant it," Summer said, her tone sassy, her expression defiant. "It's not fair that we have to stay inside and do this durned old housework, while the men around here have a good old time doen whatever the heck they please." She crossed her arms, then declared, "I resent it."

Rachel stepped fully into the room, coming into Joe's range of observation. He approximated her temper at a slow boil as she considered an appropriate response to this willful display of temper by her granddaughter.

Like the season for which she was named, Summer was strong-willed, feisty and unrelenting on occasion. Rachel was the same way. As Joe saw it, his oldest sister and grandmother were two different patterns cut from same bolt of cloth. They shared common interests, particularly sewing and needlework, but their perspectives contrasted as sharply as the difference between a summer shower and a hurricane. Fortunately, Summer and Rachel rarely butted heads, but when they did, their sameness and differences clashed like stripes and polka dots. Joe sensed such a fashion faux pas at hand.

"Fair or not, young lady, that's the way it is," Rachel admonished her granddaughter. "And you'd better get used to it cause you're a young woman and young women are responsible for keepen a clean house." She paused, no doubt, Joe figured, to let her good advice sink into Summer's hard head. "Now you finish up your dusten. Then go copy ten Bible verses, and I won't tell your Mama what you said. But between us, you should be ashamed of yourself, Summer."

Joe smiled, thinking his sister was getting off lucky for the transgression. He made up his mind to show Summer ten of the shorter verses in the Bible as he waited expectantly for her contrite acceptance of the punishment. The girl fooled him.

"Granny, I don't think I should have to write down any old Bible verses. I've got a right to be mad. And besides, Daddy says damn all the time. If you weren't so ignorant about the ways of the world, you'd probably damn all this housework, too. There's more to life than just housework, and I'm sick and tired of all this cooken, cleanen, ironen and sewen."

Summer regretted the words as soon as they spewed from her mouth. Joe saw the remorse in her expression, as surely as he saw disappointment flash in his grandmother's eyes. For a split second, Rachel and Summer were bewildered, torn by desire to make amends and conviction in their beliefs.

Joe considered intervening to restore the peace, but the sudden appearance of his mother in the doorway doomed the prospect before it fully evolved.

"Summer!"

Their mother swept into the room on a wave of carefully controlled anger, obviously appalled by the situation. "In this house, young lady," Caroline Baker exhorted her daughter, "you do not talk to anyone that way, especially your elders. Tell your grandmother you're sorry this very instant; then go to the kitchen and wait there until I decide an appropriate punishment."

"I'm sorry," Summer spat, her indignation rising to another level.

"Say it and mean it, Summer," Caroline ordered.

Summer stared at her mother, then at Rachel and back to Caroline. "Mama," she replied. "That's the best I can do right now."

His sister's insolence stunned Joe. Summer always spoke her mind, but she was never deliberately spiteful. Yet, in one fell swoop, she had committed treason against her grandmother and declared open rebellion on her mother. Joe settled back and waited for her impertinence to be quashed.

More and more these days, he found himself witness to the travails of his sisters and brothers as they plodded through rough spots in the road to becoming young men and women. He deemed such observations as a due of his birthright, an act of passage that signified his coming of age and heralded a season of coming-out parties for the long line of siblings who trailed him. Joe had traversed the path of adolescence, and the road ahead—while certain to contain a few rocky places—looked relatively smooth to him. For the moment, he was intrigued more by the idea of stepping aside as his brothers and sisters took their turns as Johnny-come-lately. He considered it an obligation and a pleasure.

In some imprecise way, his salad days had passed and Joe felt as if he were between seasons. But Summer, John, Carrie, Luke and Bonnie were chomping at their bits with impatience, and Joe looked forward to watching the performance from the shadows. That was another privilege of his birthright, a position that brought huge responsibility but endowed him with the unique perspective of having been there. Joe was young enough to sympathize with the fervency of his brothers and sisters, yet old enough to understand the wisdom of his parents and grandparents.

Indeed, when he thought about it, Joe enjoyed his domain as the oldest child. It was the perfect vista, affording him the distance of deep shadows while extending leeway around the edges, providing a jumping-off place, yet allowing him to come rushing in to the rescue at a moment's notice, of his own volition or at the beck and call of someone else.

He was on the verge of plundering this last thought with more thoroughness when Caroline abruptly ended her dressing-down of Summer.

"You've disappointed me, Summer, not to mention your shabby disrespect of your grandmother," Caroline said gravely. "Nevertheless, it's your decision to be satisfied with your feeble apology and if you are, so be it. I, however, am not satisfied. Go to the kitchen."

"Yes, ma'am," Summer answered, her comedown so low that Joe leaned back once more in his chair to observe the goings-on through the doorway.

"I don't know what gets into that girl sometimes," Caroline re-marked to Rachel when Summer had fled the room. This was not the first time Caroline had played mediatrix between her daughter and mother-in-law. She paused, expecting Rachel to give her version of the situation.

Instead, the older woman picked up the dust rag abandoned by Summer and used it to wipe away an invisible spot on the fireplace mantle.

"You two are so much alike that I guess there's always goen to be an occasional wrangle," Caroline prodded. "What started this one? Why was she so disrespectful?"

"Punish her for swearen, Caroline," Rachel said, looking her daughter-in-law in the eye. "But not for her insolence. It will pass, and Summer and I will work out our differences in due time."

Caroline considered the request for a moment, then nodded her agreement before casting her suspicions on Joe. "Son, did you hear your sister cursen?"

"She was haven a bad day," Joe suggested glibly.

"Well, that's no excuse!" Caroline retorted.

"No, it's not," Rachel agreed quickly. "And Joe, you should have told her so. You're a Christian, and you shouldn't condone such behavior."

Joe started to protest the rebuke, then changed his mind and smiled penitently. "You're right," he agreed. "Sorry, Mama. Sorry, Granny."

Seeing the two women sufficiently appeased, it occurred to Joe that while his sisters and brothers were coming into their own and taking center stage, he still had a few lessons to learn himself and would—of his own volition and heeding the beck and call of others—stay close in the wings as this drama unfolded. Joe shrugged his shoulders and told himself it was not a bad feeling at all to have such an important role.

CHAPTER 2

ON THE FIRST FRIDAY night of the new year, something happened that sent a wave of fear cresting through the Cookville community. Around midnight, Delia Turner, the wife of Dr. Ned Turner, was reading a book in bed when she heard someone knocking on the back door of their brownstone Victorian home located just off the main square in Cookville. Figuring the doctor had forgotten his house key—a frequent, annoying habit of her husband—Delia came downstairs wearing only a thin housecoat. Reaching the kitchen, she turned on the back-porch light and heard the screen door open as she entered the utility room.

Later, when explaining the incident to the sheriff, Delia would recall thinking that moment odd since Ned usually waited for her to open the door before he pulled back the screen. Nevertheless, she unlocked the door, cracked it open and was about to unfasten the chain lock when a man rammed his fist through the tight space and tore open her housecoat. Screaming, Delia glanced up at her assailant, then jerked free of the black man's grasp and fled through the dark house.

She heard the chain lock snap and the back door crash open as the man pushed his way into the house and chased after her. Seconds later, while she fumbled with the locks on the front door, the assailant collided with a stout coffee table. Cut down at the shins, the man howled in pain and cursed Delia as she escaped through the door. She ran into the middle of the street, screaming for help while the man recovered his senses and limped a hasty retreat back the same way he had entered the house.

Sheriff Paul Berrien conducted a thorough investigation of the incident, concluding that Delia had been the victim of a drifter passing through Cookville. Ned was outraged by the outcome, accusing Paul of running a slipshod investigation and refuting the sheriff's contention that the assailant likely would never set foot again in Cookville. Ned demanded an arrest, insisting that somewhere on the other side of the tracks in Cookville, his wife's attacker was running scot-free, waiting to strike again. On the basis of Delia's description of the man and his own knowledge of the colored community, Paul refused to budge from his original position.

Ned was not someone easily put off or to be taken lightly. Despite his overbearing, snobbish ways, he wielded considerable influence in Cookville. People listened when he talked, especially when he questioned Paul's capability for enforcing the law and suggested the sheriff had a knack for "kowtowing to the niggers." Paul stayed above the fray, but the doctor's talk and accusations made the rounds through the community.

Whether to believe Paul Berrien or Ned Turner was a matter of opinion, but almost everyone agreed on one thing: It was most unsettling to have crime strike so close to home. In its aftermath, more people began to lock their doors at night; several jokesters suggested the man must have been hard up to have made a grab for Delia Turner, whose stout body and homely features defined ugliness; and one man hatched an idea.

It was a farfetched, spurious thought at first, almost inconceivable. But the man was gifted with vision, and he had a talent for making the most of every opportunity and seeing the possibilities offered up by improbable situations. Once the idea entered his head, he latched onto it with increasing clarity. To execute it would require guts, risk, foresight and luck, all things he lacked but could fake well enough when the stakes were high.

He refused to think of himself as a criminal, though he had skirted the law when the situation suited him. But his past misdeeds had been indirect associations with the main event. If his latest plans were to come to fruition, he would have to be the triggerman.

On a cold, damp day in early February, Rachel sat by the kitchen fireplace in her favorite rocker, humming *In the Sweet By-and-By* as her knitting needles clicked to the melody. She was knitting an afghan of royal blue, red and white for Carrie. Last winter, she had made one of forest green and black for Summer. Next winter, she would knit one for Bonnie. In addition, she was sewing special quilts for each of her grandchildren, a project started a few weeks earlier. She did her quilting at night, and her first effort, which she would present to Joe come next Christmas, was stretched across the quilting rack that hung from the ceiling over the bed she shared with Sam.

Her mind was wandering, and Rachel dropped a stitch. Chastising herself, she corrected the mistake and continued with the work.

On another winter morning more years ago than she cared to remember, Rachel had first suspected she was going to have a baby. She had been cutting a dress pattern for a neighbor when a wave of nausea rolled through her. Becoming dizzy on her feet, she had sought comfort in this same rocking chair. A few days later, the doctor had confirmed she was expecting Joseph, her firstborn, who would perish at Pearl Harbor only a few days before his twenty-first birthday.

Similar bouts of morning sickness had warned that she was pregnant on four other occasions. She had miscarried on the first occasion, in the third month, before giving birth to Matt, Ruth and Nicholas, the baby who had died of the pneumonia at six weeks. The miscarriage and the death of Nicholas had saddened Rachel, but she had attributed the losses to God's will and plunged back into a busy life filled with the shenanigans of three boisterous children.

In those days, quiet moments had been as hard to come by as money. And unless she was certain the children were asleep in their beds, Rachel had learned quickly that moments of noticeable silence and absent children usually meant mischief was afoot or in the making.

She recalled a day when Joseph had decided his little brother was too old to take a bottle and used it to feed suckling pigs. Although Rachel would have chosen another means of breaking Matt from the bottle, Joseph's tactics had done the trick. Matt, who was approaching his fourth birthday and should have been weaned years earlier, had taken one look at the pig sucking on his bottle and lost all desire for it.

Then, there had been another day years later when Joseph and Matt took it upon themselves to teach Ruth a lesson in humility. Somewhat spoiled—especially by her father, although Rachel and the boys catered to her whims as well—Ruth had taken particular fancy to matching dresses that she received for herself and her prized baby doll as Christmas presents one year. Although Rachel had sewed the dresses and was right proud of them herself, she, too, had become annoyed by Ruth's ticky behavior and vanity. Ruth would prance around in the dress, holding her doll, putting on airs and scoffing at her brothers.

Rachel laughed to herself, remembering the day she had heard Ruth's plaintiff moan when she discovered the dresses were missing. As soon as Ruth wailed, "Dolly's naked. Where's her dress; where's my dress?" Rachel realized she had a mess on her hands. She'd had to go only as far as the kitchen window, where she spotted the boys leaning against the barnyard gate, guffawing all over themselves.

Expecting the worst, Rachel had gone outside and discovered a sow and one of her shoats prancing around the lot in the prized dresses. Ruth also made the discovery for herself a few moments later. She took one look, started to cry, then changed her mind, slapped both brothers across the face and refused to speak to either of them for a whole week.

Feeling their daughter's actions were justified, Rachel and Sam had let her off without so much as a reprimand. As for Joseph and Matt, they had received a belt across their backsides. It was one of the few times Sam had whipped any of his children.

Smiling àgain, Rachel remembered feeling as if she were on a fast merry-go-round in those days and wondering if it would ever stop. Then, without warning, that merry-go-round went whirling like a top out of control. When it crashed, Rachel was a shell-shocked veteran of motherhood, the victim of a daughter who had eloped with a stranger, a son who had lost his life to the Japanese bombs at Pearl Harbor and another son who had answered the call of a nation at war.

At first, Rachel had been too shocked to grieve properly. Neighbors and relatives had praised her for holding up well under the strain as she carried on with the everyday business of living. But her aplomb was more a dazed response to the turmoil. She might well have been sleepwalking through those dismal winter months of 1942, but spring had awakened her senses. On some days, she thought the silence would kill her. On others, she questioned her sanity, wondering if she had imagined a life filled with children.

Even after all these years, Rachel wondered from time to time whether she would have survived the losses without her daughter-in-law.

As soon as she was finished with high school that spring, Caroline had swept into the Baker home like a breath of fresh air. She had been determined to discover everything about her chosen life with Matt, and her enthusiasm for learning had been infectious. Rachel and Sam had accommodated her every wish. Although unintentionally and perhaps unknowingly, Caroline had filled a void and helped to coax Rachel back from the edge of torment.

As Sam and she had shared the stories of a lifetime with their new daughter-in-law, Rachel had begun the grieving process over her lost children. In telling those stories, Rachel had laughed; she had cried; and she had come to understand the full extent of her loss.

On occasion, she had gone for long walks, where she could bawl her eyes out in private. At other times, she needed only to walk into the yard, where her prayer stump bided a talk with God. But gradually and true to her nature, Rachel had accepted the past and adjusted for the future. In all honesty, she could never deny wishing that things might have turned out differently in the past; but neither would she give up the present to change the past.

A tear fell on her hand as the knitting needles clicked, surprising Rachel as she realized her eyes were misty. "Pshaw," she scolded herself. "You're beginnen to think like an old woman."

The self-admonishment reminded Rachel of her approaching birthday. Come Valentine's Day, she would indeed be an old woman, at least according to the government, which would declare her a senior citizen. The notion displeased her to no end. She did not feel elderly, and she had the constitution of an ox, as her husband was prone to tell anyone should the subject arise. Sam meant it as a compliment, but bless his heart, the man's poet spirit should have come up with a more flattering form of praise.

Rachel sighed and considered again her approaching birthday. Perhaps she wasn't old by her own judgment, but she wasn't young either. Still, she'd aged well.

She was slightly built, with her thinness tending to make her appear taller than she was. Although childbearing and age had robbed her of an hourglass waist, she still weighed little more than she did when Sam had carried her over the threshold forty-three years earlier. Wearing bonnets and long sleeves over the years had protected her complexion from the elements and kept her free of age spots. Her features also had softened with age, blunting the harsh effect of her sometimes-saucy disposition. While a few wrinkles creased her forehead and the corners of her eyes, her narrow face was still smooth and her green eyes sparkled. Her hair had turned a silky light gray several years earlier, and she thought the color actually more becoming than the previous jet black. Rachel wore her hair pinned into a neat bun on the back of her head, with short bangs and several wisps covering her ears. The style had remained unchanged for as long as she or anyone else remembered.

Pushing aside these rambling thoughts, Rachel examined the precise stitches of her work and was pleased with the effort. Glancing at the hourglass clock on the fireplace mantle, she saw it was time for her morning story to begin on the television. She started to put away her knitting when an outburst of furious yelping from the dog shattered the quietness.

The racket came from Pal-Two, the white and charcoal German

shepherd that watched over the Baker place with a military guard's vigilance. Like his predecessor, Pal-Two had become a member of the family. When the dog barked furiously as he was doing now, it usually meant something was amiss on the place. Setting her knitting on the table, Rachel went to the side window in the kitchen, looked out through the screened back porch and discovered the source of Pal-Two's irritation.

Several of Sugar and Geraldine's offspring had managed to break out of their pen. "Oh, good grief," Rachel groaned as one of the shoats made a beeline through Caroline's rose bed with Pal-Two nipping at its heels.

By now, the shoats probably were wishing they had stayed in the safety of the lot, Rachel thought, as the hog squealed in pain, the result of Pal-Two's incisors taking a bite out of its rump. Rachel would have preferred to let the hogs run loose until the family came home, but Pal-Two's vigilance made it impossible for her to ignore the fugitive pigs. The dog's barking and the pigs' squealing were commotion enough. But left to his own means, Pal-Two would see to it that several of the shoats were gone before their time had come. As long as the hogs and cows stayed in their place, Pal-Two ignored them. But the dog dealt severely with wayward stock.

Knowing the family could ill afford a full-course pork dinner for a dog, Rachel sighed, fetched one of Sam's jackets and headed into the cold rain to herd the pigs back into their pens while there was still an opportunity to do so.

"Granny's not very cheerful," observed six-year-old Bonnie at the supper table.

While Caroline privately agreed with the assessment, she was dutybound to scold her youngest daughter. She did so halfheartedly, then concentrated on her plate.

When Rachel was upset or feeling poorly, she was not a cheery person indeed. In fact, she could be downright ornery. Having spent an hour of her day chasing pigs through a cold rain, Rachel was both upset and feeling poorly on this night, and her disposition was worse.

"Y'all oughtta have a tobacco stick brought across your backside the way I belted those hogs," Rachel muttered for her husband, son and oldest grandson's benefit. "There's a right way of doen things and a wrong way, and y'all should have done better."

Rachel was convinced that either her husband Sam, son Matt or grandson Joe was guilty of careless repairs on the hog pen, and there was no reasoning with her. She blamed the three of them for her misfortunate morning, including a nasty fall on her backside. Chasing hogs had never been one of her preferred pastimes, and Rachel wanted her family to understand the depths of her disgruntlement. By now, everyone around the table had a good taste.

When she eschewed the supper dishes and retired to her room early for the night, complaining of a tickle in her throat and fretting about a cold, everyone was frankly glad to see her go.

"I don't feel so good," Rachel told her husband when Sam came to their bed later that night. "I'm afraid I might be comen down with the grippe."

"You're sounden chugged up—it's a fact," Sam replied sympathetically. "Let's see what we can do to doctor you."

A while later, Rachel settled under an extra blanket and tried to sleep. Sam had rubbed her down with Vicks salve and given her a tiny dose of liniment with sugar, surefire remedies for whatever ailed her.

But rest eluded Rachel. She was miserable through the night, feeling hot one minute and chilled the next. When she dozed at last, it was a troubled slumber, lasting only a few minutes before daylight peeked into the room and woke her.

Rachel lay in bed until Matt and Caroline came into the kitchen, which was next to hers and Sam's room. Not until she heard a match strike and determined sufficient time had passed for a fire to warm the kitchen was she ready to face the day. Climbing slowly from bed, she eased into her brown dress, pushed Sam awake and went into the kitchen.

"Good mornen," she greeted as Matt and Caroline returned the pleasantries.

"How you feelen this mornen, Ma?" Matt asked.

"Stove up and old," Rachel answered bluntly. "I think I've got a touch of the grippe—probably from be'en out in the cold yesterday."

"Bonnie's got a nasty cold, too," Matt replied. "Caroline was up with her a couple of times last night."

"I'm keepen her home from school today," Caroline said, peering closely at Rachel. "You do look peaked, Ma," she observed. "It might do you good to go back to bed and rest. I can take care of breakfast."

Rachel shrugged off the suggestion. "I'd rather stay up and busy. I'd just toss and turn in bed, and I did enough of that last night." In short order, Rachel helped Caroline put breakfast on the table, then ushered the older children onto the school bus and checked on Bonnie. While Caroline washed the first of several loads of dirty clothes, Rachel cleaned the breakfast dishes. She labored through a few more chores before succumbing to the tiredness that made every movement a struggle. Telling Caroline to wake her for dinner, she retreated to the comfort of her bed and buried herself beneath the covers.

While Caroline spent a busy morning taking care of the household chores, Matt and Sam idled away leisurely hours. It was their slack time of the year, and the men used the opportunity to replenish themselves for the coming spring and summer when the workload would leave little time for relaxing. They changed the oil in several vehicles and chatted with Buck Franklin while he refilled the propane gas tank. Later, they sat in the kitchen, nursing several cups of coffee while discussing the farm's need for a new tractor. Ultimately, they would put off the purchase to another time, but the discussion was progress in itself after several lean years on the farm.

Caroline kept their cups filled with hot coffee and prepared chicken soup for the noon meal.

By dinnertime, Bonnie was out of bed and well on her way to feeling better. Although she continued to suffer from the sniffles, her fever and coughing had subsided. She was restless and bored, all of which added up to an excellent prognosis for recovery according to Caroline, who sent her daughter to check on Rachel.

"Granny's asleep," Bonnie announced upon her return to the kitchen. "She's snoren."

"Well don't mention that to anybody," Caroline advised. "I've never known your granny to snore, and she wouldn't appreciate people thinken she did. Go tell your daddy and grandpa to wash up for dinner."

While Bonnie skipped away to call Matt and Sam to the kitchen, Caroline dished up a bowl of the steaming chicken broth and carried it to Rachel. As soon as she cracked open the bedroom door, she heard the sound of wheezing breaths muted by the heavy cover of blankets and quilts that Rachel had piled upon the bed. Putting the soup bowl on the dresser, Caroline sat on the edge of the bed, lifted the covers, including the electric blanket, which was turned on high, and found her mother-in-law shivering. Rachel's face was flushed and her lips parched from the burning fever. Caroline placed a palm flat against the woman's forehead and was startled by the heat.

Rachel opened her eyes at the touch. "I kept thinken I would start to feel better," she said weakly. "But I'm worse, Caroline. I haven't felt this bad in a long time."

"You're burnen up with fever," Caroline noted, "and awfully chugged up. It sounds like a bad case of the croup. We should get you to a doctor this afternoon."

Rachel nodded agreement, and Caroline's concern mounted. Over the years, her mother-in-law had shunned doctors, relying on home remedies and a resolute faith in the good Lord to keep her healthy. Her willingness to seek medical treatment was out of character, and Caroline took it as an ominous sign. She gave the sick woman a quick smile, covered her again and went to make the arrangements to see a doctor.

In times like this, Caroline wished the Bakers had a family doctor.

They took Rachel to the emergency room at the Tifton hospital, where her care fell into the hands of Dr. Martin Pittman. On first glance, Dr. Pittman appeared extremely fragile, more like a shriveled old man who probably had forgotten most of what he'd ever known about doctoring than a trustworthy physician. His body was thin and brittle, almost emaciated, and his eyes literally bulged from the sockets, coming perilously close it seemed to making contact with the thick, black-rimmed glasses that rested on a crooked nose. In stark contrast to the otherwise frail features, his ears appeared remarkably sturdy. They were gigantic flappers, so much so that people were never sure whether the doctor had excellent hearing or was ready for takeoff at a moment's notice.

Despite his odd appearance, Dr. Pittman came highly recommended by the Berrien sisters, who had warned Caroline not to be fooled by the appearances of a man who had survived the brutal Bataan Death March in the Philippines during World War II. Beneath his vulnerable exterior, the doctor possessed a keen medical mind, a heart of gold and a genuine desire to ease the suffering of others.

Nevertheless, he did little to inspire confidence in the Bakers upon first introduction.

Shuffling into the room where the Bakers were waiting, Martin

Pittman was overcome by a coughing spasm. The Berrien sisters had forewarned Caroline that the doctor was prone to spells of breathless coughing and she had passed the word to her family. But nothing could have prepared them for the violent nature of the coughing fit. Gasping for breath, Dr. Pittman lurched toward the edge of Rachel's hospital bed on rickety legs and motioned for someone to slide a chair underneath him. Matt snatched up a nearby stool and hurried to put it beneath the man, who collapsed upon the steel seat with such force that everyone feared he might have broken a hipbone. Such was the commotion accompanying his entrance into the room that even the ailing Rachel raised her head in a dismayed show of concern.

"Are you okay, doc?" Sam asked.

"Well, Mr. Baker," the doctor replied in a drawl that was a bit Southern but mostly tired. "I don't mind tellen you that I'm just about tuckered out for one day. But the fact is, I'm not the one who's sick here." Turning to Rachel, he asked, "Now what seems to be the problem, Mrs. Baker?"

With Rachel feeling too poorly to respond, Caroline launched into a description of the older woman's symptoms, as well as her travails with the hogs a day earlier and her own suspicions that her mother-in-law might be coming down with pneumonia. The doctor confirmed her diagnosis with a cursory examination, then informed them he was admitting Rachel to the hospital for treatment.

"I'm orderen a private room," he said. "It costs a little more, but I think she'll rest easier and we can give her better treatment."

"Whatever you think is necessary, doc," Matt agreed.

"Good then," Dr. Pittman said. "While you folks get her admitted, we'll get her situated in the room and start some medication. I'll see you soon."

A few minutes later as they watched a hospital orderly guide away the gurney with Rachel stretched on it, a chilling premonition settled over Sam, Matt and Caroline. Where minutes before they had been concerned about Rachel's well-being, they now were genuinely worried. Their worry stemmed from the doctor's change in manner while he examined Rachel. As he had listened to her congested chest, Dr. Pittman had abandoned his folksy attitude and taken on a sense of urgency in his approach.

That urgency hurried them through the admitting process and on to Rachel's hospital room, where they found her lying in bed beneath a contraption of steel poles and plastic. She had drifted into an uneasy sleep, hounded by short, gasping breaths.

"I ordered the oxygen tent to make her as comfortable as possible," Dr. Pittman explained. "Don't be too alarmed by the looks of it."

"She's goen to be all right then," Sam inferred.

Instead of answering, Dr. Pittman motioned them to follow him. "I don't want to alarm you needlessly, Mr. Baker," he said when they were in the corridor outside Rachel's room. "But I'm also not goen to beat around the bush with you. Your wife is a very sick woman. You know as well as I do how dangerous pneumonia can be. Medical science has made great strides in treating it, but pneumonia is still a touch-and-go proposition, especially for older people. In her particular case, the disease developed very quickly and it's in both of her lungs. Frankly, I would have preferred starten her on medication several hours ago. Sometimes hours can make a big difference in a case like this. Right now, however, we need to do everything possible to keep her condition from worsening, and I assure you we'll do that. I will tell you this, though: The next few hours will be critical. You can help by keepen her spirits up when she's awake. You might say a prayer, too. I'm a firm believer in the great physician up above. He can do a whole lot more for Mrs. Baker than I can."

"Amen to that," Caroline concurred, soothed by the knowledge that a God-fearing man was entrusted with Rachel's care.

"I have a few things to take care of," the doctor continued, "then I'll be back to check on her. You might think about getten somethen to eat yourselves. We could be in for a long night, and y'all need to keep your strength up to help Mrs. Baker."

The doctor took his leave, and Sam, Matt and Caroline began their vigil.

Joe might as well have skipped his final two classes. From the moment he was called to the school office and told to telephone his father at home, Joe had been preoccupied. Once Matt informed him that Rachel was ill enough to require a hospital's care, he lost all interest in his schoolwork. World history paled in comparison to his concern for Rachel, and twice in trigonometry, the teacher ordered him to pay attention to the problem at hand.

He mentioned to Tom Carter, his best friend, that Rachel was ill on their bus ride from the high school in Cookville to the New River community where they lived. Instead of lingering to talk with Tom when they got off the bus at the mercantile owned by his friend's family, Joe said goodbye and set off on the muddy dirt road for the two-mile walk home. Normally, he would have proceeded right past the Berrien place, but today's circumstances sent him on a detour down the graveled lane to the elegant home, where Bonnie had spent the afternoon with Miss April and Miss June, the older sisters of Sheriff Paul Berrien.

On any other day, the walk would have been an occasion for his mind to turn cartwheels over thoughts about his approaching high school graduation and the following fall when he would enter college. Today, however, Joe scanned the barren pecan orchard on either side of the road and longed for spring to restore life to these acres and acres of trees. Shaking away the dreary thoughts, he focused on the tasks awaiting him at home, making a mental list of the chores that needed his attention and assigning others to his brothers and sisters.

Before realizing it, he was approaching the Berrien home. The Berrien estate was a study in splendor, with immaculately maintained grounds and the red-bricked, Georgian house rising three stories in the distance. On his left was the guest cottage where his parents had spent their honeymoon night, and Joe paused to admire the scenic beauty. Leaving the path of the road, he cut across the lush lawn and arrived at the wide staircase that led to the front door. He climbed the brick steps, rang the doorbell and was admitted a moment later by Miss April.

She greeted Joe enthusiastically, taking his hand and leading him through the Greek archways of the foyer with its tapestries, mirrored coat rack and antique wash basin, past the white marbled stairway streaked with delicate traces of ruby red and emerald green.

They arrived at the sitting parlor, which was dominated by a grand piano and a dark mahogany mantle encasing a red-bricked fireplace. Heavily carved Gothic tables of walnut and mahogany were mixed and matched with Martha Washington chairs and Renaissance sofas upholstered in creamy white and brocaded burgundy. On top of the tables and a cherry lowboy were precious lamps and many of the family's smaller treasures acquired over the years. The room had polished hardwood floors covered by two Persian rugs, each of which had a single diamond-shaped medallion and scrolled floral borders. One rug was solid red with hints of black and ivory in the scrolling; the other was a deeper red with traces of black, pale blue and dark green in the scrolling. Two chandeliers hung perfectly over the medallions in the middle of the rugs. But what Joe admired most about the parlor was the worn black leather recliner and the new television console.

The parlor reflected the tastes of the Berrien sisters and their brother. It was fancy without the slightest show of pretentiousness, a homey, cozy room where Paul, April and June spent the majority of their waking hours at home.

Bonnie was sitting on the floor beside the huge fireplace, playing with a porcelain doll and drinking hot chocolate with melted marshmallows.

"Afternoon, Miss June," Joe greeted them. "Bonnie."

He glanced at both ladies and nodded to his sister who ignored his greeting by keeping her attention glued to the doll. "If I had to guess, I'd say y'all are spoilen my little sister."

"We're doen our best," Miss June said heartily.

"I suspect she'd just as soon as stay here with y'all than go home with me," Joe told the ladies.

"And that would be perfectly fine with us," Miss April answered. "Bonnie's an adorable little girl."

"Practically an angel," Miss June said as Bonnie favored her with an angelic smile.

Joe laughed at their flattery of his baby sister. "She is sweet," he said, crossing the room to sweep Bonnie off the floor into his arms. The little girl squealed and threw her arms around Joe's neck as he kissed her on the cheek. "Hi, pumpkin," he said.

"Granny's sick," Bonnie informed him promptly. "She might have the pneumonia."

"Pneumonia?" Joe replied with a questioning glance at the two sisters.

"I'm afraid so," June confirmed. "Your daddy called here not too long ago and said they were admitten Rachel to the hospital. He wasn't sure when they'll be home tonight but said you'd know what to do around the farm. You children are welcome to have supper with us tonight if you'd like. In fact, Bonnie could just stay here with us for the night."

"Thank you, Miss June," Joe replied. "It's kind of you to offer, but I think it would be best if we waited at home. We'll be fine."

"Indeed, you will," April agreed. "It's perfectly understandable that you'd want to stay around the house. Should y'all need anything, though, don't hesitate to call on us."

"Thank you," Joe said again.

"Do let us drive y'all home, Joe," June offered. "Bonnie doesn't need to be out in this cold weather. It might freshen up her cold."

"We'd be much obliged."

Riding home in the backseat of the Berriens' silver Cadillac was like taking a trip with Lucy Ricardo and Ethel Mertz at the wheel, and the best thing Joe could say about the experience was that it was blessedly brief.

At home, grateful to be out of the car, he thanked the women for the ride, reassured them he and his brothers and sisters could fend for themselves and waved goodbye. He led Bonnie into the house, settled her in front of the television and returned outside to begin the afternoon chores.

His other sisters and brothers arrived home from school a short time later. Joe watched them exit the bus and head for the house. Once they were inside, he began counting to himself and walking toward the porch. At fifteen, he reached the porch steps and the front door burst open, with Summer leading the charge of curious siblings, each of them with a question.

Joe told them everything he knew about Rachel's condition, which was just enough to make them suspect he was sharing only pieces of the story. He tried to reassure them all was well, but the effort was so pitiful that even his own concern for their grandmother magnified.

"Is Granny gonna die?" his youngest brother Luke asked suddenly.

"No!" Joe replied testily. "There's no sense getten ourselves worked up when we don't know the situation."

"But, Joe," Carrie interrupted. "Granny must be awful sick to be in the hospital."

"That's right," chimed in Summer. "Granny doesn't put much stock in doctors and hospitals. Are you tellen us everything there is to tell?"

"I've told y'all everything I know," Joe answered patiently. "We'll have to wait until we hear from Daddy and Mama before there's anything else to tell. Until then, though, we're gonna do what we're supposed to. There's work to do, and every one of us has a job. Summer, you and Carrie are in charge of supper and taking care of Bonnie. And Bonnie, you behave yourself. Luke, you gather the eggs and feed the dog and cats. John and I will feed up and do whatever else needs to be done outside. Let's get to it."

Even Summer, who tended toward the bossy and brash side, knew when her brother meant business. With only token grumbling, she ordered her sisters to the kitchen and began planning supper. Joe barked another round of orders at his brothers, then sent them on their way.

Luke gathered eggs from the chicken coop and the various nests that several hens had made around the place. In deference to Rachel, the eight-year-old boy worked diligently, careful not to break any eggs, and held his tongue, even when a curse word appeared on his lips after he stepped in chicken manure. Finally, after plucking the last egg from its nest, he considered the plight of his grandmother.

He was plagued by unsettling thoughts, some of which he shared with Matilda, his grandmother's favorite Rhode Island Red layer, before he carried the egg basket into the house.

Joe ordered John to give Brindy a pail of sour corn mash to keep the cow still while she was milked. When the animal was eating contentedly, Joe pulled the milking stool beside her, took hold of her teats and began squeezing streams of warm milk into the waiting pail. He then directed his brother across the road to the corncrib, telling him to fill the two tubs for the hogs.

Joe detested milking nearly as much as he despised butchering hogs. In this day and age, he thought, it seemed ridiculous to milk a single cow. But whereas Matt had been willing to leave the butchering to the abattoir, he was unlikely to abandon the milking. Brindy held a sentimental spot among the family's hearts, even in Joe's. He remembered all too well the many times Brindy provided the only milk his family could afford to put on the table.

The cow gave her milk easily. When she was dry, Joe gave the old girl a friendly pat on the rear, put away the stool and carried the pail of fresh milk to the kitchen, with orders for his sisters to strain it.

On his return to the barn, he discovered that John already had carried the tubs of corn over from the crib. Picking up the first bucket, he flung the corn over the gate behind the barn, scattering the yellow kernels so that every hog could eat its share. He divided the other bucket among three special sections of the barn, which housed farrowing sows and their litters. A series of sliding gates separated the three pins, all of which contained dirt floors and water troughs carved from large tree trunks shortly after Sam and Rachel had bought the farm.

"Thanks for luggen the corn over here," Joe told his brother as John picked up the empty pails and started back across the road to the crib. "Let me water up here, and I'll be over to feed the others."

When the troughs were filled with water, Joe went across the road and tossed four more tubs of corn to the main herd of hogs, while John took care of the watering. "Luke's talken to the chickens again," John observed as they walked back across the road to the barn. "I wonder what he's tellen them."

"I wonder what they're tellen him," Joe remarked, giving the eleven-year-old boy a playful nudge on the shoulder.

With the cows growing restless, bellowing for food of their own as they grazed in the pecan orchard, John climbed the loft stairs where the sweet hay was stored. The loft was still half full of hay that had been cut from the back pasture last fall, and the sweet-smelling, sunny aroma was ingrained in the wooden structure. John inhaled deeply, then grabbed the two nearest bales, tugged them to the edge of the porch and pushed them over the side.

Joe watched them fall to the ground, then cut apart the binding string with his pocket knife and moved on to the barn's lower crib where the scratchy peanut hay was stored. He climbed into the crib, tossed one bale out the door and returned for a second.

"Do you really think Granny will be okay?"

The question surprised Joe, who had expected his brother to be on his way down the stairs to begin feeding the clumps of hay to the bellowing cows. Instead, John was peering down at him from the loft window that overlooked the crib.

Joe gazed upwards, trying to come up with an answer that would satisfy his brother. In his contemplation, he spied a rusted nail sticking out of the wall below the loft window. Once when they had been playing in the loft, John had miscalculated a backward jump from the window, falling straight down and raking the bottom of his chin across the rusty nail. The boy carried a thin scar as a permanent reminder of the accident.

Joe pointed to his own chin. "Do you remember the time you scraped your chin on that nail there?" he asked John.

"I was showen off," John recalled.

Joe held up his left hand, pointing to a jagged scar that wrapped around the fleshy outer side to the bottom of his palm. "I was showen off, too," he said. "I jumped out of that bay tree across the road and landed smack-dab on a broken drink bottle. Needed twenty-three stitches to sew it up. I remember landen on my hand and somethen stingen like the dickens. When I looked down at my hand, there was blood everywhere. I took off runnen across the road, screamen at the top of my lungs. You'd've thought I was dyen."

"Who were you showen off for?" John asked.

"Do you remember Frieda?" Joe said. "She was Aunt Euna's grand-daughter."

John shook his head negatively.

"Her family lives in Texas now and they don't come around these parts much anymore, so maybe you don't remember her," Joe continued. "Anyway, this happened before you were born. I think I was tryen to prove that I was a better tree climber than she was, and Frieda dared me to jump. Ever since then, every time I've seen her, she mentions that day and wants to see my scar."

"I guess we've all got a few memorable scars," John remarked.

On Summer's right calf was the faded reminder of the time she had fallen through a cultivator while using it as a podium to boss her younger brothers and sisters. The front of Carrie's left thigh was marked with a perfect oval from the time she had run into a hawthorn bush and one of the prickly thorns had broken off beneath the skin. Although Matt practically had performed minor surgery, the nettle had remained lodged in Carrie's leg until the sore festered several weeks later and the thorn came out by itself. Indeed, from the eye patch that covered Sam's bad eye to the gash across the bottom of Bonnie's foot, everyone in the family had suffered in one way or another, Joe reminded his brother.

"These things happen from time to time, Bud," Joe continued, invoking his personal nickname for John. "People get hurt and they get sick. I wish I knew what to tell you about Granny. I wish I could say she was goen to be fine. But I honestly don't know. All we can do is hope and pray for the best."

"You're right," John agreed, as yet another cow bellowed for food.

Joe grabbed another bale of the peanut hay and heaved it over the crib's side. He started to climb out of the crib when John stopped him with another comment about their grandmother.

"I keep thinken about that horse," he said. "The one that belonged to Granny's brother. Do you remember that story the way Granny told it?"

"It's not somethen you can forget," Joe replied.

"Would you tell it to me?" John pleaded as the cows bellowed again for their hay.

Joe was torn between honoring his brother's request and answering the cattle's call. He glanced from the cows to John, then nodded and took a seat on the crib floor, leaning against a stack of hay. "You'll have to settle for the short version," he said.

The horse tale was part of the family's folklore. Rachel repeated the story sparingly, often with a specific purpose in mind, usually as an example of the trouble that comes when people do things they shouldn't.

"When Granny's brother, Alton—the one who drowned—was nine, their daddy gave him a filly," Joe began. "It was a quarter horse, beautiful, reddish-brown with black markens on her face. Alton loved the horse. He named her Queenie and treated her like a queen. Alton taught her jumpen tricks and snuck apples, sugar and anything else he could from under his sister's nose so that Queenie could have her treats.

"Alton loved that horse probably more than anything in the world. He would have done anything for her. Unfortunately, he also had a bad habit of smoking a tobacco pipe in the barn with Queenie. Now anybody with any sense knows that it's dumb to smoke or have any kind of fire around a barn that's filled with hay. But Alton was careless. He figured nothen bad could ever happen.

"One day, when Alton should have been busy doen his chores, he disobeyed Granny. Instead of hoe'en in the garden like she had told him to do, he snuck off to the barn to smoke his pipe. For some reason, he laid his pipe down in the barn and then forgot all about it. Anyway, he went off somewhere else, and that pipe caught the hay on fire.

"Sometime that mornen before dinner, Granny glanced out the kitchen window and saw flames shooten from the roof of the barn. She knew right away that the builden was a goner, but she wanted to save Queenie. By the time she reached the barn, however, the fire had engulfed the builden. The heat was intense, and the flames were whippen toward Queenie.

"The poor horse was scared to death. She was whinnyen and kicken savagely at the walls. But she was trapped and there was nothen anyone could do to save her. Even so, Granny was determined not to let that horse suffer. She raced back to the house, jammed a shell in her daddy's shotgun and was back at the barn in seconds flat. By then, Queenie had squeezed as far away from the fire as possible, and the flames were licken at her beautiful coat. Ignoren the heat, Granny ran to the edge of the fire, took careful aim through the flames and shot that horse dead center in the head. The poor animal died instantly, and seconds later, the barn's roof caved in and turned that builden into a crematorium.

"Poor Granny was distraught. She went back to the house, told the twins, Edna and Euna, to finish cooken dinner and took to her bed for the afternoon. Later, Alton came to see her. He was torn up about Queenie, especially knowen that he had caused the fire. Granny says he never really forgave himself for starten that fire. But regardless, Alton told Granny how grateful he was that she had spared Queenie the agony of burnen to death. He told her she was brave and courageous and had done what needed to be done.

"Now Granny had always been one who believed in doen what needed to be done. But that day made her realize that life's hardships and its joys were all the same. You take things for what they are, then you put them behind you and get on with life. That afternoon was the first time Granny ever told herself, 'It's time to get on with the business of liven.' And ever since then, she's been doen just that."

Joe and John were silent for a moment.

"Sometimes I think that's the saddest story I've ever heard," John remarked at last. "But I suppose there are worse things."

"Yeah," Joe agreed.

"Anyway, I sure do hope nobody decides that Granny's so sick she needs to be put out of her misery like poor Queenie," John continued.

Joe laughed aloud at the idea. John frowned for a moment, then smiled, saying, "That was a dumb thing to say, wasn't it?"

"I just hadn't thought about it in that way," Joe replied cheerfully. "But I think everybody probably gets somethen different from that story."

John glanced across the crib, toward the house as if he were about to share a secret. "Do you wanna know somethen else about that story?" he asked.

"What's that?" Joe replied.

"A few Sundays ago, when the preacher talked about the fire and brimstone of Hell, I thought about poor Queenie and Uncle Alton and Granny," John said. "To tell you the truth, Joe, I'm not too fond of fire, and the prospect of burnen in Hell is pretty scary. Chances are that if you wind up in Hell, there's not a bullet made that's gonna spare you from the torment. And even if there was one, I feel sure Granny wouldn't be around to pull the trigger. Honestly, Joe, it made me think long and hard about repenten and getten saved."

Joe smiled again and shook his head. "Everybody has a reason for getten saved, John," he said. "I reckon yours is as good as anybody else's."

"Well, I'm just thinken about it," John admitted. "I wonder what Granny would think about my reasonen."

"She'd be pleased as punch," Joe answered quickly. "She'd say the good Lord works in mysterious ways, and she'd probably even decide He had your salvation in mind on the day when she had to shoot poor Queenie."

"Maybe I'll mention it to her when she gets home from the hospital," John remarked.

"You do that, Bud," Joe said. "And I'm glad you asked to hear that story. I think it was a good tonic for what ails us. Now come on down from there and let's feed these cows. They're hungry, and I'm beginnen to get that way, too."

———————

Standing at the kitchen sink, Summer attacked the chicken fryer with the swift strokes of someone who knew how to use a cutting knife, while Carrie peeled the last of the potatoes and put them on the stove to boil.

The kitchen showed all the signs of a normal evening, with water running in the sink, pots percolating on the stove and a blaze popping in the fireplace. But the evening was far from run-of-the-mill. Without the familiar presence of Caroline and Rachel, the kitchen seemed hollow rather than homey. Carrie tried to fill the void, but Summer responded with muttered grunts and stone-faced silence. At last, Carrie abandoned attempts at making conversation and fled the room wordlessly, leaving Summer to herself.

Summer was thinking about the argument she'd had with her grandmother on New Year's Eve. After all these weeks, they still had not settled their differences. While housework and cooking were not high on Summer's list of fun things to do, she had never intended to criticize Rachel's rigid beliefs. Although her grandmother prided herself for honoring her wifely duties, she would have overlooked Summer's criticism of her devotion to household chores. But Summer had overstepped the bounds of criticism when she lashed out at one thing dear to Rachel, and that was sewing.

Sewing was a common denominator between Summer and Rachel.

Summer had inherited her grandmother's skills with a needle and thread. Under Rachel's tutelage, she had fashioned her first garment, an apron, at age six. Soon afterward, she had completed her first dress, and both her interest and skill for dressmaking seemed to increase proportionally with every stitch and hem.

This passion for sewing was unique to Summer and Rachel. Caroline had neither the talent nor the desire to try her hand at tailoring, while Carrie and Bonnie lacked the patience. Over the years, however, Summer had proven an eager apprentice and Rachel a willing mentor. The bond between them was strong, and their work had afforded ample opportunity for conversation. During these talks, Rachel had shared the stories of her life, and now as she prepared supper in her grandmother's absence, Summer reflected on that life.

As a child, Rachel had been carefree, with just enough spunk to get herself into trouble and charm to talk her way out of it. All that changed when her mother came down with rheumatic heart disease. While waiting a long year for her mother to die, Rachel had been forced to develop the discipline that now seemed such a natural part of her being. When Merry Willis finally died, Rachel had retreated to a safe, solitary place of the mind, where she could remember the good times they had shared and console herself with visions of her mother singing with angels in Heaven. Her escape had lasted until a few days after the funeral when the flock of mourners bade their final condolences, gathered up baskets of food and took their leave. When everyone was gone, Rachel was left with the reality of cooking and cleaning for her father, two small twin sisters and a baby brother.

Her childhood memories faded quickly, and her discipline rose to the challenge as Rachel became the woman of the house. She became the cook, washwoman, nursemaid and authority figure for her brother and sisters, who soon came to think of her more as their mother than a sibling. Often left alone in the house for days at a time while their father peddled the goods that provided the family its livelihood, Rachel learned early the value of a stern personality, terse words and disapproving frowns to keep the household under control. To casual acquaintances and even to her own family on occasion, she was an austere woman.

The one daydream Rachel indulged was of her mother singing with angels. She would imagine her mother's voice rolling across streets of gold, bringing Heaven to a standstill with its melodious flow and perfect resonance, and Rachel would remember her mother's love and sweet disposition. The memory kept her heart pure and nurtured her goodness.

Those qualities had attracted Sam. He had taught her to laugh again, to smile and to show affection. When the situation required, Rachel would slip back into her old, austere, stubborn ways. But she was known now for her tolerance.

Still, she retained the vestiges of her youth, including a stout belief that hard work brought rewards. When there was a job to do, whether pleasant or not, Rachel tackled it without complaint. She refused to consider work of any kind a hardship, and she never wished for a better lot in life. It was a characteristic passed along to all the Baker women, even Summer, who was proud to carry the mantle for her grandmother on this night. Someone had to prepare supper for the family tonight, and Summer was the best person for the job. As with most household chores, cooking was not her favorite duty, but she would complete the job and hope tomorrow might bring another task more to her liking.

Rachel believed people should be satisfied with today and hope for a better tomorrow. Never one to mince words, she felt obliged to share this philosophy with others when the situation warranted. For instance, her teenage years had been more tedious than festive and she tired quickly of hearing people praise "the good old days." More than once, she had rebuked Sam when he spoke fondly of simpler times when they were young. She even chided Miss April and Miss June when the Berrien sisters voiced nostalgic longings for the gay parties hosted by their parents.

"June, April, the time has come for y'all to get on with the business of liven," Rachel had informed the ladies. "The old days belong in the closet with all the old things. Or better yet, toss them out altogether. What's past is past, and the most you can get from it are good memories—not to dwell on, mind you, but to cherish and think of fondly. I've tried to enjoy every day of my life and wouldn't change a single thing even if I could. But I tell you one thing: My favorite day is tomorrow 'cause there's always that chance it will be better than today.

"So ladies," Rachel had concluded triumphantly. "If it's parties you're pinen for, then I suggest you go home and start plannen. The party you have tomorrow will bring a lot more satisfaction than the memories of years ago. And by the way, June, April, I'd be mighty pleased to be included on your guest list."

Two weeks later, Summer had heard a hint of satisfaction in her grandmother's voice when Rachel opened the mail and announced the family had been invited to a Fourth of July celebration hosted by the Berriens.

Her thoughts returned to the argument with Rachel on New Year's Eve. Summer wasn't sure why she had challenged her grandmother, but she regretted the outburst, especially her flippant criticism of sewing. She had not sewed with Rachel a single time since the argument, and she missed their friendship as well as the work itself.

Somehow, Summer told herself, she would find a way to atone for her blunder and make up for lost time with her grandmother. She refused to consider the possibility they might not have that opportunity.

Through the long afternoon into the evening, Martin Pittman fought for the life of Rachel Baker. He feared it was a losing battle.

The woman lapsed in and out of a coma. Her fever soared dangerously high, her lungs filled with fluid and she struggled to claim her next breath. At one point, expecting Rachel would die within the hour, Dr. Pittman decided to tell her family to brace themselves for the inevitable. He turned to motion them from the room and found himself looking into the faces of three people who expected a miracle. As much as anyone, the doctor believed faith could accomplish the impossible. Sighing to himself, he gave the Bakers a brief smile instead, asked for divine intervention, suctioned Rachel's lungs and called for more ice.

A few hours later, the fever broke; Rachel was breathing easier and resting.

"I don't mind tellen y'all—I was afraid we were goen to lose her for a while there," Dr. Pittman told Sam, Matt and Caroline. "I'm still not convinced she's out of the woods. It might be a lull, but she's definitely better for the time be'en. Mrs. Baker's a very strong woman, which is why she's alive. Now, I'm goen to get some rest, and I suggest y'all do the same. I'll check on her later."

With the doctor's temporary assurance, Matt heeded his wife's advice and went home to check on the children and get some needed sleep. The house seemed unnaturally quiet when he let himself in the front door shortly before ten o'clock, but otherwise, everything appeared normal. Bonnie and Luke had been put to bed, and the older children were gathered around the kitchen table doing their homework. Joe was showing Summer how to diagram complex sentences, and John was quizzing Carrie for a spelling test. The dishes were washed and drying beside the sink, and a fire crackled in the kitchen hearth. It was like a thousand other evenings at the house, but the picture was incomplete, missing a huge portion of the vitality that made this house a home.

A creaking floorboard between the dining room and kitchen betrayed his arrival home, and the quietness exploded with a dozen questions all begging for answers. Matt hushed his children, then told them Rachel was gravely ill and had come close to dying earlier in the evening. Now, however, the doctor seemed to believe she might recover.

It was a sobering answer to their questions, and the prognosis seemed only slightly less bleak. In their abstract worries, some gloomy thoughts had passed through the minds of each child. But the full scope of reality caused their hearts to flutter with fear. Afraid of what the answers might be, they ceased their questions and steered the conversation to safer ground.

"When can we see her?" Joe asked his father.

"I'm not sure," Matt answered. "We'll have to see how she's getten along tomorrow."

"You're probably hungry, Daddy," Summer commented, sliding off the bench. "There's a plate warmen in the oven for you. I'll get it."

Matt waved her back to the table. "I'll eat later," he said. "Right now, y'all finish your homework and get on to bed. We'll have to count on you for breakfast in the mornen, Summer. Maybe supper again tomorrow night."

"If y'all can stand to eat it, I can stand to cook it," Summer drawled.

Everyone chuckled quietly, as if unsure whether humor was appropriate at a time like this. One by one, they put away their homework, knowing it could be finished on the school bus tomorrow morning. At last, each of them kissed their father goodnight and went to bed, determined to honor his request to say a prayer for Rachel.

Sometime before midnight, Matt still sat at the kitchen table with the plate of fried chicken, mashed potatoes and gravy before him. The food was cold, and the ice in his tea glass melted. His thoughts drifted back and forth over his childhood, then settled on the single moment when he had made the largest leap to manhood.

He had been sitting with Rachel in this very room on a Sunday afternoon, listening to the radio. A brisk wind howled outside the house, echoing through the chimney. Matt was at the kitchen table reading a Superman comic book, while Rachel knitted in her rocking chair. Sam had been in Atlanta, trying to sell a truckload of vegetables at the State Farmer's Market. The trip had been a bone of contention between him and Rachel. She was staunchly opposed to commerce of any kind on Sundays, while Sam was equally determined that they needed the money.

All in all, it had been a pleasant day. Then, the news bulletin came over the radio, and their peace was shattered.

Engrossed in the end of his comic book, Matt missed the initial announcement. In fact, the whole bulletin might have escaped his attention had he not noticed a slight, uncharacteristic movement from his mother. Glancing up from his comic book, he found Rachel hunched over in the rocking chair, frowning at the radio with her knitting laying idle in her lap. Around then, his mind registered the radio announcement, especially the mention of Pearl Harbor where Joseph was stationed. He dropped his comic book, which he would never finish, and leaned forward to listen to the news.

"Pearl Harbor," Rachel said softly when the announcement had been read twice over the radio. "That's where your brother is."

"Yeah, Ma," Matt responded as if she had asked him a question.

"Oh, Lord," Rachel moaned, leaning back in the rocking chair with a dazed expression on her face. "I hope Joseph is okay."

"Don't go getten upset, Ma," Matt urged. "We don't know anything about what happened."

He'd wanted to be optimistic for his mother's sake, but actually, Matt had been struck by a gut feeling that Joseph already lay dead somewhere in Pearl Harbor. As he sat with his mother waiting for additional news and listening to the president's speech, Matt had made several decisions about his future, including marrying Caroline and joining the Army.

When dusk approached, Rachel had taken him by the hand and led Matt to the pecan orchard, where they kneeled down on the ground and she delivered the most powerful prayer her son had ever heard. Rachel had intoned God to spare her son from death, but even as she prayed, Matt sensed his mother knew in her heart that Joseph was gone. The prayer, which had begun as an appeal for Joseph's life, ended as a plea for his soul and a seat at the right hand of God.

At some point in that prayer, Matt had lost his faith. He had never given up a belief in God, but he'd lost confidence in Him. It was a scary feeling, even now after all those years of being faithless, and Matt kept these thoughts to himself so that Caroline or anyone else would not see the dark spot in his heart.

Religion had been the major quarrel between Caroline and Matt throughout their marriage. From time to time, they argued over his refusal to attend church, even on special occasions like Easter and

Christmas. And once Caroline had come right out and demanded to know whether Matt believed in God. The question had jarred him.

"Of course, I believe in God," he shouted angrily. "What kind of question is that?"

His forceful answer had calmed Caroline, and their arguments had ceased somewhat. While he still refused to attend church, Matt forced himself to take a more active role in the Christian training of his children before they came to the perception that he did not believe in God. He read to them from the Bible, listened to their prayers and took his turn saying grace at mealtimes. And somewhere along the way, Matt realized, he had come once again to believe in the power of those prayers, which probably explained why he had exhorted his children to say a prayer for Rachel earlier in the night.

Maybe Matt had started to believe again in the power of God as he gazed on the sweet faces of his children as they asked the good Lord to bless their daddy. Or maybe he had been convinced on one of those occasions when he heard his wife and mother sharing their hopes of getting him baptized. More likely, his faith had come back to him in stages. While he still had reservations that religion could comfort him as it did Caroline and Rachel, Matt knew the time had come to put his trust in a higher authority.

Years had passed since Matt had taken the initiative to pray for anything other than thanks for food. Now, when he groped for the appropriate words, they eluded him. But Matt was persistent. He was determined to put his trust in God.

"Blind faith," he murmured, remembering an intonement from his mother years earlier.

Rachel had lived her life by blind faith in God, drawing strength from it to survive the hard times and never losing sight of it through the good times. Matt knew he must count on that blind faith to carry his mother through another ordeal and return her home.

CHAPTER 3

THE TELEPHONE JARRED THE household from deep slumber to gripping fear. Matt's eyes darted open before the first short ring ended. He lay glued to the bed, hoping that grim news might disappear if he ignored the messenger. On the third ring, he remembered the phone was ringing in the Carters' home as well. The short ring belonged to the Bakers, the long to the Carters, and this one was unmistakably short.

Matt hurried from the bed to the knotted cypress table by the front door and grabbed the phone. He took a calming breath, picked up the receiver and said hello on the fifth ring.

"Matt."

It was Caroline. Her voice whispered in his ear, and she gave him time to brace for bad news.

So much for blind faith, Matt thought.

He wondered how long he had slept. He watched Joe bound into the hall, followed by John and Luke, before his eyes caught Summer. She clung to the door-facing of the girl's room, holding on for dear life.

His heart panicked. "Yeah," he answered. "What is it?"

"She's bad off, Matt," Caroline said. "You need to get here as soon as possible."

"I'm on my way," he promised. "How's Pa taken this?"

"He's holden up well for the moment," she replied. "But he's scared."

"I'll be there soon," Matt pledged again as he hung up the phone.

"Daddy?" Joe said.

"Is Granny okay?" Luke asked.

"Your mama says she's taken a turn for the worse," Matt announced calmly. "I need to get to the hospital."

"May I go with you, Daddy?" Joe asked.

"Me, too?" Summer added.

Matt considered the request, then nodded. "Okay," he agreed. "Just get dressed as fast as you can. We need to get there."

Glancing at the brass clock on Caroline's nightstand as he jerked on jeans and a shirt, Matt noted the time was just past four. A minute later, he was standing on the front porch, giving John and Carrie a forced smile, telling them to set the alarm clock so they would not miss the school bus and urging them back to sleep. He was reconsidering the decision to leave the younger children by themselves when a set of car lights came barreling down the road.

"Who in the world is that?" Joe asked.

His answer came seconds later as Amelia Carter wheeled her blue sedan into the yard, cut the bright lights and shut off the engine. Dressed in a worn housecoat with rollers in her hair, the mercantile owner was a far sight from the pretty picture she usually presented outside the privacy of her home.

"I heard the telephone," she said by way of greeting as she came toward them. "I figured you could use some help with the children."

Matt was touched by her thoughtfulness. Few people saw this side of Amelia, because they refused to look past her faults. It was true that Amelia gossiped too much, overwhelmed the timid with her forceful personality and sometimes got grand notions about herself. But she also possessed a generous spirit, a kind heart that expressed itself through deeds more than words. When the world went awry, Amelia believed in lacing up her boot strings and setting it right—a like it or lump it attitude that prevented her from making many true friends but earned the grudging respect of many acquaintances.

Thinking of her now, Matt remembered an essay Joe had written about Amelia. Joe had described her thoughtfulness as "callused compassion," and Matt thought the description fit perfectly. Except for those times when she became Queen Amelia, she was as genuine as anyone Matt knew. Over the years, he and the rest of her friends had learned to tolerate the woman's majestic moods. And, fortunately, for everyone, especially her husband and son, Amelia's royal moods were diminishing with age.

"You've taken a load off my mind, Amelia," Matt said as she stepped onto the porch. "I was gonna leave the kids by themselves, but then started wonderen whether that was the right thing to do. I appreciate you maken the decision easy. Make yourself comfortable, and go ahead and send the kids to school in the mornen."

Amelia gave him a caring smile. "What about your mama, Matt?"

"Caroline says she's bad off," Matt replied. "That's all I know."

Rachel was suffocating beneath the plastic tent. She fought for a breath of air, her arms thrashing and her body contorting on the hospital bed between fits of coughing and gagging. Vaguely, she heard the doctor order Sam and Caroline from the room, then tell a nurse they were losing her. She craved a single breath of air, to fill her lungs with oxygen, but the pneumonia had a chokehold on her windpipe. The realization came to Rachel that she was fighting for her life. And losing.

She heard Dr. Pittman's cracked voice again, this time instructing the nurse to suggest that Caroline call Matt and any other close kin to the hospital at once. Although unfamiliar with the Catholic way of death, Rachel acquired a sudden understanding of last rites. But while she felt at peace with the Lord, prepared for death as Preacher Cook put it, Rachel was not ready to die. She wanted a few more years with Sam and the children. She had a quilt to finish, and she wanted to make a dress from the blue gabardine material Caroline had given her at Christmas.

Still, she supposed if God was ready for her, then she would have no choice in the matter. Everyone had an appointed time with death and if hers was at hand, then she would leave behind unfinished work. Rachel had a vague notion that she should have planned better. Then, a gagging cough sent her thoughts swirling, and she lost consciousness.

Heat as hot as the fires of Hell itself roused her sometime later. Her throat was parched, her tongue swollen. A thin line of fever blisters stretched across her bottom lip. She was drenched with sweat, and her chest felt as if it had been beaten with a sledgehammer. Her breath came in shallow gasps, and the act of breathing caused a pain worse than childbirth.

Somewhere in the room, a coffee pot percolated. Rachel tried to smell the strong aroma, but detected only the odor of anesthesia. To her horror, she realized the noise was coming from her own fluid-filled lungs. Rachel wanted to touch her heart, to make sure it still beat, but she was too weak to lift her hand. She began to wonder if each breath would be her last, and time ceased to exist as Rachel knew it.

An eternity later, the emaciated doctor stood at her bedside, sponging alcohol across her face and forehead. Two nurses packed ice around her. Her body heat dropped quickly from the boiling point to something merely lukewarm. Soon, she felt cool and then ice-cold.

Chills shook Rachel, and her teeth chattered like a jackhammer. She was too tired to think, too numb to feel, so Rachel cleared her mind and surrendered to the deep blackness.

———————

Dr. Pittman sighed. "Sleep is the best medicine for her now," he told the two nurses who were with him in Rachel's room. "But how she can manage it while packed in ice is a mystery to me."

He pulled up his stethoscope and checked her lungs. Her pulse was almost steady, her blood pressure returning to normal. But the congestion in her chest was still thick.

Rachel's propensity for survival amazed the doctor. Two times now, he had been convinced she was at death's door, and twice she had been turned away. At the moment, a complete recovery seemed possible. But Dr. Pittman was determined to season his message with caution when he delivered the prognosis to her family. He saluted the nurses, then stepped outside the room where the Bakers were waiting.

He smiled thinly to ease their greatest fears, noting Matt had returned to the hospital with a young man and a girl in tow. "Your wife is a remarkable woman," he addressed Sam.

"Yes," Sam nodded. "She is at that."

"She's lucky to be alive," Dr. Pittman continued. "Honestly, I don't know how she did it. She's stabilized for the moment, but we have a long way to go before we're out of the woods. She's packed in ice now to lower her temperature. I hoped the fever would burn itself out, but it kept climben. The ice helped get a handle on it. Right now, she's sleepen. I wish I could tell you with certainty that everything will be okay. But I can't. I'm cautiously optimistic, but then again, this could be another calm before the storm. We'll have to wait and see."

Seconds later, the door to Rachel's room opened and a nurse called frantically for the doctor. "She's having trouble breathen again," the nurse announced. "You better suction her."

Dr. Pittman moved quickly inside the room, leaving Sam, Matt, Caroline, Joe and Summer to their collective fear. Caroline hugged her father-in-law in a protective embrace, as Matt slumped against the wall and Summer buried her head against Joe's chest.

They were hoping for a miracle, but all they could do was wait. And pray, Caroline decided. "Joe, you and Summer go to the chapel," she instructed her children. "Find a Bible, read John 4:16 aloud and then pray for your grandmother. God can make her better.

"Grandpa," she continued, looking Sam in the eyes. "You, Matt and I will do our prayen right here outside Ma's door. And if it's God's will, then she will get better."

"You're right, daughter," Sam sighed, taking Caroline's hands. "Prayer is our best hope."

"Will you join us, Matt?" Caroline said.

The question caught Matt by surprise. Startled, he frowned at Caroline, then saw Joe and Summer staring at him, perplexed by his indecision. Sensing their confusion, he knew at once this was not a time to create doubts of any kind. He pushed off the wall, nodded his children on their way to the chapel and went to stand beside his wife and father. They joined hands, bowed heads and offered their prayers to God. Matt did his best again to surrender to blind faith.

———

Rachel woke fully alert, sensing at once that she was better. She was weary from the struggle to breathe, and her chest ached with each rise and fall. But it was a dull pain, unlike the earlier crushing blows that had caved her breast. At the worst, it felt as if she had a bad case of the croup deep in her chest.

Sam was at her side, dozing stiffly in a straight-back chair that probably would crick his neck. She called weakly to him. Her voice, hoarse and strange even to Rachel, failed to rouse her husband.

She scanned the room, allowing her gaze to settle on the window blinds that shielded faded daylight. The dimness suited Rachel's mood. She felt more glum than physically sick. At a time when she should have been rejoicing over her improving health, Rachel was fretful.

For as long as she could remember, Rachel had looked to the future, hoping tomorrow or the next day would bring better times. She filled her days with hard work and sacrifice, believing those virtues would bring rewards one day—if not on this earth, then in Heaven.

Her life was dedicated to God and family, and the commitment was unwavering on both counts. Over the years, Rachel's faith in God had grown even stronger, along with her devotion to her husband, son, daughter-in-law and grandchildren. She deemed there was no price of self-sacrifice too high to serve Christ and help her family. Although Rachel believed more could always be done for the good Lord, she harbored no such compunction about her family. She had done her best, and she felt appreciated for the effort.

Still, doubts brewed in her mind.

The one thing for which Rachel had little time or patience was matters of the past. As she was prone to tell her family and friends, time tended to flavor their memories like too much sugar.

"You tell a story like my sister, Euna, sweetens tea," Rachel had scolded Sam during one of his frequent bouts of reminiscing about their early struggles on the farm. "Pour in three cups of sugar where one would have sufficed, then add six saccharine tablets for good measure. It's sweet stuff all right, but it ain't tea."

Remembering the incident, Rachel smoothed the sheets across the starchy, white hospital bed and realized she was guilty of the same thing. Except, instead of using sugar, she tended to flavor life with unsweetened chocolate or vanilla straight from the bottle. In any portion, the taste was bitter, and her conscience swallowed a double serving.

A troubling notion besieged Rachel, a sense of having traveled through a lifetime governed by her rigid philosophies rather than as master of her domain. With her expectations always put off into the future, she had managed somehow to lose sight of the business of living. She had been preoccupied with getting by and getting past, always in a hurry to get to whatever was next. In her rush to pay no mind to the past, perhaps she had forgotten dreams that could or should have been remembered.

A practical woman by choice, Rachel realized her thoughts were self-pitying. She found it odd that after so many years of refusing to subject herself to the rigors of reflection, she was now falling into the trap of second-guessing the past. It was foolish reasoning, a selfish surrender to the temptation of vanity. But nevertheless, a strong sense of emptiness plagued Rachel. She felt as if she had spent her life preparing a feast, yet forgotten to set a place for herself at the banquet table.

Without doubt, Rachel considered the family her greatest accomplishment as well as an infinite source of pride and joy. But the family was a creation of itself, and Rachel was only one of many members who were making lasting contributions to its history. As much as she felt fulfilled by those contributions, Rachel also needed to believe that she had nurtured a vital part of herself that would endure long after she was gone from this earth. And that was the crux of her melancholy: Nothing she knew validated this desire and she was beset by growing despair, the likelihood that she coveted something that did not exist.

Saddened, Rachel sought once more to wake her husband. "Sam," she called with as much energy as she could muster in that unfamiliar, throaty voice. "Sam. What time is it?"

His good eye popped open, and he flew from his chair, easing down on the bed beside her. "Rachel!" he exclaimed, relieved as he took her hand. "Thank God, you are awake at last. You've been so sick, and I've been worried sick. How do you feel?"

"Better than before," she smiled weakly. "But not very strong. What time is it?"

"About six o'clock in the evenen," Sam replied. "This is your third day in the hospital, and you've been in a coma for the last thirty-six hours or so. Until sometime early this mornen, the doctor wasn't sure whether you'd make it. Your lungs filled up with fluid, and you couldn't breathe. But you're better now, and we'll be home before you know it."

He leaned down and kissed her forehead. "You scared the daylights out of me, Rachel," he said tenderly, looking into her eyes. "I'd never before thought about you not be'en beside me." He shook his head with a fearful expression. "I need you. And I love you."

Rachel smiled softly at her husband, then pulled his big, rough hand against her cheek. She nodded, closed her eyes and drifted off to sleep.

She awoke an hour later to the booming voice of a stout nurse, whose cheerfulness irritated Rachel. Once her eyes adjusted to the glare of bright lights, she discovered a flock of relatives surrounding her bed.

"Good Lord!" Rachel said as her eyes lit on her sister from Ocala, Florida. "Euna, what are you doen here?" she asked seconds before she saw the preacher, Adam Cook, standing at the foot of the bed.

Chagrined by the preacher's witness of her obvious irritation, she apologized immediately for the outburst. "You'll have to excuse me, Preacher," she said. "It's not often I take the Lord's name in vain, but I'm surprised to see all these faces."

"Think nothen of it, Mrs. Baker," Adam Cook said. "We should be maken apologies for intruden on you. Perhaps, we should leave you to your rest."

"No need for that," Rachel said, returning her gaze to her sister.

Euna was tall and thin as a beanpole, a stark contrast to her twin, Edna, who had been short and stout. Edna had died years earlier during the birth of her third child, and Euna was Rachel's only living sibling.

"I *must* have been sick if you came up all the way from Ocala," Rachel remarked with a grudging smile.

"I wanted to make sure you were well cared for," Euna replied, giving Rachel a quick hug. "I wasn't ready to be the last of the bunch."

Rachel would have preferred solitude, but the situation called for gracious acceptance of the well wishes of her family and friends. Besides the preacher and her sister, Sam, Matt, Caroline, Joe and Summer had crowded into the room.

Soon after the nurse had taken her temperature and checked her vital signs, Dr. Pittman strolled into the room. He was seized immediately by one of his coughing spells, which caused a shock of panic among those who were unprepared for the fit.

Rushing to drag a chair under the doctor, Joe instead slammed one of his shins against the steel legs of the hospital bed. Dr. Pittman waved off the attempted help, which was just as well since Joe had crumpled into the chair himself and was already massaging his aching leg.

Had she felt better, Rachel might have laughed at the slapstick circumstances. Instead, her ire grew. She tolerated the doctor's poking and prodding, figuring he was owed as much given his role in saving her life. She was civil to her family, despite their worried smiles and stilted comments. And she was genuinely grateful when the preacher took her hand and gave thanks to the Lord for her recovering health. But when the prayer was ended and Preacher Cook took his leave, Rachel made her preferences known. Bluntly speaking, she told her family to go home where they were needed and leave her to rest.

Knowing the woman's limit, everyone left but Sam, who refused to be budged from her side. "I'm stayen right here till the doctor says you can come home with me," he declared.

"Suit yourself," Rachel replied flatly. "But that chair's gonna make a poor bed, and I'm not sharen this one."

Rachel slept soundly until early on her fourth day in the hospital, waking only when an orderly served breakfast. She forced down a small amount of the chicken broth, then pushed away the tray and took a short nap until Dr. Pittman arrived to check on her.

"I've already told your husband, Mrs. Baker, and now I'll tell you," he said when he had completed the examination. "You're an amazen woman. Two days ago, I thought your time had come to sing with angels. And now, you're gainen strength with every passen minute. You've surely been blessed with one of God's miracles. At this rate of recovery, you'll be goen home to your family in no time at all."

Sam clasped his hands and cracked his knuckles at the doctor's prognosis. "Do you hear that, Rachel!" he exclaimed with uncontrollable delight. "The good Lord obviously has been listenen to the singen at Benevolence, and he realizes our church needs your splendid voice more than Heaven does."

The doctor laughed, but Rachel arched her eyebrows at Sam. "He's exaggeraten, doctor," she said. "The singen is good enough at our church—with or without me."

After the doctor had gone, Rachel retreated into her private thoughts. Understanding her desire for solitude, Sam took a walk around the hospital to stretch out his stiff muscles. He spent nearly two hours chatting with acquaintances and strangers, reading an abandoned newspaper and eating an early lunch in the hospital cafeteria.

When he returned to Rachel, she greeted him with the same faraway look that had caused him to leave the room earlier and returned her gaze to the blank television screen. Although surprised by her reluctance to talk, Sam was not overly concerned by her inattentive behavior. Over the years, they had come to understand each other's various moods, always mindful of the need for privacy, yet close at hand to provide solace when it was wanted. He gave a brief description of his morning, then sat down in the chair and promptly fell asleep.

In the afternoon, a steady stream of family and friends visited Rachel. Caroline brought Euna, and Paul Berrien came with his two sisters and an arrangement of red roses. Pearl Walker, Rachel's best friend, and several members of the Ladies Aid Society from church brought her one of the quilts they kept on hand for members of the community who were gravely ill and needed cheer. Sam recognized several squares in the quilt as the handiwork of his wife, whom he suspected felt ridiculous to receive a gift of her own stitching.

Rachel treated each of her well-wishers with courtesy, but Sam could tell she was relieved when the last one left. He hoped she might be ready to talk in the hour they had before supper, but his wife continued her silent contemplation. Mildly annoyed, Sam took another walk around the hospital, counting the minutes until supper and the arrival of their nighttime visitors.

In the late evening when everyone had gone, Sam made up his

mind to confront his wife. He suspected Rachel was troubled by something other than her health, and her disinclination to confide in him was both worrisome and frustrating. Not since the early days of their marriage had Rachel held her tongue when she was distressed.

He tried first to prod her into conversation with pointed questions, but Rachel evaded him with simple nods or an occasional grunt. At length, his puzzlement gave away to irritation, and Sam exploded. "Enough of this dad-blamed silence, Rachel!" he railed. "I know you feel poorly, but that's no excuse to act as if I don't exist. You cannot continue to ignore me."

When she failed to acknowledge him, Sam walked to the end of the bed, crossed his arms and continued his tirade. "This mornen, the doctor said you're menden and on the way back to good health," he said stoutly. "You should be rejoicen, Rachel, but instead, you're as gloomy as English fog. Why, I haven't even heard you give a single word of thanks to the good Lord for restoren your health."

Her eyes flashed with anger, and Sam was pleased to see the spark. He had struck a nerve.

"I'll have you know, Sam Baker, that I am thankful to be feelen better, and I have indeed told the Lord exactly that," she growled. "And furthermore, I'll have you know that my prayers are between me and the Lord. It's none of your business."

"Touché," Sam agreed. "You're absolutely right. Your prayers are your business, and I'm sorry for sticken my nose into it. But, Rachel, this silence is unlike you. Somethen's botheren you, and you're keepen it from me." He sat beside her on the bed. "I just want to help. Please tell me what's wrong. Don't shut me out."

She began to cry, so softly at first that Sam almost failed to notice. First, her eyes brimmed; then the tears spilled down her face. Sam figured he could have counted on one hand the times Rachel had cried in their years as husband and wife, and these tears disturbed him. He edged closer on the bed, grasping her by the hands and holding on until she was ready to confide in him.

"Where did the time go, Sam?" Rachel asked finally, the words coming in a hoarse whisper. "And how did we get so old so fast?"

She shifted her gaze to his face, saying, "If there's one thing I always thought we'd have plenty of, it was time. But we're getten short on even that now, aren't we? I've become an old woman, Sam, an old woman who's probably goen to die with little to show for in this life."

Her head shook tiredly, and she glanced away. "All my life, I wanted to do or make or give somethen that would last, somethen I could be proud of and leave behind when I die. But here I am now, sixty-five years old ...."

She looked again at Sam with a sad-eyed smile. "Or am I?" she asked.

Sam shrugged and rubbed the black patch over his bad eye. "I don't know the date," he confessed. "I've lost track of time these last few days."

"It doesn't matter," Rachel said. "A day late, a day early—it doesn't change the facts. It's gone way past the time to do somethen grand in life."

Sam was dumbstruck by the revelation. In his wildest imagination, he never would have expected Rachel to worry about her age. Such fears contradicted her entire nature. Rachel was the most practical woman Sam knew, and this line of worry from her sounded almost like nonsense. Yet, he sensed her fretting was sincere and he wanted to ease her mind.

"May I ask what it is you would have liked to have done?" he asked gently.

"I can't say for certain," Rachel answered with a shake of her head. "It's just a feelen, a knowen that there was somethen special I should have seen to, but I never quite got around to it when the time was right. And now, the time is gone, and I can't even figure out what it was that I should have done in the first place."

Sam considered the statement. "If it's any consolation, Rachel, I think most everything you've ever done has been somethen special. You've been a wonderful wife, a loven mother, and you've created a legacy of memories that will last a lifetime or two after you're gone."

"We all touch people's lives in some way or another," Rachel replied. "And don't get me wrong, I'm thankful to have been able to do that, and I'm proud to have been your wife and the mother of your children. Still, though, I would have liked to have left behind an inheritance, something of value."

"Rachel!" Sam said sharply. "What in tarnation do you think I'm gonna leave behind when I die? Nothen but a few acres of land," he answered, "and I wouldn't have that without all your hard work and sacrifices. If it's an inheritance you're wanten to leave, then there's no more reason to fret. You have an inheritance; it's somethen real and lasten. We poured our hearts and souls into the farm, and our spirits will roam those woods and fields for years to come."

She smiled and patted his hand. "You're right, and I am proud of the farm, maybe more than I ever thought I would be. I should count my blessens that I was able to work beside you each and every day and we were dedicated to the same goal. And I do, too. But I could have been happy anywhere as long as you were there with me. The farm was your dream, Sam, and it will be your inheritance."

She hesitated, then added, "I'm be'en selfish, but still I wish I could have been blessed with an inheritance of my own, somethen that was mine and only mine."

"I appreciate the thought, Rachel, but I'm still confused," Sam remarked. "And I think you are, too."

"Yes, I am," she replied glumly. "And rather late in life at that."

Sam toyed with his eye patch, mulling over the situation. Rachel's sentiments left him bewildered. He was unfamiliar with this notion of wanting something, yet not knowing what it was. Of course, the same was true of his wife, which explained her predicament. There had been few times of doubt in Rachel's life. She studied problems and she fixed them, all with the precision of a mathematician. Now, however, the answers eluded her, and Sam was likewise stumped.

"I wish I could help you figure it out," he offered at length.

"Pshaw!" she said, waving her hand to dismiss his concern. "I'm just acten my age," she continued gallantly. "All this carryen on does indeed make me sound like a silly old woman. You should just tell me to hush up."

"I would never do that," Sam declared. "But I do think it's best that we sleep on our thoughts. Perhaps tomorrow we'll have fresh perspective."

"No, no, no," Rachel said with forced determination. "I've ranted and thought too much nonsense as it is. It's probably just the strain of be'en sick and allowen myself to give in to self-pity. Ignore me, Sam. I'll be fine."

Rachel's prophecy went unfulfilled. And Rachel went from the hospital bed to her bed at home.

She complained of feeling weak, refused to eat her meals and rejected plans for a late birthday celebration. For the first time in her life, she missed consecutive Sunday services at church. And yet, two weeks after he had dismissed Rachel from the hospital, Dr. Pittman pronounced her recovery complete and suggested she resume a full schedule of her normal routines.

Out of boredom, Rachel accepted his advice and returned to her daily chores. But her heart was elsewhere. In spite of her good intentions, she moped around the house, brooding in silence as the family tried to guess the cause of her malaise. Rachel felt full of self-doubt and robbed of self-worth, but she brushed off repeated attempts to bolster her spirits. As the days passed, however, this constant state of anxiety took a toll on her fragile health.

One month after coming home from the hospital, Rachel sat at the kitchen table with Sam, Matt and Caroline eating a snack for lunch. She felt a flutter above her eyelid followed by a stabbing pain in her left temple. She started to rub her head, then tried to stand. But the pain intensified, and sudden dizziness overcame her.

"Sam!" she gasped.

It was the last thing she remembered, except for the sensation of falling through air. She never felt the linoleum floor, which stopped the flight of her body, and she was unaware of being rushed to the hospital by her worried family. She regained consciousness a few hours later and was blessed to have all her faculties intact.

Dr. Pittman diagnosed the seizure as a mild stroke. He hospitalized Rachel for three days, ran a battery of tests and released her, again with an excellent prognosis for recovery.

The doctor's words of encouragement, however, fell on deaf ears. Rachel seemed resigned to ill health. It was almost as if she had given up on life. At home, she retreated to the bed, with a request for peace and quiet.

Almost overnight, the home turned into a funeral parlor, with everyone cautious of their every word, fearing they would be the one who disturbed Rachel and triggered a worsening of her illness. They were strung across a long line of caution, walking on eggshells. Caroline and Matt took out their frustrations on each other and on their children to some extent. The children battered each other with insults and occasional blows, while Sam harped like a bleating sheep on the need for family harmony.

Entombed in her room, Rachel was oblivious to the family tumult. Like a loose seam, her family was coming apart—in desperate need of a fine seamstress to mend the frayed ends.

CHAPTER 4

SUMMER FIXED HER GAZE on the blackboard, looking past Mr. Barnes, the eighth-grade history teacher who was lecturing on Georgia's rivers. For two days now, the class had heard point after point about the influence of rivers in shaping Georgia's history. As far as Summer was concerned, the discussion was pointless. She'd never so much as set eyes on any of the waterways mentioned in the history book, and she was unimpressed to learn that three nations had fought for control of the St. Mary's River or that Stephen Foster had immortalized the Suwannee River in the song, *Old Folks at Home*, without ever even laying eyes on its black waters. Furthermore, she questioned the wisdom of any history book that failed to mention the rivers close to home—New River, the Alapaha, the Willacoochee and the Withlacoochee, or Little River.

She acknowledged Mr. Barnes with an interested nod, then resumed her thoughts. At some point, she'd figure out what she needed to know about Georgia's rivers. If worse came to worst, she would humble herself and ask Joe, the family history buff, who probably knew all the pertinent facts about the 75 major rivers in Georgia and a few of the minor ones as well. But for now, Summer's mind was preoccupied with a more important matter—her grandmother's health.

In a way, it seemed as if Rachel had decided to die. Summer felt guilty for having this thought, but the truth was the truth as her grandmother had reminded her and almost everybody else on more than one occasion. And while no one at home would come right out and admit it, everyone was thinking along those lines, except perhaps Sam, who was in the process of worrying himself and everyone else to the sick bed.

For several days now, Summer had been mad at her grandmother's behavior. She considered it tacky for someone to decide to die without first consulting the ones who would suffer the consequences. And she was more than put out by the sorry state of affairs at home, all because

Rachel had decided she was ready to meet her maker. Brash as these thoughts seemed, Summer knew they were nothing more than bluff and bluster. Deep down, her grandmother's illness frightened her, not so much the physical ailments but rather Rachel's apparent crisis of faith.

"A crisis of faith—not in God but rather in her own self-worth," Preacher Cook had suggested to Caroline and Sam last Sunday afternoon following one of his frequent visits to Rachel's bedside since she became ill. "Mrs. Baker is struggling with self-doubt."

Summer's instincts suggested Rachel would weather this crisis, but there was just enough doubt to keep her worried about the outcome. And it was that hint of fear driving Summer's thoughts, motivating her to search out the root of Rachel's depression.

Summer had a good idea of where the search would end. But she decided to start at the beginning anyway, hoping to discover something new or perhaps rediscover something special.

Rachel came from a long line of seamstresses. Her maternal grandmother had used a needle and thread to support three young children after being widowed at an early age, and her fondest memories of her own mother dwelled inevitably on times they had sewed side by side. As a young girl, even as a young woman charged with running a household in the wake of her mother's death, Rachel had dreamed of someday owning a dress shop and sewing the kind of clothes worn by women of high society. She would pore over each edition of the Sears, Roebuck catalog, identify the most exquisite dresses and then create perfect replicas for her twin sisters and herself. In time, her services were being sought by dozens of neighbor women.

Faced with the opportunity of a lifetime, Rachel had immersed herself in the work. Before too much time had passed, the majority of women in her Baptist church, as well as those of the Methodist persuasion, wore dresses made by Rachel. Eventually, her sewing attracted the attention of a downtown shop owner, who hired Rachel to do alterations and suggested she might make a handsome profit by allowing the boutique to sell some of her dresses. Excited and flabbergasted by the idea, Rachel had been ready to plunge headlong into the venture when Sam Baker made an abrupt entrance into her life. Soon afterward, Rachel was sewing her most exquisite and elegant creation of all—her wedding dress.

"If I had but one vanity, then I suppose it would be my wedden dress," Rachel had confessed on the day she first showed the garment to Summer.

She kept the dress stored away in her cedar chest and had waited deliberately until Summer was old enough to appreciate the artistry and technique required in the sewing. Fashioned from the finest broadcloth of the day, the wedding dress was a masterpiece of pure white beauty in simplicity. Long-sleeved, with a fitted bodice and a full tea-length skirt, the dress flowed with elegance and featured the richness of tiny seed pearl buttons and embroidered lace roses on the neckline and sleeves.

"It is by far the prettiest dress I've ever made," Rachel had told Summer. "I spent months on it—not so much sewen but tryen to imagine what it must look like. I thought long and hard about each cut of material and every stitch along the way. And if I do say so myself, the dress is close to perfection. I've worn it only once in my entire life, and that was on the day I married Sam. Maybe it was foolishness to put away such a beautiful dress, but I believed then and now that some things are intended for once-in-a-lifetime occasions. My wedden dress was one of them."

Rachel had lapsed into silence as she returned the dress to its protective cover, while an awestruck Summer committed details of the garment to her memory. When the dress was returned to its rightful place and the cedar chest closed, Rachel had made an admission from deep in her soul.

"I'm not one to wish for things that might have been," she told Summer. "But I would have liked the opportunity to make more dresses like that."

Finding her voice at last, Summer had asked, "Why didn't you, Granny?"

"I don't know, child," Rachel replied. "Perhaps I should have. It just seemed frivolous to me back then, an extravagance that I had neither the time nor money to indulge. First off, your grandpa and I were busy clearen fields. Then, I started haven babies. I was so busy back in those days that I could scarcely keep my head on straight, much less think about sewen beautiful dresses. At one point, we were so poor that I used flour sacks to make shirts for the boys and dresses for Ruth. Later, when times were better, I planned to make some fancy dresses—for Ruth, if no one else. Somehow, I never got around to it, though. Then Ruth was gone and I just never saw the need after that. When you're plain people liven on a farm, there's not much need for fancy dresses."

While the full significance of Rachel's answer escaped Summer, the wedding dress had captivated the girl. Long after the dress was re-turned to the cedar chest, Summer remained fascinated and enthralled by its beauty, the delicate embroidery, and the rich texture of the broadcloth. She felt as if she had discovered a secret door leading to a place filled with treasures of silk, lace and velvet. It was a magical feeling of knowing she possessed a key that would admit her to this realm, a sense of coming home to a place that she had always known existed for her.

Part of her discovery was the knowledge that she wanted to make many dresses, which, as Rachel put it, should be worn only once in a lifetime. But essentially, Summer made the glorious discovery of beauty, beauty in the material sense to be sure but still grace and ele-gance shaped from yards and yards of lovely fabrics. It was a marvelous feeling, the beginning of something special and a sense of destiny.

———————

Like the arrival of daybreak, the reason for Rachel's melancholy dawned on Summer.

If she wanted to place blame, Summer supposed she could have accepted responsibility for the lately wistful ways of her grandmother. She was the one, after all, who had sown seeds of doubt in Rachel's mind about the value of dedicating her life to the needs of her hus-band and her family. Perhaps Rachel had never voiced her doubts, but it was easy to imagine the questions that likely claimed her attention.

Certain that Rachel had forgiven her for the angry outburst, Sum-mer was similarly convinced her grandmother had been hurt to the core by the girl's ready rejection of sewing. At the time, Summer had lashed out with the first words that came to mind. Her denouncement of all that was dear to Rachel had come in a moment of frustration; she had rebelled against the confines of her predicament.

Regardless of the harsh words spoken, Summer would have ex-pected her grandmother to sense the shallowness of her tirade and realize the depth of her appreciation of the beauty produced by a nee-dle and a thread. Perhaps Rachel had, too. But hindsight told Summer that Rachel would have deemed even the slightest rejection of sewing as a personal failure, especially from the prized apprentice she had nurtured every step of the way.

Whether sewing a man's work shirt or a formal evening gown, when Rachel took a needle and thread in hand, sat down at the sewing machine or laid out a piece of material, she transformed into the young woman with big dreams. On the day she first showed her wedding dress to Summer, Rachel had glowed with the pride of accomplishment and a sense of fulfillment. Remembering the moment, Summer recalled the sense of destiny enveloping her as she had slipped into her grandmother's dreams. It was a memory tempered by the knowledge that Rachel had put aside those dreams to concentrate on more worthwhile pursuits such as loving her husband and nurturing their family.

No one should have second-guessed such a decision, and Summer didn't think for one second Rachel would make that mistake. Still, it was easy to conclude that Rachel would have felt her dreams trampled by the relentless march of time, especially when the one person with whom she had shared those dreams had made light of the legacy. If Summer had been able to tell her grandmother that she wanted to be a dressmaker on the day Rachel brought out the wedding dress from its hiding place, then the older woman's dreams would have found a refuge of safekeeping. But Summer was only twelve years old, and she had required time to figure out the future.

Rachel might have simplified the process by impressing on Summer her hopes that the granddaughter would fulfill the grandmother's dreams. But Rachel, despite all her strict, set ways, was a woman of conscience. She had shared her dreams, her skills and her talent with Summer, but she would never foist expectations on the girl. If Summer chose to become a dressmaker later in life, then she would make the decision of her own free will, without the expectations of anyone but with all the support and encouragement of everyone dear to her.

When she thought about the situation with her grandmother in those terms, Summer understood more than ever the wisdom of Rachel's decision to devote her life to God, Sam and family—even at the expense of lifelong dreams. Clothes were clothes, after all, and beautiful dresses were nothing more than that. They were lovely to behold, to touch and to wear, but it was the people who wore them that mattered most.

Having come to this conclusion, Summer supposed she could march into her grandmother's room and tell Rachel these things. But to Summer's way of thinking, actions spoke louder than words. Somehow, she had to find a way to help her grandmother remember just how important was the business of living. And somehow, she had to make Rachel realize that the dreams they shared were still within the reach of both women.

On the same day Summer decided to put purpose back into Rachel's life, the Cookville chapter of the Veterans of Foreign Wars decided to move the annual county fair to mid-April from its traditional fall dates. The reasons were unclear to Summer, who was in her home-room class preparing for the bus ride home when the announcement was made.

Later, Summer would think how often the fortunes of fate fell her way. At the time, however, she saw only the opportunity to give new life to her grandmother's dreams.

Summer adored the fair with its carnival rides, sideshows, caramel apples and cotton candy. But she gave only fleeting thought to these thrills and instead focused attention on the various competitions that were equally important to the fair.

The Baker family had claimed their share of prizes over the years. Joe had won best of show with one of the family's prized shoats sev-eral years ago, and Summer had earned top honors in the junior dressmaking event last year. Caroline had captured blue ribbons with her pepper jelly on two occasions as well as one each for her tomato preserves and a special coconut cake.

Rachel's pear tarts had won blue ribbons several times, and she had carried home another blue ribbon three years ago for a yo-yo quilt. But the prize Rachel coveted more than any other was for specialty sewing, an event that rewarded creativity as well as technique. So far, Rachel had failed even to place in the competition, where the winning entries had ranged from a purse to a tablecloth and a formal evening gown in recent years. As she regretted every year, Rachel simply could not come up with an entry that would set her work apart from everybody else's.

With all that in mind, Summer set her sights on the competition.

As soon as the bus rolled to a stop in front of the Baker house that afternoon, Summer charged off it and headed straight for Rachel's bed-room. "Where's Granny?" she shouted as she walked down the hall.

"Hush up, Summer," Caroline admonished as her daughter entered the kitchen. "She's in her room, and you know we're not supposed to disturb her."

"I know," Summer replied. "But I've got important news, and it can't wait. We don't have much time as it is."

Dropping her books on the table, Summer marched over to Ra-chel's bedroom, barged through the door and announced matter-of-factly, "Granny, they're haven the annual fall fair this spring. I think we ought to team up to enter the specialty sewen. There's nothen in the rules that says teams can't enter, and I need your help. I was thinken a collection of doll clothes is just the thing that might win us first place."

Summer crossed her arms and held her ground as Caroline stormed into the room, apologizing to Rachel for the girl's behavior and ordering her daughter from the room.

"Well, Granny?" Summer insisted, ignoring her mother. "What do you think?"

"Your grandmother's not up to it this year, Summer," Caroline remarked. "Are you forgetten that she's been very sick?"

"She's not very sick at the moment," Summer diagnosed boldly. "But if you want, Granny, you can sit in bed and do your part of the sewen. The important thing is to get started as soon as possible. Will you help me? Don't you think a collection of doll clothes will do the trick for us?"

A flash of anger lit Rachel's eyes, giving way instantly to serious consideration of the proposition. She pulled herself into a sitting position against the headboard, glancing from Summer to Caroline.

Rachel frowned slightly, then said, "It's a grand idea, Summer. When do you want to get started?"

"The sooner, the better, so how 'bout right now?" Summer suggested. "I've already come up with several ideas. We can discuss designs and materials and maybe come up with a schedule to keep us on track."

"Are you sure you're up to this, Ma?" Caroline asked for the sake of caution.

Rachel shook her head affirmatively and motioned Summer to the bed. "It's time, Caroline," she nodded. "Way past time if I say so myself."

Caroline gave her mother-in-law and daughter each a hug, then left the two seamstresses to their work.

———————

Later that evening, Summer invaded Joe's room for a private chat. Without knocking on his closed door, she pushed it open, marched into the tiny room and fell onto the twin bed with a heavy sigh.

"I became a woman today," she announced, slinging a forearm across her forehead and letting loose another exaggerated sigh.

Used to one or two of these interruptions a night from his brothers and sisters, Joe detected a hint of seriousness beneath Summer's dramatics. He pushed aside his research paper, leaned his chair against

the wall and cupped the back of his head with his hands, more interested in her thoughts than his unstirred expression revealed.

"Should I offer congratulations or condolences?" he said, drawing
a puzzled stare in response. "Are you haven cramps or anything like
that?" he asked to break the silence.

"Oh, that," Summer replied, understanding his intent. "I got my
period the week after Christmas, Joe—around New Year's, when I was
so grumpy."

Joe cocked his eyebrows. "So why all the melodrama tonight?" he
inquired. "It seems a bit late in the game for that."

Summer flipped onto her side, resting on her elbow. "Will you take
me serious, Joe?"

"Sure I will," Joe answered, resting the chair on the floor and clasp-
ing hands in lap, a sure sign she had his undivided attention. "What's
on your mind?"

"What I should have said," Summer began, "is that I understood today what it means to become a woman. You're a man, and you can do
pretty much what you want in life. But it's different for me. I know I'll
have more choices in life than Mama did when she was young or Granny,
too. I might end up as a famous fashion designer or maybe nothen more
than a housewife. But either way, I'll be expected to nurture my family.
You on the other hand will be expected to provide for your family."

"I can nurture, too," Joe commented.

Ignoring his remark, Summer continued: "I'm not sayen there's a
right way or a wrong way, but men generally go about the business of
maken a liven for their family, while women run the household. But
regardless, it's this idea of nurturen that fascinates me. I think I'll be
good at it."

"Frankly, I've always thought of you as more bossy than anything
else," Joe interrupted.

"Maybe sometimes you have to be bossy to do a good job of nurturen," Summer shot back. "And maybe you have to be tender and
loven, helpful and caren, patient and understanden, too. I know I've
got a lot to learn about it, but today I realized how important it is to
nurture your family. Maybe it sounds dumb to you, Joe, but this is
somethen I look forward to and want to be good at doen, maybe more
than anything else I'll ever do in life."

Joe stared at his sister, dumbfounded by her remarks.

"Well?" Summer prompted a pregnant moment later. "Does it
sound dumb or not?"

"It sounds very grown-up," he answered at last. "Exactly what I would expect a good woman to say. In fact, though I've never heard them put the thought in those exact words, it sounds very much like Mama and Granny. They're both excellent nurturers, and you'd do well to learn from them." He paused. "But it appears you've already figured that out for yourself."

Summer gloated, pleased by the compliment.

"So what brought you to this understanden about yourself, little sister?"

"In a roundabout way, it was Granny," Summer replied. "I was in my Georgia history class today—which, by the way, we need to talk about later—and she was pretty much on my mind through the whole class. I was thinken about that argument she and I had on New Year's Eve. Do you remember?"

Joe nodded his recollection of the debacle.

"Plus, I was thinken about her be'en sick and all, and then some of the things we have in common, especially our love of sewen," Summer continued. "Granny's spent her whole life taken care of other people, which is as fine a thing as anybody could ever do. But did you know she wanted to be a dressmaker when she was young?"

"I know she was worken for a dress shop when she and Grandpa got married," Joe remarked. "Guess it's not surprisen that she would have wanted to make dresses."

"You want to be a journalist, right?" Summer asked.

Again, Joe gave an affirmative nod.

"Known you, Joe, you'll probably be a great one," Summer admired, bringing a blushing smile to her brother's face. "But what if for some reason, you couldn't be. What if you had to choose between a career and your family?"

His smile faded, replaced by a doubtful shrug.

"Let's put it this way," Summer went on. "What if you made a choice to stay here on the farm instead of becomen a journalist because you wanted to get married more than anything and have six kids? Even if you had no real regrets about that decision, you'd probably always wonder what might have been."

"Probably," Joe agreed. "But I can't see any of this happenen, can you?"

"No," Summer replied. "But that's exactly what happened to Granny. She had a dream, but she had to give it up for somethen else more important."

"True," Joe said. "But *she* decided what was most important to her."

"Probably," Summer agreed. "But I've never asked her about that. Have you?"

"No, and I never will," Joe remarked with force. "That's her business."

"Agreed," Summer said. "Still, I'd like Granny to see some of her dressmaken dreams come true in one way or another."

"I smell somethen strange," Joe said suddenly. "What exactly are you cooken up, little sister?"

Summer smiled mischievously, then told her brother about the plans to enter the specialty sewing competition at the county fair, including one significant detail that she had withheld from Rachel as they discussed the project earlier in the day. When she had finished outlining the plan, she promised Joe to secrecy and predicted with confidence the Baker team would bring home the blue ribbon.

"Rowenna Rowan has won two years runnen, includen last year with the most gosh-awful purse you could ever imagine," Summer explained matter-of-factly. "The thing had feathers on it. It was ugly as sin, but it was also very different. That's what the judges seem to favor year after year—whatever's unusual. I can't ever remember anyone enteren a collection of doll clothes, and I just bet no one else will this year, except for Granny and me. We're a shoo-in to win that blue ribbon."

Joe leaned his chair back against the wall, once more relaxing his neck against his cradled hands. "You know what, Summer?" he remarked. "I don't doubt it one minute."

Summer grinned, folded her arms and sat up cross-legged in the bed. "If he heard me boasten like this, the preacher would probably tell me to read the first chapter of Ecclesiastics," she said.

"I forget that one," Joe replied.

"Vanity of vanities, saith the preacher," Summer quoted scripture. "Vanity of vanities, all is vanity."

"Vanity is not one of your faults, little sister," Joe said. "I suspect Preacher Cook would pat you on the back and ask how you managed to get Granny out of her sick bed."

"To tell you the truth," Summer admitted, lowering her voice, "Rowenna Rowan probably had more to do with it than me. She's not one of Granny's favorite people, and I'm sure she'd love to take that blue ribbon from her."

Joe laughed aloud, and Summer seized the opportunity to change the subject to something on her mind.

"So tell me, Joe," she asked, "if you had to choose between haven a family and a career, which would it be?"

"A career, hands-down," Joe answered quickly. "But since I'm a while away from having that choice, it's an easy question to answer. Ask me ten or fifteen years from now and I might have to rethink it.

I've never imagined myself as a married man with children, but I think it's important."

"Do you consider yourself a man?" Summer asked, with obvious curiosity.

Joe thought a moment. "Since I can't point to an obvious rite of passage like you, I guess my best answer is that I'm worken toward it," he said. "Just from talken with Daddy and Grandpa, I get the feelen that it's a gradual process. Obviously, when I turn twenty-one, I'll be considered a man. But it's a lot more complicated than that, don't you think?"

"Yeah," she admitted. "Despite today's revelation, I've gotta long way to go to full-fledged womanhood. I suppose these things won't ever be easy, will they?"

"Probably not," Joe remarked, "but you're well on the way, Summer, and you'll be a better one tomorrow and the next day after that."

Summer grinned. "So are you, brother."

Using Barbie dolls as models, Summer and Rachel fashioned their collection of clothes—evening gowns of pale yellow and green satin, a suit of blue velvet and dresses of red paisley print, pink chiffon and black silk. They sewed with painstaking perfection, creating replicas of the most elegant fashions in the pattern books they collected from cloth stores.

"These are just beautiful," Summer told her grandmother one afternoon as they thumbed through the pattern books. "Maybe someday I'll design clothes that appear in these books."

The suggestion put a gleam in Rachel's eye, and her health and spirit returned in almost measurable quantities as the fair's grand opening drew nearer. She became her bustling self around the house and was once again in attendance at Benevolence Missionary Baptist Church.

In the privacy of Joe's room, Summer worked on the signature piece of the collection, a flawless replica of Rachel's wedding dress. It was a miniaturized masterpiece, faithful to every detail of the original.

At last, the day of the fair's grand opening arrived. In the living room where the family gathered shortly after breakfast for last-minute discussions of the day's activities, Summer and Rachel unveiled their collection.

Probably everyone had seen some snippet of the doll clothes over the last several weeks, but this was their first opportunity to view the collection in its entirety. Spread across a line against a backdrop of black velvet, the tiny clothes dazzled the eye, each piece an exquisite example of design and sewing perfection. From the rich texture of materials to the elegant lines of stitching, the collection radiated an aura of excellence. In more simple terms, prizewinner was sewed all over it, even among those who did not know a backstitch from a whipstitch or basting from tacking.

"Rowenna Rowan doesn't stand a chance of winnen that blue ribbon this year," Joe declared, the first among them to find a voice of congratulations.

"Goodness gracious no," Caroline echoed him. "It's everything y'all wanted it to be and more. The technique's perfect, and the idea is not only unusual but plumb awestriken. I don't know when I've ever seen finer work."

In the midst of rounds of hearty congratulations and well-wishing, Summer cried out suddenly, "We forgot somethen, Granny."

The noise subsided instantly to dead silence as everyone looked to Summer, wondering about the missing creation.

Rachel looked over the collection piece by piece. "No, honey," she told Summer, shaking her head. "This is everything."

"What on earth else could there be, darlen," Caroline added, as everyone caught the suddenly unmistakable gleam in Summer's eye. "It's already perfect," she added, almost as a curious afterthought.

"Not quite yet," Summer replied mysteriously, looking to the hall, where Joe was walking toward them holding a brown paper bag.

Moments earlier, he had slipped away unnoticed as the family congratulated Summer and Rachel on their excellent work. Now, coming to a stop behind the Victorian couch, he handed the bag to Summer, with a wink of encouragement.

"I have somethen I'd like to show Granny before we go to the fair," Summer said coyly to her mystified family. "I know how much this meant to her, and I wanted to find some way to show how much it meant to me, too. I thought maybe we could add it to our collection."

Without further delay, Summer reached inside the bag, pulled out the tiny wedding dress and placed it on the velvet backdrop, which was draped across the coffee table.

Accustomed as they were to sharing moments, both tender and robust, none of the family was prepared to acknowledge this breathtaking tribute to their matriarch. The level of care, devotion and love resonating in the garment struck a chord of silence, even among those who were unaware the dress was a perfect copy of Rachel's wedding dress.

This time, it was Sam who first found his voice. "Your wedden dress, Rachel," he said, his words touched with the reverence of memory.

"Summer," Caroline gasped, awed as much over the obvious talent of her daughter as the sheer beauty of the dress. She wanted to thank the girl and sing her praises all at once. She settled for a crushing embrace. "It's beautiful, darlen," Caroline said before releasing her daughter. "Just beautiful."

Matt and Carrie added their voices to the swell of rave reviews, but Summer barely heard them. She was focused solely on Rachel's reaction to the dress, waiting for her grandmother's stamp of approval. Absorbed by the mastery of detail in the dress, Rachel seemed oblivious to everyone and everything around her. At last, however, she gave her blessing to the project, doing so in the crusty style of her younger years.

Almost without thinking, Sam reached for the dress only to have his hand slapped away by Rachel. "Don't you dare touch that, Sam!" she exclaimed. "Just the slightest bit of dirt on your hands, and you would stain it to ruin."

Ignoring her husband's quick sulk, Rachel took the tiny wedding dress in her own clean hands, marveling at its exactness to the garment she had created so long ago. She caressed the folds of soft broadcloth, admired the tiny seed pearl buttons and traced the delicate lace embroidery. Something happy and fulfilling deep inside brought her close to tears, but Rachel figured she had cried enough for the time being. So instead, she opted to celebrate her granddaughter.

"Land sakes, child—it is beautiful," she said with deep-felt sincerity. "It's a prize-winner on its own without any of these other dresses as garnishment." She hesitated, still trying to absorb the significance of Summer's gift. "If gamblen weren't a sin, I'd be willen to bet we do bring that blue ribbon home where it belongs," she said at last.

Still clutching the dress but careful to protect it, Rachel hugged Summer tightly, stroking her granddaughter's long brown hair as her cheek pressed against the girl's forehead. "We may have a real dressmaker in this family after all," she said at length, smiling toward Sam, watching his face narrow with puzzlement.

"We always did, Granny," Joe remarked softly, unexpectedly. "Now we have another, I think."

Rachel acknowledged her grandson, eased her embrace of Summer and looked again to Sam with a conscious smile. At once, the clouds broke on his face, replaced by a beam of full understanding.

"Yes, now we have another," he agreed with Joe. "And you have a legacy of your own, Rachel. You always have."

Giving her granddaughter a tender kiss on the cheek and a quick squeeze of the elbow, Rachel released Summer and walked into her husband's open arms. "It's a fine thing to have a legacy, Rachel, especially one as full and complete as yours," Sam said. "I hope you're proud of it."

She laid her head against Sam's shoulder and nodded.

———

In a way, the judging of the specialty-sewing event was almost anticlimactic for the family. It seemed inevitable that Summer and Rachel would walk away with the blue ribbon. Regardless, the family understood the real prize had been handed out and accepted many times over, long before the judges reached their decision. Still, everyone was on hand to applaud and congratulate the winners when the judges, after brief consideration, laid the blue ribbon across Summer and Rachel's collection of doll clothes.

With Rachel and Summer's approval, Caroline purchased an expensive glass case, framed the collection and hung it on the living room wall.

A few days later, Sam splurged on a new electric sewing machine for Rachel. Presenting it to her at suppertime, he attached two strings to the gift. "Number one is that you retire that old push-pedal machine, so I don't ever have to hear another complaint about the sorry state of the contraption," he said.

"I'll consider that," Rachel agreed.

"If you decide to get rid of the push-pedal, I'd be glad to have it for myself," Summer suggested.

Rachel regarded the girl with an affirmative nod, then cast her gaze on Sam. "What else did you have on your mind?"

"Number two," Sam said, "is that you take in enough sewen from our neighbors to pay for this high-priced gadget and earn your keep."

Rachel stiffened at the suggestion. "I shall sew whenever and for whomever I please," she said coolly. "Without any regard for your feelens on the subject. And furthermore, old man, I intend to keep every last dime I might earn off that machine. I've patched enough holes to pay for one new sewen machine in my lifetime, and I've more than earned my keep around here."

Somehow, the words were lost and their familiarity ignored by those gathered in the kitchen as the family's hum began to rise around the table—though not by everyone. Watching their grandparents exchange the briefest of smiles, Joe winked at Summer and received a wrinkled nose in return.

THE GARDEN

1963

CHAPTER 1

BONNIE DECIDED THE ENTIRE Baker family needed a strong dose of castor oil—or some such elixir that would cleanse their ill attitudes the way the medicine emptied the bowels. In these days when they should have been rejoicing over Granny's renewed health, everyone seemed to have their noses out of joint. Mealtimes had become quieter than a funeral home as everyone chose to maintain a careful silence instead of risk rebuke over the most benign of comments. The family had forgotten how to be kind.

"Good evenen, everyone."

Bonnie glanced up as Preacher Adam Cook strode up to the front-row church pew where she and other members of the primary class—mostly first- and second-grade students—were busy making sandals similar to the ones Hebrews had worn during the days of Jesus. The craft project was part of Vacation Bible School, which the preacher had initiated at Benevolence for the first time this year. One more night of the special school remained, and already Bonnie regretted that it was ending so soon. She had enjoyed the experience, even if it had taken place during spring vacation from regular school.

"Hello, preacher," Bonnie said, her voice joining the greetings of seven other classmates.

Bonnie liked the church pastor. He smiled often and always had a cheerful word to say, unless he was preaching one of his hellfire and brimstone sermons. While Preacher Cook rarely shouted in the pulpit, he had a way of putting the fear of the Lord in people. Frequently, Bonnie understood his sermons. Often, even when the sermon did not make sense to her, she still paid attention to the preacher—drawn by his kindness and sincerity as well as the knowledge that he refused to tolerate rude behavior in church. On more than one occasion, he had called talking teenagers to the floor and admonished them to hush up or leave.

Unlike some adults, Preacher Cook also seemed to enjoy children and young people. He somehow always knew what was important to them at the moment, whether it was a big football game or simply time for report cards at school. And he took time to offer encouragement and support.

Throughout the week of Vacation Bible School, the preacher had visited Bonnie's class each day, telling various stories about the crucifixion of Christ and the days that followed. This evening's story was about Doubting Thomas, the disciple who refused to believe Jesus had risen from the grave three days after He was crucified. The preacher said Thomas had demanded proof that his Lord was alive after being dead, and that Thomas had believed only after the resurrected Jesus allowed him to feel his nail-scarred hands and pierced sides. Last, but certainly not least, Preacher Cook claimed that while Thomas had been fortunate to have his faith substantiated by touching and feeling Jesus, today's Christians must believe on faith alone that Jesus had died and was resurrected so that all might have eternal life in Heaven.

Listening to the story, Bonnie decided Thomas was a lucky soul, whereas she was getting a raw deal. Believing was one thing, but honest-to-goodness proof was quite another.

Take her household. On faith alone, everyone accepted that all was well with the world. Rachel's health was restored, and their lives once again strummed along at a happy pace. Unfortunately, the proof of all this happiness was sorely lacking.

Rachel was well again, but the Bakers still suffered from her illness. It had something to do with Rachel's depression during her period of ill health. Her self-doubt had shaken the family at its very roots, replacing boundless faith with confusing uncertainty. At least, that was the way Bonnie had overheard Joe describe the family turmoil one day when Tom Carter chanced an off-handed remark about the recent unpleasantness.

"It's kind of like everybody all at once decided their life is in need of spring cleanen," Joe told Tom as they fed hogs one late afternoon, "and they're goen about it with all the energy of a female getten ready to give birth. Nobody takes anything for granted anymore, even things we've done virtually every day of our lives. And it's like taken your life in hand to tease somebody, make a simple observation or even answer a question in some cases. To tell you the truth, Tom, it's kind of like we're all at war with each other: We're all as volatile as wartime alliances and as fragile as peace treaties."

It was a highbrowed explanation—the kind her oldest brother was given to in these last days of his senior year in high school—but Bonnie understood the message. Attitudes were rotten around the house and everyone was grumpy, despite their insistence that things had returned to normal. Bonnie hoped the situation might improve, but she was reserving her opinion until she saw evidence of it.

Finishing his story about Doubting Thomas and urging the children to believe with all their heart that Jesus had died on the cross and risen from the grave for them, Preacher Cook asked if anyone had questions. Bonnie thought a quick moment, then raised her hand.

"Yes, Bonnie?" the preacher asked.

The church suddenly seemed awfully quiet. A sideways glance allowed Bonnie to see her mother and grandmother. Caroline was reading a story to the beginner's group of VBS scholars, and Rachel was helping the juniors with a craft project. Both women forgot their work temporarily, beaming with pride as they waited for Bonnie to discuss the story with the preacher.

"I enjoyed the story, Preacher, but I have a question," she said at last. "How in the world are we supposed to believe in somethen that we can't see, somethen that there's no way of knowen if it's real or not?"

"That's what Christianity is all about, Bonnie," Preacher Cook replied patiently. "Haven faith and trusten in the Lord even though we can't actually see Him as you and I see each other."

Bonnie pursed her lips in serious contemplation. "I suppose that's well and good for some folks," she said finally. "But I'm like Doubting Thomas. I prefer to see things for myself." She paused, then added loudly, "Guess this means I'll never be much of a Christian."

Her declaration resonated through the tiny church. An audible gasp greeted the assertion. Rachel snapped a child's stick house, and Caroline's book slid off her lap.

Noting all the fuss, Bonnie suddenly realized she had committed what the ladies of the church would describe as a serious breach of decorum. Her eyes widened as she glanced from Caroline to Rachel before the gaze settled on the preacher.

Preacher Cook watched her with a curious expression on his face. Then his features broadened into a big smile, and he threw back his head to release a hearty chuckle.

"Forgive me, sweetheart, but I beg to disagree," he said finally, with obvious amusement. "You have all the makens of an exemplary Christian, Bonnie, and I believe that one day you will find your faith. I may not have any proof of that at the moment, but I believe in you with all my heart."

For a long moment, the preacher regarded Bonnie with twinkling eyes. Then he patted her head and moved on to deliver another lesson in faith.

Bonnie wanted to trust his judgment. She almost believed him—but not entirely.

———————

In less than a month, Joe would graduate from high school. By rights, this should have been the time to kick back and coast until graduation. Unfortunately, trigonometry, physics and a college-prep research paper—not to mention his ego—were making these last few days of high school more burdensome than pleasurable.

The classes would have been challenging in themselves, but Joe faced the added pressures of work on the farm and his own desire to finish as salutatorian of his class. From day one of high school, no one had ever doubted that Denise Culpepper would end up as valedictorian of the Cookville High School Class of Sixty-Three. The three-way race for salutatorian, however, had come as a complete surprise. Karen Baxter had been the favorite, but, undone by chemistry, geometry and home economics, of all things, her grades had faltered slightly in the tough junior year. Meanwhile, after a slow start his freshman year, Joe had begun acing every course in sight, while Deborah Faircloth had run a close third in the class academic rankings all three years.

Joe considered himself the underdog in the race for salutatorian, although not for lack of effort. He was contending with physics and trigonometry, while Deborah had only trig to worry over this year, and Karen had bypassed both courses in favor of easier credits.

While it could be debated who had the toughest classes, Joe knew that his workload at home was more demanding than anything Deborah or Karen could fathom. He was used to hard work, but the last few weeks had been brutal. Without Lucas Bartholomew around to help, the bulk of work fell upon Matt and Joe. His grandfather pitched in and so did his brothers, but one was too old and the others too young to tackle the hard work.

Joe found himself rising early to do chores, gulping down breakfast and dashing for the school bus. After school, he came straight home and usually was in the fields a good forty-five minutes before his brothers and sisters arrived, clamoring for a snack to tide them over until supper. He worked until dark, ate supper and hit the books until long after everyone else was fast asleep.

"It's nearly more than I can stand," he complained to Peggy Jo Nix as they lay in a secluded spot by the banks of New River one warm April night.

"You can take me home then," Peggy Jo replied, nibbling his ear. "I hate to take up so much of your valuable time and keep you away from the really important things."

Peggy Jo was a big-boned, buxom blonde, a high school classmate who had caught Joe's eye on the football field their freshman year. She had been a majorette in the marching band. From the moment he first saw Peggy Jo tromping across the field in a red-sequined uniform with short white boots, twirling her baton and jiggling like a bowl of firm jelly, Joe had been smitten by her generous presence.

Peggy Jo had proved to be as lighthearted as she was voluptuous, striking an instant friendship with Joe in the months following his career-ending injury on the football field. For three and a half years, they had been good friends, close like a brother and sister, with a hint of something incestuous and provocative lurking in the shadows.

Their romantic interplay had bloomed with the springtime. On a whim, Joe had asked her to go with him to the prom. The invitation had surprised and delighted Peggy Jo. Now they cavorted in the throes of a spring fling. It was a pleasant way to pass time as they waltzed through the final few weeks of school, each giving and receiving an education that couldn't be found in books.

It was all in good fun, too, a case of old-fashioned lust, from which each expected to walk away without remorse when they graduated in a few weeks. Both planned to attend college in the fall. Joe would pursue a degree in English. Peggy Jo was aiming for an M.R.S., with a specialty in P.H.D.-M.D.

Joe rolled onto his side and kissed her. "There you go again, jumpen to conclusions," he drawled. "I tell you, Peggy Jo, I got all the time in the world."

Later, when they had explored each other thoroughly and expanded their education, Peggy Jo cuddled against Joe.

"It's too bad I'm dead set against becomen a doctor," he remarked.

"That thought crossed my mind, too," she replied. "Then I thought about it some more, and let's face it, Joe. We're really nothen more than friends when you get right down to it. I love you in a way, but we're kind of like kissen cousins. It's fun to fool around, but nothen good would come of it if we carried things too far between us."

"I suppose so," Joe agreed.

"Besides, your mama and grandma aren't too keen on me," Peggy Jo added. "They think I'm a floozy."

"They think no such thing," Joe argued. "They just happen to find you a little suggestive. That's all."

"It's my chest," she lamented. "It's not my fault I'm so well endowed."

"I don't think Mama and Granny have anything personal against your chest, Peggy Jo," he explained. "They just get a little riled up over the tight sweaters and all that cleavage. And I think the way you flirt gives them a little indigestion. They worry and maybe wonder, but they think you're a nice girl."

"And what do you think about me, Joe Baker?"

"It depends," Joe replied slyly.

"On what?" Peggy Jo inquired.

"On the moment," he said. "When you're all dressed up in red sequins marchen across the football field with your baton, I tend to think of you as a cherry tart, ripe for the picken. When we're in the cafeteria at school talken and eaten lunch, I consider you a good friend. But when you're lyen next to me—like now—I don't like to think too much, Peggy Jo."

"Want to know what I think about you?" she asked with a leer.

"What's that?"

"I think you have strong taste for cherry tarts," Peggy Jo said. "And you're very good at picken them."

Joe shrugged. "I have a very good and willen teacher," he replied.

They regarded each other for a tender moment, then dissolved into giggles and fell into a tangled mass.

At supper one Friday night, Sam casually mentioned that Good Friday had come and gone. "I can't remember the last time we didn't plant our garden on Good Friday," he said. "But with all the carryen-on around here, it's no wonder that we just plumb forgot."

"It's bad luck not to plant on Good Friday," John remarked. "Ain't it, Grandpa?"

"No, that's not the case," Sam replied. "It's just good luck to plant on Good Friday. It makes for the best gardens. We'll do okay, though, even if we are a few weeks late getten it into the ground."

Matt pushed back from the table and tried to rub away a headache. He was tired tonight. For weeks, he had done nothing but plant crops and fix ragged, worn-out equipment that he could not afford to replace. He had planted his fields once, before having to turn around and do it all over again after a solid week of torrential rains had washed away seed and flooded the fields.

He was working from sunup until sundown, then coming home to bickering children, nagging adults and an endless assault of bills. A garden was the last thing he wanted to think about. But if his family was going to have food on the table, a huge summer garden was a staple more valuable than sugar or flour. He leaned back in his chair, yawned and took a drink of iced tea. "We do need to get it in the ground," he commented.

"If I were you, Daddy, I wouldn't bother," Bonnie remarked absentmindedly as she picked at the last mess of the previous year's butterbeans.

"What makes you say that, honey?" Matt asked.

"It's not gonna grow, so why bother with it?" she suggested.

"Why won't it grow?" Matt responded.

"All that stuff you planted the first time around didn't," Bonnie pointed out. "And I haven't seen hide nor hair of anything you've planted this second go-round."

"It'll grow," Matt said, trying to sound patient, yet irked because everything she said was true, despite the farfetched ideas that fed her conclusions. "The seeds simply haven't been in the ground long enough to come through yet."

"I doubt it," Bonnie persisted. "I won't believe it until I see it."

Sensing his son's mounting frustration, Sam intervened in the debate. "Since you've decided to be our family's Doubting Thomas, Bonnie, I'm gonna give you a little summer experiment," he proposed.

"What kind of experiment?" Bonnie asked cautiously as supper ground to a temporary standstill.

"A garden all your own," Sam replied. "We'll fix you a little plot in the corner of the field, but you'll have to do all the planten yourself and then take care of it through the summer. I'll oversee to make sure you do everything the way it's supposed to be done, but it will be your responsibility."

"What can I plant?"

"Anything you want," Sam said. "You come along with your daddy and me tomorrow, and we'll get the seed."

Bonnie considered the suggestion. "A garden could be fun," she agreed. "I'll go along with it, Grandpa, but I still have my doubts that anything will ever come of it."

As everyone returned to their supper, Matt made a few plans in his head, hoping to accomplish the task in the quickest way possible. "Joe," he finally said. "First thing in the mornen, turn that piece across the road and get it ready for planten. Pa and I'll go into town to get the seed. Ma, Caroline, if y'all have any special requests, make out a list. I want to get through with this in one fell swoop."

His daddy's request irritated Joe, who already was ill natured because the day's work had forced him to cancel a date with Peggy Jo. Now this garden business threatened to spoil his Saturday plans.

"Can't John or Luke do it, Daddy?" he proposed. "I had somethen else planned for tomorrow."

"It'll go a lot more quickly and smoothly if you help out," Matt replied firmly to his son.

That suggestion angered Joe, who was beginning to feel put upon by the incessant demands. "We really ought to wait till Monday to worry about it," he persisted. "There's hogs in that field, and we need to move them first."

It was a feeble excuse to avoid the work, and Matt stared blankly at the boy, trying to keep his temper under control. "Well then, son," he replied with a touch of sarcasm, "I suggest you get up early and move those few shoats. Just open the gate and shoo them in with the others. It shouldn't be too much of a strain. Then you can turn the land, and we can plant a garden so you'll have something to eat this summer and next winter. That's a little bit more important than whatever you have planned."

"Yeah, yeah, yeah," Joe muttered, his tone a trifle bit more disrespectful than intended. "That's usually the way things work around here."

"Don't use that tone with me, son," Matt said sharply, "or you won't ever see the light of day."

They glared at each other with clinched jaws. Sensing the charged tempers of father and son, Sam tried to avert a crisis. Matt and Joe never exchanged cross words. Weariness was talking for them. "What's so important about tomorrow, Joe?" Sam asked.

Joe challenged Matt's gaze a second longer, then looked to Sam. "Nothen anymore. I had planned to do some fishen, maybe relax a little bit since we're almost all caught up."

"Well you can go fishen and relax on Sunday," Matt informed him. "Tomorrow, we're planten a garden."

"There'll be no fishen around here on Sunday," Caroline reminded Joe. "That's not what the Sabbath is for."

Joe rolled his eyes and shook his head. He took one last gulp of tea, rising from the table with the glass in hand.

"Don't you want dessert, Joe?" Rachel asked, trying to coax him back to good humor.

"I do not," Joe replied.

"Where are you goen?" Caroline called as he walked out of the room.

"To take a shower," he said tersely. "And then to bed unless anybody has any problem with that."

———————

The thick hedge of red tips on the backside of Dr. Ned Turner's gabled and turreted brownstone mansion needed trimming, but the bushy shrubs provided excellent cover for the man to approach the house without being seen. He moved silently across the lawn, nervous and excited over the prospect of pulling off his first burglary, grateful for the moonless night. Once inside the house, he would have free run of the place because Ned and Delia Turner had left earlier in the day for a fishing trip to the Gulf Coast. But the actual act of breaking into the house scared him.

He quickly found a ground floor window leading to a spare room in the three-story house. Using the handle of his flashlight as a battering ram, he knocked out a small piece of one pane, then removed the remainder of the glass piece by piece and reached his gloved hand inside to unlock the window. To his dismay, the latch was missing. He rolled his eyes in disbelief, realizing he could have gained entry into the house simply by lifting the window. Knowing he should have checked first to see if the window was open, he attributed the blunder to inexperience.

Undaunted, the man edged the window open, unnecessarily concerned the creaking would reveal his presence. He pulled himself onto the ledge, pushed through heavy curtains and stepped onto some kind of trunk. He took a deep breath, realizing he had passed the toughest hurdle of the night.

His eyes adjusted quickly to the darkness, and he went to work. He canvassed the bottom two floors, paying particular attention to the bedrooms on the second floor, concluding the doctor and his wife slept in separate quarters.

Next, he tried to think like a thief to determine the things he would take from the house. He started with a jewelry box in one of the bedrooms, emptying the contents on the bed, picking out the most expensive pieces and dropping them into the burlap bag he carried. He took a pearl-handled, silver-plated pistol from the nightstand, then scattered the contents of a few more drawers and moved into the next room, where he found a coin collection in a bottom drawer. He put the coins in his sack, then moved to the downstairs rooms.

The dining room contained the best loot, including a silver tea set and goblets, plus what appeared to be expensive candlesticks. When the bag was filled, he considered for the first time the lucrative side of tonight's venture. He had come to the Turner house with a plan in mind. He was leaving with several valuables that could be pawned for cash. The idea pleased him.

Finally, he was ready to go. Glancing around the living room one last time, he decided the place appeared extremely neat. He considered and rejected the possibility of upending furniture and trashing drawers and cabinets. He had left his mark. There was no need to go overboard, especially when he planned to pay another visit on the good doctor and his wife.

In spite of himself, the man shook his head and laughed. He was blessed with vision, he thought, as he made his exit.

CHAPTER 2

OVERNIGHT, A SOFT RAIN fell, providing the perfect moistening for planting a garden. When the sun appeared on the horizon, it dawned on a storybook spring day, complete with a gentle breeze and stacks of fluffy white clouds.

By eight o'clock, Joe was in the field across the road, trying to drive fifteen shoats into the adjoining wooded land. He spread a pail of corn to entice the hogs near the gate. Given their piggish manners, he expected to have a relatively simple task of herding the hogs through the gate one by one. The shoats were feisty and ornery this morning, however, refusing to cooperate with his plans.

Joe argued and pleaded with the hogs, but they ignored the gate, continually running in the opposite direction every time he tried to push them through the opening. Making matters worse, the rain had turned the slop holes into slushy mud. Several times, Joe barely caught himself from stumbling into the muck. His sneakers were ruined within minutes, and he scolded himself for not having worn work boots.

After twenty minutes, he had moved only four shoats onto the other side of the fence. The others had gobbled down the corn and were drifting across the field. Joe fetched another pail of corn, spread it on the ground and opened the gate to shove through another hog.

The pig was extremely cantankerous, refusing to pass through the gate. Finally, Joe grabbed the hog by its ear, shoving and pulling the squealing animal through the gate. Instead of heeding its natural instinct to head for open space, the shoat somehow turned around and tried to slide back through the gate. Cursing the hog's pigheadedness, Joe rammed his knee against the animal, pinning its head against the wooden gatepost, intending to close the gate before the shoat gained freedom.

Seconds later, something hard slammed into his groin, knocking Joe head over heels. He went airborne before landing face down in a muddy slop hole. Before he could regain his faculties, several hogs trampled past him, stomping against his arms and back with their hoofs as they raced for their fair share of the corn.

Dazed, stricken with a sick feeling in the pit of his stomach, Joe needed a couple of minutes to come to his senses. He struggled to his knees, using a hand to steady himself against the gatepost. Finally, he pulled to a standing position and managed to close the gate before more hogs escaped into the field.

Still suffering from severe pain in his gonads, Joe took several cleansing breaths and tried to surmise the situation. In short order, he realized that Big Male, the huge Duroc hell-bent on protection of his charges, had butted him. In his preoccupation with pushing the shoat through the gate, Joe had failed to notice that the pig's high-pitched squeals had turned the other hogs into slobbering swine ready to defend their own. Big Male had led the charge.

Joe tried to rub away the pain in his groin and swallow the nausea in the pit of his stomach when he became aware of the mud clinging to him. He wiped his eyes clean, then pushed the sludge away from his forehead and mouth. His clothes were coated with mud, and his good disposition was declining.

"Mama!"

Even inside the house where she was washing dishes, Caroline heard the fury in her oldest son's voice.

Joe hollered once more, loud enough this time to attract the attention of everyone in the house. Caroline dried her hands on a towel, then pulled open the kitchen door and stepped onto the back porch. Joe stood a few feet from the porch steps, covered with mud from head to toe.

"Goodness gracious, Joe!" Caroline said as Rachel arrived to investigate the commotion and let out a short gasp.

"What in the world happened?" she whispered to Caroline.

"I don't know, but he's mad as a wet hen," Caroline answered back.

"Mama!" Joe yelled for the third time. "Tell those young'uns of yours to get on their work clothes and get their sorry tails out here with me. I need some help with those blasted hogs."

"Okay, Joe," Caroline replied calmly. "What happened, son?"

Joe gaped incredulously at his mother, a little wild-eyed, with his nostrils flared and one foot tapping furiously against the ground.

"What does it look like happened?" he yelled. "The blasted things nearly killed me. I need help, Mama. Send those children out right now."

All at once, the back porch exploded with laughter as his brothers and sisters joined Caroline and Rachel. Joe simply waited for the laughter to stop, then ordered the children to help.

"They'll be out in a second, Joe," Rachel assured her grandson. "In the meantime, you might think about getten Pal-Two to help. He has a knack with wayward hogs."

Joe bit his lip, realizing his grandmother had the right idea. The German shepherd had a ruthless streak when it came it to rounding up hogs. Joe figured he could put the animal in the field with those shoats and sit back to watch the fun. Temporarily forgetting his indignation, Joe whistled for the dog, turned his back on his laughing family and headed back across the road with Pal-Two on his heels.

By the time his daddy, grandpa and little sister returned home from the seed store, the dog had chased the hogs from the field, and Joe was halfway finished plowing it.

Once the land was turned, Joe hooked the harrow to the tractor and disked the field to smooth out the plowed ground.

Across the road under the pecan orchard where the farm equipment lined the back fencerow, Matt and Sam prepared the two-row planter to lay a garden. The planter resembled a cultivator, with seven plows of varying sizes stretching across the front end to make neat rows and dig furrows for the seed. Behind the front line of triangular plows were the two planters, which created troughs in the ground, dispensed the seed and fertilizer and covered the crops with a layer of dirt, leaving orderly rows. Each planter contained two bins, with the larger ones used to dispense fertilizer and the smaller ones to apportion the seed.

In preparing the contraption to plant the garden, Matt and Sam filled the two large bins with guano fertilizer, then removed the two seed cylinders. When the planter was used to lay field crops, the cylinders were vital to dispense the seed. When planting a garden, however, Matt and Joe walked behind the planter, dropping the seed by hand through the chutes that fed into the trough. Matt had few superstitions, but he did believe in a hands-on operation when it came to planting the family garden.

By the time Joe finished harrowing the field, Matt and Sam had the planter ready. Although the two older men had been apprised of Joe's earlier misfortune with the hogs, they fell into sidesplitting laughter when they finally saw Joe.

"I've seen worse, but I don't know when," Sam commented when Joe had hitched the planter to the tractor. "You look like a dried mud cake."

Joe ignored the remark.

"Consideren everything, son," Matt said, "I think we can get by without you if you want to go fishen this afternoon. But I wouldn't get too near the water because you'll scare away the fish."

The feeble humor plunged the men into another round of choking chortles. Joe merely waited until they calmed down. "By gosh, Daddy," he said at last. "You were all-fired hot to plant a garden last night, so let's do it and be done with it."

"You heard the boy, Pa," Matt told Sam. "Let's plant a garden."

They required most of the afternoon to plant the four-acre patch with all the staples of the summer garden. Sam drove the tractor, while Matt and Joe walked behind the planter dropping the seed. When the seed had been planted, the younger children pitched in to transplant a variety of tomato, onion, eggplant and pepper plants. They worked until the patch was crammed with enough food to carry the family through another year.

When the garden was planted, Joe joined his daddy and brothers under the shade of two pecan trees in the field, watching as Sam helped Bonnie prepare her small garden. With a little coaxing, Joe provided the details about his futile efforts to move the hogs and the subsequent run-in with Big Male. He gave an embellished version of the ludicrous chain of events, sending everyone into fits of laughter. This time, Joe howled with everyone else.

"You're the only person I know who's been stampeded by hogs," Matt remarked when the laughter subsided.

Joe grinned. "Now that everyone's had a good laugh at my expense, I expect I'd better get cleaned up," he said. "Mama's not likely to let me in the house looken like this."

"That's for sure," Luke agreed.

"I think I'll go swimmen in the river," Joe said. "Who wants to join me?"

"I do!" John answered.

"Me, too," Luke added.

"What about it, Daddy?" Joe asked. "Come go with us."

Matt bunched his eyebrows. "It's warm enough today, but I bet that river water is cold as ice," he replied.

"It'll put some get-up-and-go back into you," Joe said persuasively.

Matt grinned at his sons. "Let's go!" he said.

John let out a whoop.

"Last one there's a rotten egg," Luke shouted.

———————

Under Sam's watchful eye, Bonnie planted corn, butterbean, cucumber, okra, pumpkin and sunflower seeds in her garden plot, along with tomato, cabbage and onion plants. Grandpa predicted the seeds would sprout within a week.

On the following Saturday, Bonnie woke with the full expectation that her garden had sprouted overnight. She was disappointed to find nothing but the same old patch of gray dirt when she went to investigate after breakfast.

"We should have planted radishes," Sam said, urging his granddaughter to be patient. "Radishes grow quickly, and they would have pushed through the ground by now."

Pushing aside her misgivings, Bonnie lugged the water hose across the road and gave the garden a good soaking. Later, she made a scarecrow out of tobacco sticks and a ragged pair of her daddy's dungarees.

In the back of her mind, the garden had become a test of faith. She was determined to believe, even without proof.

When Monday came and the garden remained barren, her faith wavered. Sam shored up her spirits, though.

"Just wait until we get a good rain," he promised. "Then you'll see nothen but peaks of green."

On Tuesday morning, the patter of rain on the tin roof woke Bonnie. Remembering her grandfather's prognostication, she hopped out of bed and went to the front door. The gentle rain quickened her heart and brought a rush of hope.

With only scant thought that she was barefooted and still in her nightgown, Bonnie opened the door and ran to her garden. Her breath caught as she came to the garden plot, where dozens of fresh green sprigs poked up from the rich earth. Gradually, she became aware of the hundreds of other shoots sprouting from the family garden.

In that moment, Bonnie felt her heart fill up with faith. She understood what Preacher Cook meant when he spoke of "things seen and unseen." And she understood that while doubts were an unavoidable part of life, faith in God was an eternal blessing.

————————

On a scorching day in late summer as he carried two buckets of corn to the hogs, Joe noticed his baby sister sitting amid the remnants of her garden. Bonnie's fascination with the garden had touched the family that spring and summer. In some way, she had rekindled their passion for life and deepened their understanding of the forces shaping it.

Joe was acutely aware of all this as he watched his sister, wondering what occupied her thoughts. Bonnie had been a whir of motion throughout the summer. Now she seemed subdued, which concerned him.

He tossed the corn to the hogs, then set the buckets on the grass beside the gate and went into the field where Bonnie sat.

"Hey, there," he called. "May I join you?"

Bonnie glanced over her shoulder, then looked straight ahead again and motioned Joe to sit beside her.

"You seem deep in thought, honey," he remarked, sitting down beside the girl. "Anything you want to talk about?"

"My garden's about all played out," Bonnie said. "I'm a little sad."

"Gardens do that," Joe replied. "They come and they go."

"But this was a special garden, Joe," she explained. "It's the first one I ever took care of all by myself. I didn't want it to end. I wanted it to keep on growen."

"It was a humdinger, all right," Joe said cheerfully. "You did a great job with it. Your corn was the best I ever ate. And I know those cabbages must have been good because rabbits ate every one of them."

Bonnie smiled. "I hope they enjoyed them."

Joe pointed to two fat pumpkins still growing on the vines. "I don't think we've ever had a pumpkin quite so big on the place as those two," he pointed out. "They're spectacular. I bet Mama and Granny can make some kind of pumpkin pie out of them."

Bonnie nodded.

"Don't feel too sad about your garden, Bonnie," Joe urged. "It was your first garden, which makes it special. But you'll raise plenty more gardens if you want. Some will be bigger and better than this one, and some won't. I think part of the fun is the anticipation of it—getten the ground ready, putten in the seed, waiten for it to sprout and then watchen things grow."

"Do you know what's really on my mind?" she asked.

"I'd like to."

"When you get right down to it," Bonnie explained, "gardens are like people, Joe. They're here for a while and then they play out. No matter what, people die—always."

"But life goes on—forever," Joe said quickly. "I think that's most important to remember."

"Do you mean Heaven?" she asked.

"Just life, Bonnie. Heaven and earth and people—even you and me. It never ends, no matter what." He hesitated, then suggested, "Maybe not even your garden has to end. We could save some of your pumpkin seed and plant them next year if you want. That way, part of this garden would carry on."

"We could do that?" Bonnie asked hopefully.

"Absolutely. When you get ready to carve those pumpkins, let me know, and I'll help you with the seed."

Bonnie nodded. "I could make that one of my traditions," she said. "Do it year after year, so that it's never-ending."

"You could," Joe agreed. "It's an excellent idea."

"It's been a wonderful summer," Bonnie said in a while, a small sigh escaping her. "I hate to see it end."

"We've got fall to look forward to," Joe reminded her with cheerful optimism. "And there'll be other summers, too."

A huge smile settled on Bonnie's face. "One thing's for certain," she concluded. "There'll never be another brother like you."

Joe glanced up and bit his lip, acting puzzled. "Probably not," he grinned. "But there'll also never be another sister like you."

"Well, I suppose we should be thankful for that," Bonnie suggested.

"Among other things."

"Joe?" she asked a moment later. "Do you think we'll remember this summer when we're older?"

"I imagine we will," he said. "I certainly know we'll never forget *this* time."

FAITH AND GRACE

1964-1965

CHAPTER 1

TOWARD THE END OF February in 1964, Florence Castleberry paid a noontime visit to the Bakers. It was a blustery day, and she knocked for a solid minute on the front door without an answer. Finally, she walked around the house to the side porch entrance and knocked on the kitchen door. Rachel answered almost immediately, inviting the neighbor woman into the warm kitchen where she was received with a round of greetings from Sam, Matt and Caroline.

"That wind cuts right through a body," Florence commented as she shook off the chill and took a seat on the table bench beside Matt and across from Caroline. "We'll have rain by nightfall."

"Probably before," Sam predicted as Rachel set a glass of iced tea before their neighbor. "These cold, damp days make my bones ache. I'll be glad for warm weather."

"It won't be long now," Florence replied, making herself at home, even though she had interrupted the family's dinner.

Florence was plumpish, grayish and in her mid-sixties. She was married to Slaton Castleberry, a struggling farmer much like Matt and Sam. The Castleberry place backed up against the western flank of the Baker place, the two farms separated by the railroad tracks. Florence and Slaton lived in a large white house that fronted Highway 125 between the mercantile and the New River school. Their three daughters and son were grown, married and living elsewhere.

The neighbors chatted for several minutes, discussing family and the upcoming revivals at Benevolence Missionary Baptist Church and the Holiness Baptist Church, where the Castleberrys attended—as well as twelve-year-old John's recent first-place prize in an art contest sponsored by *The Tifton Gazette*.

"I recognized the picture as y'all's orchard as soon as I saw it in the paper," Florence remarked. "It was a right nice picture. I didn't know John was so talented."

"He's been drawen and painten practically since he learned to pick up a color crayon," Caroline replied. "I don't know where John gets his talent, but we're proud of him."

"Florence, how's your children doen?" Rachel inquired. "Weren't they all home for the holidays?"

"They were," the woman said. "They wanted to be close to their daddy. Cheryl calls every day. It's nice haven her close by in Cookville. She's expecten again—around August. They're hopen for a girl this time."

"Do they have two or three boys?" Caroline asked.

"Two," Florence answered. "They're both pistols."

"How does Cynthia like Atlanta?" Rachel asked. "Is she adjusten to the big city?"

"She loves it," Florence said. "Her works for the power company, and they live in Doraville. husband Candace is still in Valdosta. She turns forty next month. I can't believe I got a child forty years old."

"Time sure does fly," Matt remarked. "I hit forty last year."

"My David had a ball with your Joe over the holidays," Florence said. "He's back in California now, tellen all his Air Force buddies about the deer he killed over the Christmas holidays. I think Joe and him and Tom Carter went hunten every day for a solid week."

"Joe thinks the world of David," Caroline said. "Always has ever since he was a little boy, and we swapped off help in the tobacco patch that summer. They're kindred spirits."

"Military life seems to suit David," Matt commented. "I guess he likes liven in all those faraway places, always be'en on the go. I was ready to get back home the whole time I was in the Army."

"He enjoys the lifestyle," Florence agreed. "David's gonna make a career out of the Air Force. He'll have nine years of service in June and will transfer to the Philippines this summer. I hate see'en him so far away, especially since Slaton had the heart attack."

"How is Slaton?" Sam asked. "I keep meanen to stop by and see him more often, but the winter's just slipped right past me."

"He's not doen too good," Florence confessed tiredly. "He's some better, but it's been a slow recuperation."

"We've been prayen for him at church," Rachel said.

"A lot of people have," Florence replied, "and I fully believe that's what's kept him goen these last few months. To tell you the truth, though, Slaton has a leaky heart. He's never gonna be his old self, and I guess we're finally admitten to that." She paused slightly, then added, "That's why I barged in on y'all today."

"Is there anything we can do to help, Florence?" Matt asked, setting aside his eating utensils and giving her his full attention.

"I hope so, Matt," she replied. "The truth is that Slaton's farmen days are over and done with. He'll never raise another crop."

"I was afraid of that," Sam said.

"We'll get along okay," Florence said. "We've got a little money set aside, and all our bills are paid."

"There's somethen to be said for security," Sam agreed.

"What we really need is someone to rent our land," Florence continued. "We've had several people ask about it since January. Slaton kept thinken you'd come around, Matt. When you didn't, he sent me over to see if you'd be interested. Y'all are good neighbors, and it would mean a lot to Slaton and me to have you worken our fields."

Matt crossed his arms and rubbed his chin as he considered the idea. "The only land I've ever rented is that ten-acre field behind the mercantile," he said at last. "I've always wanted to tend a little more, but it's been pretty much all Pa and I could do to keep up this place."

Florence reached into her sweater pocket, pulled out a folded sheet of paper and handed the note to Matt. "That's the price Slaton's hopen to get per acre," she explained. "We've got an even two hundred acres, Matt, plus a ten-acre allotment for tobacco. There's two tobacco barns on the place, which would be yours to use."

"That's more than a fair offer, Florence," Matt said.

"We're just looken to make ends meet," she replied. "The only other thing I'd ask is that you'd plant us a nice garden and maybe plow it once or twice to keep down the weeds."

"Honestly, Florence, I don't even know if we've got enough equipment to farm your place and ours," Matt said. "If we took on your fields, that'd almost double what I'm farmen now."

"You'd be welcome to use our equipment," she offered, "but I have to warn you, Matt: It's old and worn out, too—just like Slaton and me."

Matt smiled slightly, nodding at the woman. "You've certainly given us somethen to consider, Florence," he said. "I'm mighty tempted, but I'll need to think on it a day or two before I give you an answer."

"You do," she agreed, rising to her feet. "I just wanted to plant the seed in your mind. I know it's late in the year to be maken big decisions like this, but Slaton believes this is an arrangement that could benefit us all. You give it careful thought and let us know your answer. We hope you'll take the place, Matt, but if you decide not to, we'll understand."

Sam practically clapped his hands in anticipation the moment Florence Castleberry was ushered from the house. "It's manna from Heaven," he said to Matt, Caroline and Rachel. "We'd have more than four hundred acres of crops, plus the extra tobacco allotment. You could double your income, son."

"Or double your loss," Rachel warned.

"It's an unexpected opportunity," Matt agreed with his father. "I'm excited, but we'd have to make some adjustments. We'd definitely need a bigger and better tractor—some new equipment, too. That would mean borrowen from the bank."

"I hate to go in debt," Caroline remarked.

"I don't look forward to owen money either," Sam agreed, "but the truth is we needed a new tractor and new equipment last fall. Then we couldn't justify the loan. With two hundred extra acres to farm, we can justify the expense."

At the conclusion of the previous fall's harvest, Matt and Sam had taken stock of their equipment, and the result had been grim. They operated the farm with an aging two-row John Deere and an even older one-row Farmall. The tractors had served them well for many years but were becoming inadequate to shoulder the farm's mechanical burdens. Still, they had agreed the tractors would have to carry the load for one more year. If he tended the Castleberry place, however, Matt could justify the new tractor—a larger, stronger machine that would increase the efficiency of his operation and not break down in the middle of the growing season.

"Pa's right, Caroline," Matt said, his calm tone concealing a growing excitement. "We've got ragged equipment on this place, and, frankly, I'm not sure some of it can be fixed up to last another season."

Caroline and Rachel glanced at each other, sensing their husbands' anticipation, yet still lukewarm to the idea. "We'd be tenden ten more acres of tobacco, Matt, on top of what we already have," Caroline fretted. "We'd spend the whole summer worken in tobacco—probably six days a week."

"Since when have any of us ever been afraid of hard work?" Matt asked. "Carrie and John will be able to carry a full load this year. Lucas and Beauty will be around to help, and so will Tom Carter. We can do the work, and it'll mean extra money come fall—maybe the difference between barely getten by and getten by."

"Come fall, we'll also owe the bank a small fortune," Caroline worried still.

A silence settled around the table as Matt and Sam waited for the women to give their blessing to the proposition. Caroline and Rachel stared again at each other, then at their husbands.

Finally, Caroline sighed. "I guess my bookkeepen's gonna be a little more complicated this year," she said. "It probably is too good an opportunity to pass up, but let's think about it for a day or two before we commit ourselves."

"Fair enough," Matt agreed before grinning broadly at his family. "I have a good feelen about this. Maybe this is what we've been worken for all these years."

"Just make sure you plant a nice, big garden for Florence and Slaton," Rachel instructed her son. "And keep it plowed for them."

"I'll do that, Ma, regardless of whether we rent their land or not."

"There are some practical matters to consider before we decide for sure," Sam said. "While I can still hoe a pretty long row, the truth of the matter—which I reluctantly admit—is that you will need extra help to get those fields prepared and planted this spring, Matt. Lucas Bartholomew would be perfect for the job, but he's tied up until the first of June with his contract work. We're gonna need full-time help, son, someone strong and capable to work with you."

"Couldn't Joe do it?" Caroline suggested.

"He could, and I'm sure he would," Matt answered truthfully. "I wonder if it's fair to ask him, though. He'd have to take off from college, and that's the most important thing in the world to him. I hate to tie him down on the farm, even if it's only temporary." Matt sighed. "I suppose we had better think about everything a day or two before we give the Castleberrys an answer."

A gleam suddenly entered Caroline's eye. She glanced at Rachel, then back to Matt. "Come with us to church Sunday, and we can pray about it, Matt," she suggested, renewing a decades-old quest to entice her husband to darken the doors of Benevolence. "The Lord will lead us to an answer."

Matt grinned at his wife, knowing her suggestion had ulterior motives. "Now, honey," he replied patiently, "I got you, Ma and Pa sayen prayers for me. I think that's enough divine intervention for the time be'en."

"It's a fact, son," Sam said. "I offer up a prayer for you most every Sunday, and I'm sure the Almighty listens. Still, it might not hurt you to plead your own case occasionally. And it certainly would be beneficial to seek His guidance every now and then, especially now."

"You act just like a Catholic, Matt," Rachel remarked brusquely. "I'm not sayen that's all bad, but you seem to think that somebody else can pray you into Heaven, son. Well, it ain't so. I've read the Bible from one end to the other, and there's only one way for a body to win salvation. It's a personal matter between you and the Lord, Matt, and you need to start thinken about it."

"You're right, Ma," Matt agreed diplomatically. "It is a personal matter. And that's just how I intend to keep it."

———

"Do you think about God very often?"

John's question surprised Joe. The two brothers were fishing off a rowboat in a water hole in the middle of the farm's largest field. The pond was full from winter rains, and the fishing was excellent on this first Saturday in March. The water hole's snaky reputation usually spared the fish any likelihood of winding up on the end of a hook, but the brothers had made up their minds to go after a big catch on this day. They had been rewarded with several huge channel catfish, as well as a long line of perch and bream. Twice already, a brazen snapping turtle had attacked the string of fish, making off with half a perch before Joe and John wised up to its antics and pulled the line into the bottom of the boat. On three occasions, they also had observed water moccasins gliding across the small water hole.

"Probably not often enough," Joe answered his brother as the cork on his line bobbed under the water and he hauled in another catfish.

"What does it mean to be a Missionary Baptist?" John asked when Joe had baited his hook and returned his line to the water.

Joe took a long time to answer the question.

The Bakers attended Benevolence Missionary Baptist Church, where Adam Cook presided over services on the second and fourth Sundays of each month. On the first and third Sundays of the month, Adam led services at Poplar Springs Church on the other side of the county. Prayer meeting was held the first Wednesday night of each month at Benevolence and on the second Wednesday at Poplar Springs, while Sunday school took place every week without fail. On those few five-Sunday months, the preacher got a respite from his pastoral duties, while fidgety children rejoiced over consecutive Sundays without church.

While Benevolence and Poplar Springs enjoyed their own identities, there was little theological difference in their beliefs. The Poplar Springs Baptists seemed a tad more liberal with their "Amens," but members of each persuasion felt comfortable in the other's service. They shared the services of Adam because neither church could afford a full-time preacher. During revivals, which occurred twice a year on back-to-back weeks in spring and fall, the congregations virtually became one, filling the tiny buildings to capacity to hear the exhortations of some visiting preacher.

Besides revivals, both churches were united in their desire to maintain distinct identities from the powerful Southern Baptist Convention and the hardline Primitive Baptists.

Several years earlier, Joe had asked his grandmother the same question now posed to him by John: What did it mean to be a Missionary Baptist?

"It means we're not Southern Baptists, Primitive Baptists or Methodists," Rachel had told him curtly. "And it means we're not snake handlers."

Mindful that God worked in mysterious ways, Rachel respected the path to salvation chosen by most any congregation—even the Catholics. While she believed Southern Baptists, Primitive Baptists, Methodists and snake handlers would wind up in Heaven right along with her, Rachel had preconceived notions about all four groups. The Southern Baptists and the Methodists argued too much over issues that had little to do with leading a God-fearing life; the Primitive Baptists misinterpreted the Bible's teachings on grace; and Rachel simply could not justify a place in church for rattlesnakes.

Joe agreed wholeheartedly with his grandmother on those accords, so he now told his brother: "It means we're not Southern Baptists, Primitive Baptists or Methodists. And it means we're not snake handlers."

John considered the answer for a long moment. "I can live with that."

"I wonder why people try to complicate religion so much," he added a moment later. "It's such a simple, foolproof thing if you approach it with the right attitude."

"The Lord's dealen with you," Joe commented matter of fact.

"Are you maken fun of me?" John asked quickly, skeptically.

"I am not," Joe answered strongly, smiling warmly at his brother. "It was a simple statement, John. Don't complicate it."

John considered the familiar advice, then grinned. "I see what I mean," he said. "What saved you, Joe? Why did you join the church?"

Joe lit a cigarette. "Everybody's got a different reason," he answered. "I made my public profession of faith and repented my sins, John. My reasons for doen it were between the Lord and me, and I'd prefer to keep it that way."

"I can live with that, too," John said with a sly smile. "Do you still feel saved?"

Joe took a long drag on the cigarette and checked his hook. "When you get right down to it, I guess I'm a backslider," he said at last. "I'm lusten for too many worldly things, I suppose, not prayen like I should, not readen the Bible like I used to do. But I do try to pay attention to the Sunday sermons. Adam Cook has a way of inspiren you."

"He sure does," John agreed. "He has a way of maken a person want to do good."

"I take it you are thinken about joinen the church," Joe surmised.

"Do you think I'm too young to be saved?" his brother asked.

"You're twelve," Joe began.

"Closer to thirteen," John pointed out, as he frequently did to any and every one these days.

"If the Lord's knocken on your heart, John, then you're old enough to answer," Joe suggested.

"He really is knocken," John said with wonder. "I can't rightly explain it, but I've felt so close to God lately. There's this feelen of peace and comfort and faith inside me. It's with me everywhere I go these days—walken through the woods, taken a test in school, even here today while we've been fishen. I've never felt like this, Joe, but I just know everything will be okay, no matter what happens."

Joe eyed his brother for a long moment, knowing the boy was sincere. A higher power obviously was working on John, and Joe was awestruck at the thought—as well as unsettled by the whole idea.

"I sound ridiculous, don't I?" John said suddenly.

"God is walken with you, John," Joe replied. "Follow your heart."

John searched his brother's face, found sincerity and gave Joe a shy smile. "I don't know what to make of it either, but I'll take your advice."

"I think you've hooked another one," Joe remarked suddenly, noticing the cork bobbing on his brother's line. "Let's see what you got."

A short time later, when he had caught another fish himself, Joe made a conscientious effort to lighten the serious mood of their conversation. "The decision is yours entirely, little brother, but if you do decide to join the church, I'd appreciate it if you could manage to get baptized before revival comes around," he said. "They always have foot-washen on Thursday night, and while I understand it's a beautiful gesture, I'd like to avoid a repeat of last year."

"What happened?" John asked.

"I wound up washen Mr. Millard Webb's feet," Joe said. "He had one corn after another and the longest toenails I've ever seen. Honestly, it grossed me out. I'd be more comfortable with your feet, John, and I think you could break into the routine a lot easier on my feet than on somebody like Millard Webb."

"Give me cigarette, and I'll think about it," John promised.

Against his better judgment, Joe obliged him.

One week later, Joe stood with his family and members of the Benevolence congregation on the banks of New River, singing *Shall We Gather at the River* as Preacher Cook led John into the cold water. It was almost like watching John the Baptist baptize Jesus Christ, and Joe chanced a skyward look, half expecting a dove to come flying toward his brother. The sky was clear, however, except for the radiant sun, which shone brightly over the occasion.

His brother's spiritual side impressed Joe. Clearly, the Lord had called John to serve a purpose. That purpose remained a mystery, however, and Joe had an uneasy feeling about it. Standing there, as John was lowered beneath the water, Joe uttered a silent prayer for his brother and turned the matter over to the Lord.

Benevolence Missionary Baptist Church was nestled amid a grove of mature pine trees. The church charter dated back to the turn of the century, but the current worship place had been erected in 1933 after fire destroyed the original building.

The community had always known hard times, but 1933 had been the year the Great Depression finally finagled its way into the economy of Cookville, making times harder than usual. As a result, the Benevolence congregation had taken pennywise measures when rebuilding the church. The building was constructed of sturdy pine timbers, with hardwood floors and, some people said, even harder pews. Knots and gaps in the timbers kept the church drafty and cold in winter, yet offered little relief on hot summer Sundays. The church was supposed to be painted white, but mostly it was gray due to a neglectful congregation that believed trappings were totally unnecessary to worship God.

Two long rows of rickety tables sat behind the church, where the womenfolk spread massive dinners on Big Meeting Sundays in spring and fall. The cemetery lay to the right, separated from the church by a clump of pine trees. The oldest grave dated to February 4, 1890, and a host of others appeared nearly that old.

In the fall of 1963, the congregation had decided Benevolence needed some sprucing. During the months since, they had restored the walls to a pearly white—outside and inside—installed ceiling fans and built a new altar. The crowning touch was a graceful steeple donated by the Berriens.

As the spring revival approached, the congregation looked forward to showing off and dedicating their refurbished sanctuary. Caroline had something more consequential on her mind in those days. She wanted to get her husband baptized.

The Bakers rarely missed a church service, except for Matt, who had not darkened the door to Benevolence since his first Sunday home from the war. His rigid avoidance of church was a source of great mystery and worry for Caroline and Rachel. When the mood struck them—and it frequently did—they fretted that Matt had never been baptized. Baptism was essential to salvation, and Caroline and Rachel believed staunchly that while God would overlook long absences from church, he would not forgive the lack of a public profession of faith in Christ and submergence in the pure waters of New River.

"Matt is a good man with Christian values, Caroline, but he is not a Christian," Rachel told her daughter-in-law one morning as they prepared dinner a few days before the revival was to begin at Benevolence. "We have to find a way to make him realize that."

"Every year—twice a year—it's the same old story at revival time," Caroline lamented. "I try to get him to attend just one service, but he simply refuses. Sometimes, I feel like I'm at my wits' end. Over the last few years, Matt has become as much a stickler as you and I over church matters and the children. He expects his family to be in church, makes sure we're on time and doesn't tolerate any lame excuse for missen a service. He has told me for a fact that see'en Joe and John baptized were two of the happiest occasions of his life, yet even on those days he refused to set foot inside the church. At home, however—and you know this as well as I do, Ma—he sets a Christian example. He blesses meals, he has even read our nightly devotionals. I just don't understand why he refuses to attend church with us."

"Likely, he doesn't either," Rachel replied sadly. "But we can't give up on him, Caroline."

"I'll never do that," Caroline said, reaffirming her convictions. "I want to share my happiness with Matt in Heaven one day."

Over the next few days, Caroline coaxed and prodded, blatantly asked and gently reminded her husband to attend one of the upcoming revival services, always careful never to cross that thin line where her efforts would turn into harping and sour Matt on the whole deal. In one moment of frustration, she even volunteered to turn Methodist if Matt would agree to get sprinkled.

"I appreciate the gesture, honey, but the Methodist church ain't for me," Matt replied patiently. "If I ever do decide to join up with a church, I promise it'll be the Missionary Baptists. As I hear tell, y'all have about the only choir around where I could sing out loud and not sound off key."

"Humph!" Caroline groused a minute later when his appraisal of the Benevolence choir became clear in her mind. By then, Matt was gone, having fended off another attempt to get him into church.

On the Saturday before revival services began on Sunday night, Caroline's persistence turned into nagging and Matt took offense. They quarreled loudly, fiercely, their general disagreement rapidly evolving into outright anger. The battle of wills ended with Matt cursing and stomping from the house, while Caroline wept and retreated to their bedroom.

Sam went after Matt, while Rachel tried to console Caroline. Both were told to mind their own business.

The children were disturbed. Their parents rarely shared a cross word with each other, much less yelled, cursed and cried—especially over religion. They all went to bed early, hoping the dawn would restore the peace between their parents.

Matt returned home late that night with whiskey on his breath. Caroline started to rebuke him, then changed her mind when he confessed to drinking. Instead, they apologized to each other, reached a quiet truce and quickly surrendered to complete forgiveness, making up and making love.

Matt never made it to any of the revival services.

The revival reached its high point on Thursday night. Day services were planned for Saturday and Sunday, with dinner to be spread both days on the church grounds, but Thursday was the pivotal night.

Instead of summoning a visiting preacher, Benevolence had opted for Adam Cook to lead the spring revival, and the result had been overwhelming. On Monday night, the preacher had delivered a stirring hellfire and brimstone message, saving Summer Baker and five other people in the process. He followed with an inspirational message on Tuesday, breathed fire again on Wednesday and delivered the promise of Jesus Christ on Thursday. Sixteen people had repented their sins over five days of preaching, and they would be baptized Sunday in New River.

Matt vowed to be by the riverside when Adam baptized Summer, but he would miss Sunday's Big Meeting service.

His daddy's refusal to attend church preoccupied Joe's thoughts as he waited to take communion, a semi-annual event at Benevolence, always offered on the Thursday night of revival week. He was seated next to John in the Baker family pew as Paul Berrien and Dan Carter passed the plates with bread and tiny cups of grape juice. He ate the bread, drank the wine and offered a hasty prayer for the Lord's Supper.

Earlier in the afternoon, Joe had almost asked Matt why he refused to attend church with the family. The question had been on the tip of his tongue as they repaired a broken chain on the tobacco transplanter. Unfortunately, Matt made an errant move with the screwdriver, the tool slipping and puncturing the fleshy part of Joe's hand between the thumb and index finger. Joe had cursed, Matt had cursed and they had both wound up laughing before sharing the last cigarette between them and finishing their work.

"It always amazes me how much we have in common," Matt had told his son. "And how that tiny bit of uncommon makes all the difference in the world between us."

Joe had felt the same way for a long while now, and the thought was firmly on his mind tonight. Despite their differences, father and son were kindred souls at heart. The notion made Joe more than a little uncomfortable as he reflected on Matt's attitude toward church, so he changed his thoughts.

On this day, he had written his final English essay and completed his second quarter of classes at Abraham Baldwin Agricultural College—commonly known as ABAC. Tomorrow, he would become a full-time farmer, embarking on a six-month mission to help his father tend their expanded operation.

When Matt had made the request for his son's assistance a few weeks earlier, Joe had volunteered without hesitation. Joe did not regret the decision to leave school temporarily to help bolster his family's fortunes. Still, he wondered what it would be like to spend six months away from classes. He expected to miss school, but he also looked forward to the hard work ahead of him. His instincts told him something special was afoot for his family, and he wanted a front-row seat to whatever it might be. Somehow, he knew, this was the year when that elusive promise of *next year* would prove fruitful for his family, and he needed to be part of the fulfillment. His future would wait awhile longer.

Instinctively, he bowed his head again, this time in silent prayer for the good Lord's blessing on the farm. When he opened his eyes a short time later, John was poking him in the ribs.

"It's time to wash feet," his brother whispered. "Let's go get a tub together. I don't wanna get stuck washen Mr. Millard Webb's feet."

Joe washed his brother first, removing John's shoes and socks, bathing each foot with water, wiping them with a soft, white cloth and finally taking the towel draped over his shoulder to dry the feet. The entire act played out in silence and when Joe finished washing his brother's feet, he glanced up and discovered John regarding him with a sincere smile.

John placed a hand on his brother's shoulder. "I dreaded this tonight," he confessed. "I thought washen somebody else's feet was a silly thing to do, but it's not. I understand it now. When you wash another person's feet, you show them how much you're willen to do for them—maybe how much you love 'em. I've always believed I could count on you for anything, Joe. You're always there, maken all the right moves, sayen all the right things. I don't know what your secret is, but I hope it rubs off on me."

Joe cocked his head, holding his brother's gaze. "I'm flattered," he admitted at length, "but what a strange thing for you to say, John. Why?"

John glanced around the sanctuary, where the women sat on one side and the men on the other as they participated in the religious act. "Because this is a special night. We could wash each other's feet and let it go at that, without ever given it another thought. But it's supposed to mean somethen. I just want us to always remember this one night."

"We will then," Joe promised. "When we're old and sitten on the porch in our rocken chairs, strollen down memory lane, we'll remember this night, John. And recall how special it really was."

They exchanged places then, Joe sitting on the church pew while John kneeled before him with the basin of water and washed his feet. When the ritual was finished, they cleaned up their space, returned to their seats and joined the congregation in singing hymns.

On a typical revival night, the service ended with an altar call as members of the congregation moved forward to kneel and pray, while others sought to confess their sins, seeking baptism and membership in the church. As was customary on the final night of the Benevolence revival, however, the congregation spread out in a crooked circle through the sanctuary, holding hands and praying aloud in a chain prayer. When Preacher Cook concluded the prayer, the singing began again with *Amazing Grace* followed by *The Old Rugged Cross* and other hymns.

Preacher Cook started the final procession, making his way from one person to the next in a parade of tearful, happy hugs and gladsome handshakes. One by one, the congregation peeled off behind the preacher, singing and acknowledging each other as brothers and sisters in Christ. It was an emotional, spiritual parade of the Christian heart, and everyone surrendered to the power of the moment.

Joe figured he must have hugged a hundred people that night— friends like the Berriens and the Carters, all of his family members, a host of neighbors, fellow Benevolence members and several strangers, even Mr. Millard Webb. He teared up right along with everyone else, thanked the Lord he had been able to humble his heart and prayed he would find the way back to the straight and narrow.

CHAPTER 2

IN EARLY APRIL, ADAM Cook paid a call on the Baker farm to deliver the family's tax returns. To supplement his preacher's income, Adam and his wife ran a small accounting business in Cookville. The minister was tall and rangy, in his mid-thirties, with brown hair worn a little longer and shaggier than most men in the community. He wore blue jeans whenever possible, hunted, fished and led lost souls to the Lord.

The preacher's father had married Matt and Caroline, and his two congregations had called Adam to succeed his father six years ago when Fred Cook took ill and died.

Matt regarded the young minister with deepest respect. Adam was an easygoing, sincere man, who provided a conscience for the community without dictating the way it should be.

"I'd be pleased to have you join us for services on Sunday," Adam always told Matt when their paths crossed.

Nothing else, nothing more—just a simple invitation. Matt always thanked him politely, never committing to or rejecting anything.

He was planting cotton in the field beside the house when Adam drove into the Baker yard. Adam walked into the field, carrying the tax forms and standing at the edge as he waited for Matt to reach the end of the row.

It was the busy time of the season for both men, so they greeted each other, chatted quickly and got down to business. Adam explained the tax returns, answered a couple of questions for the farmer and got Matt's signature on the forms.

"I wish all my work was as easy as your tax returns, Matt," the preacher said. "Your wife keeps excellent records. It's a pleasure doen business with y'all."

"Caroline is precise," Matt remarked. "She pretty much keeps track of every penny that comes on or goes off the place. How much do we owe you, Preacher?"

Adam started to hand the bill to Matt, then stopped suddenly and grinned. "How does one Sunday in church sound?" he asked. "I'd forgo the bill in exchange for haven you at next Sunday's service."

Matt eyed the preacher with a bewildered expression.

"Adam Cook!" he exclaimed a moment later. "I don't know much about your line of work, but blackmailen someone sure doesn't seem like the preacherly thing to do."

Adam laughed heartily. "I saw somethen like that in a movie," he confessed. "It worked well on Henry Fonda, so I thought I'd give it a try."

"Have my wife and mama been talken to you?" Matt inquired.

"They only ask me to remember you in my prayers, Matt," the preacher answered. "This isn't part of some conspiracy to get you to church. But you have been on my mind lately, probably because you were at the river when John and Summer were baptized."

"I see," Matt said.

"I wonder if you really do," Adam replied sincerely. "I don't want to belabor the point, but I'd like to say somethen to you so I can satisfy my conscience if nothen else. In a way, you and I are a lot alike, Matt. You plant your seeds in hopes of harvesten a good crop. I'm always looken for a good harvest, too, only I'm out to get a crop of souls for the Lord. I've come to realize lately that you're a crop I've neglected for one reason or another. I'm not gonna badger you, Matt, but I am goen to urge you to give some serious thought to your soul. It's not for me to judge and if that seems what I'm doen, please forgive me. But I believe you live a Christian life, Matt. Liven it is not enough, though. Christ laid a few ground rules for salvation, and I owe it to the Lord—and my conscience—to ask you to consider how those basic rules apply to your life."

"I worry about it myself, Preacher," Matt conceded. "Somethen keeps holden me back—maybe hardheadedness, maybe laziness, maybe even a little fear that I won't or can't measure up."

"The mystery of Christ is somethen to behold, Matt, but this much is clear in my mind," Adam replied. "You won't ever measure up. We are saved by the grace of Christ, but it is a matter of our faith that allows us to experience that grace."

"Faith is a difficult thing, Adam."

"Only as difficult as we choose to make it, Matt."

They were silent for a careful moment, then Adam laughed. "I'm sounden like a preacher, which is the last thing I wanted to do," he admitted. "Just give it some thought, Matt. You know your needs and the Lord knows your needs better than anyone else, including Caroline, your mama or me."

Adam offered his hand, and Matt shook it. The preacher took several steps toward his car, then turned back to the farmer.

"I've always admired you, Matt, ever since I was a kid," he said. "Your strength, your compassion, your general caren for people. Back when you did attend Benevolence, I took it for granted you were a Christian. My sermons won't save you, but I sure would like to look into the congregation on Sundays and see you looken back at me."

Matt laughed slightly. "We'll see. I'll think about it."

Adam grinned broadly. "Watch out for preachers with ulterior motives," he teased.

"You could never have an ulterior motive if you tried, Adam," Matt suggested lightly as the preacher started to walk away from him. "Keep us in your prayers, Preacher."

Adam stopped again, turned slightly sideways and glanced one last time at the farmer. "I'll do that," he vowed. "And you keep me and mine in your prayers."

The two men nodded again, then returned to their busy days.

———

"Weather's worken like a well-rehearsed play," Joe told Matt and Sam just before dinner on the day his brother and sisters ended another school year. "This might be one of those seasons, Daddy, when we have money left over come next winter. This could be the year you've been waiten for."

The three men stood on the edge of the field located directly on the south side of the house, surveying a swath of new cotton. Matt was one of the few farmers in these parts who continued to plant King Cotton.

"You may be right, son," he replied. "You may just be right about that."

Given the fickleness of the relationship between farming and profits, their expectations seemed overly optimistic. But the young season was moving along perfectly, with full cooperation from the weather. Abundant rain had ushered in the spring, followed by a dry spell that allowed ample time to plant the crops. As soon as the last seed was sown, plentiful rains had returned to nurture the young rows of cotton, peanuts, corn, tobacco and other crops that lined the family's fields.

Their hopes sprang from the knowledge that the obligations await-ing the family in the fall were larger than ever. By taking on the Castleberry place, they had nearly doubled the size of their farming operation. Matt had financed the land rent, the crop, a new tractor and equipment with an enormous loan from the Citizens and Farmers Bank in Cookville. The debt was staggering, more than the family had ever owed, and they needed a prosperous year to pay the bill. The risk came, however, with considerable opportunity for profit—certainly greater than they had ever experienced.

Without a doubt, the spring of his nineteenth year had been the most incredible time of Joe's young life. Everything within his realm filled him with exhilaration, especially these difficult days of helping his daddy accomplish twice the amount of work that previous springs had required of them. He had crisscrossed one field after another on a hard-seated tractor, lugged countless bags of seed and fertilizer into the planter and tracked once more across the same fields. He had spent long days hoeing weeds and breaking thousands of tiny suckers and flowering tops from the tobacco patch. The work had honed the boy's rangy form into a man's body. He was lean and hard, with muscles bulging in his arms and chest, while the hot sun had baked his upper body a leathery brown.

The toil of the labor exhausted Joe—for about ten minutes each night after the workday ended. Then, filled by some inexplicable and inexhaustible source of energy, he went in search of new fields, per-haps horseplay with his brothers and sisters, a quick swim in the river or a quiet moment with a book or a fishing pole. But usually, boister-ous business bordered his playing fields.

"You're downright annoyen," a weary Matt told his son one night after a playful moment at the supper table.

"The world is my oyster, Daddy," Joe teased back.

"But, Joe, you don't even like oysters," eight-year-old Bonnie re-marked earnestly, unknowingly, as the family dissolved into laughter around her.

Joe's enthusiasm was infectious and rampant, spreading far beyond the confines of his family and the farm.

Unable to provide his son a salary, yet wanting to reward him some way, Matt helped Joe buy a used Volkswagen Beetle. The bright red car became Joe's passport to a whole new realm.

On Friday and Saturday nights as well as some weeknights, he bounded into the car and disappeared, always careful to return home by midnight to avoid the ire of his parents. He saw movies, loitered in crowded parking lots with friends and acquired a taste for Blue Ribbon beer, preferably when a pretty waitress served it.

Often, he passed the hours in the company of Peggy Jo Nix. A year ago, they had embarked on a spring fever romance. The feelings still lingered. It was a fling between good friends, a learning experience preparing them for something more substantial in the future—with someone else, of course. They spent hours discovering each other, usually on a blanket in some secluded place.

"We're probably spoilen each other for the future," Peggy Jo told Joe one deliciously satisfying night as they shared a cigarette. "Do you think we'll ever find anyone to measure up to our standards?"

"At the worst, let's have fun tryen," Joe suggested. "And then we'll teach them everything we've learned."

"If somehow, I reach the ripe old age of thirty without ever finden a well-to-do husband, preferably a doctor, and you're still single, too, let's marry each other," she suggested.

"It's a deal," Joe promised.

As luck would have it, Tom Carter became romantically involved with Liz Barker, one of Peggy Jo's best friends. The four of them spent many evenings by the banks of New River, skinny-dipping and falling in lust, bragging and daring, pondering and reflecting, mixing pure innocence with the slightest trace of decadence to create the best of times. No one had expectations or made demands. Freedom rang, especially between Joe and Peggy Jo, and they often went their separate ways, yet always kept in close touch and made their plans accordingly.

Frequently, Joe traded Peggy Jo's company for tamer activity with his brothers and sisters or something wilder with Tom. Sometimes, the whole bunch of them crowded into the Volkswagen and disappeared for hours, leaving an empty, silent house that unsettled their parents and grandparents. On other occasions, Joe discriminated, picking a single companion or perhaps two of his siblings to frolic away the night. He ignored no one.

The spring unfolded gloriously, and the summer beckoned with an appeal all its own. Joe reckoned he was enjoying a glimmer of immortality. He lived in the moment and thrived during every minute of it.

After years of racial calm in Cookville, signs of unrest appeared. Aided by the National Association for the Advancement of Colored People, or NAACP, a small group of blacks petitioned the county to remove the "For Whites Only" signs on the public restrooms and water fountains at the county courthouse. The effort failed, but the group made a lasting impression, which was reinforced a few weeks later by the American Civil Liberties Union.

The ACLU provided an attorney for the trial of a Negro man accused of burglarizing the home of an influential white citizen. At the attorney's urging, the community's colored people came down out of the courthouse balcony to swamp the pews of the courtroom floor on the trial's opening day. The act enraged Judge Wilson Avera, who prided himself on courtroom decorum as much as his knowledge of the law. Judge Avera ordered Sheriff Paul Berrien and his deputies to remove the Negroes from the courthouse.

Paul had filed the charges against the burglary suspect in question and considered it an open-and-shut case. The ACLU's intervention first surprised, then angered him as the slimy lawyer sought to create distrust in the colored community by slandering Paul's sincere commitment to dish out justice fairly and impartially. Feeling betrayed by the very people he had tried to help, Paul wanted to uphold the judge's order. His conscience, however, forced him to remain true to his beliefs.

"I can't do that, sir," he told the judge when Wilson Avera ordered him to remove the colored upstarts.

"Why not?" the judge demanded to know.

"Because there's not a single law in the land, including our county ordinances, that says these people don't have a right to sit where they want to in this courthouse," Paul declared. "Tradition is not the law, Judge, and I'll have no part in any scheme to railroad them out of this courtroom."

Judge Avera threatened Paul with contempt of court, but the sheriff stood his ground. Finally, the judge relented, and the trial proceeded in quick order. By the day's end, the suspect had been found guilty as Paul expected, and Judge Avera had handed down the harshest prison sentence available under the law.

Bobby Taylor maintained a close watch on the proceedings, milking the integrationist efforts for every political advantage possible, always careful to refrain from any direct attacks on Paul Berrien.

Bobby and Paul were in the midst of another heated election battle, and Bobby believed he could unseat the sheriff.

Bobby had campaigned for the job ever since the bitterness of his 1960 defeat vanished—or at least subsided to the point where he could deal with it. In retrospect, Bobby had found triumph in the close outcome of the previous election. Even when all had been said and done in that bitter fight, Paul Berrien remained one of the most respected men in the county. Yet, only a few votes had kept Bobby, a relative upstart, from claiming victory. Ever since coming to this realization, Bobby had waged a steady campaign to mend fences and become more respectable while still promoting his prejudiced beliefs. He already had increased his share of votes for the next election, and now, fate appeared on his side as well.

Given the tone of the last election, Bobby concluded the public was unlikely to tolerate any more slander of Paul's credibility. So instead, Bobby unleashed his attack on the NAACP and the ACLU, two organizations with motives and means that even some of the South's staunchest civil rights supporters distrusted. He deftly pointed out the current sheriff's support of these outsiders' courtroom demonstration tactics, then shrewdly reminded voters of a handful of unsolved crimes in which Negroes were the prime suspects. In particular, he cited two incidents at the home of Dr. Ned Turner, which was located right off the square in Cookville.

"People, it's time to wake up!" became the rallying cry of his campaign.

"These outsiders, carpetbaggers and scalawags, all of them, are peddlen their evil ideas all across our beloved way of life," he repeated to anyone who cared to listen. "We are under siege right here on the main square in Cookville. You need look no farther than the home of Dr. Turner to find the evidence. And while the crimes go unsolved, our sheriff spends his days in the courthouse, defenden the rights of those who spread dissension and cause turmoil in our justice system."

Paul speculated he could become the first one-term sheriff in the county's history.

He had dropped by the Baker home to visit Matt one night after prayer meeting. Politics were an unavoidable subject, and the sheriff was frank about his chances of re-election.

"The trouble is that Bobby's runnen a fairly respectable campaign this time," Paul explained. "Except for his insinuations that I'm in cahoots with the ACLU and the NAACP, everything he's done has been legitimate as far as politics goes. It is the sheriff's job to solve crimes after all. Bobby's just keepen a handful of those unsolved cases in the public eye. Pretty smart tactic if I say so myself. And effective."

"I think you're be'en too generous, Paul," Joe said. "Bobby's running a racist campaign. The only thing notable about it is that his campaign is not nearly as ugly as it could be—or may be before it's all over."

"People will see through Bobby," Matt added. "Surely, he can't pull the wool over enough eyes to win the election."

"I don't know," Paul worried. "Ned Turner is solidly in Bobby's corner this time around, and Ned supported me in the last election. The doctor wields considerable influence around Cookville, and he's been successful at getten town folk to believe they're not safe in their homes."

"The pompous Dr. Turner and the bigoted Bobby Taylor," Joe remarked scathingly. "What a partnership. It's just crazy enough to be believable, especially since the good doctor is as prejudiced as they come."

"You know the old sayen: Politicians make strange bedfellows," Paul opined. "I guess it's true."

———

On an early morning in the middle of June, Joe jumped out of bed at the first ring of his alarm clock and slipped quickly into a clean pair of ragged blue jeans, a faded red T-shirt and a comfortable pair of worn work boots. He was still feeling randy following the previous night's date with Peggy Jo.

Without bothering to tie his shoes, he pulled open the bedroom door and tapped his two sleepy brothers from happy dreams as he passed through their room. His daddy and grandpa were already in the kitchen when Joe arrived. Both men grunted inaudible greetings, which Joe returned as he poured a cup of coffee. While waiting for the sleepyheads, they drank the steaming black liquid in silence, each pondering the day's work.

A few minutes later, Sam went to milk the cow while Matt and his sons piled into the cab of a two-ton truck that needed a new muffler. The truck was used primarily to haul heavy loads and transport crops to the markets. Joe steered the vehicle down the pot-holed road, while his two brothers bounced around in the bed of the truck, trying to ignore the predawn chill that pimpled their arms. They were headed to the Castleberry place to unload a barn of freshly cooked tobacco.

Tobacco was the family's greatest source of income and biggest burden. Everyone pitched in to help, all of them working in the tobacco field, except for Rachel, who took care of the housework and cooked three meals a day—a filling breakfast, a huge dinner and a light supper.

With the additional ten-acre crop allotment acquired from the Castleberrys, the Bakers were growing twenty acres of tobacco this summer. Harvesting the crop would tax their sanity from the first of June until the first of September. They worked anywhere from five and a half to six full days each week during the tobacco season, gathering the crop from the fields and filling four barns, where the leaves were cooked over open flames that cured the tobacco to a tawny, golden brown color in five to seven days.

Over the years, as he acquired gumption and experience, Joe had come to understand that the law of averages did not apply to the tobacco. On a typical day in a typical year, he presumed the worst would happen, tried to prepare and still was usually surprised by whatever went wrong on any given day. Equipment malfunctioned sometimes, people got hurt occasionally and everything turned back-asswards every now and then. Yet, as difficult as the task was, Joe enjoyed working in tobacco. He figured his passion for the leaf was some form of deranged hedonism, and he believed that—if cotton was king, then tobacco was a kind of god. It was just a thought, without a single shred of sacrilege intended.

The golden leaf lured prey with seductive charms, like a spider with its web; then consumed the victim in a sensual orgy.

Tobacco was a way of life among the Bakers. Like his daddy and grandfather before him, Joe enjoyed the pleasures of smoking. Now John was leaning toward the habit, although he would be discouraged, particularly if caught by his mother or grandmother, who preferred not to see children smoking. Still, no son of Matt Baker would suffer a severe reprimand for smoking. It was a different story for his daughters, of course. While Rachel dipped snuff—as did many Southern women of her era—it simply was not proper for women to smoke.

"It looks trashy," Rachel often said with a frown—but only when the subject came up in conversation, never as a judgment.

On barn-filling days, which were every day but Sunday, the family got additional help from Lucas, Tom and either the dependable Peggy Jo Nix or the increasingly unreliable Polly Tuckerman. Peggy Jo and Polly were supposed to alternate workdays on the Baker farm, but the Tuckerman girl frequently came up with an excuse to miss her turn in the tobacco field, leaving Matt in a lurch and Peggy Jo in more demand than she wanted.

Four days a week, the men in the crew rose early to unload one of four barns—two of which were on the Baker farm and the others on the Castleberry place. On this morning, they would tackle the "chocolate barn," so named for its brown-colored shingled sides. The chocolate barn was the smaller of the two barns on the Castleberry place. The barns were tall, box-shaped buildings, containing "rooms" that were actually row upon row of wooden tiers with open walls. The tiers were horizontally spaced four feet apart and vertically separated about two feet. Three of the tobacco barns contained five rooms with eight tiers. Each tier held eighteen to twenty sticks of tobacco. The second barn on the Castleberry place was gigantic, with an extra room and nine tiers, each of which easily held twenty-one sticks of tobacco. The Baker crew needed almost two days to fill that monster.

Arriving at their destination, where Lucas and Tom were already waiting, Joe pulled the truck into place beside the barn and shut off the engine as everyone piled out of the vehicle. Except for another round of mumbled greetings, no one said a word in those first few minutes as they drifted into their accustomed places, adjusted their eyes to the dark and went to work with the first light of dawn.

While his family and friends cleared the bottom tiers in each room—taking two sticks at a time and carrying them to the truck, where Matt laid them in layers across the truck bed—Joe climbed onto the barn's lower tiers.

Joe relished a fresh-cooked barn of tobacco. He took a deep breath of the sweetly, pungent tobacco, savoring the aroma. It was an enticing, sensual fragrance, tingling his nose in the same way that Joe supposed the salty seawater of an ocean would.

Minutes later, the thrill was gone as he straddled the tiers, passing the sticks of cured tobacco down to Lucas. Joe had forgotten his cap, and the barn contained the last cropping of sand lugs, those bottom leaves on the tobacco stalk that grew on the ground and were covered with grit. Sand stung his eyes and itched his body unmercifully, especially down the nape of his neck. Joe growled, secretly suspecting the surgeon general was at the bottom of this mess.

———————

They unloaded the barn in less than an hour, then transferred the tobacco to the Castleberry packhouse. The availability of the spacious Castleberry packhouse was especially satisfying to the Bartholomews who had lived in the packhouse on the Baker farm for the past three years.

Lucas and Beauty had two children. Annie was two and Danny one.

JIM BARBER | 121

Living conditions were cramped enough in the one-room shed without having to share it with a barn-full of cooked tobacco. Beauty spent her days in the Castleberry packhouse and various outbuildings on the Baker place, unstringing the tobacco and stacking the loose leaves in neat piles along the walls. In their spare time, the menfolk packed the leaves into neat circles on burlap sheets, tied the ends, loaded the tobacco onto a truck and carted it off to the huge warehouses in Cookville for sale.

When the tobacco had been stored in the Castleberry packhouse, the men returned to the Baker home where they ate a quick, filling breakfast of streaked meat, grits, eggs and toast. Before eight o'clock, they were on their way to the tobacco patch—the whole crew packed into the pickup truck, except for Joe and John who had left earlier on the new John Deere tractor.

On a typical day, the entire crew climbed aboard the double-decker harvester and was riding through the fields cropping tobacco by eight o'clock. Joe, John, Tom and Lucas sat in two rows of metal seats, picking three to five tarry, greenish yellow leaves from each stalk along their respective rows. They were the *croppers*, placing their hands of tobacco into metal clips attached to a chain that revolved around a series of fearsome cogs.

The cogs occasionally chewed up people's fingers, but such a misfortune had never befallen any member of the Baker crew. They were cautious around the cogs, always mindful of the gruesome stories they knew to be true about people who had been careless on other harvesters. The worst story was about Roy Pearson, whose finger had been chewed off by one of the cogs and circled around and around in the chain until someone made the effort to pick it off.

The chains carried the tobacco *hands*—three to five leaves—to the top floor of the two-story harvester, where Caroline, Summer, Carrie and either Peggy Jo or Polly tied them to sticks. They were the *stringers*, always careful to tape their fingers to prevent the tough twine from cutting the flesh between the joints. Each stick held anywhere from twenty-four to thirty hands of tobacco, equally spaced on either side.

Matt ramrodded the operation, taking full sticks from the stringers and hanging the heavy poles on steel tiers at the back of the harvester. Luke and Bonnie took turns driving the contraption through the fields, with the idle one expected to walk behind the harvester picking up any dropped leaves.

After making one round through the field—down fours row at a time and up another four rows—the men unloaded the full sticks from the top of the harvester and placed them on wooden pallets. Using a tractor and forklift, Sam then transported the tobacco to the barn. Twice a day—at dinnertime and the end of the day—the men hung the tobacco in the barn.

This was not a typical day, however, because Polly Tuckerman had telephoned a short time earlier with another flimsy excuse for missing work. Since they were short a stringer for the time being, John would have to spend the morning pulling weeds in the peanut patch instead of cropping tobacco.

Still, it was well before eight o'clock when the short-handed crew piled into the pickup truck and headed for the tobacco patch a few minutes after Joe and John drove away on the new John Deere tractor.

As Joe drove the tractor along the field road, he savored the first cigarette of the day and tried to figure out why he found it difficult to light up in front of his mama and grandmother. Both women knew he smoked, but they had never witnessed him in the act. And even though he smoked freely in front of his daddy and grandpa, Joe still felt uncomfortable lighting a cigarette in the house.

Caught up in his thoughts, Joe ignored John, who stood beside him on the tractor floorboard and muttered a complaint about having to pull weeds. Joe never bothered to glance his brother's way, but the complaint did alter the course of his thoughts. Instead of concerning himself over John's plight, he thought about the possibility that Peggy Jo would end up working with them today. He was determined to persuade the girl to devote her summer to working alongside him in the tobacco patch.

As he considered which arguments of persuasion to use on Peggy Joe, the radio blared some tune by the Beetles. The tractor bumped along the path, and the sun shimmered in the east, burning away the early morning coolness. It was a perfect day.

––––––––

"Have fun by your lonesome," Joe called merrily as John jumped off the tractor.

It was a ridiculous parting sentiment, and John refused to acknowledge his brother as Joe drove away on the tractor. The fact that Joe did not have the common decency to realize he had been snubbed infuriated John even more.

At the moment, John was in full agreement with his father: Joe was indeed annoying. How else to describe someone who virtually ignored you all morning, then turned into Mr. Sunshine the moment he was rid of you. John never knew where he stood with his older brother these days. One minute, they were the best of friends; the next, like aliens from different worlds.

Daddy and Grandpa blamed Joe's condition on spring fever; Mama and Granny pinpointed a more specific cause—Miss Peggy Jo Nix. Joe was feeling his oats, and his frisky behavior made everyone else dizzy.

John released a pent-up sigh of frustration, wishing he could have some of his brother's energy. He felt weary, and the day was just beginning.

His lassitude derived from the rows of peanuts stretched before him. No one had pulled a single weed from this patch, and it seemed unlikely that he could make a dent in the problem. The chore reeked of busy work, a yoke John resented. But since resentment was a waste of time, he trudged into the field.

As he walked up and down the rows, bending to pluck offending weeds wherever they appeared, John filled the time with reflection on the family and himself. At heart, John suspected most people, including his family, perceived him as a loner. The perception was wrong. He valued companionship, especially family ties, although his friendships extended beyond the family. He had a gift for gab, a penchant for frankness and a knack for dry humor that everyone but his relatives noticed. Among the family, John had been tagged inappropriately as shy, right along with his middle sister.

Carrie was truly shy. She went out of her way to avoid unfamiliar people and strange situations. John was merely quiet. He could strike up a conversation with President Lyndon Johnson and never miss a beat if he wanted to.

As far as John knew, the only difference between his brothers and himself was the role of destiny, which had placed him in the middle. When the genes had been allotted, Joe and Luke had received the excesses while John had been doled a perfect balance.

Their excesses gave Joe and Luke a commanding presence, which came across as brash and cocksureness in Luke and boldness and quiet charisma in Joe. With his quietness and solitary ways, John often felt like a pale shadow of his brothers, even though the three of them shared far more common characteristics than differences.

Had he chosen to, John could have resented his brothers' bright stars, but he was too satisfied with his own lot to waste time on jealousy. He enjoyed privacy, which both his seventh-grade reading teacher and Joe had recognized toward the end of school. Mrs. God-win had acknowledged the recognition first, giving John a picture of a young man standing on a rocky seacoast lashed by waves. Beneath the picture was a quote that said: "When you find me here, do not think me to be lonely—only alone."

Joe had noticed the picture lying among scattered schoolbooks on the floor of his brothers' room. A few days later, he had presented John with a sheet of notebook paper containing a handwritten quote from someone called Omar Khayyam: "The thoughtful soul to soli-tude retires."

"Think about it, John," Joe had said. "It's a huge common denom-inator between us, I believe."

Such gestures endowed John with deep respect for his brother, convincing him they would become the best of friends one day. They were pretty close as it was, especially considering the almost six-year age gap. Nevertheless, the age difference, coupled with subtle person-ality clashes, occasionally caused conflict.

Joe was one of those people who seemed to have been born know-ing exactly what direction his life would take. He was the most purposeful person John knew, always preparing, always aiming, always achieving.

John was purposeful to a point, but he was also only twelve years old, although closer to thirteen, as he preferred to tell people these days. Sometimes, Joe lost sight of the fact that John was still a boy who had yet to grasp the full meaning of the future.

Their most recent skirmish had come over John's budding artistic talent. Already a wizard with sketching, he was now winning praise and awards for his paintings. His subject was nature, and he painted the beauty of the world—an interest fueled early by countless walks through the woods with his grandfather and later through similar sol-itary journeys.

Next to Sam, no other Baker family member knew the lay of the land as well as John. Together, they had stumbled across playful black bears, mating deer and other natural wonders that few people ever witnessed firsthand. From his grandfather, John had learned to iden-tify virtually every plant and tree that grew on the Baker land. Sam had instilled in his grandson a strong reverence for the land, and the boy had cultivated an artistic touch to go with his passion.

John had begun to get an inkling of his talent during the winter when he sketched the pecan orchard behind the house. By happen-stance, Joe had seen the picture and suggested John enter the drawing in an art competition sponsored by the Coastal Plains Regional Library in Tifton. John had not been interested in the contest, but Joe had badgered him into it. No one had been more surprised than John when the picture won the overall first place prize in the contest. On top of that surprise, *The Tifton Gazette* had published pictures of the contest winners, including a review written by an art professor who was one of the judges. Of John's sketch, the critic wrote:

"The stark barrenness of the pecan orchard screams with longing, which in itself makes the sketch a prize-winner. But the picture's true greatness lies in the artist's ability to convey the perception of a prideful orchard that will rise anew. This sketch is the work of twelve-year-old John Baker, and I urge you to remember that name. He has the potential to become an artist of renown."

John only half-understood what the professor meant to say, but the words had impressed his family and friends. No one had been more responsive than Joe.

"You've got real talent, John," Joe had told him again and again. "But you have to work hard and then work some more to develop it."

John harbored no grand illusions about his work. He viewed artwork as a pleasant way to fill idle hours. Instead of acting on his brother's advice to work hard, he had put away his sketching pencils and paintbrushes for several weeks, which eventually prompted Joe to yell at him about a lack of motivation and commitment.

"You're talken Greek to me, Joe," John had snapped. "I'm twelve—it's a little early for me to be motivated and committed to the future. I'm happily stuck in the present, so get off my back."

"Well ... you're closer to thirteen," Joe had shot back, the sharp edge gone from his voice.

Pausing to wipe away sweat from his forehead and freshen his cap, John smiled at the memory of his brother's clever comeback. Perhaps more than anything, Joe was disconcerted by a lack of ambition. Perhaps, too, John should heed his brother's well-intentioned advice. Talent was potential, but the true proof of success was the effort that went into the accomplishment.

He glanced upward, judging by the sun's position that precisely half an hour stood between him and dinner. There was still time to cover three more rows.

John weeded to the end of one row, then started another. The weeds were scarce in this part of the field, allowing him to cover the ground quickly. He reached the far end of the field and started back up the row.

The green peanut plants were thriving, their vines running in every direction and mingling with those on the next row. Sighting a clump of wild grass, John kneeled to pull the offensive weeds. Frenzied burring erupted all around him. It was a rattlesnake, nearby, hissing, spitting, slithering closer.

Before John could move, something slammed against his tennis shoe with startling force, piercing the cloth, stabbing the fleshy meat between the heel and ankle of his outer foot. He heard a thud, then screamed as pain exploded in his foot and spread like wildfire up his leg.

John crashed to his hands and knees as more stings slapped his leg. The burring began again, roaring around him as John crawled toward black blotches forming in the distance.

He tried to think calmly, rationally, but dizziness overpowered his desire. His left leg throbbed, stinging currents running from the bottom of his foot to the pit of his stomach. He struggled to his feet, stumbled forward and collapsed to his knees. Dropping his hands to the ground, he struggled forward another yard on his last reserves before flopping face-first in the dirt. The warm soil felt like a featherbed, comfort to the cold creeping into his body. Darkness descended, a powerful, consuming force, claiming his last conscious thought.

CHAPTER 3

AT NOON, MATT SHUT down the harvester. The women went to the house, and the men went to hang the tobacco in the chocolate barn.

The crew's hanging process varied little from day to day. Inside the barn, Joe climbed into the top tiers, while Lucas took a position beneath him on the lower poles. On the ground, Matt started the hanging process by taking the tobacco off the pallets and handing it to the first link in the human chain. Each stick eventually made its way to Tom, who handed it up to Lucas, who pushed it on up to Joe. Straddled across the higher tiers, Joe hung the bird roosts as well as the top three rows in each room. Then, he took a position on the lower tiers, and hung the bottom rows.

Usually, enough available bodies existed in the human chain to allow each man to hold a virtually stationary position as they passed the sticks onto the next person. As the position between Joe and the pallet increased or decreased, men dropped in and out of the line. No one was ever idle, using free time to pick up leaves that fell off the sticks. The leaves were placed in a pile and restrung onto sticks at the end of the day. Matt did not tolerate a messy barn floor or wasted tobacco.

On this day, because they had been shorthanded in the morning and had fewer full sticks than usual, the hanging moved quickly and they wound up with only the tops of two and a half rooms filled by dinnertime. Matt grumbled about the slow-go of progress, not wanting to fall behind and having to play catch-up as the tobacco burned in the field.

Returning home, the men found a bar of Lava soap and clean towels waiting on the back porch. They took turns washing the black tar off their hands beside the well pump, then made their way into the house, eager to dive into the feast that Rachel had prepared for dinner.

The table was set with fried chicken, mashed potatoes and gravy, creamed corn and butterbeans. Rachel was taking homemade biscuits from the oven, and the girls were setting jelly glasses of iced tea at every place.

No one noticed John's absence until they all gathered around the table and his place remained empty.

"Where's John?" Caroline asked.

"I figured he was here," Joe replied. "I drove by the peanut field to pick him up earlier but didn't see him. He's probably taken the long way home."

"You better go check again," Matt instructed his oldest son. "Your granny rounded up Peggy Jo to help us after dinner, so we're gonna need him in the baccer field."

Joe muttered something, grabbed his glass of tea and left the table before the blessing was said. He was disgusted with John for pulling this stunt and delaying their dinner as he climbed into the pickup. He drove recklessly down the lane, expecting to see his brother walking toward the house every time he rounded a corner. The way remained clear, however, and Joe's disgruntlement gradually turned to apprehension as he slid the truck to a stop near the shady water oak where he had last seen his brother early this morning.

Although John was apt to wander off in his leisure time, the boy put work before pleasure. He understood his responsibilities, and Joe began to feel uneasy.

Hopping from the truck, setting the empty tea glass on the hood, Joe moved across the edge of the field, scanning the rows. Just as he almost satisfied himself that John was elsewhere, his eyes hung on something amiss. He did a double-take and sighted the boy, collapsed near the middle of the field.

His heart stopped, then lurched into his throat. His stomach churned, and Joe sprang into action, tearing through the field in a dead run. His first fear was that his brother had suffered sunstroke. Less than twenty yards from the stricken boy, however, he saw that was not the case.

A snake had bitten John. It was obvious.

His brother's left leg was swollen grotesquely, nearly twice its normal size, constricted against the denim of his blue jeans.

Joe fell to his knees, rolling John onto his stomach and pulling the boy into his arms in one motion. He touched his neck, finding the pulse instantly. It beat like a jackhammer. His brother's face was deathly pale, suggesting Joe was too late to help. Then, instinct took over.

He wiped away the vomit dribbling from the side of John's mouth and stretched his brother on the ground. Wedging the blade of his pocketknife between the fabric and John's knee, which protruded from a hole in the jeans, he cut the tough denim. Finally, he cut a swath large enough for leverage, then ripped apart the pants leg from the knee all the way down.

The entire effort took no more than thirty seconds. Joe took one look at the leg and realized a hospital was the only hope for his brother. He picked up the thin body, hoisted the boy over his shoulder and sprinted for the pickup.

Sam was winding up an amusing anecdote about the life of a farmer, which he had read in the *Progressive Farmer*, and a spill of laughter drowned the first faint blasts of the truck horn. Seconds later, though, the urgent blaring pierced the racket around the dinner table, silencing the clatter with heart-stopping abruptness.

"Somethen's wrong," Caroline gasped, rising spontaneously from the bench and racing toward the kitchen door with everyone else in tow.

As soon as they rounded the corner of the house and cleared the obstruction of the smokehouse, everyone realized how right she was. The truck barreled down the field road with alarming speed, and soon, they glimpsed John slumped against his brother's shoulder.

Joe braked the truck to a sliding halt beside the house, yelling for his parents to get inside the cab.

"A snake got him," he informed them breathlessly through the window. "It's bad. We have to get him to the hospital."

His parents dashed to the other side of the truck, with Matt hollering orders for someone to call the hospital in Tifton and alert them what to expect.

Caroline had feared the worse, but she froze upon first sight of the swollen leg, which had turned such a deep shade of purple that it almost looked black.

Matt pushed her into the truck, and motherly instincts took over. With Joe's help, she pulled the boy into her lap and twisted his body so that Matt could examine the leg.

Joe floored the accelerator, and they were gone.

Matt found two sets of fang marks right away, one on his son's lower calf and the other on the backside of the knee joint. Then, while trying unsuccessfully to remove the sneaker from the swollen foot, he saw a ragged tear in the shoe and groaned with disbelief.

"Gosh, almighty," he muttered. "Near as I can tell, he's got three sets of marks on him."

The leg was a bloated mess of deep purple and distended blood vessels. Blood oozed from the two visible bites. The swelling started at the foot and extended to the hip, distorting the leg almost beyond recognition.

John convulsed twice on the way to the hospital, vomiting, choking and stiffening like a board in his parents' arms. Blotches appeared on his dark skin, his breathing turned into short gasps and more swelling began to puff his neck and eyes.

Nobody said it, but they all believed he was dying.

A stretcher, orderlies, nurses and the reassuring presence of Dr. Pittman waited for them outside the emergency room door of the Tifton hospital. The orderlies placed John onto the stretcher and rushed him inside the emergency room with everyone else following closely on their heels.

"How long ago did it happen?" Dr. Pittman asked.

"Thirty minutes at the least," Joe answered. "Beyond that, there's no way of tellen. He was by himself."

"He's got three bites, I believe," Matt added. "Two on the back of his leg—a third on his foot near the ankle. I couldn't get the shoe off."

They arrived en masse at an open door, which the orderlies pushed the stretcher through as Dr. Pittman wheeled around to face Matt, Caroline and Joe. The doctor promised to do what he could, then vanished inside the room.

Caroline insisted she needed to remain at John's side, but a nurse rejected her pleadings with a sympathetic promise to keep the family posted on John's condition.

Matt placed a calming hand on his wife's arm, led her to a nearby couch and cradled her in his arms as Caroline wept against his shoulder. Joe paced before them, chain-smoking cigarettes.

They waited and waited and waited.

"Honey," Matt said in a while. "If ever there was a time for you to have faith, this is it. I'd feel a lot better if you said a prayer instead of cryen."

The suggestion silenced Caroline's tears. She gazed into her husband's eyes, nodded agreement and hugged him fiercely for support.

"Prayer does work better than tears," she told him. "You pray, too, Matt."

He nodded, and they closed their eyes in silent pleading for a miracle.

Inside the emergency room, Dr. Pittman prayed, too, as he examined John.

Nurses attached a heart monitor to the boy, started him on oxygen and used shears to cut away the sneaker. John's foot looked like a grotesque balloon on the verge of popping.

The doctor examined the bite marks, re-examined them and shook his head in disbelief. He administered a dose of antivenin, relying on all the standard procedures for treatment. In all of his years of practice, Dr. Pittman had never come across a rattlesnake bite. He would have preferred someone else in his place, but he was in charge. He ordered a nurse to call for a surgeon, then plunged ahead with his treatment.

First, he made two parallel incisions through each set of fang marks, applying suction cups in hopes of drawing out some of the poison. It was standard procedure, but probably too late to do any good at this point. The extent of swelling and the irregular heartbeat confirmed the obvious: The poison had circulated throughout the body.

Next, the doctor made two long incisions on either side of the engorged leg, hoping to ease the pressure of the swelling and to protect the blood vessels and tissue from more damage. The venom already had destroyed large chunks of tissue near the bite marks. There was no telling what damage the surgeon would find when he opened up the leg. Perhaps muscle and nerve tissue had been destroyed as well.

Almost two hours later, the doctor concluded with certainty, and amazement, that John would survive the ordeal. The boy's vital signs were stable, the swelling had subsided and he was breathing easier.

Once, during the treatment, he had regained consciousness, moaning something inaudible and trying to sit up on the bed. The struggle had been blessedly brief, and he had slipped back into unconsciousness.

Ted Thacker, the young surgeon with a sunny disposition and an earnest desire to make sick people well, concurred with Dr. Pittman's assessment of the boy's condition. Surgery was necessary to repair the leg, but the patient first needed to recuperate from the shock.

"Do you know his family very well?" Ted asked the older man.

"Fairly well," Dr. Pittman replied. "I've been their family doctor for the last couple of years."

"Then I'll count on you to help prepare them for the surgery," Dr. Thacker said. "There's a lot of damaged tissue and blood vessels. It could mean the boy's foot, or even his leg."

Dr. Pittman emerged from the emergency room door with Ted Thacker at his side. Both men wore grim smiles.

"Your boy is gonna make it," the older man informed Matt and Caroline.

"Thank, God," Matt sighed as Caroline slumped against him and Joe closed his eyes in relief.

"You'll never know just how much to thank Him, Matt," Dr. Pittman said quickly. "It was a higher power that saved John. It's another miracle for your family as far as I'm concerned."

"It is," Dr. Thacker agreed. "By all rights, your boy probably should have died. No matter what else happens from here on out, you have his life to be thankful for."

Dr. Thacker's tone contained a warning, and Matt, Caroline and Joe braced for whatever it might be.

"Ted is tellen you the honest truth, folks," Dr. Pittman continued. "The venom has done tremendous damage to John's leg. Your son needs surgery. Matt, Caroline, if y'all agree, I'd like Ted to perform it."

Matt and Caroline accepted the recommendation at face value.

"How bad is it?" Joe asked.

"I want to be straightforward with y'all," Dr. Thacker replied before launching into a graphic explanation about the damage John's leg had suffered. "The leg is in extremely bad shape. You should prepare yourself for what might happen. When that boy comes out of surgery, he could be minus a foot. Or possibly part of his leg."

The surgeon's warning cut through them like a scalpel, without the benefit of anesthesia. Still, they forced themselves to remain composed, trying to focus on the blessing of John's life instead of the part he stood to lose.

Now that Matt, Caroline and Joe had been prepared for the worst, Dr. Pittman sought to encourage them. When he again reminded them that John's life was the true blessing, that anything else might be asking for the impossible, they clutched their stomachs and nodded like satisfied simpletons.

"Thank you, doc," Matt said finally when he was able to push down the lump in his throat. "We appreciate everything. We are grateful. But we have to hope for more—for John's sake."

"I would expect nothen less," Dr. Thacker replied with an honest smile.

Caroline cleared her throat and smiled at the two doctors. "Prayer gave us one miracle," she remarked. "I believe it can deliver another."

"So do I, Caroline," Dr. Pittman confirmed.

"Please do everything you can," Joe urged. "My brother's a great kid. And he happens to love nothen better than a walk through the woods."

"I'll remember that," Dr. Thacker promised.

"We'll get John to a room shortly," Dr. Pittman said. "You can see him then."

"Okay," Matt breathed.

The doctors turned to leave, then Dr. Pittman paused. "I have to tell you this," he said. "I debated whether to, but it's not somethen I can keep to myself."

He had their attention.

"There are four sets of fang marks on John's leg," the doctor explained. "Two are similar in size, the other two considerably larger. It's probable that John stumbled upon a mama rattler and her babies. He may be more fortunate than any of us realize."

On the night after a female rattlesnake and her babies took four bites out of John's leg, Dr. Ned Turner was sleeping alone as usual in his Cookville house. His wife occupied the room next door.

A shuffling noise roused the doctor from a dreamless sleep.

Assuming Delia had come into the room, Ned concluded his wife was having another bout of insomnia, which was the primary reason they no longer shared the same bed. The sounds of someone fiddling with the pocket change and billfold on the dresser across the room piqued the doctor's interest. He struggled to a sitting position and reached over to switch on the bedside lamp.

A few feet away, a man dressed in solid black turned slightly askew, continued rummaging through Ned's wallet and removed two hundred-dollar bills. Dropping the wallet on the floor, the man turned fully toward the doctor, and Ned recognized him.

"What are you doen?" Ned asked. "Have you taken complete leave of your senses?"

The man regarded the doctor with detached amusement. "You've been preachen loud and clear how unsafe people are in their homes, doctor," he said, walking to stand beside the bed. "What is needed is a little proof to back up your high-and-mighty claims."

"You're crazy," Ned observed, the first hint of fear entering his pompous tone. "Get out of here! Right this instant!"

The man merely laughed, crumpled the bills and stuffed them in his pocket. When his hand reappeared, it held a pistol.

The doctor went wide-eyed with terror. And in that instant, the gun discharged a single bullet into his right temple.

The loud bang woke Delia Turner. She sat up in bed as footsteps shuffled past her door and headed for the stairs. The steps were light and quick, a sharp contrast to her husband's plodding movements.

Fear seized her thoughts as she tried to recreate the exact sound that had wakened her. The front door opened downstairs, then shut, and her heart hammered.

Rising from bed, Delia crossed the carpeted floor, pulled back the curtain on the front window and witnessed a single man running down the street toward nigger town.

"Ned! Ned!" she screamed, concluding their home had been violated once again.

Delia rushed from her bedroom, ran into the hall and took two steps toward her husband's room. The light coming from the Tiffany lamp in Ned's room halted her.

She told herself to return to her own room, to call for help, but genuine concern prevented her from heeding the advice. She crept toward the light, peered around the corner and saw her husband. Blood flowed from the wound in his head, already clotting in a purple shade of blue on the side of his face.

She screamed, backed away and broke into convulsive sobs as she fled down the stairs and out the front door. On the sidewalk, she shrieked again, like a wounded animal's peal for help. Car lights came toward her, coming from colored town, even as the porch lights flashed on the house next door.

Delia Turner collapsed in a sobbing heap on the sidewalk. Her neighbors reached her quickly, moments after Paul Berrien, who had happened by the house on a routine patrol.

Ted Thacker was a gifted surgeon, and he performed heroically during almost two hours of surgery on John's snake-bitten leg. He removed numerous layers of tissue destroyed by the venom and used skin grafts taken from the backs of the boy's thighs and buttocks to repair the damage. When John emerged from the surgery, his leg and foot were intact, but he faced a lengthy period of rehabilitation and a long haul on crutches and braces.

John was still groggy from the anesthesia when nurses placed him in a private hospital bed. As he became more alert, he had a strange feeling of omission, as if time had stood still since his face pressed against the warm soil in the peanut patch. He was confused and frightened—until the moment the door opened to his room and his parents, grandparents and Joe stood before him.

Their presence comforted him. And a surge of serenity brightened his face, emerging as a grin, so honest and unassuming that it filled his family with unwavering confidence and unshakable belief in the possibility of miracles.

Late that afternoon, when John was fully alert, Matt and Caroline informed their son about the drastic turn his life had taken. They explained about the crutches and the braces waiting for him, the painful rehabilitation in store and the likelihood that he would walk with a limp.

John accepted their warning with his usual aplomb. "Like you said, it could have been worse. When can I go home?"

Four days later, he did go home and was strong enough to carry himself into the house on crutches.

A steady stream of visitors dropped by the house all afternoon and late into the evening, welcoming John home and wishing the boy a speedy recovery. His last visitor was Paul Berrien, and Matt could not remember a time when his friend appeared so haggard.

A week's worth of black beard had collected on Paul's face, his hair needed a comb run through it and he seemed several inches shorter. His emerald green eyes, which Caroline often complimented for their vividness, were dimmed and marred by dark circles. The strain of the murder investigation had worn Paul down, a feeling with which Matt could empathize as he realized he probably appeared similarly frazzled.

Considering their friendship, it was ironic that neither man had been available as a sounding board for the other during one of the most trying weeks of their respective lives. Their sole contact had come through messages relayed by April and June, who had inquired daily about John's condition while providing only scant details about the murder.

What's the world coming to? Matt wondered as he considered how something so evil could occur right off the main square in a sleepy town like Cookville.

Paul joshed with John momentarily, then gave the boy a dozen packs of Blackjack chewing gum. His son and best friend were the only people Matt knew who enjoyed the licorice taste of Blackjack.

"Just between you and me," Paul told John, "I believe Blackjack can cure anything—even snakebites."

Eventually, the conversation turned to the murder of Dr. Ned Turner, and Joe asked, "What can you tell us about it, Paul?"

"Not very much substantial, and that's only because there's not much to go on," Paul replied. "From what we've pieced together, someone came into the house and robbed him. Ned must have woken up and surprised whoever it was. He was shot once in the head. It killed him instantly."

"There's not a suspect, then?" Matt questioned.

"Not a single one," Paul said. "The gunshot woke Ned's wife. Delia heard someone leave the house and says she saw a colored man runnen off down the street. She's still shook up and not too coherent.

"Of course," he continued a moment later, "the GBI folks are just about convinced that whoever killed the doctor is also the same person who robbed the Turners' house last year—maybe even the same man who tried to attack his wife a few years earlier. Do y'all remember that?"

"Vaguely," Sam said. "The robbery occurred while Rachel was sick with the pneumonia. We sort of lost touch with everything else back then, much like this week."

"One of the things taken in the robbery last year was a twenty-two pearl-handled, silver-plated pistol that Ned had given to his wife," Paul explained. "The GBI has determined the bullet that killed Ned came from a twenty-two. It could be nothen more than coincidence, but their feelen is that someone used that stolen gun to kill the doctor. Unless we find a murder weapon, there's no way to prove any of this. And frankly, we're not close at all, to finden a weapon or a suspect. At this point, we have nothen but a lot of speculation and fabrication."

"I guess this will make the election that much more difficult," Matt commented.

Paul nodded. "It's less than two weeks away," he surmised, "and there's a killer runnen loose on the streets of Cookville. You have to admit: It doesn't exactly inspire confidence in the local sheriff."

"Don't lose your spirit, Paul," Matt instructed.

"Or your confidence," Sam added.

Paul responded with a grim nod and tight smile.

"What's Bobby Taylor sayen about all this?" Joe inquired, trying to shift the focus off Paul. "I supposed he's pleased as punch, especially if everybody believes it was a black man who killed Ned."

"Actually, he's been fairly understated about the whole thing," Paul replied. "And why not? He probably realizes there's a noose around my neck, just waiten for me to pull the string."

The Bakers had never seen their friend so downhearted.

"You'll still win the election, Paul," Sam tried to reassure him.

Paul shook his head in obvious doubt. "I don't know," he replied. "Maybe I don't need to be sheriff anymore. And to tell you the honest truth, I'm not even sure I want to be. When you get right down to it, the election doesn't mean diddly-squat to me right now. I just want this whole business over and done with."

On election day, Bobby woke with a victorious feeling. He had conducted the perfect campaign, giving careful attention to every move he made and each thought he uttered. He had held his temper and never once questioned the saintly virtue of the respectable Paul Berrien.

This time around, Paul had cooked his own goose, with plenty of help from the NAACP, the ACLU and the good Dr. Ned Turner.

Bobby chuckled at his good fortune. All he had done was remain respectable and keep a solemn face as one uproarious event after another unfolded. And now, everyone had questions about Paul Berrien's ability to enforce the law.

Next to him, Martha stirred, and Bobby rolled onto his side to observe his wife. He wondered how he had managed to end up with a wretch like her as the woman in his life. Martha was such a plain Jane that Bobby was grateful for and encouraging of her reclusive behavior. He wanted as few people as possible to know she was his wife. Tonight, however, he supposed Martha would have to stand beside him as they waited for the election returns. Perhaps he could persuade her to stay home tonight. Bobby laughed obnoxiously. Of course he could.

He had never wanted to marry Martha. He had intended to screw the woman and leave. But she had proved to have an alluring quality, coming across like an anxious puppy ready to please her master. And more than anything, Bobby loved feeling masterful.

These days, Martha made a miserable mess of almost everything, but she still had that dutiful quality, especially when Bobby showed the slightest affection toward her. Though his feelings for Martha had died long ago, Bobby still felt the need to possess her. He leaned closer, with his eyes closed, and nuzzled her neck. Martha usually did whatever he said, showed whatever enthusiasm he asked of her and, as long as he closed his eyes, Bobby could imagine he was making love to anyone he wanted—but never to the homely woman who was his wife.

It was the closest election of any kind ever in the history of the county. So close that every single ballot was recounted to make sure there was no mistake in the outcome.

On the first balloting, Paul won by five votes, and Bobby was livid, reverting to his old self, demanding a recount. He calmed down as the votes were counted the second time, resuming the cool posturing that had been his trademark throughout the campaign. The new totals added one vote to Paul's margin of victory.

Genuine disappointment prevented Bobby from exploding in rage, dampening the animosity that simmered below the surface of his consciousness. Even with all the odds stacked in his favor, Bobby had been rejected. For the first time in his life, he was ready to put a battle behind him. Then and there, he decided to find another goal—something that would bring him more satisfaction than the responsibility of being a sheriff who had to worry about keeping the peace and solving every crime that came his way.

Bobby wanted to tell Paul Berrien that he had gotten everything he deserved with the victory. Instead, he masked the smug feeling and offered a handshake to the victor.

"You whipped me fair and square, Paul," he said, gazing intensely into the face of his conqueror. "Enjoy it."

Paul could only nod an acknowledgment, and a shiver ran up his spine. Bobby's eyes contained something unsettling, a glazed look to the future and a cold, empty disdain of the past. Beneath the complacency, those eyes presented a challenge and held a devil-may-care attitude.

As Bobby moved away toward his three sons, uncertainty overwhelmed Paul. The sheriff had a feeling of having overlooked something of vital importance. And while he believed Bobby was definitely the wrong man to have the sheriff's job, Paul could not help questioning whether he himself was the right man for it.

CHAPTER 4

DURING THOSE DAYS WHEN John's life was at the mercy of God, the Bakers had fallen behind on the farm. More tobacco ripened in the field than was picked; almost overnight, other crops begged for attention; and machinery suddenly required repairs. The days seemed to have no logical end, and the weeks went on without pause, prompting Caroline to remind her husband that too many Sundays were being spent working the fields instead of honoring the Sabbath.

To make matters worse, the family work crew was short a hand in the tobacco field. John was confined to the house to convalesce under Rachel's watchful eyes. Peggy Jo Nix became a permanent fixture around the place, which pleased Joe but still left the family in need of one more hand. At Paul Berrien's suggestion, help came unexpectedly from his sisters.

April was sixty-four that summer, June sixty-two; yet they insisted they could string a stick of tobacco. Out of desperation, Matt accepted their generous offer, even though he feared the ladies' help might be more trouble than it was worth. To everyone's surprise, however, April and June caught on quickly, needing less than half a day to get the hang of tying tobacco to the stick. For the remainder of the season, the two sisters alternated their days in the tobacco field, always reliable, always bringing a freshness to their work that made the long, hot days somehow more tolerable.

Then, before anyone realized it, the work slackened, a waning so slight that it was hardly noticeable—except suddenly the days seemed shorter than usual and the weeks were long enough to get the most important work done in six days.

In addition to the long days on the farm, Joe began working nights in the Planter's Tobacco Warehouse in Cookville, hoping to earn enough money to pay for his college tuition and books when he resumed classes at ABAC in the fall. Five nights of the week, he walked out the door at a quarter till seven, returned home shortly after midnight and climbed into bed. Less than six hours later, he was up again, working alongside his family as they struggled to meet the obligations of their most pressing season ever in the tobacco field.

Finally, with one week to spare before the children returned to school, the Bakers stripped their last stalk of tobacco and paused for a brief moment of rest before the fall harvest season.

These things occupied Matt's mind as he sat at the kitchen table, alone again on another Sunday morning.

He recalled Joe's prophecy from early spring. "This might be one of those seasons, Daddy," his son had predicted. "This could be the year you've been waiten for."

And it had been. Matt reckoned he might never see another year like it—when the weather cooperated perfectly and the crops thrived as never before. His fields were bursting with a bumper crop, so beautiful that he almost hated to run a combine through them. Tobacco was bringing top price, and the leaf was heavy. He would exceed the government quota for pounds, and that was his most pressing concern. As concerns went, this one mattered little and was shrugged off without a second thought.

Matt should have been on top of the world, yet he felt oddly let down. More than anything, he was restless, torn between what he should have done on this day and why he had chosen to do otherwise.

He should have gone to church with his family, as his wife had requested. It was the first Sunday John had been able to attend services at Benevolence since the snakebite, and Caroline wanted the whole family to be with him. Even Joe, who probably was more tired than all of them, had dragged out of bed and gone to church to please his mother and support his brother. Matt had spurned the request, however, and Caroline's disappointment had been bitter. She had started to pick an argument with Matt, then stopped short as he became defensive.

"I don't see why we have to have this same old argument over and over again," he told his wife. "You see things one way on this matter, and I look at it another way. I'm not a churchgoen man, Caroline. You knew that when you married me."

"No, Matt," she replied sternly. "I did not know that when I married you. I believed the man I married counted his blessens and knew where those blessens came from. I believed we shared the same faith. I've always believed that, Matt, but I won't bother you again about it."

Caroline had not been the only one disappointed. The entire family had acted coolly toward Matt throughout the morning, almost as if they regarded him through newly opened eyes.

For the most part, Matt had been an exemplary role model for his children. He was hardworking, understanding and comforting, a man of integrity and honor, who taught his children about idealism as well as how to reconcile dreams with reality. He showed his children the virtues of compassion, caring and generosity through a never-ending series of good works and goodwill.

He had earned the respect accorded to him, but Matt was human after all and susceptible to mistakes like everyone else. In the solitude of that Sunday morning, Matt faced the consequences of his most glaring mistake—the hypocrisy of his life, the false notions given to his children by a man who taught them all the right things in life but selfishly refused to embrace the essential reason for their being.

The contradiction ran against the grain of everything Matt had been taught by his parents as well as the values Caroline and he had tried to instill in their children. Hard work, relatives, fate—a person did not have much choice in things such as those. But when the matter came down to beliefs and convictions, especially those where commitment was necessary, the decision depended entirely on choice. How many times had he told his children exactly that? And how many times had he told them about the importance of making those choices of your own free will? That commitments made when you were backed into a corner or as an easy way out of a jam often proved worthless in the long run? And that worthless commitments were the worst kind of all?

Yet, from the first moment Matt had doubted God on the day the Japanese bombed Pearl Harbor, every decision about his Christian faith had been made when he was backed into a corner or as the easy way out of a jam. There was no ready explanation for his past actions, but the time had come for an honest decision on this matter.

Either, he had faith or he did not. The decision was that simple.

If he chose to believe, however, then he had to make the commitment, too, without any suspicions and reservations as well as with the understanding that searching for the answers to the mysteries of faith was part of faith itself. And if he lacked faith, then he had to end the pretense and quit confusing his family with mixed messages.

The choice was Matt's to make—of his own free will.

On a similar Sunday well over a year ago, Matt had wrestled with this same decision. Burdened by worry over Rachel's illness and other concerns, he had been equally restless, with absolutely none of the usual desire to quell his uneasy spirit with busy chores. He had gone for a drive, taking back roads to Cookville and winding up by chance at a tiny block building on the outskirts of town. It was the African Methodist Episcopal Church where Lucas Bartholomew worshipped with his family.

Spotting Lucas' truck, Matt had stopped, intending to leave an overdue paycheck on the dashboard. Something about the preacher's voice booming from the open church doors had captured Matt's interest, however, and he had listened intently to the message based on the biblical story of Job.

It was a simple sermon of one man's blind faith, faith so strong that it had overcome the worst of trials and tribulations. Listening to the black preacher intone his flock to have the faith of Job, to believe their dedication would earn them the ultimate reward one day, Matt had felt the desire to trust a higher authority for help in dealing with life's hardships.

He had gotten back into his truck and headed toward Benevolence, determined to make his public profession of faith in Christ and repent his sins. By the time he reached the church, however, services had ended and the congregation was milling around the outside grounds. Matt had passed on by the church. Soon afterward, his mother had become her old self again, and the thoughts of repentance and forgiveness had given way to the daily rigors and joys of life.

On this day, Matt arrived at Benevolence with plenty of time to spare and with better reasons to justify his decision. He came seeking a God who would grant him inner peace for every day of life rather than provide a quick fix during the difficulties. He came as a believer in Christ, with faith restored and repentant of his sins. He needed redemption through God's saving grace, and he was humbled enough to set aside his pride.

With sweaty palms, Matt opened the front door and stepped into the church sanctuary for the first time in a long time. A lump rose in his throat as he stood there, oblivious to the few curious looks generated by his sudden appearance this late into service. For a moment, he was self-conscious, wishing he had changed into more suitable clothes than his everyday jeans and work shirt. From the altar, however, Adam Cook smiled and nodded Matt toward a seat, his actions so subtle that hardly anyone noticed the acknowledgement.

Gathering his courage and remembering his mission, Matt moved to his left and took a seat on the back row. Already, he felt the first stirrings of fellowship.

Felled by despair as never before, Caroline hardly heard Preacher Cook's sermon on *The Bounty of Living in Christ.* Her husband's stubbornness baffled Caroline, and his hard-hearted resistance worried her. For the first time, she truly doubted whether Matt would find his way to Christ. For most of the service, she agonized, bereft of reason and hope. The sense of loss and failure was demoralizing, but something prevented her from conceding defeat in this battle for Matt's soul. Mustering up her faith, she renewed the silent, continuing prayer that her husband would see the light one day and surrender his will to a greater power.

In the middle of this prayerful contemplation, Caroline heard the doorknob turn as the church door opened. Inexplicably, her heart gladdened and filled with anticipation of the miracle for which she prayed. She risked a sideways glance, and there was Matt, completely unaware that his family occupied the pew beside him. In the happy rush of her heart, she watched her husband claim a seat on the pew opposite his family. Intuitively, she clasped Rachel's outstretched hand, bit her inside lip to keep from weeping tears of joy and stiffened to keep her body from becoming a quivering mass.

"The Lord's been worken on him hard, Caroline," Rachel whispered in a voice chockfull of emotion. "You could tell it all summer, even long before that. We knew it would happen. Sooner or later, the Lord was bound to reach him."

Caroline merely squeezed the older woman's hand one more time, unwilling to trust her own voice as the preacher concluded the sermon.

Adam Cook felt the Holy Spirit enter into Benevolence the moment Matt Baker walked through the church door. Sensing works of a greater power were at hand, he finished the sermon, offered up a prayer and issued the altar call as the congregation went through the ritual of finding page eighty-one in the hymnal—*Just As I Am,* a song the church members knew by heart.

As soon as April Berrien struck the song's first note on the piano, Matt rose and headed toward the preacher. An overwhelming urgency compelled him forward, building with every step, rising up from deep inside his heart and soul. Tears came of their own accord, unabashedly.

A teary-eyed Adam welcomed Matt into the body of Christ with a crushing embrace, brother to brother as they silently acknowledged the presence around them.

"I need this," Matt said. "For a long time, I've needed it."

"Unburden yourself, Matt," the preacher advised as the congregation sang.

Strength of mind and body failed Matt then. Emotion overcame him as the sense of something pitiful and wretched dominated his every thought. He was a broken man, and the congregation was humbled. People understood the cleansing taking place, especially those who had been at this low point in their own lives.

Caroline went to stand with her husband, holding Matt as he wept, then encouraging him with a gentle touch as Adam ministered with words of salvation.

In a while, something else stirred within Matt, the first feelings of comfort and encouragement, faith and hope, grace and consecration. As their tears subsided, Adam and Caroline led Matt to the altar. The three of them knelt and prayed silently before the preacher offered another prayer on behalf of Matt, Caroline, their family and the entire congregation.

When his prayer was finished, Adam lifted his lanky frame off the floor, reclaimed a center position and urged others to unburden their souls, correctly sensing that a spirit of revival and restoration was moving through the congregation.

April heeded the call first, halting her piano playing to move to the front of the church to offer up prayers to the Lord. Others quickly followed, coming one by one and then hand in hand, as it became apparent that something extraordinary and intimate was occurring within the tiny church. Tears came in torrents, and prayers of every kind filled the sanctuary.

Sam and Rachel went to pray with Matt and Caroline, while Joe helped John to the altar to plead for his leg to be restored to full capability. Their brothers and sisters found their way to the altar as well, each on a personal mission, as did their closest friends.

On this day, everyone felt the power of the Lord and was struck by the enormous sense of awe and respect it commanded, as well as innate belief in the strength and miracles it possessed.

Eventually, the entire congregation was drained but also refreshed.

Everyone reclaimed their seats, and the day's business continued. In quick order, Adam proposed church membership for Matt. The proposal was motioned by Paul Berrien, seconded by Dan Carter and rousingly approved by the whole congregation. Then, as they sang *Amazing Grace* and *Faith of Our Fathers*, Matt stood in front of the congregation and was welcomed into the fold of Benevolence Missionary Baptist Church. A short time later, the service moved outside, where the congregation sang the standard, *Shall We Gather at the River*, and the preacher baptized Matt in the saving waters of New River.

As he did with everyone he baptized, Adam spent a private moment with Matt after he lifted the man out of the water and offered an appropriate piece of scripture.

"Fight the good fight of faith, Matt," the preacher advised. "You'll find those words in the Bible. I'm not goen to tell you exactly where, but I trust you'll come across it on your own."

Matt nodded his understanding, knowing that he had just embarked on a search for the mystery of mysteries.

Among those to whom it mattered most, everyone reckoned it was about the best Sunday dinner they had ever waited for as they finally got around to spreading food on the church grounds.

In bed later that night, Matt shared with Caroline the whole story about his road to salvation. When he was finished, she hugged him tightly, and they sealed the wonderful day by making love.

Finally, when they were satisfied and snuggled close to each other, drifting toward a peaceful sleep, Matt made one last observation to his wife.

"One thing surprised me more than anything else, honey," he told her. "I never once figured you and Ma for back-row Baptists."

Caroline laughed softly and started to suggest they would move up one row beginning next Sunday. Then, she changed her mind. As long as they were filling up the church, with Matt anchoring the family pew, she reckoned the good Lord would not mind where the Bakers sat.

With nothing but time on his hands, John discovered a passion for his artwork in the fall of the year. His paintings and sketches captured the season—the gathering of the harvest, the changing landscape and the people at work. His technique improved, and he experimented with different styles, shades and textures. He painted and sketched countless pieces, yet saved only a select few that appealed to his basic instincts.

His leg was healing slowly as he followed the doctor's schedule of tiring exercises and relentless physical therapy. He faced the rigorous routine with a cheerful attitude, as if it hardly mattered when he next walked without crutches, as long as he would walk again by his own power. His family regarded John as the epitome of patience. As John saw it, he simply had no other choice.

One warm day in early October as he sat on the front porch doing homework, he noticed a commotion in the field across the road where his brothers and sisters were digging sweet potatoes. Suddenly, Joe burst into a trot across the field, coming toward the house.

"It's another rattlesnake," he informed John as he approached the porch. "The place is crawlen with 'em this year."

The rattlesnake population did seem unusually large this year. Various members of the Baker family had killed eight so far—three Eastern Diamondbacks and five timber rattlers—not to mention four moccasins and a rare coral snake.

Joe went inside the house and returned quickly with his pistol in hand, loading the gun on the porch before trotting back to the sweet potato patch.

Observing from the porch, John watched his brother shoot the snake. The children then spent a few minutes poking and prodding at the dead rattler before Joe picked the snake up with a stick and brought it to the house for everyone else to inspect. It was a five-foot-long diamondback, as big around as a grown man's fist with fourteen rattles and a button.

John half-hoped it was the *mother* that had bitten him.

Later that night, he suffered through another nightmare about snakes. The scene was familiar. He was sitting in the glider on the front porch when he noticed the first snake slithering down the road. Others soon followed in all shapes and sizes, and John was beginning to feel the first urges of panic when the burring erupted in his dreams. Frantically, he glanced around and found the snake coiled below him ready to strike. At the precise moment the snake lunged toward him, John woke with a terrified cry, coming to a sitting position in bed, awash in a cold sweat, trembling uncontrollably as his heart pounded.

In an instant, Joe was beside him, offering words of reassurance and a protective embrace. As always, John calmed quickly, realizing his mind had played tricks on him.

"That was a bad one," he said a while later, falling back into the bed. "I thought I was a goner."

Joe crawled onto the double bed beside his brother, providing a comforting presence for John as they lay in the dark. "You know what might help," he suggested. "Try thinken of what happened as one of life's vaccinations—like for polio or smallpox. Rattlesnakes strike at very few people, much less take a bite out of them. I think the odds are on your side the rest of the way, little brother."

"That's one way of looken at it," John agreed as they began to drowse. "I've just got to find a way of convincen my dreams that it's not likely to happen again in my lifetime."

At school recess the next day, John sat on the walkway, soaking up the sunshine while his friends played football. The previous night's bad dream occupied his thoughts, and almost without thinking, he began doodling on a piece of notebook paper. Gradually, a form emerged on the paper, and an image of the grotesque captured John's imagination.

Over the next few days, the pencil sketch turned into a full-fledged color picture and then into a vivid painting of a coiled rattler surrounded by her babies. Every detail registered precisely and menacingly—the flat, triangular, golden head that rose hissing out of the coiled mass of brown skin and black diamonds, gleaming amber eyes with a hypnotic quality, the pinkish membranes of the split mouth, the forked tongue and raised rattles. Smaller rattlers flanked the female diamondback, each stretched to full length with angry heads rising off the ground.

"It looks as if they're about to slither off the canvas," Sam observed when John showed the painting to his family one night after supper.

"That's what I was aimen for," John replied. "The good thing is that they're stuck right where they are for the duration. There's no need to worry about them."

"It's more than a little unsettlen," Rachel suggested. "What are you goen to do with it?"

"I thought I might hang it in my room," John answered.

"Then you'd better think again," Luke declared fiercely. "I don't care what you do with the ugly thing, mister hotshot painter, but it's not stayen in the room where I sleep at night."

"What's the matter, Luker?" Joe teased. "Are you afraid they're gonna getcha one night while you're sleepen?"

Everyone laughed but Luke. To keep the peace between his brothers, Joe volunteered to store the painting in his room.

Two days later, he began reconsidering the decision after a second consecutive restless night. Now, snakes were slithering through his dreams, and Joe wanted to rid himself of the painting.

Recalling an advertisement he had seen while reading the previous month's edition of *Progressive Farmer*, Joe thumbed through the magazine and located the notice. As far as he was concerned, the art contest provided a perfect opportunity to get the ghastly painting out of his room and the house as well.

Bombarded by the full extent of Joe's persuasive powers, John reluctantly agreed to enter the painting in the contest. With one day to spare before the entry deadline, the brothers wrapped the painting carefully, placed it in a large box and mailed the package to a Birmingham, Alabama, address.

———

The hunter's moon of October turned into November, and John's recovery stalled. At the suggestion of Drs. Pittman and Thacker, Matt and Caroline carried their son to Crawford Long Hospital in Atlanta. A team of specialists examined John's leg, and their prognosis was disheartening. The nerve damage had been more extensive than previously thought; John might end up as a cripple.

For the first time, the youngster felt discouraged.

His family rallied around him, however, and their faith renewed John's spirit. He put aside his artwork, preferring to spend his free time perched alongside his daddy or Joe as the men guided the combine through fields of cotton, soybeans and grain sorghum. He accompanied his grandpa to various farms and warehouses as Sam conducted the dealings of his pecan business, always learning from and amazed by the man's strength of character and perspective.

At prayer meeting one Wednesday night, the Benevolence congregation pleaded with the Lord specifically on John's behalf, praising the glory of God and asking that the boy be made whole again. John went away from the church feeling blessed beyond measure, knowing he belonged to something vast and special.

One week before Thanksgiving, John received a letter from the *Progressive Farmer*. He opened the envelope at the supper table, read the letter in silence and casually informed his family that his painting had been selected as the overall winner in the art contest. In addition to the notification letter, the envelope contained the first-place winner's check for fifty dollars, a form requesting his permission to reprint the painting in the magazine and a handwritten note from an Atlanta art patron. The man praised the quality of the painting, predicted great success for John in the future and proposed to buy this early work for an additional one hundred dollars.

No one knew quite how to take the success. Winning a contest sponsored by the local library had been surprising enough, but this latest accolade put John's artwork in another dimension.

"You're an artist, John," Joe declared as the family celebrated the accomplishment. "A real, honest-to-goodness artist who gets paid for doen what you love."

"Enjoy it, son," Sam advised. "Not everyone is so fortunate."

John nodded at the sage advice. He felt blessed, and more than a little amazed.

———

One Saturday in mid-December, John woke early, hauling himself and a warm blanket to the front porch. He settled in the porch swing, wrapped the blanket around him and waited for the sunrise, enjoying the wintry atmosphere. It was a chilly morning, perfect weather for snagging a deer, which Joe and Tom Carter hoped to do later in the morning.

A few minutes later, the front door opened, and his sleepy brother emerged from the house.

"What the heck are you doen up this time of day?" Joe asked, leaning his shotgun against the wall and taking a seat in the glider to wait for Tom's arrival.

"Woke up early," John explained. "I always do on days like this when the hunten's gonna be good. I bet you snag a big one today."

For several minutes, the brothers lost themselves in a discourse on hunting. They spoke about the deer that got away, the shot they missed and the one they could not fire at all. From deer hunting, their conversation rambled onto dove, rabbit and squirrels before lighting on quail.

Neither Joe nor John considered himself a good shot at quail, but both loved to eat it, especially the way their grandmother prepared the birds. Rachel stuffed the quail with pork sausage, then baked the birds brown and served them with gravy made from the pan drippings, butter, grape jelly and a touch of vinegar. Their mouths soon watered, anticipating a feast, and they made plans to set bird traps, hoping to entice a covey of quail lurking in one of the cornfields.

"We'll do it this afternoon," Joe promised, "as soon as Tom and I are finished butcheren that deer you seem so sure we're gonna get."

John smiled, then his face clouded with disappointment. "You'll have to do it without me," he said. "My crutches work well on solid ground, but they're not worth a flip in soft fields."

"I guess the goen would be tough," Joe replied. "It won't be too much longer, and you'll be walking with me."

"Do you really think so?" John asked.

"You have to keep believen, John," Joe said firmly. "Stay determined, keep your faith."

"I'm tryen," John said. "I keep tellen myself everything will be okay. I don't want to be a cripple. I don't even want to limp." He hesitated, then said, "But somethen doesn't feel right. It's not simply that my leg is weak. It's as if somethen's not connected down there—whatever it is that makes my leg cooperate with the rest of me."

He paused again, scanning the horizon across the field beside the house. "I'd give almost anything just to feel a breeze against my face from a good run," he said finally, turning back to Joe. "Lately, though, I'm beginnen to believe it's not meant to be."

"I felt that way when my leg was broken," Joe replied. "The strength will come when it's time, John, when the healen's ready for it. One day, you're gonna be overwhelmed by a knowen feelen that you're ready to walk again. You'll take that first step, and the leg will be strong enough."

"You sound entirely sure," John remarked.

"Oh, I could be wrong," Joe admitted. "You know yourself and what you're goen through better than anyone else. More than anything, I'm just urgen you to keep encouraged and not give up. Give yourself a chance and see what happens."

John nodded, returning his gaze to the dark horizon, waiting for the dawn to come.

———————

John's prediction proved correct. At mid-morning, Joe and Tom returned home with a nine-point buck that had wandered into sight of Joe's shotgun. Soon, everyone was engrossed in carving up the animal for the freezer, and John used the busyness to seek a quiet moment. He planned to read a book on the front porch, but his natural instincts sent him on a different path, and the boy and his crutches followed a course that led eventually to the Old Pond.

He welcomed the solitude like a long-lost friend, soaking up the beauty of the land. A slight breeze stirred the crisp air, chapping his lips and face with a feeling of freshness that had been absent since that summer day when he almost lost his life to the rattlesnakes. The wind rippled the pond water, and an occasional fish broke the surface. Beyond the pond, cows grazed in the back pasture.

The mood was gentle and peaceful, lulling John into a deep slumber as he lay on the grassy bank, basking in the direct line of warm sunshine.

He woke sometime later with the sun directly overhead and his soul rested and refreshed. Warmed by the sunshine, he thought of the approaching winter solstice. Like his grandpa, John had keenly noted every equinox and solstice for several years now. Sam saw those days as beginnings and endings, "portending"—Grandpa's favorite word—a sense of something lost and something found, of happiness and sadness. Strictly speaking, John believed his grandfather's viewpoint gave too much weight to mere days. Nevertheless, he vowed then and there to view those seasonal markers as opportunities to take stock in what was and set his sights on what would come.

Earlier this morning, his brother had predicted the leg would heal when the timing was right. Recalling their conversation, a Bible verse came to John: "To everything there is a season, a time for every purpose under Heaven." The verse had provided the vision for John's prize-winning painting of the pecan orchard in winter. He remembered setting out to capture on canvass the beauty and quality of every season—the robust winters, promising springs, relentless summers and bountiful falls. The memory stirred a sudden anticipation about the paintings still to be done, filling John with an eagerness to move forward and leave behind this dreary season of his life.

Rising to a sitting position, he experienced a keen awareness of his faith in God, a connection to all that was good and real in life. He knew then that God existed wherever people looked for Him—in the here and now, in the woods and the fields, in church and home, in hearts and minds, even in the mountains and oceans that John had never seen. He was beauty, grace and natural order. Or as the preacher put it: God was and is and will be—His hand always extended and waiting for all who sought Him.

John felt conviction and power behind these thoughts, even wished he might find a way to share the knowledge so that everyone would realize the power of God and seek His grace. It was the mystery of faith being revealed, and in that moment, John felt the beginnings of

healing. One day, he might even understand the purpose for his encounter with those rattlesnakes. For now, he was content with this
inner peace that his world would right itself in God's time.

A movement on the pond's far side caught his attention, and John
saw his older brother emerging from the path in the woods at a trot.
He pulled himself to a standing position, waving to Joe.

"Are you okay?" Joe called across the pond.

"A-Okay," John said.

"You had us worried," Joe said when he reached his brother. "You
shouldn't wander off like that without tellen somebody where you're goen."

John chuckled. "Since when, big brother? Wanderen around this
place is what I do best. I'm pretty good at—I think you put it—haven
fun by my lonesome."

"I put what?" Joe asked, perplexed.

"The day it happened," John answered, tapping his foot with a
crutch. "You dropped me off at the peanut field that mornen, and the
last thing you said was, 'Have fun by your lonesome.'"

"Really? I said that?"

"I wanted to punch you," John said. "I resented like crazy haven to
pick weeds by myself that day, and you were totally oblivious."

"Still feel that way? Joe asked.

"Nah. I get over things pretty quick." John glanced down at his
feet, then back at Joe. "Thanks for comen to get me that day, Joe."

"Least I could do since that fun thing by your lonesome didn't
work out so well," Joe shrugged. "You sure you're okay, John?"

John beamed with knowing. "I'm good. God and I just had a
meeten of the minds right before you got here. It eased my mind. And
you were right this mornen, too, Joe. The leg's getten better, and I'll
be walken soon enough."

"You will," Joe agreed. "And runnen and wanderen and, hey, next
summer, you'll even be picken weeds in the peanut field."

John grimaced. "I don't doubt it."

"Dinner's waiten for us," Joe said.

"I'm hungry," John said. "Can I ask you for a couple of favors?"

"Anything?"

"Could you set those bird traps this afternoon? I could really go
for some quail," John said.

"Right after dinner," Joe confirmed. "What else?"

"How about a piggyback ride back home?" John asked. "My arms
are worn out from these old crutches."

"Hop on," Joe said, dropping to a crouch.

The healing came slowly, sometimes grudgingly, it seemed, certainly slower than Christmas, which passed with John still in need of crutches. Indeed, all of winter came and went, and he missed most of the planting season, too. He wasn't the only one.

Facing the prospect of being drafted, Joe volunteered to join the Marines. He enlistment and departure happened so swiftly, the family never really had time to process it. One day, he was there, finishing up his winter quarter classes and helping set out tobacco; the next, he was gone to boot camp at Parris Island, South Carolina.

For a short time, his absence felt like the vacuum of a huge black hole, and then the space filled up with everyday life. Matt offered Lucas Bartholomew a full-time job on the farm to replace Joe, and everyone adjusted to the new family dynamic.

For most of the spring, John felt like an empty canvas, blank and waiting to be filled. He wanted healing for his leg, but even that prospect failed to excite him. He needed something more basic, and couldn't quite wrap his thoughts around it.

Like the healing of his leg, it took time to sort through the cobwebs tangled in his head. Finally, one night in early June when a warm breeze was blowing, John observed a new moon hanging high on the horizon. Though distant and dim in the nighttime sky, the new moon beckoned with the promise of brighter times to come. The moment stirred his thoughts, the breeze blew away the cobwebs and he felt a future filled with possibilities.

The next afternoon, after a taxing therapy session, John set aside his crutches and began walking with a limp. He never again used the crutches. Still limping in July, he nevertheless worked alongside his family every day, helping to gather the tobacco and even pulling weeds from a field of peanuts without fear of rattlesnakes. At night, he relaxed by sketching and painting, each day's work an inspiration for a series of paintings that captured this season of life. By the time he started high school in September, the limp had disappeared and John was eager to see how his leg would hold up during tryouts for the basketball team.

THE FIRE

1967

CHAPTER 1

SOMETIMES LATE AT NIGHT as he either waited for Caroline to join him in bed or listened to the quiet rhythm of her sleep, Matt Baker wondered why he bothered with farming. Almost always, these doubts followed stressful, backbreaking days on the farm.

"There's got to be an easier way for a man to earn a liven," Matt would tell his wife.

"There is," Caroline would answer affectionately, "but not for men who have dirt in their veins."

On these rare nights, Matt wanted to make love to his wife, but he was usually exhausted, bone-tired to the point that no amount of red-bloodedness could will his body to carry out the wishes of his heart. Maybe the problem was old age. In his younger days, Matt reckoned he could have worked forty-eight hours straight and made love for the next twenty-four without missing a beat. At forty, however, he and Caroline would hold each other for a while and drift into a dreamless sleep that left them rested and replenished for another long day of toiling beneath a hellish sun.

On the morning after such a night, Matt sat on the front porch. The younger children had just boarded the school bus, and Joe was waving goodbye as he began a new day of college, another step in the journey that would lead him away from the farm.

As the school bus and Joe's Volkswagen disappeared down the road, Matt wondered once again why he bothered with farming. He knew the answer, of course. Farming was more than an occupation to Matt, something other than a simple job. It was a way of life, an opportunity for independence and self-reliance. Maybe dirt did course through his veins as Caroline claimed. Or maybe, as Joe once suggested, he was a slave to the earth. But pure and simple, a farmer's life was the only one Matt ever wanted.

So even though he knew the answer, Matt still liked on occasion to reflect on the reasons why he bothered with farming. If nothing else, the exercise allowed Matt to consider what farming meant to him and, of more importance, to his family.

In the role of family provider, Matt began his rumination on the dollars and sense of farming, both of which were sorely lacking. The financial rewards for his sweat and toil had been scarce over the years, with Matt earning barely enough money to keep his family from being classified as poor by the government. Without gardens and livestock to feed the family, the Bakers very well might have been impoverished. As it was, they lived frugally, enjoying a few luxuries during the harvest season and praying they would have enough savings to meet their obligations in those months when there was no money coming into the farm.

Though Matt hated to admit and never resented it, the truth was that he had too many mouths to feed and care for on the income generated by one farm. When the children had been younger, Matt and Sam had labored like mules to get the job done, managing most, but not all, of the work by themselves. Year after year, they paid hired hands to help with the tobacco, and each harvest season they waited breathlessly to see if their work would earn enough money to make ends meet. Once in a great while, harvesttime arrived with money still in the bank from the previous year, seasons of satisfaction, which usually preceded the breakdown of a key piece of equipment or a cruel joke of nature. In either case, their savings, always meager at best, dwindled to near nothing. For the most part, though, Matt had managed.

Then, in 1964, fate had allowed Matt to double his operation, and the children had been able to replace the hired hands. In one year, the farm's income doubled. Another good year had followed, with the bills paid and a small nest egg laid in the bank. Prosperity beckoned as never before, and Matt acknowledged it with a spending binge, buying a new pickup truck and combine, replacing the back-pasture fence and remodeling the house. While seemingly extravagant, the investment compensated for years of necessary neglect.

His reward for too much money spent in a single season came as a grim reminder that while a farmer can work tirelessly to raise his crop well, ultimately, he is a slave to things he cannot control. A year ago, the uncontrollable had been a late spring freeze, an unexplainable blight in the corn and low prices at harvest. By the time Matt tallied receipts against expenses, the family nest egg had shrunk.

Matt took nature's follies in stride. Weather was a farmer's best friend and toughest adversary. Back in sixty-three, a spring flood had drowned the young crops, and a summer hailstorm had shredded a full-grown crop of tobacco. Two perfect years of rain had followed, and except for the spring freeze, 1966 had been a good weather year as well.

The economics of farming were an entirely different story. Matt never understood why the cost of raising a crop was almost more than it was worth to harvest. While he could count on paying more for seed, fertilizer and everything else needed to raise a crop, the job came with no guarantees that this year's corn, cotton or anything in his fields would command prices equal to or better than the previous year's receipts.

Last year, for instance, every bushel of corn, every bale of cotton and pound of peanuts had brought prices lower than the previous year's harvest. Apparently, prices fluctuated according to the whims of men with far more power than Matt could even fathom. Certainly, these forces were more worrisome than the weather, maybe even unfair when he compared the prices charged in grocery stores with the prices paid to farmers for their crops. Someone profited from the food business, but it wasn't the people who grew it.

If the economics of farming were not enough to drive a man crazy, then the government could finish the job. Every which way he turned, Matt found the government staring over his shoulder. The government decided what crops could be planted, where and how much. On occasion, the powers that be even decreed the nation was producing too much food and offered incentives to leave fields empty or to plow under crops already in the ground. This notion of food aplenty irked Matt. With people hungry in America and millions starving all over the world, he found it hard to swallow the idea of producing less when more was needed.

As it was, Matt reckoned he could tolerate the whole process, but he sure couldn't make sense of it. Even so, as long as he could make ends meet for his family, the so-called experts could worry about the economics of farming. All he knew was how to raise things, and that was enough. He could tolerate the government's interference, and he could survive the market's whims. Leeway existed on both ends. Besides, Matt farmed for something more valuable than dollars and sense. Farming satisfied his basic desires.

Once, Matt had felt as if he were inheriting a life on the farm rather than choosing it. Then, he had gone away to fight the war and, while soldiering in Northern Africa and Europe, discovered the value of fields and family.

Farm work and his parents had instilled in Matt a sense of pride that showed as strength and caring, not vanity or conceit; a kind of know-how that could solve problems well beyond those found in the fields; a work ethic that allowed him independence; and the will to succeed. The farm gave general direction to life, yet preserved the freedom to choose one or many paths.

In Matt's case, his course had paralleled the direction chartered by his father, but their individual paths were marked by different approaches. While both men shared an equally strong attachment to the land, Matt wanted to conquer it, to extract life from the soil. Sam preferred to preserve the land and keep it wild. This single difference explained Matt's superiority as a farmer, a fact freely acknowledged by Sam. Under different circumstances, Sam might have become a forest ranger or a zoologist. As it was, he had taken up the farming life as the means to pursue his dreams while making an honest living for his family. Matt had chosen to farm for the same reasons, and he wanted his children to have the same values and opportunities whether they remained on the farm or followed paths leading elsewhere.

————————

"You plannen to sit there all day, or are you goen out to earn this family a liven?"

Caroline's question surprised Matt, who wondered how long he had been sitting on the porch. She had come outside to empty a pan of dirty dishwater on the array of petunias lining the walkway.

"I was just thinken there must be an easier way for a man to make a liven than the one I chose," Matt said.

"Strange time of day for you to be thinken like that," Caroline remarked.

"Yeah," Matt agreed with a tempting grin. "You know what else? I'm not tired at all."

Caroline required a moment to read her husband's thoughts, the full impact of Matt's suggestive tone coming only when she observed the glint in his eyes. While the idea of making love to Matt on this morning appealed to Caroline, she concealed her desire. Summoning her most prudish posture and false airs of disinterest, she turned away from him and emptied the soapy water on the red and purple petunias. After inspecting the flowers, she marched chastely past her husband's seductive grin, setting the pan on the hall floor and allowing the door to slam close as she returned to Matt. Falling onto his lap, she nuzzled his neck and playfully bit his ear.

"This ain't helpen matters," Matt remarked as they kissed.

"It's not supposed to," Caroline said, laughing as she broke away from the embrace. "But first things first, mister: Go out there and earn us a liven."

"Work, work, work—that's all you ever think of, woman," Matt joked as she came to her feet.

"Where's Pa?" he asked a moment later.

"Ma's rubben him down with the liniment," Caroline answered. "He's all worn out and sore from yesterday. He had no business worken that hard."

"I tried to get him to take it easy, but you know how he is," Matt responded. "When he gets a notion to do somethen, it's hard to get it out of his head. I'll have to be firm with him next time."

"I heard that!"

Sam's booming voice resonated through the screen door as he stormed down the hall. Partly on the advice of Dr. Pittman and primarily to escape the nagging of Rachel, Matt and Caroline, Sam had eased his workload considerably. He was close to seventy-one this spring and enjoyed his emeritus status, offering advice, running errands and working hard until he took a notion to go fishing, pick blackberries or traipse around the farm. On occasion, however, he showed everyone he still could do an honest day's work, and, while loath to admit it, he had lifted and stacked too many hundred-pound bags of guano the previous day.

"I'll have you know that I haven't yet reached the point where my son is goen to be *firm* with me," he declared crossly. "I can fend for myself, and I know my limits. Now what needs doen today?"

If Matt knew anything, it was when to use caution with his father. In his present frame of mind, Sam was likely to strap a plow to his back and start marching through the fields.

"To tell you the truth, Pa, we're pretty much caught up," Matt said. "Tom's finishen up the first cultivation of the corn. There's some sprayen to be done, but I don't have the chemicals for it. Maybe you can go into Cookville this afternoon and get them. This mornen, though, I'd appreciate it if you'd take a look around the place with me. It's getten dry around here, and I'm wonderen if we might ort to get us an irrigation system."

"Dry as I've seen in many a year," Sam mused, appeased by Matt's respectful appeal. "We've been short on rain since last summer. I keep thinken we're gonna have a belly-washer to get caught up. Last time we had such a dry winter and spring was in fifty-four, and you know what kind of year that was 'round these parts."

"Don't remind me," Matt worried.

"Let me get my hat, and we'll take a look-see," Sam replied.

"Everything will work out," Caroline suggested to her husband while Sam opened the front door.

Matt nodded his agreement, kissing her on the cheek. "We'll be back around dinnertime," he called as she followed Sam into the house.

Alone again on the porch, Matt returned to the rocking chair. The dry spell was just one of the strange state of affairs. Winds of change had blown furiously across the farm, sweeping away the cast of characters who had formed the backbone of Matt's operation for many years. As a result, he now relied on a trio of more youthful, enthusiastic and inexperienced workers. Matt felt as if he understood some of what Job must have experienced when the tribulations ceased and God blessed him with a new family and greater riches. Above everything, he appreciated his newfound fortunes, yet a small part of him longed for the familiarity of the past.

Gone from his fields that spring were Joe, Lucas Bartholomew and to a great extent, Sam, who had made concessions to his age. Matt had worked closely with the three men over the years, and he knew what to expect from them. Their experience had eased the pressure of tending hundreds of acres of crops, including a burdensome twenty acres of tobacco.

Lucas had worked for Matt on and off through the years. Over the winter, however, he had cleared a section of land on the Berrien estate, agreeing to farm the acreage on shares for Paul and his sisters. Matt welcomed the opportunity for Lucas, understanding the man's yearning to work for himself. While sharecroppers often fared poorly, Lucas stood a better chance than most to succeed. The Berriens had funded the entire operation upfront and were asking only to recoup their investment when the harvest was sold. Any profit above expenses would belong entirely to Lucas. Working for Matt had given Lucas security. While that security was at risk working on his own, Lucas was poised to reap greater rewards.

Meanwhile, Joe had begun his junior year at Valdosta State College in March, following his discharge from a two-year stint as a combat correspondent for the U.S. Marines and *Stars and Stripes* newspaper. His enlistment—an alternative to being drafted—had come as a complete surprise to everyone, especially when he managed to pass the physical despite the broken leg suffered in high school. Yet, Joe had made the most of the opportunity, parlaying his high scores on the military entrance exam into the coveted correspondent's position and spending the majority of his service at bases in California and North Carolina gaining experience in his chosen profession. His discharge from active duty had come in February and he had returned home eager to resume his college education. While Matt would have preferred having Joe work side-by-side with him on the farm that spring, he never gave the idea any serious consideration. It was time for his oldest son to pursue the life he wanted in earnest, and there was no reason to keep him tied down in the fields. Matt missed his son's companionship, but he took comfort in knowing Joe would have his college degree by the end of next summer.

In Lucas and Joe's absence, Matt had not looked far to find the full-time help needed on the farm. Tom Carter had been a fixture around the place for years, cavorting with Joe, working in tobacco or listening to the tall tales that Sam spun like silk. Although he was the son of storekeepers, Tom had no intentions of succeeding Dan and Amelia in the mercantile.

Tom had graduated from high school two years earlier. Adhering to his parents' wishes, he enrolled at Abraham Baldwin Agricultural College—ABAC—aiming to obtain a degree in business. His college education lasted almost two years before he succumbed to his own desires. Just prior to the beginning of the spring quarter, Tom had informed his parents that he was dropping out of college to pursue the life of a farmer.

The news came as no surprise to Amelia and Dan. "Your daddy and I won't argue with you or try to persuade you otherwise," Amelia said when Tom broke the news. "However, we will make one request. Since you have no interest in runnen this general mercantile, we'd be much obliged if you found yourself a wife who would be."

"I promised them I'd keep that in mind when and if I ever get around to looken for a wife," Tom told Matt after they worked out the terms of his employment.

Knowing full-time help was needed on the farm, Tom had approached Matt in early winter. "I want to farm but the way I see it, there's a lot I need to learn before I could even think about striken out on my own," he explained. "I can't think of a better place to learn the things I need to know than right here. I'd appreciate the opportunity to work with you, and I believe you know I'd work hard."

Matt never doubted Tom's word, and the young man had proved himself with hard work. He had harrowed land for ten hours a day, six days a week, then plowed that land, harrowed it again and planted it. He had repaired machinery, castrated shoats as well as steers and made one or two mistakes along the way, such as running the planter for a solid hour straight without realizing cotton seed had clogged one of the seed dispensers, leaving every other row seedless.

With Joe or Lucas, Matt took for granted they would know to do certain things that he now had to explain to Tom. But Tom was a quick learner, sufficing on one explanation and never making the same mistake twice. His enthusiasm was also appreciated as well as his dry sense of humor.

"Yeah, but did you notice how straight the rows are," he had drawled without missing a beat when Matt and Sam discovered the planter was jammed. The three of them had laughed off the mistake, and Tom had worked a long day to replant the seedless rows.

In this season of change, Matt also was learning to rely more on his two youngest sons. He had overlooked their abilities in the past by depending too much on Joe's experience and willingness. As the spring unfolded, however, he realized just how capable John and Luke were around the farm and he saw more clearly than ever the subtle similarities and differences among his three sons.

John, now fifteen, and Luke, almost thirteen, shared a strong affinity for farm work, whereas Joe tolerated it. While his youngest sons might very well tread their lives in furrows plowed by Matt, his firstborn was destined for different fields. At the same time, Joe and Luke possessed a natural talent for farming, while John approached each task with caution and planning. Faced with the same problem, Joe and Luke would solve it quickly with instinct. John would find the solution, too, but he needed extra time to study the situation.

Of all the differences and similarities among his sons, one stood out as the most obvious and unsettling to Matt. Whether working or playing, Joe and John approached life with a full degree of purpose. His two oldest sons had staying power, and they were diligent to a fault. At times, they could turn something as simple as fishing or hunting into a full-blown production. One time, when they had exasperated Sam with their preparations for fishing, their grandfather had forced them to spend a day at the pond with a fishing pole and an empty hook. On another occasion, he had made them spend the morning in a deer stand without the benefit of their guns. While unorthodox in his methods, Sam had instilled a new respect for leisurely pursuits in the boys. Over the years, his influence had tempered Joe and John's approach to the less serious side of life.

Luke, meanwhile, had yet to discover the serious side of life. He was diligent when the moment suited him, which usually was in the fields, guiding a tractor down a row, loading seed into a planter or feeding animals. Luke thrived on such work, but even then, the boy had a wild side. He bogged tractors for fun, drove recklessly and complained readily when he believed a more interesting chore required his attention than the one at hand.

Matt knew he should be stricter with the boy, but he could not always bring himself to make the extra effort. The trouble was that Luke reminded Matt of himself too much. As a child, Matt had caused his parents many headaches. Remembering his own youthful frivolity, Matt sympathized with Luke, understanding firsthand the problems faced by a free-spirited boy who raced toward adventure, often without ever looking where he was headed Frequently, Luke was blindsided in his haste.

Sympathy aside, Matt would have used the belt more if he had any inkling that Luke might not grow out of his wild ways. As it was, however, his mind was made up to tolerate a few minor inconveniences caused by bogged tractors and the like. He had noticed Luke's pranks tended to occur when there was time to spare.

Luke's one bad habit, which Matt refused to tolerate, was the boy's indifference toward school. Luke ignored homework, flunked tests frequently and was perilously close to failing the seventh grade. None of the other children—not even Matt himself—had been disdainful about schoolwork. Matt and Caroline had lectured the boy, punished him and watched over him to make sure Luke did homework. His brothers and sisters also pitched in, helping Luke study for tests and encouraging him to do better. The simple truth, however, was that Luke refused to apply himself, and his parents had reached their wit's end over the problem.

"You intent on spenden the day in that rocken chair, or are we gonna go see how dry it is around here?"

For the second time in the last few minutes, someone reminded Matt that he had more pressing business than passing time on the front porch. This time, it was Sam, who had gone inside the house to find his cap and wound up eating the last piece of breakfast toast smothered in blackberry jelly.

"I was just thinken, Pa," Matt said.

"It certainly behooves a man to do that once in a while," Sam suggested. "What's special on your mind this mornen?"

"Getten Luke through school this year," Matt answered. "Caroline got another call from his teacher last night. She says that unless Luke buckles down and shows a big improvement these last few weeks of school, he's gonna have to stay back a year."

Matt shook his head, slightly discouraged. "We've tried everything to make him do better, but he's not a bit interested."

"Luke's just sufferen from a bad case of spring fever," Sam replied. "Trouble is, he came down with it last spring and it's still runnen high. Face it, Matt. The boy can't tolerate be'en cooped up all day. I wouldn't worry too much about him, though. Luke's full of common sense. He'll come around soon enough and show his smarts."

"He's got to apply himself before he can show his smarts, Pa," Matt said. "If he doesn't come around soon, he's gonna spend another year in the seventh grade."

"There's a point well taken," Sam agreed. "If we can find a way to make Luke understand the seriousness of the situation, then he might just straighten up in time to get promoted. I'll put on my thinken cap and see what I can come up with. Now, though, let's decide if it's time to get into the irrigation business."

"Let's do it," Matt said.

––––––––––

Sam valued three things most in life—his family, his religion and his farm. The order of importance depended entirely on the circumstances of the moment. Religion came first when he was singing a hymn, listening to a good sermon or praying. Family mattered most when he had a rare moment alone with Rachel, Matt, Caroline or any of his grandchildren. And the land meant the world to him during those times when he was privileged to walk through the fields and woods, marveling at the beauty—fine earth that yielded a livelihood for his family, majestic forests that concealed treasures some people would never understand and hidden coves that contained mysteries still unexplored.

His most precious moments occurred when Sam experienced congruency among everything that mattered most to him. On these occasions, he saw how the family needed, used and appreciated the land, while the land sustained, unified and strengthened the family. He envisioned this trust between family and land spanning generations, decades, centuries, even millenniums. And he realized his vision fulfilled a young man's dream. At such times, Sam would thank God for giving him a small part of the world and the family with whom he shared it.

The road taken to find his dream was pocked with obstacles, sacrifices and hardships. A pioneer spirit, the companionship of a good woman and a little luck had pulled him from the deepest valleys and pushed him over the highest hills along the way.

In 1920, using his life's savings for a down payment, Sam had mortgaged his family's future for a section of prime land carved from the vast estate owned by Britt Berrien. Sam stumbled across the place by accident. Yet the very moment he turned onto the dirt road leading to his farm, Sam realized he had found tranquility, about eight miles north of Cookville in a community named New River after the tributary that meandered through it. His instincts were confirmed less than two miles down the dirt road when he came across an abandoned house obscured by weeds and run down from years of neglect. Sam had spent the entire day hiking the land, marveling at its diversity.

At the end of the day, he had approached Britt Berrien with an offer. The banker laughed, claimed he had no intentions of selling any part of his vast holdings and sent Sam on his way. Undaunted by the banker's brusque manner, Sam returned the next week with a higher offer. Once again, Britt turned him down, but Sam's persistence and genuine love for the land won the man's grudging respect. Two months after their initial meeting, Britt proposed a deal for one hundred acres—the price deliberately steep to discourage Sam.

"It's not negotiable," Britt had declared, believing Sam would reject the offer. "Take it or leave it."

"That's a ridiculous amount of money you're asken," Sam shot back, "but the land's worth every penny and more. If you trust me enough that you're willen to let your bank extend me a loan, then I'll take it."

Britt shook his head in dismay. The two men sealed the agreement with a handshake and the struggle to succeed had begun for Sam.

Sam's purchase of those first one hundred acres in 1920 coincided with a national collapse in farm prices and the ravages of the boll weevil on Georgia's cotton fields. In the early years, he had doubted his ability to keep up with the payments. On the bad days, he would curse Britt for making such an unfair offer and then berate himself for accepting the deal. But always, the appeal of his dream and Rachel's constant support would spur him forward.

In 1925, his family went an entire winter without sugar, tea, coffee and other store-bought goods because every penny was needed to make the monthly payments to the bank and still have enough money to buy the seed and fertilizer to make a crop when spring came. By the next year, Sam believed the battle had crested, and his confidence soared. He refinanced the balloon payment on his original five-year loan and bought another one hundred acres from Britt Berrien. Then the Depression hit, along with the worst drought on record in Georgia.

At first, the hard times brought on by the collapse of the nation's economy mattered little in the tiny Cookville community, which was used to being poor. Slowly, however, the poor community became Depressed. In 1933, money disappeared and commerce came to a halt. With food on their table every night, Sam and Rachel fared better than many of their neighbors. But few of the neighbors owed such a huge chunk of money to the Farmers and Citizens Bank.

A day finally arrived when Sam could not meet his obligations to Britt Berrien. Refusing to make excuses, he explained his plight to the banker. "If you want me off the property, I understand," Sam said. "All I ask is for a few days to pack my things and find a place for my family to stay."

"Let me think about it," Britt had replied.

Throughout those early years, Sam and Britt had lived as strangers, exchanging nods of acknowledgment here and there and even fewer words. Sam knew the banker had a ruthless streak. Only a few years earlier, Britt had foreclosed on a nearby piece of property owned by Henry Anderson, a hardworking man who often performed handyman jobs on the Berrien estate. Understanding Britt had been reluctant to part with the land in the first place, Sam fully expected the man to reclaim the property through foreclosure. However, Sam had underestimated the effect his hard work had on the banker. Two days later, Britt had proposed a one-year moratorium on the loan payments with an understanding that interest would accrue on the unpaid balance.

"Farm prices should improve next year, and I continue to have every confidence in your ability to repay the loan," the banker had written in a short note explaining the terms of his proposal. "As far as I'm concerned, our handshake is still good."

When all was said and done, it had taken Sam well over twenty years to pay for the first two hundred acres and Britt had profited enormously from the deal, with interest payments alone dwarfing many times over the land's original value. Yet, Sam never failed to acknowledge the financial lifeline from the banker. It was the closest gesture of friendship to pass between the two men, and Sam appreciated the opportunity. Soon afterward, the Bakers and Berriens began living in a more neighborly way. April and June began swapping recipes and gossip with Rachel, while Joseph and Matt became good friends with Paul. Britt occasionally would join Sam for hunting or fishing, but they remained mere acquaintances to his dying day.

Two decades later, when Sam sought to buy an additional two hundred forty-eight acres in 1940, Britt had readily agreed to the deal, without any persuasion required. Again, however, he had parted with his land only for an excessive price, a ready reminder that Sam and he were just acquaintances after all. As Sam once dared to observe to his wealthy companion, Britt preferred an acquaintance to a friend.

On county plats, the Baker place appeared as a perfect rectangle, with the long lines serving as east-west markers and the short sides showing north and south. Carved from the thousands of acres in the Berrien estate, the farm backed up against timber owned by Paul, April and June on its southern and eastern flanks. The north side bordered property owned by Ruby Davis, a cantankerous widow who possessed almost as much money and land as the Berriens, while the railroad tracks ran along the farm's western edge, separating the Baker place from the Castleberry place.

The farm contained a blend of pastures, ponds and seven cultivated fields, all stretched between woods of pine, oak, sycamore, cypress and fat lighter stumps left over from trees harvested by Britt Berrien many years earlier. Except for the small patch across the dirt road in front of the house, which was the lone piece of cultivated land on the farm's eastern flank, the fields were all vast expanses of fertile land dotted only with lines of fence and trees. The largest of the fields required nearly four days to harrow or plow, while the smallest took two days to do the same work.

The Old Pond—so dubbed because it had been in place when Sam bought the land—was on the southwest side of the farm, its banks shaded by towering pines and majestic oaks. Primed by underground springs, the pond eventually turned into a huge bog of pitch-black water, mud and decay from some ancient swamp. Home to black bears, bobcats and rare plants among other things, the bog contained a few acres of inaccessible swampland. Having such a mysterious place plunked down in the middle of their farm had provided fodder for more than one restless night for every member of the Baker family.

Another oddity on the farm was a small water hole placed squarely in the middle of the farm's largest field. Too many large, cranky water moccasins inhabited the water hole. Twice, their poisonous bites had killed cattle. Every so often, the boys would grab their guns and spend a few minutes sighting the moccasins for target practice. By and large, however, everyone avoided the water hole or kept a close watch for snakes when they ventured near it. The beneficiaries of their reluctance to fish in the water hole were some monstrous catfish, most of which went through life never once tempted by a worm dangling on the end of a hook.

The New Pond, which had been dug in 1954 from a grove of aged cypress trees, lay on the extreme northern side of the place, concealed within a stand of virgin pine trees and merging eventually with a swamp on neighboring land known as Bear Bay. Filled with ragged stumps and dead tree trunks, the pond simmered like an English moor on foggy mornings.

On this early May morning in 1967, however, the entire farm baked beneath a merciless sun. Wherever Matt and Sam looked, they saw crops begging for water. Tobacco had already wilted, with the hottest part of the day still to come. The slightest gust of wind sent swirls of gray dust across fields of corn, cotton, peanuts, soybeans, cantaloupes and sweet potatoes. Ponds that should have been full were far below their normal levels, lower than either man could remember in many years.

Each year, Matt depended on a tricky mix of rain, warmth and sunshine to bring life to the crops and put money in his pockets for the next year. Perfect weather was not required for a good crop, but some balance of rain and sunshine was needed. So far this year, dark storm clouds had been a rare commodity, yielding dry heaves for the most part. The short supply of rain had seemed like a blessing last fall as Matt raced to bring the harvest home, but the absence of winter rains had left the fields plenty dry when planting time arrived in early spring.

Matt counted on several days or weeks each winter and spring when the fields would be too boggy to work, meaning long days ahead later as he scrambled to prepare his land for another crop. This year, however, the weather had been dry enough that Matt had his fields harrowed and turned by the end of February. Early spring rains, while lighter than usual, had allowed the newly planted crops to take hold, but water had been sparse ever since, limited to a few afternoon showers that evaporated almost as quickly as they fell on the thirsty ground.

With his foot propped on the front fender of the pickup truck, Matt now scanned the patch of droopy tobacco, then cast his eyes skyward in a futile search for signs of an approaching rain. "Pa, these crops need water or they're gonna die," he surmised. "If we expect to make any crop at all, we'll have to irrigate, and we'll have to do it soon."

"No doubt, you're right," Sam agreed. "It's even drier than I suspected."

"Then you agree we need to invest in an irrigation system?" Matt asked.

"Did you notice how low the ponds were?" Sam replied. "Even the water hole is lower than I've ever seen it at this time of year. We probably can get two, possibly three good waterens out of them as it is now. But, son, what happens if we don't get some good rains to replenish what we take out? Then we'll have an expensive irrigation system on our hands, no water to run it, and no decent crop to help us pay for it."

"It's a gamble we have to take," Matt insisted. "Look at that tobacco. If these crops don't get water soon, they won't be worth what it cost us to plant them."

Sensing his father's continued reluctance to the idea, Matt abandoned any serious attempt to get his father's blessing. "Don't fret too much about the cost," he said. "We've got some money saved, and you know how it's always bothered us to have money in the bank."

He winked at Sam, then added with a chuckle: "Besides, Pa, I think our current situation qualifies as a rainy day. Don't you?"

"I hope we're still laughen come fall," Sam remarked.

————

"Lu-u-uke!"

The cry exploded with the pent-up fury of a launching rocket, and everyone knew Luke was in trouble again. In this last month before he became a teenager, trouble lurked around every corner for Luke. Sometimes, it blindsided him; occasionally it caught up with him. But more often than not, Luke ran smack-dab into the middle of more trouble than he could handle, frequently ignoring the warning signs pointing to an easier way.

Hearing Caroline holler for her youngest son, Sam peered down from the barn loft where he was storing the chemicals he had bought a short time ago in Cookville. His daughter-in-law was standing by the back porch, tapping her foot as she waited impatiently for Luke to answer her summons. Having long ago learned to gauge Caroline's anger by the pace of her foot-tapping, Sam judged she had reached the boiling point.

"Luke!" she shouted again. "Get out here this instant. You and I are gonna get a few things straight around here, mister."

"Poor, Luke," Sam muttered to himself as he deduced the cause of Caroline's rage. She had stopped tapping her foot and was scraping the bottom of the shoe against the porch edge, which meant one thing.

Unable to master the art of inhaling cigarettes, Luke had taken to chewing tobacco. While no one cared about his tobacco habit, everyone had tired quickly of his nasty tendency to spit used plugs anywhere the notion struck him. This was not the first time someone had stepped onto a messy clump of salivated tobacco, but it was the first such misfortunate step for Caroline.

The screen door opened, and Luke stood mystified before his mother. "Yes, ma'am?" he drawled.

Caroline pointed to her shoe, then delivered a stern lecture, managing to touch on responsibility, carelessness, cleanliness and manners in a sixty-second tirade that ended with her declaration that she would not tolerate nastiness in her backyard. When she had delivered a sufficient scolding, without any interruptions from Luke, Caroline ordered the boy to get rid of the tobacco and then wash down the back porch. Without any protest or acknowledgment, Luke obeyed her.

Luke's spiritless attitude toward Caroline annoyed his grandfather. Sam would have preferred the boy show remorse or even defiance rather than bland acceptance. While he normally would not condone disrespect to one's elders, Sam could tolerate almost anything but indifference. He abhorred people who showed neither spunk nor regret when they made a mistake, and Luke's recently acquired insipidity was particularly distasteful. The boy would fight at school, ignore homework or flunk a test, then accept his punishment without any explanation or protest. Luke needed an attitude adjustment, and Sam decided to provide it.

"Luke," he called from the loft. "I need you to help me with a little project before it gets dark."

"Can't right now, Grandpa. Mama's got me cleanen up the porch."

"Never mind with that," Sam said. "Just put that tobacco out of harm's way, and no one will be the wiser. Water's too scarce around here to waste on a porch that's clean enough. Grab a couple of hoes and the field rake, then meet me at the blackberry bramble."

"Yes, sir," Luke sighed.

The bramble consisted of about fifty blackberry bushes clustered along the fence between the far edge of the pecan orchard and a small meadow of sweet grass and broom sage. Each summer, the bushes yielded enough berries for jelly, cobblers and homemade ice cream. Sam had planted the blackberries over many years, and he kept the fencerow spotless to make sure no snakes took up residence in the bramble. He also picked most of the berries himself, contending everyone else tended to eat almost as many as they put in their baskets. When the berries ripened in early summer, Sam made a point of reminding everyone that hundreds of bushes grew wild all over the farm, the point being, of course, to stay away from the bramble.

"It's time you and I had a little talk," Sam said as Luke and he worked on either side of the fence, pulling weeds and raking away dead leaves.

"What about, Grandpa?"

"Do not play dumb with me, Luke," Sam replied testily. "You know exactly why we need to talk. It's partially about your poor work in school. But mainly, it's about your attitude, son, or I should say your lack of attitude."

Luke focused intently on his work, but Sam knew the boy was listening. One of the pleasures of being a grandparent was the knowledge that his grandchildren listened carefully to his words of wisdom. Sam would tell Luke virtually the same thing the boy had heard from his parents on countless occasions. However, because the words came from someone who rarely reprimanded or lectured, they tended to make a stronger impression coming from Sam.

"Luke, I know you're not as dumb as the grades on your report card indicate," Sam began. "But the truth of the matter is that your smarts are measured by those grades, and what's written down on your report card determines whether you pass or fail in school."

"It don't matter to me whether I pass or fail," Luke retorted. "As soon as I get sixteen, I'm quitten school."

"Maybe so; everybody's got a right to be ignorant, you included," Sam said. "But I'd think twice before tellen your mama and daddy that. In the meantime, you're only twelve right now, so you have to go to school."

Luke gave an indifferent shrug.

"You and I are alike in a lot of ways, Luke," Sam continued. "We both like worken outdoors, usen our hands. When I was a young man, I had a job in town. It was a good job, but I always felt cooped up and caged like a wild animal. It drove me crazy at times."

"That's the way I feel," Luke muttered with an understanding nod. "I can't stand it. I'd rather be home duren the day, worken around here."

"Then I suppose spenden the summer in school would be especially hard on you?" Sam suggested.

"There's no way I'd ever go to summer school," Luke said defiantly.

"Well, between you and me, I'm afraid you're gonna wind up in summer school if you don't buckle down and pass the seventh grade," Sam said. "Your mama and daddy are none too happy about it because we need you in the tobacco field, but your teacher says you're gonna fail unless she sees a vast improvement in your effort these last few weeks of school. Summer school will make up what you missed and get you promoted to the eighth grade in the fall."

Sam sometimes justified a white lie, but this suggestion of summer school was an outright deception. As far as he knew, no one had mentioned summer school. In fact, he doubted New River Elementary even offered such a thing. If he had guessed correctly, however, the mere possibility of attending summer school would light a fire under Luke and he would finish the seventh grade.

"Summer school," Luke moaned incredulously. "That'd be more than I could bear."

"I would think so," Sam replied, using Luke's sober silence to reflect on his deception.

Knowing he had broken one of the Ten Commandments bothered Sam, even though he had a good reason and had simply allowed Luke to draw his own conclusions. Of course, Rachel would disagree with his reasoning, contending there was no good lie. She would be right, too. Nevertheless, Sam would confess his sin to her anyway, just as she would say a prayer of penitence for him. His wife delivered a powerful prayer, and Sam always felt better to have her working on his side in matters with the Lord.

When they had cleared half the fencerow, Sam broached the main concern on his mind, which was Luke's lackadaisical attitude. "Now that I've got you all worried about school, Luke, let's discuss the real reason I brought you out here," Sam said. "When it comes to school, I don't have room to brag. I never graduated from high school—not that I didn't want to, mind you. Things were just different when I was younger."

Luke looked intently at his grandfather, expecting some wonderful yarn about the past. But Sam had spun enough tales for one day and figured the boy was overdue a word to the wise.

"Your attitude has changed of late, Luke," Sam said abruptly, casting a stern eye on the boy. "And I, for one, don't like it a bit. As a matter of fact, if you were my son, I'd've probably taken a belt to your hide a few times more than your daddy has these last few weeks."

Sam paused, allowing silence to emphasize the uncharacteristic harshness of his reproof. Unaccustomed to such forceful reprimand from his grandfather, Luke appeared sufficiently slack-jawed for Sam to continue his admonishment.

"Watchen you grow up is pretty much like watchen your daddy grow up all over," Sam said. "He was just as rambunctious as you are, a regular rooster. Your daddy did things and got away with stuff you've probably never dreamed of doen. And do you know why, Luke?" The boy shook his head.

"Matt was a firecracker, but you could always count on him haven a reason for doen the things he did—even if it was a really dumb reason," Sam said. "Now reasons, even dumb reasons, don't excuse bad behavior. But, son, you don't seem to have a reason for anything you do of late. I don't know why that is, and frankly, I don't care. All I'm sayen is that a man's got to have reason in his life, a purpose for doen the things he does. I don't care if it's somethen as simple as hunten. When I hunt, Luke, I hunt because I enjoy the sport or because my family needs meat on the table. I don't go kill an animal without any reason whatsoever.

"Do you understand?" Sam asked.

"Sort of," Luke answered.

"Either you do or you don't," Sam replied firmly. "Let me put it to you this way: Next time you decide to spit out a nasty clump of tobacco right beside the back porch, think first. Ask yourself, 'Why there,' when you've got a thousand other places you could spit. Or if you miss a homework assignment, tell people why you didn't do it, even if it means admitten you were just plain lazy. Excuses won't get you far, Luke, but I'd rather hear a bad explanation from you than see that tired shrug of your shoulders and hear you say, 'I don't know.'

"The good Lord gave you a brain, son, but it's up to you to use it," Sam continued, his sharp tone softening considerably. "You may never be a scholar, and that's fine. Sometimes, I think there are too many scholars in the world as is. But there's also too many dumb and ignorant people in the world. You've always been a smart boy. Now's the time to decide if you're gonna become a smart man.

"Do you understand?" Sam asked again.

"I understand, Grandpa," Luke said.

Sam eyed the boy fiercely, wielding his pirate's face to maximum advantage, a tactic he used rarely, only when the moment was of grave importance.

Almost involuntarily, Luke nodded, again indicating he understood his grandfather, and Sam sensed half the battle had been won. With the daylight fading, they finished their weeding in silence.

CHAPTER 2

TOM FLUFFED A PILLOW cushion, yawned loudly and stretched his lanky frame across the black leather sofa in the front parlor of his home. It was a warm Saturday in the middle of May, the first time in nearly two months he had not worked a six-day week, and Tom had volunteered to mind the mercantile so that his parents could go to town. On the television, Mickey Mantle belted a home run and started his obligatory run around the bases. As the announcer started to say how many homers Mantle needed to reach the five-hundred career mark, the bell jingled on the store door, drowning out the information Tom wanted. Rolling his eyes in disgust, he pulled himself off the couch and went to wait on the customer.

It was Summer Baker, and she wanted cloth.

"Cloth?" Tom said, his mind still preoccupied with how many homers Mantle needed to reach five hundred.

Summer nodded and repeated her request. "Cloth," she said. "I'm enteren the Miss Golden Leaf beauty pageant, and I'm gonna make my own evenen gown."

"That's nice," Tom remarked absently, almost surprised to realize he knew nothing about selling material. In fact, Tom felt unusually out of place around the mercantile these days. Months had passed since he had helped his parents do any kind of work in the store, except for manning the cash register for a few transactions here and there.

As Summer babbled about the beauty pageant, Tom regarded the store, beginning with the "Carter's General Mercantile" embellished on the plate glass window beside the door. General mercantile aptly described the establishment. Dating back to the early 1920s when Tom's grandfather had set up shop in this crossroads community, the building had been razed and expanded over the years to accommodate increased traffic. The store contained a soda fountain, an over-the-counter pharmacy and the remnants of a post office. The U.S. Postal

Service had discontinued the New River community postmark during the Korean War.

Children especially delighted in the store's treasures, beginning with the glass case beside the front door that prominently displayed a large selection of candy. Frequently and never with complaint, Amelia took a minute out of the day to wipe away tiny blotches left by children who had pressed their faces against the glass to obtain a better look at the candy bars, suckers and other goodies inside the case.

From the candy counter, children typically moved on to investigate the soda fountain with its ice cream box and the two drink machines. To attract adults, the store offered a cracker barrel prominently displayed in the middle of the floor—as well as a sandwich counter in the rear of the building where a refrigerated case stocked with fresh meats, vegetables and dairy products hummed. The mercantile also carried a solid line of groceries, clothing, hardware and convenience items that saved many country families a trip to Cookville or Tifton. Dan and Amelia ran a tidy, profitable store, designed to satisfy their customers.

The store's one exception to convenience and practicality was a collection of crystal, porcelain figurines and dolls, handmade quilts and other treasures that occupied a special glass counter near the soda fountain. Amelia had acquired the collection through two decades of shrewd bargaining and bartering. She set great store by the collection, regarding each piece as a prized possession, almost dreading to part with any of her precious valuables. Still, the prizes came and went, her business instincts frequently turning a hefty profit on every piece of merchandise that graced the treasure counter.

In the store's far back corner near the storage room, Tom finally spotted the cloth, realizing at the same moment that Summer had asked him a question. "Huh?" he asked.

"Do you think I can win?" Summer repeated impatiently.

"I don't know," Tom replied. "I haven't thought about it."

Whenever possible, Tom paid little attention to Summer. As children, she had bedeviled him with her quick tongue and sassy style. Over the years, he had learned to deal with Summer simply by ignoring her teasing and feigning indifference to her good-natured sarcasm. His strategy had worked for the most part. While Summer spared no one from her clever, rapier-like wit, she had developed a standoffish approach to Tom, which suited him just fine. As much as he felt a part of the Baker family, Summer had become the sister for whom he never had time, and Tom suspected she felt similarly about him.

For those reasons then, he found himself surprised for the second time in almost as many minutes. To his utter amazement, Summer Baker turned into a beautiful woman before his very eyes. She had long, thick chocolate brown hair that usually cascaded down her shoulders—but today was pulled back hastily it seemed, piled on top of her head and held in place with a rubber band. Tom resisted an impulse to push back a wayward strand as he observed her face, which managed to be round and lean at the same time, with cheeks that arched and dimpled deeply when she smiled, which Summer did frequently. Light brown eyes radiated from her face, which was clear, silky smooth and carried a healthy tan, not nearly as brownly toned as her bare shoulders, arms and legs. She was a good half-foot shorter than Tom's six-foot frame, but Summer carried herself with the regal grace that distinguishes beauty from mere prettiness.

Tom suddenly sensed without a doubt that Summer would become the next Miss Golden Leaf beauty queen.

"You're staren, Tom," she barked abruptly, obviously annoyed.

As they met face-to-face, his own midnight blue eyes clashing with Summer's sparkling brown, Tom blushed with embarrassment, feeling like a little boy who had been caught with his hand in the cookie jar just before supper. Summer giggled, and Tom felt his face flush red hot under her gaze.

"Uh, I'm sorry," he stammered. "I was just thinken."

"Well, that explains everything," Summer said with mounting sarcasm. "I realize what a strain that must be on you, but I don't have the time to wait for all that brain activity to take place." She smiled with sickening sweetness, then added quickly. "Although I'm sure that like a total eclipse of the sun, your thought would be equally spectacular, especially knowen how one comes about as often as the other." She crossed her arms. "Cloth, Tom!" she said in demanding tones. "I need to see the cloth. Are you gonna help me or not?"

He started to tell her the thought was not worth pursuing, then changed his mind, knowing she would win a battle of words, even more afraid his comment would invite further questioning. "Awe shucks, Summer," he complained. "You know I don't know nothen about cloth. You know where it is. Help yourself."

"Some storekeeper you are," Summer nagged. "If I'm gonna spend my money here, then I expect help in deciden what I want. Come on back here and help me decide."

Wordlessly, Tom followed her and unfolded one bolt of cloth after another. At a whirlwind pace, Summer sought his opinion on each piece, flustering him with a series of questions that she answered herself before Tom even had time to consider the possibilities. After ten dizzying minutes, she calmly announced, "I'll wait for your mother. She has good taste. You can put all this stuff back."

Tom shook his head in dismay, returning the cloth to the shelf while Summer inspected the refrigerated counter. This kind of whimsical behavior was infuriating, reminding him exactly why he kept his distance from Summer Baker. As he silently rebuked himself for allowing her to get the upper hand, the doorbell jingled again and he escaped to the front to wait on a real customer.

The woman and her two children obviously were passing through New River on their way to somewhere else. Tom pumped five dollars' worth of gasoline into their car, then sold a bag of potato chips, a sucker, a candy bar and three small Cokes, pleased that he remembered to collect the deposit on the bottles.

"Your wife was showen me the quilts while you gassed up the car," the woman remarked as Tom handed her change from a ten-dollar bill. "They're lovely. How much are you asken for them?"

"She's not my wife," Tom said stoutly.

"Oh, I'm sorry," she replied, smiling at Tom, then at Summer, who returned the pleasantry.

"Anything else I can help you with?" Tom asked, anxious for everyone to leave.

"The quilts?" the woman reminded him, looking quickly to Summer for assistance. "How much are they?"

Tom was slow to reply, so she continued, her tone growing more uncertain. "I've been looking for a quilt for some time now, and that wedding pattern is really beautiful."

"Oh, yeah," Tom replied at last. "Well, ma'am, my mother does the buyen and sellen from that part of the store. I really don't know the first thing about it. I'm sorry. I'd help you if I could, but I can't."

The woman's face crinkled with disappointment.

"Tom," Summer suggested. "Why don't you get her telephone number and address? That way, Amelia can get in touch with her."

"That's a splendid idea, and I'd appreciate it," the woman said, setting her drink bottle on the counter and opening her purse to retrieve a pen and paper. When she had written down the information, she handed the note to Tom and received his assurance that he would give the note to Amelia as soon as she returned home. Finally, the woman returned two of the drink bottles to the storage rack, collected her deposits and ushered her children out of the store.

"Now I know why you have no intention of taken over the store someday," Summer teased lightly when they were gone. "The place would fall apart in a matter of months, maybe even weeks or days."

"Probably so," Tom agreed with obvious disinterest. "If there's nothen else I can help you with, I'll see you later."

"Are you tryen to get rid of me?' she asked.

"The thought crossed my mind," Tom answered. "I'd like to see the end of the baseball game."

"Okay, okay," Summer conceded. "Before I leave though, you still have to answer one question for me."

"What's that?"

"Since you obviously have doubts about my ability to win the Miss Golden Leaf pageant, are you plannen to come see how I do?" she asked.

"I'll probably go—if your daddy doesn't have any work for me to do," Tom replied.

"It's at night; that shouldn't be a problem," Summer said. "Will you root for me, Tom?"

"Depends," he answered, shrugging his shoulders.

"On what?" she replied, irked by his lack of support.

"On who else is in the pageant," Tom said. "Anyway, that's more than one question. How 'bout letten me watch the game, Summer?"

"I ought to wait for your mother to get home, but I don't have time," Summer remarked. "I have to get ready to go out tonight. Oh well, when Amelia gets home, ask her to give me a call. Bye-bye now."

"Bye," Tom called as Summer opened the door to leave.

"And good riddance," he muttered when she had gone.

Summer enjoyed flirting. But walking home from the mercantile, she tried to reassure herself that nothing of the sort had passed between Tom and her. Her intentions had been purely innocent, nothing more than everyday conversation—until that moment Tom's eyes had pored over her like a hungry man eyeing a steak dinner. She was accustomed to approving glances, even occasional whistles from boys who found her attractive. But Tom had appraised her with the eyes of a man. And whether he meant to or not, his obvious attraction stirred new feelings in Summer.

Boys had always desired Summer. She had dated plenty of young men who wanted more than a goodnight kiss, and she had rejected every advance with ease. Now, two weeks before she graduated from high school, Summer experienced new feelings and felt the tug of old-fashioned desire.

Although subtler in her appraisal, Summer had responded to Tom's lure by looking at him in a way she had never looked at another man. She had started with his hands, which were rough, chapped and stained from his work. But they were good sturdy hands, with long fingers, huge knuckles and chewed nails. Although naturally fair complexioned as evidenced by his bare white feet, long days in the sun had darkened Tom's face and arms to a light tan. His hair was golden blond, a shaggy mass of curls because it needed a cut, and his eyes were midnight blue. A series of generous angles, with classic cheekbones and dimples, set his face, while his frame was too thin but hard and agile.

While she had never before given him more than a second glance, she was vaguely aware that girls considered him handsome. He was no Romeo, but Tom rarely lacked female companionship. Summer understood the physical attraction to Tom. The puzzling part was her sudden desire to know him as a companion. The surprise was that while she considered Tom a friend, almost a member of the family, she had lost touch with him somewhere along the way. He was Tom, a constant presence in her life, yet nothing else.

In English class earlier this year, Mrs. Gaskins had asked Summer to describe herself with a single word. Without hesitation, she had answered, "Forthright." She was bold and direct, and she tended to be drawn to similar people. Tom seemed the exact opposite, but maybe she was mistaken with her opinion.

A long time ago, Summer had categorized Tom as shy, a true country bumpkin who found pleasure in watching the wheels go round and round. Having never bothered to reconsider her views, she now realized her notions of Tom were outdated, certainly not in tune with the more recent images of a young man who bickered playfully with her brothers, joshed her sisters or charmed the family with hilariously exaggerated tales about his parents and their store. Tom still retained a certain amount of shyness, a bit of self-doubt when he ventured toward the unfamiliar and a larger portion of reluctance that often showed up through his smiles. Yet, his shyness came across as a quality, and it no longer overshadowed the confident young man he had become.

Suddenly, Summer was determined to know this man. Naturally, she began scheming.

Summer found Joe fishing at the New Pond. Or at least he presented a good impression of a fisherman. He was leaned against a pine tree, dozing with an open book by his side and a cigarette dangling precariously from his mouth. He had taken off his shirt to soak up the sun's warmth, and the fishing pole rested against his naval, expertly propped on the edge of his blue jeans and the tip of his sneaker.

If Tom Carter had become a mystery to Summer over the years, then Joe had become her closest friend. Their age difference had shrunk over the years, bringing them closer in spirit, and though they moved in different circles to different tunes, Summer could count on her brother for anything. She relished quiet moments like this when the opportunity allowed her to contemplate him in complete solitude. She wanted to etch these moments in her memory, so they could help fill the lonely hours ahead when the day came for Joe to leave the farm.

As much as she dreaded that day, Summer hoped it would come soon for Joe. She understood his craving for something else. Occasionally, she shared the same feelings of restlessness, but the urge was strongest in Joe. He needed new places, new people and new experiences before the desire would be satisfied. Her brother wanted to write the first draft of history, to tell people about the important stuff that shaped their world. Without a doubt, his journey would carry him far from Cookville.

Her own future seemed entirely uncertain. On some days, she imagined herself as a famous dressmaker, watching beautiful women model her designs on the runways of fashion salons in New York and Paris. The possibility dazzled her with excitement, yet Summer doubted her ability to obtain such heights and wondered whether she even wanted to try. A part of her sensed she could find contentment simply designing and making dresses for women in Cookville. Right now, Summer was glad to have time on her side. She would graduate from high school in a few weeks and begin college next fall. Long-term decisions about the future could wait until she had a better understanding of her wants and needs.

Glancing at her watch, she realized time was running short on her most pressing problem. She edged next to Joe and nudged him awake.

"Any luck?" she asked.

"Yeah, but I threw 'em back," Joe answered, rousing himself from the catnap with a loud yawn and a long stretch, the fishing pole falling to the ground between his legs. "I don't want to clean fish tonight."

"I'm glad to hear it because I have a small favor to ask if you don't have any plans for tonight," Summer said quickly, rushing her brother awake with a playful tug of the tiny hairs that lined the bottom of his stomach.

"Ouch!" Joe yelped, pushing away her hand, then casting a suspicious eye on his sister. "Small favor? Summer, you always scare me when you come asken for small favors."

"I just want you to take me to the movies in Cookville tonight," she said, frowning pretended offense at his suspicions. "*Bonnie and Clyde* is playen, and it's supposed to be really good. You can drool over Faye Dunaway, and I'll fawn over Warren Beatty. What could be more perfect?"

"That's it?" Joe asked cautiously.

"Honestly, Joe!" Summer huffed. "Let's take Carrie and John along with us. Heck, why don't you even invite Tom along?"

"Tom Carter!" Joe exclaimed, suddenly intrigued.

"Do you know any other Tom?" Summer replied casually.

"You want me to invite *Tom Carter*?" Joe puzzled aloud. "Why?"

"Don't invite him then!" Summer bristled. "It was just an idea. I was only tryen to be nice."

"Darlen sister of mine, you have never been nice to Tom," Joe replied with droll sincerity. "But that's beside the point. Tom's daten Liz Barker. I imagine he's busy tonight."

"Good grief, Joe," Summer sighed. "Even Granny knows Tom and Liz are old news. That's been over for ages."

Joe grinned, reading her mind, and a sneaky smile broke her face, her motives no longer a secret. "The truth?" he coaxed.

"Tom and I had an interesten conversation at the store a little while ago," she confessed. "I thought it might be fun to see him in a social situation."

"A social situation with Tom," Joe murmured, considering the idea. "Sounds like you have a crush on him, little sister."

"No, not yet," Summer replied. "But he might be worth a crush."

"I'm not sure if I should do this to Tom," Joe mused.

"Just call him up and see if he wants to go to the movie, Joe," Summer demanded. "But don't tell him that I'm goen with you."

"And what if I don't?" Joe asked.

Summer sighed. "Then I suppose I'll have to tell Mama and Daddy that you've been drinken beer, hangen out in shady places and the like."

"Just how did you find out about that, Mata Hari?" Joe inquired, frowning.

"You came home dead drunk a couple of weeks ago," Summer explained. "I just happened to be haven trouble sleepen that night. I heard your car, but you never came inside. Finally, I went out to check on you and found you fast asleep in your car. You smelled awful by the way, and you had red lipstick on your collar and a hickey on your neck. It was just like a scene from some tasteless movie. Of course, be'en the gracious, nonjudgmental person that I am, I helped you stumble to your bedroom."

She hesitated a moment. "You don't remember any of this, Joe?"

"I remember the night well, the mornen after painfully well," Joe groaned, recalling the hangover. "But that one little detail seems to have escaped me."

"It wasn't one of your better moments," Summer remarked.

"I won't argue with you over that," Joe agreed. "You wouldn't really tell Mama and Daddy about that, now would you?"

"Of course not, silly," she smiled. "That was entirely for your benefit—to make sure you give me the proper respect I deserve. Early or late show?"

Joe looked at his watch. "Better make it the nine o'clock show," he answered. "That should give you plenty of time to make yourself beau-ti-ful, daa-lin."

Summer kissed him on the cheek. "I really do love you, big brother of mine," she said. "Now put on your shirt and escort me home. You have a call to make, and I have to get ready."

————

Joe, Summer, John, Carrie and Tom saw *Bonnie and Clyde* at the Majestic Theater in Cookville. If Tom was surprised that Summer joined them, he gave no indication. For her part, Summer was unusually subdued, preferring to listen and watch the rapport between her siblings and Tom. In the theater, she wiggled her way between Joe and Tom, clutching both of them by the arm during the final shoot-out that left Warren Beatty and Faye Dunaway dead on the big screen.

Following the show, they went to the Dairy Queen for sodas, and Tom sat between Summer and Carrie in the crowded booth. Deciding against his better judgment to do his sister a favor, Joe gave John and Carrie money for the sodas and made an unnecessary trip to the bathroom. While he figured her infatuation with his best friend might be nothing more than a passing fancy, Joe also had decided that Summer could do far worse than pick Tom as a boyfriend.

"I thought you had a date tonight," Tom said when they were alone in the booth.

"What made you think that?" Summer asked coyly.

"You mentioned getten ready to go out, and I assumed you had a date," Tom replied. "Usually, that would be a safe assumption."

"Usually, but not tonight," Summer said. "Were you jealous, Tom?"

"What makes you think I'd be jealous?" he asked.

Summer tilted her head and smiled. "Just a hunch," she said truthfully. "Were you?"

"Nah, I wasn't jealous," Tom said at last, glancing down at the table, then flashing her a shy smile. "But I'm glad you came with us to the movie."

Moments later, Carrie and John returned to the table with a tray of chocolate sodas, and the talk turned to *Bonnie and Clyde*.

On the following Thursday, Summer volunteered to help her father, Joe and Tom set up the new irrigation system. The task seemed simple enough. Matt and Joe put the pumping engine in the New Pond, while Summer and Tom laid metal pipes through the woods, along the edge of the field and through the dry tobacco patch. But as Summer attached the last two pipes, she regretted volunteering for the job. The long metal pipes had been heavier than she anticipated, and her back already ached from several long afternoons of hoeing and thinning acres of cantaloupes.

She checked the last pipe once more, then signaled Tom to tell her father he could begin pumping water anytime and started walking from the field.

Her path followed the trail of pipe snaking through the tobacco field, and she came across two pieces that were not attached properly. Straddling the pipe, she bent over and fidgeted with the metal hinges, trying to make the connecting latches catch on the tubes.

At that precise moment, Matt cranked the irrigation pump. The engine roared to life, creating a powerful suction that snapped the loose hinges into place, snaring Summer's fingers between the metal edges.

Pain seared her breath momentarily, and then it was if someone ripped a scream from the bottom of her chest. She snatched her hands from the pipe. The flesh around her fingers ripped and, for a terrified second, she feared her fingertips had been sliced off. Closer inspection, however, showed her fingers were intact, but the pain, blood and ragged flesh frightened her. She stumbled backward, tripped over a tobacco stalk and landed on her rear in the soft dirt of the sled row.

————————

Tom's first thought was that a snake had bitten Summer. Her scream attested to severe pain. He started to yell for Joe and Matt, realized they would not hear him above the drone of the pump and tore off down the sled row. He found Summer sitting on the ground, sobbing and rocking as she cradled her bloodied hands. By then, the irrigation system was raining torrents of pond water across the field.

"Good Lord, Summer!" he exclaimed, dropping to his knees beside her. "What in the world happened?"

As best she could between sobs and the patter of water being pumped across the field, Summer explained the situation. "I was afraid my fingers were cut off," she concluded, her sobs dwindling to sniffles.

"Let me see," Tom said gently, taking her hands and laying them crosswise on top of each other so he could examine the cuts. "It probably hurts worse than it really is," he concluded. "All eight fingers are gashed all the way around, but the cuts aren't deep. I imagine your mama or grandma can fix you up good as new without haven to see the doctor."

Summer took a moment to inspect her hands more closely, satisfying herself that Tom's diagnosis was correct. Finally, she nodded agreement with him. "It hurts like the dickens," she said, "but I guess I'll live."

"That's the spirit," Tom said with an encouraging smile as he cupped his hand beneath her elbow and helped Summer to stand. Her eyes were red-rimmed, and he surrendered to the impulse to push a wayward strand of hair off her face. He took off his T-shirt, using it to wipe away the tear stains, then wrapping it around her hands to slow the bleeding before putting his arm around her waist as they began walking toward the end of the row.

"I know this really isn't the time to ask, but I'm gonna do it anyway," he said a short time later when they were drenched and near their destination. "If your hands are okay by Saturday, would you like to see a movie or somethen?"

Summer stopped dead in her tracks, her mouth agape with disbelief. "Here I am at my absolute worst—hurten like crazy, cryen and soaked through and through on top of everything else—and you dare to ask me for a date, Tom Carter?" she huffed.

"I guess that was a pretty stupid thing to do," he remarked, clearing a spray of water from his face.

"I can't call it one of your finer moments," she replied with airs.

"Anything wrong down there?" Matt called suddenly.

"Summer's cut her hands," Tom yelled back at his boss. "We need to get her home, so someone can look after them."

Turning back to Summer, he repeated his request as Matt rushed toward them. "How 'bout it, Summer? You interested in a night out with the hired help?"

Despite herself, Summer smiled. "What time?"

"Seven," Tom suggested.

"It's a date," she agreed a few seconds before Matt reached them.

"What happened, honey?" Matt asked quickly, worried about the blood.

"Here's the long and the short of it, Daddy," she replied, her tone pouty even though she already felt better. "Somebody almost cut off my fingers when they started those irrigation pipes. My back aches, my fingers feel like they've been detached from my hands and I'm wet as a mad hen. On top of everything else, Romeo here just asked me for a date. All in all, it's been one heck of a day, but I would appreciate it if someone took me home now. This ain't no way to treat a future beauty queen."

Matt stared blankly at his daughter, then at Tom as the water cascaded down around them. Suddenly, all three of them burst into laughter. They were still laughing a minute later as they arrived at the end of the row, where Joe waited on the tractor.

At precisely seven o'clock Saturday night, Tom arrived at the Baker home. He was shaved, doused in cologne and dressed neatly in gray slacks and a white pullover. Luke answered the door.

"Hi," Tom said.

"Since when do you knock?" Luke remarked through the screen door.

"I'm here for Summer," Tom explained.

"What for?" Luke asked.

"We have a date," Tom said.

"Oh," Luke shrugged, finally opening the door. "She's still getten ready, I guess. Come on in."

Tom stepped inside the house and found himself facing the entire

Baker clan, except for Summer and her mother. It was like walking into the middle of an inquisition. He mumbled greetings, trying to appear relaxed, finding it a difficult proposition, especially since he had to stand for scrutiny in front of everyone. He looked to Joe for help and received a frothy grin in return.

"If you're feelen a bit uncomfortable, we planned it that way," Sam said finally as the rest of his family yielded their silence to whelps of laughter.

"Do all of Summer's dates get such special treatment?" Tom asked when the laughter subsided.

"Not usually," Carrie answered. "With Summer, dates are like a re-volven door, so you quit payen attention after a while. But this is different. She's never gone out with anyone we know as well as you."

"Is that good or bad?" Tom asked.

"We'll let you know in good time," Sam said cagily.

"Are you gonna kiss her?" Bonnie inquired. She was eleven, with an increasing penchant for asking embarrassing questions at the worst times.

"I doubt it," Tom answered, suddenly at ease among friends. Scooping Bonnie into his arms, he planted a sloppy kiss on her cheek as the girl squealed in delight. "That'll probably be the only kiss I get tonight," he teased.

"It better be," Matt growled.

Everyone laughed once more, and then John asked the question that had all of them guessing for an answer. "I want to know why you asked her out in the first place. Y'all can hardly tolerate each other."

Every eye and every ear converged on Tom, who knew they ex-pected a truthful answer. He had no intention of being serious, though, especially since he was still trying to figure out this sudden attraction to a long-time nemesis. Taking his time, first putting Bonnie back on the floor, he finally replied, "It was like this, John. Summer was screamen, cryen and carryen on so that I didn't know what in the world to do. So, I thought of the most outrageous thing possible, which was to ask her for a date. I had no idea she'd actually say yes. But when she did, I was more or less obligated to see it through. And here I am."

"I heard that!" Summer cried as she emerged from her bedroom door with Caroline in tow. She was smartly dressed in a short-sleeved yellow blouse with a blue-green plaid skirt that fell just above her knees.

"You look very nice," Tom told her, noticing the white gauze wrapped around her hands.

"Compliments will not get you out of this, buster," Summer replied sassily. Turning to her family, she explained, "The truth of the matter is that he misunderstood my stunned reaction to his silly question. I said, 'Uh,' and he heard, 'Yeah,' so I'm stuck with him for the night. Any way you look at it, I'm the injured party in this predicament."

"Me thinks you both doth protest too much," Sam teased as the room grew suddenly suspicious about Tom and Summer's intentions toward each other.

"Y'all better get out of here while you still have a chance," Caroline urged with a cheerful smile.

"Bye, Mama," Summer said, kissing Caroline on the cheek. "Bye, Daddy."

"Home by eleven," Matt called.

"Yes, sir," Tom replied.

Instead of seeing the movie as planned, Summer and Tom never made it past the Shady Lane drive-in restaurant in Tifton. They sat in the cab of his pickup truck, munching hamburgers and French fries, downing vanilla milkshakes and engaging in the kind of conversation that occurs when two people are intent upon learning about each other.

They were like two old best friends, who had been separated for too long and wanted to catch up on the past. More than friendship was at work, however. The night crackled around them, sizzling like a power line on a hot summer day. They teased, tempted and tested each other, then surprised themselves with quiet moments of reflection and discovery.

Perhaps their common past put them at ease, but the entire date unfolded as naturally as the night closed around them. Summer flung the full force of her forthrightness at Tom, deciding he would like her for who she was or not like her at all. Tom discovered he liked her more than he had ever believed possible.

"So why *did* you ask me out?" Summer asked finally, late in the night.

Tom eyed her carefully, thinking the simple answer to her question was lust. "Truthfully?" he replied.

"The truth is always best, Tom," she said.

"I never thought of you as be'en pretty or anything like that," Tom said. "Honestly, I never thought about you much at all unless I had reason to, and then I generally was irritated with you. Last Saturday, however, I took a good look at you, Summer. And I liked what I saw."

"I'm flattered," Summer replied modestly.

"Now it's my turn," Tom said. "Why did you say yes when I asked?"

"Because I could tell that you liked what you saw when you looked me over last week," Summer answered unabashedly. "That caught my interest. Then, I realized I don't really know you very well, Tom. And I wanted to get to know you."

"Am I tolerable?" he inquired.

"A lot more so than I ever imagined," Summer replied, then added quickly, "Not that I ever imagined."

Tom deliberately cleared his throat. "We're be'en truthful," he said. "Remember."

"I never did imagine," Summer said. "I'm not tryen to burst your ego, but I've always thought of you as plain old Tom. Part of the family." She smiled slightly, then explained further: "You know those relatives that you're always tryen to ignore."

He laughed lightly.

"Besides, I should be offended," she continued. "You wanted to go out with me entirely because of my looks. That doesn't speak well of my personality."

"Honestly, Summer, I never thought you had much personality," Tom said. "Just a big mouth."

A feisty retort appeared on her lips, but Summer stopped short. "A little honesty never hurt anyone," she concluded, with uncharacteristic humility. "I hope you change your mind after tonight."

Tom shook his head. "You're the real thing," he commented, a shy smile on his face.

His words came as a casual compliment, but his blue eyes revealed the depths of the man's desire. Summer saw danger in those eyes, and her heart constricted. Shock waves coursed through her because she was not prepared or ready for such feelings, either from Tom or within herself. She tried to ease the moment with some flippant remark, stammered instead and forgot her thought in mid-sentence.

"This must be a first—Summer Baker at a loss for words," Tom teased as a warm breeze drifted through the open windows.

"Don't tell anyone," Summer said, quickly recovering her composure. "It could be damagen to my reputation."

The late hour took care of the unanswered thoughts between them. With Summer due home in twenty-five minutes, they gathered their empty food wrappers and cups, using a trip to the wastebasket to stretch their legs and cool down the sparks flying between them.

———————

Many words had passed between Summer and Tom; many more remained to be said. But the ride home was dominated by silent contemplation.

"I had a great time," Tom said when they were standing on her front porch. "I hope we can do this again."

"I'd like that," Summer agreed.

For the first time that night, an uncomfortable feeling arose between them as they tried to decide how to close the night or even if they wanted to end it. "I should go," Tom said finally. "It's getten late. I'll see you at church tomorrow."

"If you're there," Summer chided. "I believe you've missed more Sundays than you've made recently. The Lord gives you seven days a week, Tom. The least you can do is give him back an hour of it."

"Maybe I should start callen you Sister Summer," Tom replied as he backed away from her.

"Aren't you goen to try to kiss me goodnight?" she asked boldly as he reached the porch steps and turned to leave.

The question stopped Tom in mid step, and he wheeled around to face her. "You wouldn't let me," he stated. "Would you?"

"Of course not, silly," she replied, "but you ort to at least make the effort. It's a man's obligation to try and a woman's prerogative to say no."

Summer had backed against the screen door, and Tom slid up close to her. He braced his hand against the doorframe over her shoulder, dipped his head to kiss her and almost fell against the screen as Summer ducked away at the last moment.

"Geez, Tom!" she said, laughing as he righted himself. "It's only our first date. If you're lucky, I might let you kiss me on the second date." She pointed to her cheek. "Right here, mister."

Tom spun toward her. "Gosh darn it, Summer!" he exclaimed a little more loudly than intended. "You shouldn't oughtta do stuff like that. I don't know what in the world to make of you."

"Shh!" Summer said, pointing to the window on the left side of the door. "Mama and Daddy sleep in that room. They might hear you and think somethen's goen on."

Tom crossed his arms, staring through her with those blue eyes.

"Summer?" he said softly, his tone serious and questioning. "Somethen is goen on?"

She looked away from him, across the porch to the other side of the road where the hazy light of a full moon shone on the woods. Quickly, she nodded her agreement and reached behind her back to open the door.

"Goodnight," she whispered before escaping into the house.

———

Once in a while, the Bakers respected each other's privacy and kept their curiosity to themselves. On the morning after her date with Tom, Summer came to the breakfast table prepared to fend off a barrage of questions. Only one was asked, however, and it was nothing more than a polite inquiry from her mother as to whether she had a good time. No one bothered to ask the obligatory follow-up of whether they could expect more dates between Tom and her, and she refused to answer the unasked.

On the following Friday, Summer and Tom had their second date, an almost burdensome outing, so fraught with uneasy feelings that both of them welcomed the opportunity to sit through a bad movie. "Maybe we expected too much," Tom suggested as they stood beside her front door a good half hour before she was expected home. "How 'bout if we try again tomorrow?"

Summer offered him her cheek for a kiss.

On Saturday, they were relaxed and carefree with no plans. At Summer's suggestion, they went only as far as the New River Elementary School, stopping there to visit the playground that had been their childhood stomping grounds. Turning back the years, they played like children, balancing on the see-saw, flying down the slides and running through the warm night in a spirited game of chase that exhausted itself when they wound up at the swings. Plopping into side-by-side seats, they launched into fond reminiscing about their school days.

"This has been a wonderful evenen," Summer said sometime later. "Most people probably would think it's childish stuff, especially for someone who's just one week away from graduating high school."

"It'll be our secret," Tom promised. "Besides, I wouldn't want everyone to know how cheap I am."

"Push me for a while, and I'll tell everyone you're extremely extravagant," Summer said, giggling. "Then all the girls will want to go out with you."

Tom rose from his swing, walked behind Summer and began pushing her lightly. "Are you excited about finishen high school?" he asked.

"Mostly," she replied. "Everything seems so wide open at this point in life. It's exciten but also a little scary. Right now, I'm just looken forward to the summer and to Miss Golden Leaf."

"That pageant means a lot to you?" Tom inquired.

"I know it's vain, but I'd like to have that crown," Summer said. "If they awarded the title based on who actually worked in tobacco, I'd be a shoo-in."

"Well, if it means that much, then I hope you bring home the crown," Tom replied. "Did you pick out the material for your dress?"

"Your mama gave me good ideas," Summer answered. "Pink satin with a chiffon overlay. Sleeveless, long evenen gloves, the works. Granny's helpen me with the dress."

Tom murmured a polite reply, and they drifted into silence for several minutes. Finally, Summer asked, "What are you thinken about?"

Tom stopped the swing, walked around to face her and put his hands above hers on the chains. "You mostly," he said. "Pretty much lately, Summer, you're *all* I've thought about. Two weeks ago, I wasn't even sure whether I liked you. Now I'm thinken I'm in love with you, and none of it makes sense because people aren't supposed to fall in love just like that."

"Maybe it's not supposed to make sense," she replied, smiling softly. "Maybe that's what makes love so special."

In the long silence that followed, they basked in the joy of new-found love. Their relationship had moved swiftly to this important point. Now they wanted tenderness, time to savor the moment at hand and each new discovery to come. Tom stroked her hair, cupped her face and kissed her. It was a gentle, slow, uncomplicated kiss, lingering like the taste of a sweet dessert.

"I love you, Summer," he said.

"And I love you, Tom," she said.

He pulled her from the swing, and they embraced, their bodies becoming familiar and intimate, all while understanding that a certain caution was necessary. Tom buried his face in the sweet scent of her hair, and Summer pressed her cheek against the roughness of his evening beard. When they kissed again, it was passionate, ardent and forceful, and it made their hearts and bodies clamor, anticipating the day they would forgo caution.

CHAPTER 3

THE COMING OF SPRING had always meant the beginning of a new adventure for Matt. He regarded the season's arrival as the start of a pilgrimage, an expedition in which he would reap the rewards that usually beckoned to him under the pretense of *next year*. More often than not, the full rewards came cleverly disguised, with just enough promise to leave him hopeful for better times to come. Without some sense of sameness to serve as a guide, the journey might well have become an endless cycle of insanity.

As long as he knew what month it was, Matt could anticipate the work. In January, he limed fields, fixed fences and repaired machinery, greasing equipment, replacing and tightening bolts. In February, he planted Irish potatoes and sugar cane, while beginning to prepare the fields for the crops, harrowing, plowing and fumigating the ground. The corn and tobacco were planted in March; sweet potatoes and peanuts in April; cotton and cantaloupes in May; soybeans and grain sorghum in June after the winter wheat and oats had been harvested. When he was not planting, he mixed chemicals and sprayed, fighting the annual battle to beat down the teaweed, cockleburs, ragweed and sand spurs that choked the fields, as well as the hornworms, armyworms and boll weevils that invaded his crops. At some point, the tobacco and cantaloupes had to be hoed; the flowering tops and tiny suckers had to be broken out of the tobacco so that the stalks would grow tall and heavy; and all of the crops had to be cultivated at least twice, preferably three times.

By the time summer arrived and the children finished the school year, he was already tired from the effort. Still, the hardest work remained, with the bulk of it waiting in the tobacco field. Tobacco yielded a high profit, but the crop also exacted a heavy toll on those who grew it. In June, July and the first half of August, nothing mattered more than gathering tobacco. Unless it was critical, everything else waited or was accomplished either in the spare hours of the six-day workweek or on an occasional Sunday.

When the tobacco had been gathered and packed off to the warehouse, the family picked cantaloupes. If the summer ran smoothly, in the relative meaning of the idea, then the children got a few days of rest before returning to school in late August.

In early September, Matt picked and graded sweet potatoes, then enjoyed a temporary lull in the middle of the month before the harvest season began. Out of tradition and perhaps some superstition, he usually waited until the Harvest Moon arrived to begin combining, starting with the corn and then working his way through the peanuts, cotton, soybeans and sorghum. In his spare time, he bailed hay and harrowed the harvested fields so they could be sewn in grains and greens.

By early December, the combines had been put to rest for another year and the children were picking up the last of the pecans. At some point, Caroline and Rachel had taken care of the garden, cramming two freezers and the pantry with the vegetables that would feed the family through the coming winter. In addition, Sam had found time to gather the cane and make several kettles of syrup. Around this time, the boys often took a notion to begin plowing the empty fields, hoping to get an early start on the next year. Occasionally, they burned a field or some section of woods in the constant battle to keep the land clear of weeds and undergrowth.

Matt usually took several days to relax, hunt or fish, but his mind was never far from planning for the next year, which always began between Christmas and New Year's, when they prepared and sewed beds for the next year's tobacco plants.

Matt thought about this routine as he walked through his tobacco field, checking for hornworms and signs of disease. On this first Monday in June, dark storm clouds gathered on the horizon. If this had been any other day, he would have expected the clouds to follow their springtime precedent and yield nothing more than a dry thunderstorm. Since it was Summer's high school graduation day, however, with the ceremony scheduled for the Cookville High School football field, Matt figured rain would dampen the festivities. If his cynical forecast held, he only hoped a few drops would fall on his dry fields.

Matt was trying hard to keep a stiff upper lip about the weather. There was still time for rain to make a difference in determining whether the year would be a lean or a losing proposition. The corn already was critical, but a good rain could salvage it, while most of the other crops were still a few weeks shy of the critical time when moisture was vital for their development. Irrigation had revived the tobacco, cotton and a portion of the peanuts. But the ponds were low. In fact, the Old Pond was so low that fish were popping up dead daily. The place stank with decay, and buzzards scavenged freely, eating their fill.

The New Pond was in only slightly better condition. Matt hoped to get one more watering for the tobacco before fish began to die there as well. To avoid the waste, the boys and he planned to seine the pond before irrigating from it.

When would rain come? Would it come? When his father had posed that concern several weeks earlier, Matt had dismissed the idea as improbable, to the point that the suggestion did not even warrant worry. Now he wondered if he had been wrong.

Except for the drought of 1954, enough rain had always fallen to keep them from utter ruin. But for seven straight days now, the skies had made liars of the weather forecasters. Each afternoon, dark clouds rolled across the skies, taunting with a few drops of rain every now and then but mostly yielding dry thunderstorms. As if the unhealthy fields were not enough to cause worry, the dry clouds had added insult to injury two days ago, spawning a violent lightning storm that had zapped the well pump, which provided running water for the house and animals. Replacing the pump had taken a few more hundred dollars from their dwindling bank account.

Accustomed to praying for rain, Matt did so now as he trudged through the fields. Yet even as he sought divine intervention, doubts troubled him. He could not help wondering if nature had dealt his family a cruel sleight of hand this year.

As Matt predicted, the spring's only significant rain forced the high school graduation ceremony into the Cookville gymnasium. Nothing dampened their spirits, however, as the Bakers watched Summer take her place on stage with the honor graduates. She received a home economics award that came with a three-hundred-dollar scholarship, then grabbed her diploma and marched into the waiting arms of Tom Carter.

Tom had sat with the Bakers during the ceremony, and his was the congratulations Summer sought first. He responded with a tight hug and a chaste kiss on the cheek. In the initial awareness of their love, the couple intentionally had concealed their feelings about each other. Both had wanted to shout it for the world to hear, but they first needed time to acquaint themselves with the idea. Now their hesitation vanished, and the aura of new love revealed their commitment. Everyone sensed the significance of the moment.

"Next thing you know, we'll be goen to her wedden," Caroline said softly to Matt, fighting back tears that were a reflection of happiness, sadness and the emotion of the day.

Without giving her husband an opportunity to respond, she left him standing there openmouthed and went to give her oldest daughter a congratulatory hug. "If the time ever comes when you feel like talken woman to woman, I'm always available, and I'm a good listener," she whispered to Summer. "But right now, honey, I think your daddy could use a big hug from his little girl."

"Oh, Mama!" Summer said as her mother's hand touched her cheek in understanding. "Is it that obvious?"

Caroline nodded, and Summer beamed with happiness. Then she embraced her father, with tears shining in their eyes.

In the middle of June, the air conditioner at the Carter's Mercantile rumbled loudly into a state of disrepair. A repairman confirmed the machine's demise, and Dan followed him to Cookville to look into buying a new cooling system for the store.

Alone in the mercantile, Amelia set up fans and began moving the candy bars to the drink machine from the glass case to prevent them from melting in the building's increasingly hot confines. Hearing a car pull up beside the gas tanks, she glanced at her watch, closed the cooler door and went to greet Gary James. The mercantile was the halfway point of the postman's route through the New River community, and he routinely stopped there for his morning break, always buying a Coke and a pack of peanuts.

"Good afternoon, Gary," Amelia greeted him.

"Good day to you, too, Amelia," he responded. "I trust Dan and you are well today."

"We're languishen in this gosh-awful heat just like everybody else," Amelia said. "Our air conditioner's gone kaput on us, and Dan's off in Cookville to get a replacement. The thing was old as Methuselah anyway, so we're likely better off all the way around with a new one. I just wish I could hurry things along to beat the heat."

"I'm thinken about getten me a new truck, and you can bet I'll make sure it has an air conditioner," Gary replied. "All my fan does is blow hot air. The summers are miserable."

"What you got for us today?" Amelia asked.

"A pile of it," Gary answered, handing her a stack of letters and circulars, all bundled with a rubber band.

Out of politeness, Amelia laid the mail aside while Gary fetched his drink, opened the bottle and dumped a small bag of roasted peanuts into the Coke. He took one thirst-satisfying taste, then asked, "How much do I owe you?"

"Same as yesterday," Amelia replied as the postman handed her a shiny dime and an Indian-head nickel. "You sure you don't want to keep this?" she asked, admiring the coin.

"I have one or two put away," Gary said. "Besides, I don't like to break a dollar if I don't have to."

"Dollars are harder to come by in the long run," Amelia agreed.

When the postman had gone, Amelia riffled through the mail, finding a bill from their meat supplier in Cookville and a new product announcement from the grocery wholesaler in Valdosta. But the third envelope pushed every other thought from her mind. Her most basic maternal instincts urged Amelia to shred the letter and pretend it never existed. Knowing her son would never forgive an intrusion into his privacy, however, she clutched the letter to her chest, locked up the store and headed for the Baker place.

Tom hated cropping the sand lugs, those bottom three or four small leaves on the tobacco stalk that grew on the ground and were covered with sandy soil. Sand coated him from head to toe, the tiny granules working their way into every open crevice in his clothes and grinding against his skin. He was scratchy and itchy, plus his back ached from having to bend his tall frame at a severe angle to reach the low leaves. The work would be easier when they were working higher on the stalk.

Despite the discomfort, Tom saw no reason to complain. With a good job to prepare himself for the future and the love of a good woman to share his life, he had everything he needed or wanted for the moment.

The mere thought of Summer aroused his passion. He felt intoxicated these days, almost giddy with fortune. Best of all was the sense of permanency, the growing belief that this good feeling would always exist even in difficult times.

Tom peered upwards, trying to get a glimpse of Summer through the cogs and chains that carried the hands of tobacco to the top story of the double-deck harvester. He was admiring the form of her slender legs in snug blue jeans when she sensed him looking. Glancing down, she smiled, a warm and glowing acknowledgment that she felt the same way, the same desire.

Then all at once, sand fell in his face, blinding Tom, stinging him senseless. He buried his face in his hands, vigorously trying to rub away the dirt that filled his eyes. As he waited for tears to cleanse them fully, he heard Summer bubble over with laughter that was loud, infectious and full of affection.

"Hey, Joe," he called to his friend in the front seat. "Keep up my row a second. I got sand in my eyes."

"If you'd keep your eyes off my sister, stuff like this wouldn't happen," Joe grumbled, straining to carry two rows by himself.

"Thanks," Tom said a long moment later when his eyes were clear enough to see.

"Yeah, yeah," Joe muttered. "You've got it bad, Tom."

"No, Joe," he disagreed. "I've got it good."

The two friends bantered back and forth as the harvester ebbed toward the end of the row, then drifted into the comfortable silence of the work and private thoughts. Finishing his row, Tom shoved the last hand of leaves into the metal clip, which conveyed the tobacco to the top floor of the harvester. He jumped off his seat, brushed off the sand and started toward the pickup truck, which contained empty sticks that needed to be handed up to the stringers. He saw his mother then.

Amelia was short but statuesque and very stylish. She was wearing a plain white dress and sandals, with a wisp of her dyed-blonde hair uncharacteristically out of place. Her slender face was pinched with concern, and the heat had blotched her makeup.

Tom first feared something was wrong with his father. As his mother walked toward him, however, he saw the letter and guessed what the envelope contained. When he had decided to leave college, he had realized the possibility of being drafted. Several of his high school classmates had received orders. One already had served in Vietnam, and another had just been shipped over there.

"This came for you," Amelia said as she reached him. "I thought it might be important."

Tom accepted the Selective Service System letter with a wan smile. He tore open the envelope, pulled out the form letter and read it twice. The Army wanted Tom to report to the National Guard Armory in Tifton for a physical examination two weeks from Saturday.

Feeling more unsettled than he appeared, Tom shrugged and handed the letter back to his mother.

"Looks like I'm gonna be a soldier, Ma," he told her. "You can read it if you want. Just put it in my room when you're finished."

Amelia resisted the urge to hug her son, instead telling him, "You'll look right handsome in uniform."

"What's that?" Summer hollered from the top of the harvester.

Both Tom and his mother looked at her, and Summer shuddered with apprehension.

"I've been drafted," Tom shouted over the roar of the engine.

The color drained from Summer's face. Tom sighed and returned to work.

Tom passed his physical and was inducted into the Army for a two-year hitch of active service. Shortly afterward, he received his orders to report to Fort Benning near Columbus, Georgia, for six weeks of basic training.

"It's not so bad," he tried to reassure Summer. "We've got six weeks between now and when I report. Fort Benning is not that far away, Summer. I'll get a few days off between boot camp and infantry school, and there's a good chance I'll be stationed at Fort Benning. Who knows? We might even be able to spend Christmas together. I'd love to spend Christmas with you, sweetheart."

His voice was steady and calm, and Summer tried to appear comforted. She kissed him. "You'd better save your money then and buy me some ridiculously expensive present," she said.

The remark was completely out of character, yet Tom responded sincerely. "I'd give you the moon and the stars if I could," he vowed.

"I know," Summer said, hugging him tightly. "And that's enough, Tom."

Lucas Bartholomew craved a drink of whiskey. Even though he was not a drinking man, he wanted to feel liquor on his lips and let it slide down his throat, stinging all the way to his belly. Drowning himself in liquor would ease the disappointment and frustration of his failed hopes for a few hours. The idea held more appeal than he wanted to admit.

Ever since Paul Berrien had agreed to let him farm a few acres on shares, Lucas had worked—like a man possessed—to succeed. He wanted to impress Paul and Matt Baker with his drive as well as his ability. He wanted to earn money working for himself instead of someone else.

Lucas had no complaints about his years working with Matt. The man had treated him well, giving Lucas a free place to stay with his family and paying wages that were more than fair. Still, he would never feel complete satisfaction working for Matt. As long as he worked for any man, Lucas would never achieve the freedom he desired.

Besides his lofty ambitions, something else gnawed at Lucas. Despite all his hard work, his best efforts, he had nothing to show for the toil. If a man came into the fields where Lucas worked, he surely would deem the black man a sorry excuse for a farmer. The man would not see the straight rows that Lucas had planted, weeded and tended like a mother watching her child. But rather, the man would see scraggly crops and believe they withered from neglect. And more than one man would view the ruined crops as confirmation that a black man should not be left to guide his own destiny.

These feelings came from a dark spot, troubled and deep in his mind. Lucas knew such thoughts never crossed the minds of Matt, Paul or a few other men who he respected and counted among his friends. Why was it then, when he had earned the unflagging respect of respectable men, that Lucas could not push aside the feelings of inadequacy, incompetence and ineptitude that preyed on him from time to time? Was he doomed to measure life by his failures instead of his accomplishments? Those fears played with his mind all too often, so much so that he was learning to answer the doubts with an even more important question. Could he rise above the nonsense that cluttered his mind, cast off his demons and meet the next challenge, which was the ultimate measure of any man?

Without a doubt, misfortune was to blame for his dying crops. Only an unreasonable man would believe otherwise and if Lucas chose to cast his lot with that line of thinking, then he deserved to wallow in misery and self-pity. Likewise, while several stiff drinks of whiskey would help him forget his troubles, the problems would still exist when he woke tomorrow morning. He would have a splitting headache and a queasy stomach, but nothing would be changed. Paul Berrien would still be out the money he had paid to buy seed and fertilizer, and Lucas would have done nothing to make a better life for his family. Besides, Lucas knew what too much liquor could do to men. Whiskey sapped a man's strength, thwarted his resolve, stole his incentive and sent him to an early grave in some cases, such as his father.

Lucas had vowed long ago never to abandon his family. So instead of whiskey, he would settle for a soda pop.

To safeguard against the possibility of an unplanned detour to the liquor store, he took Danny with him to Carter's Mercantile. Danny was four, one year younger than Annie. The boy worshipped his father, dwelling on his every deed and every word, which was fortunate since Lucas rarely treated his children in a childlike way. When he talked to his children, Lucas spoke as if they were grown-ups who understood and followed his every word. If he did nothing else for Annie and Danny, he would teach them that even though life sometimes made no sense at all, they still had to make heads or tails of the confusion and get on with it.

Lucas made one exception to this rule of thumb in raising his children. When he tried to teach them their ABCs or reading or counting, he explained the lesson with childlike simplicity. When it came to imparting knowledge in his children, Lucas had the patience of a saint. The more Annie and Danny learned as children, the easier they would find it to succeed in the confusing world of grown-ups.

As Lucas and Danny bumped along the dirt road in a beat-up pickup truck that should have been retired along with President Dwight Eisenhower, Lucas aimed a steady stream of commentary at his son. "If we could just get enough water, then the corn would form kernels and the puts would develop in their pods," he lectured. "With that river so close by, there oughtta be somethen I can do to take advantage of the situation."

Having figured out his daddy was talking about corn and water, Danny was content to listen to the rhythm of his father's voice. His round black eyes rose and fell with every change in cadence. The voice was a security blanket, and nothing else mattered. As long as he could hear his daddy's voice, regardless of the words, Danny was safe.

Wayne Taylor liked fast cars, fast money and fast women. Unfortunately, his experience was limited to cars, so he made the best of the situation. Wayne was a reckless driver. He knew it, and he liked it that way, especially now that he could drive with the state's permission.

Actually, the legality of his driving status or lack thereof had never troubled the oldest son of Bobby and Martha Taylor. Wayne had required three tries to pass the written portion of the test for his driver's license. He considered the exam a stupid waste of time and effort. If the government in its infinite wisdom believed niggers should vote without first demonstrating their ability to read and write, then why should respectable people have to pass a test just to get a driver's license.

Any fool could drive, Wayne thought, as his car careened past Benevolence Church, fishtailing on the sandy road as he rounded the sharp curve right before the general mercantile. The big Pontiac straightened out on the road, and Wayne gunned the engine, quickly reaching eighty miles an hour before bringing the car to a sliding halt—inches from the railroad tracks. Before crossing the highway, he waited until a fast-approaching truck passed, using the delay to light a cigarette, then catching sight of a little nigger boy playing near a beat-up truck parked beside the store's twin set of gas pumps.

"Five points if you play your cards right," Wayne told himself. "Or you could have some real fun and games."

Driving slowly, Wayne crossed the highway and parked several yards behind the truck. Cautiously checking his surroundings, he slid out of the car, threw down his cigarette and headed toward Danny Bartholomew, who stopped playing and turned to observe Wayne.

Danny watched Wayne carefully, awed by his size and the cocky way he moved. Wayne was a burly youth, big of bone and tall, with a Marine's haircut. He carried himself with a bully's swagger, but it was his eyes that frightened Danny. They were green and burned with hatred. Instinct sent Danny scurrying behind the closest gas pump. He felt better out of sight and decided to join his father inside the store. Before he moved another step, however, Wayne's harsh voice commanded his attention.

"You come on out and show yourself, boy," Wayne ordered. "Or I just might tan your hide."

Frightened as never before, Danny peeked around the gas tank.

"Did you hear what I said, boy?" Wayne demanded, his tone menacing. "Come 'ere!"

Unable to think clearly, Danny did as told, moving slowly toward Wayne, who squatted to be face-to-face with the little boy. "You got no right to be around this place," Wayne sneered. "What's your excuse, nigger boy?"

"My daddy's getten us a soda pop," Danny answered.

"That ain't here or there," Wayne fired back. "Your kind don't belong here. You best remember that and figure out where your place is, boy, or one day you'll wind up sorry of it."

Wayne pressed a finger hard against the boy's gut, and Danny gasped, more out of fright than pain. "Are you listenen, boy?" he asked, his voice scathing. "Do you understand me?"

Now wide-eyed with fear, Danny nodded several times in rapid sequence.

"Don't you forget it, boy," Wayne hissed. "And you tell your daddy, too."

The store door opened then, the bell jingling as Lucas emerged from the mercantile followed by Tom and Summer, who were minding the business for Dan and Amelia.

Lucas moved toward Wayne like a tiger stalking prey. Lucas had fought rarely in his youth, never since marrying Beauty. In all his thirty years, however, he had never struck a white man. Now he was ready to kill one.

"He don't have to tell me nothen," Lucas said, his words clipped and threatening. "I heard it all from the goat's mouth."

Wayne rose quickly, weighing whether to stand his ground or retreat. His heart pounded, and his indecisiveness cost him any advantage. Before he realized it, Lucas was upon him.

His palm flat against the white boy's chest, Lucas shoved hard. Wayne stumbled and sprawled backward, landing on his back. Scrambling to his feet, he saw Lucas cock his fist and prepared to defend a blow. Before any punch was thrown, however, Tom grabbed Lucas from behind—momentarily restraining him and giving Wayne time to lurch backward, out of reach of the man's anger. Lucas slung away from Tom, starting once more toward Wayne. But again, Tom intervened, running in front of Lucas, placing himself as a buffer between the two men.

"Not this way, Lucas!" Tom shouted, his voice hard to command his friend's full attention. "Not this way," he repeated. "You got too much to lose to waste time on that kind of trash."

"Who you callen trash, you nigger lover?" Wayne screamed.

"Get out of here, Wayne!" Tom yelled. "Or you may just end up dead."

Wayne stood his ground, trying to decide if further action was warranted. He eyed the rage in Lucas' expression, took note of the black man's curved lip and wisely chose to back down. If they fought, Wayne suspected he would lose badly. He backed up to his car and opened the door, deciding there was sufficient distance between them to have the last word. Leaning across the car door, he sneered contemptuously at Lucas and Tom.

"You still ain't nothen but a nigger, Lucas Bartholomew," he growled. "And you ain't much better, Tom Carter."

"Go!" Tom yelled, afraid of what would happen as Lucas shrugged away from him.

Sensing the danger, Wayne dropped into the seat, slammed the door and cranked the car. Gunning the engine, he spun the car onto the highway, spewing a trail of dirt and gravel in his wake.

Neither Tom nor Lucas said anything or looked at each other until the dust settled and the doorbell jingled once more. Summer came down the steps with Danny in her arms. Fearing a fight, she had grabbed Danny the moment Lucas pushed Wayne and carried the boy inside the store. Now she put him down on the ground, and Danny ran to his father.

Not trusting his voice, Lucas lifted his son into his arms and held him tightly until the boy's shaking subsided.

"It's not right, Lucas," Tom said at last, "but be glad there was no fight."

"Sometimes, you have to fight for what's right," Lucas replied, his anger clear and determined.

"I know," Tom replied. "And you had more than enough cause. But facts are facts, Lucas, and the law don't look kindly on fights between a man and a boy—no matter what the circumstances. No matter how it seems, your fight's not with the boy. Your fight's with the man behind the boy. And as much as I hate to say it—as wrong as it is—let it go this time, friend. Just let it go."

"You can't forget things like this," Lucas said bitterly.

"Go home and take care of your son, Lucas," Tom pleaded. "It's over and done."

Lucas breathed deeply, considering the advice. "For now," he said at length, then nodded curtly at his friends and took his son home.

Wayne spent the afternoon on the rickety front porch of his house, trying to decide whether to tell his father about the confrontation with Lucas Bartholomew. His father would demand all the details, but it was difficult to gauge how Bobby would react. He might be angry that his son had backed away from a fight, and the last thing Wayne wanted was to appear cowardly in his father's eyes.

At supper, Wayne bided his time until the subject of "damned niggers" came up in the conversation. When his father reached the boiling point of his rage, Wayne interrupted.

"If you want to talk about uppity niggers, Pa, then let me tell you about Lucas Bartholomew," he said. "I weren't goen to mention it, but me and him had a run-in today at the store. He tried to push me around, but nothen came of it."

"That nigger came at you!" Bobby said, seeking clarification.

"He pushed me, then backed off," Wayne revealed. "There were people around us, and I guess he thought better of what he was doen. Or maybe he got scared."

"Who saw what happened?" Martha inquired.

"Tom Carter and Summer Baker," Wayne answered.

"Well, hell, son," Bobby cried. "Everybody knows those Bakers and Paul Berrien are the biggest nigger lovers in the county. They ain't likely to be on our side in this."

"I don't know much about Lucas Bartholomew, but I've always heard he's not one to go looken for trouble," Martha remarked. "Did you do anything to rile him, Wayne?"

"Hell, woman. Are you plumb crazy?" Bobby said with disgust, shaking his head in disbelief at the strange notions Martha sometimes had. "That don't matter nary one bit. You think it's okay for a nigger to come after your son?"

Martha accepted the reprimand without comment and busied herself by pushing the food on her plate from side to side. Experience had taught her when to keep her mouth shut.

"This is interesten," Bobby said to himself as he gnawed a pork chop bone. "Now tell me again what happened, Wayne. From start to finish."

The celebration of the Fourth of July in Cookville was a modest occasion, especially when the holiday fell on a Tuesday, as it did in 1967. With most of the county busy in the fields, only a handful of people turned out to hear a short speech by Mayor Curtis Gaddy and a rusty rendition of *The Star-Spangled Banner* played by the Cookville High School Marching Rebel Band, of which half its thirty members were absent.

A patriotic heart was the last reason Bobby Taylor came to take part in the celebration. He gathered several of his best cronies around him, then worked the men into a frenzy with an embellished tale of Wayne's run-in with Lucas. Some urged him to press charges, while others wanted Bobby himself to right the wrong. Bobby waffled back and forth on the issue, loudly weighing the merits of each option, always with a belligerent preference toward taking justice into his own hands.

More than anything, Bobby was enjoying the attention, with no intentions whatsoever of following through with either idea. As it turned out, his plans were scuttled.

"Speak of the devil," Hugh Williams said, interrupting Bobby in mid-sentence.

The interruption ticked off Bobby. "What is it, Hugh?" he asked.

"Just thought you'd like to know Mr. Lucas Bartholomew is right here in the flesh and blood," Hugh replied, pointing across the street. "Here's your chance to settle the score."

The challenge for Bobby to back up his words was clear in Hugh's voice.

"Come on, Bobby," another man urged. "We're behind you all the way."

Bobby had no choice. He had to pursue Lucas. If he backed down, his reputation would suffer irreparable harm. "Where the hell is he?" he asked, pushing forward for a clear view across the street where Lucas was walking with his wife and children.

"Well now, boys," Bobby said, "I think it's time to teach Lucas Bartholomew a thing or two about acten so uppity."

Beauty was the first to see the men coming toward her family. She tugged on her husband's shirt, alerting him to the danger.

"Take the children and get out of here," Lucas ordered quickly. "And see if you can find Paul Berrien or one of his deputies."

Beauty grabbed Annie and Danny by the hand, pulling them down the street, demanding they look straight ahead. Scared, wanting help for her husband, she made a beeline for the courthouse.

Lucas crossed his arms and waited for Bobby, willing to fight if necessary, determined not to throw the first punch.

"I got a bone to pick with you," Bobby said, halting a safe distance from Lucas. "My boy tells me you jumped on him the other day."

Lucas remained silent.

"Well?" Bobby asked loudly.

"I did what was necessary to protect my son," Lucas replied, measuring his words to ensure there was no challenge issued.

"That's not how I heard it," Bobby said, accusing. "My boy tells me you intended to beat the tar out of him and would have tried it if nobody had been around to stop you. He says you came at him for no reason."

"That's not true," Lucas claimed.

"Are you callen my son a liar?" Bobby asked, outraged by the allegation, then advancing closer to Lucas as he spied Paul Berrien emerging from the courthouse.

"If your boy said I had no cause to go after him, then he lied," Lucas replied firmly. "He's lucky someone was there to stop me. But I'll tell you this now, Bobby: If he ever messes with my child or my family again, he'll be sorry for it."

"That's a threat," Bobby said, cocking his fist, then dropping his hands as somebody warned Paul was coming toward them. He took a backward step, then hissed a parting shot. "Someday, somewhere, Bartholomew, your colored ass will rue the day you ever crossed me. You can consider that fair warnen."

"What's goen on here," Paul Berrien interrupted roughly, pushing his way between Bobby and Lucas.

Bobby sneered at his old political rival. "Lucas and me are just exchangen a few friendly threats, sheriff," he sneered. "But it's not a damn thing that's any of your business."

Paul glared at Bobby, then stared at Lucas for clarification, but the black man refused to meet his eyes. Finally, he turned back to Bobby. "If y'all don't get out of here and break it up, then I'll make it my business, Bobby," he said with authority. "And I'll make you damned miserable in the process."

Sensing Paul meant what he said, Bobby's friends abandoned him and retreated across the street. Bobby glared at his two foes, then spit on the sidewalk and spun away from them.

In a minute, Paul pressed Lucas for details about the situation. "Anything I should know about?" he asked.

"Same old stuff, Paul," Lucas answered. "And there ain't a thing you can do about it."

With that said, Lucas went to find his family.

———————

Searing heat continued to scorch the land, and the sun seemed to creep closer to the earth with each passing day. When even the clouds disappeared, Matt quit looking for signs of approaching rain. Every day, he plodded across his sunbaked fields and heard the brittle crops crunch beneath his feet. He had worked himself and his family to the point of collapse and mostly their efforts had been for naught.

For a while, Matt had believed the tobacco would keep them from utter ruin. The irrigation appeared to have saved their most important crop. But then black shank attacked, and another hope was lost. In a matter of weeks, healthy stalks withered like dried grapes. Leaves turned prematurely yellow and shrunk on the stalk. Matt figured he'd be lucky to make half the poundage allotted to him annually by the government.

The drought caused other problems, too. The hot, dry air had parched his main pasture, leaving nothing but brown stubble and bare patches of dirt for the cows to graze. Matt sold half the herd to keep the other half from starving. It was money in the bank, but only a fraction of what the cattle were worth in good times. Meanwhile, the remaining cows were wasting in the heat, with ribs protruding under scruffy coats and snouts sunburned and irritated. Worst of all, they bellowed for more water in the late afternoon, a painful wail that seemed almost as sad as an injured baby's cries. Matt figured he would have to sell a few more before the situation improved.

Several of Rachel's prized laying hens also perished in the heat, but the hogs fared better. While dwindling corn supplies forced Matt to sell some of his sows and a few feeder pigs before they had reached the preferred weight, the other hogs had a shady place to spend the hot days—even if their wallows were all dried up. The boys were hauling water every day to keep them quenched, and when fall arrived, Matt would turn the hogs and the cows into the fields of corn, which would not yield sufficiently to make it worth his time to run a combine in the fall.

"When it rains, it pours," Joe quipped one day, a rare trace of bitterness in his voice, as Matt, Sam and he prepared to fire a tobacco barn.

"Don't worry so much, son," Matt replied. "We'll get by. Somehow."

"Your daddy's right, Joe," Sam added. "This, too, shall pass."

Of course, they would get through the hard times. Matt knew that. The year might be a losing proposition, but they would survive. And with a little luck, things would get better next year. They certainly could not get worse.

With the days routine, everyone began looking for ways to beat the heat. The task was not easy, but they faced it with humor and ingenuity. On a Saturday when the temperature soared past the century mark for the umpteenth day, Sam proved an egg would fry on a paved road. No one wanted to eat it, but there was no doubt that it was fried, or at least well poached, with crusted edges and a gooey yolk.

Rachel scolded her husband for wasting an egg.

Still the heat was relentless. It woke them in the morning, burned through the day and made everyone downright uncomfortable during the night.

And through it all, Tom and Summer shivered—from an entirely different kind of heat.

———

A day arrived when there was very little water in the well that fed the house. It was a particularly grimy day, when everything went wrong and tensions rose.

Long after he had hung the last heavy stick of tobacco in the barn, Joe still smelled the sickly odor of the diseased leaves. To make matters worse, his hat had disappeared mysteriously during the day, and his hair was matted with black tar. With no water for a shower, he proposed a dip in New River to his brothers and Tom.

New River was an obscure tributary with densely forested banks thick with cypress and oak trees dripping Spanish moss. The water was pure, deep and cold. And even though the river level was down sharply this summer, the water in their favorite cove remained deep enough to prevent the young men from finding the bottom.

Soon, a quick romp in the swimming hole became a daily ritual. One day, Summer, feeling wearier than usual and unnaturally subdued, asked if her sisters and she might join them.

"The more, the merrier," Joe quipped, stunning Tom and his brothers.

While waiting for the girls to change into their bathing suits, Joe explained his proposal. "We need a little fun and games to liven up things around here," he suggested as his companions guffawed over themselves.

New River meandered through the Berrien estate, about a mile away from the eastern edge of the Baker farm. To reach the swimming hole, the group trooped across the road, through the patch of sweet potatoes and across the first of two fences. Next, they cut through the woods, crossing the second fence near the spot where Joe had shot the panther. On the Berrien side of the fence, the woods became inhospitable, filled with briars and dangling tree branches. Finally, they emerged into a back-country glade of lush wild crabgrass and sandy beach beside the gurgling river.

Nature had carved the cove from a sharp bend in New River. A tangled mesh of brush and tree roots made the far side of the cove forbidding, a sharp contrast to the inviting beach area. The shaded, sandy beach turned into slippery red clay on the steep incline of the riverbank, and a huge oak tree curled high over the water. Easily accessible, the lower tree branches provided a perfect diving platform. For the more adventuresome, Joe had hung a rope swing from the higher branches and built a tree ladder that led skyward to a makeshift platform near the top of the oak.

"I'd forgotten how beautiful this place is," Summer remarked as they arrived. "It's been ages since I've been back here." Then spying the rickety boards in the top of the tree, she asked incredulously, "Do y'all jump off that thing?"

"We do," Joe answered. "It's part of our initiation into a secret society."

"That's pure crazy," Carrie said. "You could break your neck."

"Oh, we're real careful," replied Luke, who himself had yet to work up the courage to jump from the towering platform.

"And you girls be extra careful in the water," Joe added, slipping off his dirty T-shirt and snapping open the top button of his jeans. "It's deep as the dickens."

"Wait a second!" Summer objected, discerning something amiss as Tom, John and Luke tossed off their shirts. "Y'all don't have any shorts or anything. What are you gonna swim in—your underwear?"

Joe gave his sister a puzzled look. "Our underwear?" he repeated. "You're joken, right?" he continued, stripping down to his jockeys. "What do you think we swim in? Don't be offended, but we go skinny-dippen around here."

"That's disgusten," Carrie commented, her eyes growing wide with disbelief as Tom and her brothers dropped their pants in a heap.

"We're not goen swimmen without our clothes on, and neither are y'all," Summer declared loudly. "Tom! Put your pants back on."

"Gosh, Summer," Tom said sheepishly. "I just figured you knew. There's no better place in the world to get necked than a cold river on a hot day."

Joe faked a movement, suggesting he was fixing to remove his underwear. The girls screamed disapproval, turning their backs as the four young men peeled off their underwear.

"I tell you what," Joe said. "Just so y'all don't get offended, we'll keep the important stuff under water at all times. That way, there's no harm done, and we can all enjoy the river."

Summer delayed an answer, using the extra time to think. "Deal," she said finally.

"Summer!" her sisters squealed. "We can't do that."

"I'm hot, and I want to go swimmen," Summer declared. "They won't do anything. Besides, it's not like they've got somethen we've never seen before.

"Okay, Joe," she said. "Y'all go ahead and get in the water. And make sure you stay there!"

With loud whoops of laughter, the four young men turned and raced toward the river. Only when she counted four splashes did Summer turn toward the river. "It's our turn to have the fun," she whispered to her sisters. "Just follow me and act like you're fixen to take off your shorts. When we get to their clothes, grab 'em and run like the wind."

"All of them?" Carrie asked.

"Every last stitch—shoes and all," Summer replied.

Bonnie giggled as the girls advanced toward the river's edge. When they stood among the discarded clothes, Summer stopped. Placing hands on her hips, she summoned up her most haughty tone of voice and addressed her boyfriend and brothers.

"Y'all are pretty funny, but the joke's on you," she said. "When you boys get ready to come home, we'll be waiten for you on the front porch—with your clothes."

In a flash, the three girls grabbed every piece of clothing and pair of shoes, then fled with howls of protest coming from the black waters of New River.

"Dang!" Joe muttered as his sisters disappeared into the thicket.

"Double dang!" Tom added. "Joe, we should have knowed that Summer always gets the last word."

"What are we gonna do?" Luke lamented.

"Really," John chimed in. "We can't go prancen back to the house without our clothes, Joe. Granny would have a heart attack, and Mama would be fit to be tied. Even worse, Daddy and Grandpa won't ever let us live it down."

"Don't panic," Joe told them. "Even Summer wouldn't leave us out here buck-necked."

Half an hour later, Joe knew he had underestimated his sister, and they crept out of the water, embarrassed and depressed by the situation. They trekked back along the path through the woods, waging an unsuccessful battle against the briars and branches that attacked and attached against their naked skin.

"Be careful," Joe cautioned as they climbed over the first fence. "Whatever you do, don't get hung up."

"And be thankful there's no barbwire strung across the top," Tom commented with utmost sincerity.

Finally, they arrived at the edge of the sweet potato patch. Joe led his troops along the edge of the woods, and they were forced to navigate a thorny stand of hawthorn bushes to avoid open exposure to the road. At last, they reached the rear of the corncrib across the road from the house. Carefully, they peered around the corner of the building and saw their clothes bundled on the step walls of the porch, with Summer, Carrie and Bonnie rocking lazily and laughing delightedly.

Moments later, as the young men pondered their course of action, horror of horrors happened. The screen door opened, and their parents and grandparents joined the girls on the porch.

"What are those clothes doen there?" Caroline asked as she took a seat next to Matt in the swing.

"We're teachen your sons a lesson in humility," Summer replied, launching into a rip-roaring version of their escapade by the river, with her sisters providing pertinent observations along the way.

While the distance between the porch and themselves prevented the four young men from hearing the girls' version of events, the roar of laughter was loud and clear. It was equally obvious that their clothes would remain on the porch until someone retrieved them. Joe was nominated for the task.

"This was your brilliant idea in the first place," John observed dryly. "Now get us out of it. Save our faces."

"It's not my face I'm worried about," Luke muttered.

"Well I'm not about to go walken up there without any clothes," Joe said defensively. "We'll stay here till midnight before I do that."

"There's tobacco sheets in the corncrib," Tom reminded him. "You could wrap one of those around you if we can get in there."

"We can do that," Joe said, eyeing the barn's rear window, which was covered by a sturdy shutter that resembled a half-size door. Unable to scale the straight wall, Joe considered his limited options. He glanced around at his stark-naked brothers and friend and exhaled pent-up indignation.

"You can't make this stuff up," he said finally, with a disbelieving shake of his head, followed by an almost genuine laugh. "Come here, Luke."

Reluctantly, Luke stepped in front of his brother, and Joe hoisted him up to the window.

"It's locked," Luke said when the door refused to budge as he tried to push it open.

"Just knock it loose," Joe ordered testily, straining to keep his naked brother aloft. "I'll fix it back."

Using both hands for leverage, Luke hammered at the shutter, finally succeeding in breaking the inside latch. Scampering out of his brother's arms, he disappeared inside the crib window, shuffled across the remnants of the previous year's corn and reappeared moments later with one of the large burlap sheets.

"Here goes nothen," Joe said as he wrapped the course brown sheet around his body. "Lord, I hope nobody drives by and sees me like this."

Mustering up his last bit of dignity, Joe stepped from behind the crib and began walking toward the house. Summer spotted him immediately, pointing for everyone else to notice. Except for an occasional twitter, they observed his progress in silence.

"Lose somethen, did you, Joe?" Sam asked finally when his grandson stepped onto the concrete walkway.

Joe smiled thinly.

"Or have you just taken a fancy to walken around in tobacco sheets?" Matt inquired. "If that's the case, son, then you and I need to have a long talk."

"Oh, I don't know, Daddy," Summer said with relish. "I think it's rather becomen. Who knows? Your oldest son could have just stumbled onto the fashion rage of the year."

"It does give you a certain flair, Joe," Rachel remarked unexpectedly.

Joe reddened beneath his grandmother's teasing. Coming from Rachel, who was not known for poking fun at the ridiculously absurd, the comment seemed all the more astonishing—almost like license for everyone to have a good laugh at Joe's expense, which they did.

As if properly cued, their muffled giggles erupted into uncontrollable mirth. Joe chuckled, too, with as much merriment as his wounded pride would permit. Twice, he mistook temporary lulls, when everyone was catching their breath, as an end to the ordeal, only to watch his family dissolve once more into outright chortling. Finally, though, they more or less exhausted themselves, and Joe moved to retrieve his clothes. He merely provided fodder for the fire, however, while trying to keep the sheet wrapped around him with one hand and balance the clothes with the other.

"Need some help?" Bonnie asked, with absolutely no intention of providing any.

"I've got it under control," Joe said, forgetting the shirts and underwear, settling for the collection of the ragged and faded blue jeans.

Finally, he gathered the duds, nodded to his family with an embarrassed grin and headed back across the road, leaving behind an accidental exposure of his backside in the process. It was too much for his family. They fell apart with laughter; a complete recovery was a long time in coming.

Later that night, Caroline came to her oldest son's room and privately admonished him for allowing the prank to get out of hand. "If it had been just your brothers and you involved, Joe, I'd think it's the funniest thing I've ever seen. And it was terribly funny, regardless. But Summer and Tom are daten now, and it's improper for them to be in situations like that."

"Mama!" Joe protested. "It was purely innocent. She didn't see a thing. None of the girls did. I mean nothen like that never crossed my mind or anybody else's for that matter."

"It's the principle of the matter," Caroline said firmly.

"Yes, ma'am," Joe conceded, suddenly conscious of his mother's cause for concern. A short laugh escaped him. "I suppose things used to be a lot less complicated when we were younger," he said.

"Oh, I don't know," Caroline replied. "The concerns were different, but things pretty much stay the same, Joe."

Mother and son thought about that idea for a long moment.

"By the way," Caroline said at last, "I agree with your sisters and your grandmother, son. The tobacco sheet did give you a certain flair. And it certainly put you in a somewhat new—if still familiar—light."

Joe rolled his eyes, and they laughed, genuinely and unencumbered. Then, they began to talk, something they had not done nearly enough as of recently.

CHAPTER 4

IN LATE JULY, THE three shallow wells and an old cistern on the Baker farm ran dry. The pump well, which supplied running water, dried up first. Two days later, Rachel lowered her water bucket into the older well beside the house and brought it up filled with silt and mud.

Along with their neighbors, the Bakers discovered every conceivable way to save water. Baths became a luxury, with the daily swimming forays becoming a substitute. Instead of skinny-dipping, however, Joe, his brothers and sisters, as well as Matt and Sam, often swam with all of their clothes on, using the river in place of a washing machine and a bathtub. Even Caroline and Rachel took a dip in the cool river water, considering their predicament the ultimate humiliation. To avoid the waste of flushing the toilet, which had to be filled manually every time it was used, the men did their business in the privacy of the fields. The women coordinated their calls of nature, so that one flush might take suffice for all.

"Never thought I'd say this, but it kind of makes me long for that old outhouse we tore down," Sam remarked one day, with a rare trace of disgruntlement in his voice. Even more than electric lights, indoor plumbing shone as the ultimate modern convenience in his estimation of things.

Twice a week, Matt went to the school and drew water from a new deep well, which was tapped into one of the world's largest underground aquifers. One day, Luke and he arrived several minutes after Bobby and Wayne Taylor, who were nowhere to be seen. Failing to recognize Bobby's pickup truck, Matt pulled his water trailer near the well, unhooked it from the truck and left Luke to fill it while he drove to the mercantile to buy tobacco twine.

Luke sat down on the trailer wheel, popped a plug of tobacco in his back jaw and began contemplating the dreaded prospect of returning to school in a few weeks. He would enter the eighth grade, having passed the seventh by the skin of his teeth.

While not exactly hating school, Luke did find learning a burdensome proposition. A large part of his problem was laziness. The idea of concentrating on nouns and verbs, sums and differences as well as dates and places bored Luke, especially on warm days when he preferred to be riding a tractor through the fields or working with his father. Even so, laziness was not entirely to blame for his poor grades. Every time he mastered one idea, such as learning the names and locations of all fifty states and their capitals, the teachers thrust something new at him, like all the countries in Africa or Asia—as if it mattered.

Still, even when he buckled down and tried to learn his lessons, the task was a chore. Numbers suddenly reversed themselves in his head. Sometimes, he groped for the meaning of the simplest of words. While refusing to admit it to anyone else, Luke suspected he was just a little bit dumb, a reasonable deduction he figured since all of his brothers and sisters were fairly smart. With six children in the family, one very well could have missed out when the brains were distributed.

Luke was considering all this when Wayne Taylor rounded the nearby corner of the school. Wayne halted at the sight of Luke, giving the boy a smug stare. Luke simply leaned back against the tank and resumed his thinking. Wayne was four years older than Luke. Since they barely knew each other, the younger boy saw no reason to concern himself with Wayne's presence.

Wayne sauntered over to his water tank, checked to make sure the hose was still secure and then turned to regard Luke. With his bully instincts, Wayne could not resist this opportunity to scare the daylights out of some little ignoramus, especially when the mutt's last name was Baker.

"Hey, baby Baker boy!"

Wayne's call jolted Luke back to reality, setting off warning bells in the process. But he refused to cower.

Like Wayne, Luke carried a tough reputation, although not an ounce of bully in him. While Luke fought more often than necessary, he did so only when he felt he had been dealt with unjustly or when someone else, who could not take up for himself, had been treated cruelly.

Without batting an eye, Luke sprayed the ground with a stream of tobacco juice and allowed his eyes to wander lazily toward Wayne.

The show of disinterest annoyed Wayne. "I'm talken to you, baby Baker," he said with force.

"Am I supposed to be impressed?" Luke replied finally, feeling victorious in the initial parry.

"You will be, smart-ass, if you know what's good for you," Wayne hissed. He took a couple of steps toward Luke, then stopped and crossed his arms with a great show of superiority. "There's somethen I've been meanen to ask you Bakers for a long time. Now seems as good as any."

Luke's pride forced him to respond, ignoring his own good sense to avoid the challenge in Wayne's voice. "What's that?" he asked in his toughest tone.

"How come y'all are such nigger lovers, baby Baker?" Wayne asked. "The whole bunch of y'all coddle up to that uppity Lucas Bartholomew like worms in a rotten apple. Next thing, you know, your women probably will run off with some colored man. Maybe you already have a little nigger girlfriend, Luke."

Fueled by insults the likes of which he had never heard, anger swelled like lava in Luke. He wanted to wrap his hands around Wayne's throat, then squeeze until he crushed the windpipe, heard the last breath seep out and felt the body go limp. Luke kept his fury below the surface, however, devoid of any emotion that would reveal the soulless rage in his heart.

"I could give you an answer, Wayne," he replied finally, "but it wouldn't do a bit of good. Everybody's knows you Taylors ain't got the sense God gave a cat to get out of the rain."

Wayne bristled at the ridicule, quickly advancing to within a few feet of Luke. "You watch your mouth, baby Baker, or I'll be on you like stink on manure," he threatened.

Luke rose slowly from his seat on the trailer wheel, sniffing the air. "I thought I smelled it," he said defiantly, with a disparaging grunt.

There was no doubt Luke would lose a fight with Wayne. Luke was small for his age, while Wayne could have held his own with most grown men. Still, Luke was prepared to fight if necessary, and he intended to leave his mark, even if he was battered black and blue in the effort.

Somewhat amused by the fire in the eyes of his young foe, Wayne unwittingly stifled his first impulsive rage, opting to wage a battle of words with Luke. "Calm down, baby Baker," he urged with exaggerated mollification. "I'm just curious. Your family's about the only real-life nigger lovers I know, Luke. Just answer my questions, boy, and I'll leave you to your business with no harm done. First off, baby Baker, tell me, why your daddy cottons so much to Lucas Bartholomew."

Wayne paused, baiting the question with mocking silence, but Luke refused to take the worm.

"No answer," Wayne said a moment later. "You don't understand either, do you, Luke? There may be hope for you yet, baby Baker." He gave a disdainful snort, then continued. "I've heard all kinds of stories about you Bakers, Luke. Is it true that y'all let that nigger eat at your table? I even heard the whole bunch of you drink from the same glass in the tobacco field. Ain't you worried about catchen disease?"

Luke laughed shortly. "Wayne, that's about the stupidest, most ignorant thing I've ever heard in all my born days," he answered, the words rolling from his mouth with newfound clarity, sheer amusement and total disrespect. "First of all, son, my daddy don't cotton to nobody. Never has, never will. He just happens to respect Lucas. And so do I.

"Secondly, Lucas eats dinner with us sometimes," Luke continued. "He's even had a bite of supper on a few occasions, and breakfast, too. But you're wrong about us haven just one glass in the tobacco field, Wayne. We have two—both plastic, so they don't get broke—and we all drink from them. Every last one of us—my daddy, mama, grandpa, brothers, sisters, me, Lucas and anybody else who helps us gather tobacco and wants a drink of water. Nobody's ever gotten sick. And while we're at it, *Taylor, baby,* I'd a heap rather have Lucas at our dinner table or share a glass of water with him than with trash like you."

The verbal assault rendered Wayne into temporary do-nothingness.

"Now then," Luke added, pressing the upper hand. "Is your curiosity satisfied? Or did I speak too fast for you to take it all in?"

If nothing else, Wayne understood the fighting tone in Luke's impassioned defense of his family. With surprising swiftness, he rushed toward Luke with a clearly stated purpose. "I'm gonna beat the shit out of you, Luke Baker," he said. "And then I'm gonna beat some sense into you."

Luke blocked Wayne's first punch, but the bigger man grabbed his wrist, twisted it and threw Luke to the ground. In an instant, Wayne pounced on the boy, landing astride his chest, pummeling him with several quick slaps across the face.

Clearly, he held the advantage, but Wayne underestimated Luke's fighting spirit. In the very instant he slowed his attack, Luke landed a heavy punch on his right temple. The roundhouse blow stunned Wayne. In a flash, Luke wiggled free, gained his feet and exacted revenge with a flat-handed slap across his attacker's face.

"That's the price you pay," Luke declared with bared teeth.

Wayne rose slowly, more cautious now as he approached Luke for a second time.

His good sense urged Luke to turn and run. His pride made him hold his ground.

With determination and brute strength, Wayne overpowered Luke, first wrapping him in a suffocating bear hug, then jabbing his kidneys twice in quick succession. Luke gasped for air, then went limp, and Wayne hurled him backward.

Luke flew through the air in an arc, landing like dead weight against the dangerously jagged edge of the water trailer. A ghastly moan escaping him as the ragged steel gashed his back. Luke's eyelids fluttered, and he slumped to the ground in a nearly unconscious state.

"You're the one who's gonna pay," Wayne vowed, again stalking his victim.

Grabbing the boy by the hair, Wayne pulled Luke away from the trailer, flipped him onto his stomach and pinned him against the ground with the weight of his knee. The second vicious assault somewhat restored Luke's senses as Wayne grabbed him under the chin and pulled his head backward, blocking the boy's supply of oxygen. When Luke's arms flailed, Wayne momentarily released him, then repeated the chokehold a second time. Laughing scornfully, he released the hold again, then pushed Luke's face in the dirt and wrenched the boy's arm behind his back, again using his weight as leverage, applying enough twisting pressure to draw a loud groan from Luke.

Bobby heard the boy's first terrified cry. He witnessed firsthand the second scream. For a second, Bobby started to berate Wayne for picking on the small boy. Then, he recognized the kid and promptly changed his mind.

Instead of pulling his son off Luke, Bobby ambled over to his water trailer, pulled the hose from the overflowing tank and turned off the faucet. In his own sweet time, he finally went to see what needed to be done between the boys.

"Now here's an opportunity to teach you two boys a couple of important lessons," Bobby commented as he approached Wayne and Luke. "First off, never get in a scrap with somebody way bigger than yourself because it's almost always a losen proposition. Second, always press the advantage when you've got it, because you never know when you'll lose it." He paused, then asked casually, "Y'all understand what I'm sayen, boys?"

"Yeah, Pa," Wayne replied with enthusiasm. "I understand."

"Well then, Wayne," Bobby continued, "if you really do understand, then rub his face in the dirt a little bit and tell me what started all this."

"He called us scum, Pa," Wayne explained, grabbing Luke's hair with both hands and scrubbing his face across the rocky clay. "Said we were stupid and didn't have the sense God gave a cat to come in from the rain."

"Is that a fact?" Bobby asked with an exaggerated show of interest. "You're Matt Baker's boy," he remarked after a slight hesitation, a statement of fact rather than a question.

"He is," Wayne sneered. "I call him baby Baker boy."

"Which one are you, boy?" Bobby asked.

Luke was fully alert now, disbelieving the situation, taking note of his surroundings, praying for his daddy's quick return. "Luke," he answered.

"What makes you think we're stupid, Luke?" Bobby asked.

When no answer was immediately forthcoming, Bobby added, "A little pressure, please, Wayne. I'd really like to know why Luke here thinks we're stupid and don't have the sense God gave a cat to come in out of the rain."

Wayne wrenched the boy's arm again, and Luke screamed. "I don't know why," he wailed. "I just said it."

"It's not polite to call people names and spread lies about them, Luke," Bobby said with bad pretense of offended sensibilities. "Your parents obviously haven't taught you any manners. Maybe when Wayne's through with you, you'll think twice the next time you resort to name-callen and lies. Give him a little reminder, Wayne, about the importance of politeness."

Again, Wayne twisted the boy's arm, stretching the limb until Luke hollered and burst into tears.

"Oh, great scot," Bobby muttered, shaking his head with disgust as the boy cried. "Don't cry," he ordered. "Men aren't supposed to cry; only sissies do. And while you Bakers may be a lot of crazy things, I've never thought of any of y'all as sissies. Ease up, Wayne, and let little Luke catch his breath."

Luke willed away the tears, trying again to get his bearings. As much as it hurt, he could stand the pain. But he was scared nonetheless. The whole situation seemed unreal. Bobby Taylor and his idiot son obviously were warped beyond belief. For the first time in a long time, Luke prayed, silently pleading for his father's quick return, promising the Lord to do better in school, vowing to do all of his homework.

As Bobby resumed his interrogation, the boy's prayers vanished but not his fears.

"Luke, I know you're haven a hard time, but there's one other thing on my mind," Bobby said. "Do you like niggers, Luke?"

"He does, Pa," Wayne answered quickly. "He told me so. His whole family thinks that Lucas Bartholomew is just swell. They eat at the table with him. Drink after him, and who knows what else?"

"Is that so?" Bobby exclaimed, looking horrified by the revelation. "I've always figured your daddy was a nigger lover, Luke, and now it seems as if I was right all along. What do you say to that, boy?"

"I say let people think what they want," Luke replied, quoting an oft-used phrase by his father.

"Sounds to me that's the same thing as sayen Matt Baker is a nigger lover," Bobby said. "But just to make sure there's no doubt about it once and for all, I want you to do somethen for me, Luke. Then Wayne and I will leave, you can fill up your water tank and we'll all forget this little unpleasantness ever happened. How does that sound?"

"Good enough, I reckon," Luke answered, hopeful the ordeal would end soon.

"Atta boy," Bobby replied. "Now, Luke, what I want is to hear from the mouth of the man's very son that Matt Baker is a genuine, bona fide nigger lover. Can you do that for me?"

"My daddy does his own talken," Luke replied, heartburn rising in his throat.

"That's fine and dandy, but your daddy ain't here right now, boy," Bobby said fiercely. "It just you, me and Wayne, and we don't got all day to wait."

Taking his father's reference to him as a signal, Wayne promptly inflicted another round of pressure on Luke's arm, eliciting another howl of pain from the boy.

Bobby kneeled in front of the boy. "Come on, Luke," he urged, his expression evil and his tone wicked. "Just say the words, boy. My daddy is a nigger lover."

Luke knew he was licked. Closing his eyes, he muttered the words for Bobby.

"That wasn't so hard now, was it?" Bobby said. "A little louder this time, though, please. I couldn't hear you quite as clearly as I would have liked."

"My daddy is a nigger lover," Luke said, the words clearly audible.

"Louder, Luke," Bobby coaxed, like a crazy man. "Shout it at the top of your lungs, Luke; spread the good news. Tell the world the truth about your daddy, boy. Tell everyone what Matt Baker is."

"My daddy is a nigger lover," Luke repeated for a third time, then a fourth and a fifth as Wayne wrenched his arm.

"Thank you, Luke," Bobby said at last as if nothing extraordinary had occurred. "Let him go, Wayne."

Wayne obeyed his father, delivering one last vicious twist of the boy's arm before he released him, then scampering away as Luke lay motionless, his spirit broken.

"Oh, there's just one more thing," Bobby remarked suddenly as he started to walk away from Luke. He turned on his heels and ordered, "Look at me, Luke Baker."

Luke struggled to his back, too frightened to ignore Bobby's demand.

"I wouldn't mention this little episode to anyone," Bobby suggested. "I've heard all the talk about you, son. People already think you're none too bright. Nobody would believe your word against mine—not even your family. They'd just think you were maken up lies. And you can bet your bottom dollar, boy, that it would cause a heap of trouble for your daddy. You keep that in mind now—you hear me?"

"You hear me," Bobby repeated, this time making a statement as he turned and walked away from Luke.

———

From his vantage point as he turned the pickup into the school's parking lot, the first thing Matt saw was Luke's crumpled form lying on the ground. By the time he slid the truck to a stop, Luke had achieved a sitting position against the trailer tire and was wiping away a mixture of dust and tear stains from his face. Several yards away, Bobby Taylor was berating his oldest son, holding Wayne by the shirt collar and shaking him as he yelled at the boy.

"Son, I've told you one too many times about picken on people smaller than you," Bobby hollered as Matt exited the truck. "Don't you have any sense at all? You know the difference between right and wrong."

"But he started it, Pa," Wayne howled as Bobby twisted his ear. "He jumped on me. I was defenden myself."

"What's goen on here?" Matt asked, moving protectively toward his son as Luke managed to pick himself off the ground.

"I don't rightly know, Matt," Bobby replied. "When I got here, they were goen at each other like cats and dogs. That son of yours is a feisty one to be so small," he added, interjecting a touch of praise. "I just now got 'em broke apart."

Matt regarded Bobby with marked skepticism. Faced with the same situation, he would have given the benefit of doubt to almost any other man. With Bobby, however, he could not help wondering if the man himself had thrown a blow or two against Luke. Instead of accepting Bobby's explanation at face value, Matt turned to the one person he trusted for the truth.

"What happened, son?" he asked Luke, unaware of the full extent of the boy's pain, especially the bloody gash on his back.

Before Luke could answer, Wayne offered his version of events. "He called me and my pa, stupid," Wayne said in a disrespectful tone. "Said I was trash, too. When I told him to shut up, he came at me."

Matt recognized his youngest son had a temper like a keg of dynamite, as well as a short fuse. However, Luke tended to fight only when he had provocation. Considering who was involved, Matt figured it was more likely that Wayne had taunted Luke into a fight. Still, Matt wanted to hear what his son had to say about the situation.

"Luke? What happened, son?"

Luke stared wildly at Wayne, then at Bobby. "More or less like he said," he shrugged at last. "I wouldn't exactly call it self-defense, and he left out a few of the more important details—like how he walked over here while I was minden my own business, insulted me, you, the rest of the family. But hey, that's pretty true to character for Wayne Taylor. He's good about forgetten the really important facts. And everybody knows he's quick to pick a fight when the odds are stacked in his favor."

"You little liar," Wayne said accusingly, making a sudden move toward Luke, then stopping cold when Matt stepped in front of his son.

"Listen, Matt," Bobby said with utmost seriousness. "My boy ain't perfect. I'm willen to admit that. But Wayne's no liar. If he said Luke started it, then it must be so."

Luke laughed bitterly, clearly disrespectful of Bobby's opinion on the subject.

Matt sent him a hard look, suggesting the boy keep quiet, and Bobby picked up on the moment.

"Now that's a fine way to act," Bobby said self-righteously. "I don't let my children treat their elders like that, Matt. I've heard the talk about Luke. He's hardheaded, no doubt about it. You'd better do some disciplinen, or you're gonna have problems down the road."

"Don't tell me how to raise my son, Bobby Taylor," Matt retorted. "I don't know everything that happened here, but I know my son. He doesn't fight without cause. I'd be willen to bet your nonsense is at the bottom of all this in one way or another."

"Always have an excuse, don't you, Matt?" Bobby shot back, the tension clearly escalating between the two men. "You and your kind think you can do whatever you please because you're always right. Well, let me tell you this, Matt Baker: Sometimes you're flat out wrong. And you and your holier-than-thou attitude make me sick."

Anger flashed in Matt's eyes, but he checked his rage.

Sensing his foe's reluctance to engage in a protracted battle of wills, Bobby grabbed Wayne by the shoulder and pushed his son toward the truck. "Come on, boy," he growled, glaring one last time at Matt. "It's beginnen to stink around here too much for me."

When they were gone, Matt turned his full attention to Luke. "Are you okay, son?" he asked, inspecting the boy's skinned face and busted lip, then noticing blood on the ground. "Where'd all this blood come from?"

Recalling Bobby's earlier promise of trouble for Matt if he divulged the details of the fight with Wayne, remembering the sharp words between the two men just moments earlier and aware of the long-simmering ill will between the two families, Luke opted to conceal the worst of his injuries even though his back was soaked and sticky with blood.

"He busted my mouth," he lied. "It bled a lot, but it's okay now."

Matt accepted the explanation. Except for looking slightly ashen and skinned on the face, Luke appeared reasonably well. "Tell me what happened, son," he said. "Everything."

"Wayne started it, Daddy," Luke said. "He called us nigger lovers and stuff like that. You know all their tough talk. I said somethen back, called him stupid or somethen like that. And then he came at me."

Luke hesitated slightly, almost as if he were holding back details. "We just fought," he added, subdued. "That's all there was to it."

"What did he do to you?" Matt asked.

Ignoring the throb in his back as well as his wobbly knees, Luke gave a sanitized version of events. "Nothen too bad," he said. "Twisted my arm, slapped me around and rubbed my face in the dirt. But I'm okay, Daddy. Don't worry anymore about it."

Matt felt uneasy. "Are you sure you're not leaven anything out?" he pressed. "Is there anything else I should know?"

Again, Luke hesitated.

"No, sir," he said finally with a shake of his head. "I'd just like to forget all about it, Daddy. It's over and done with, and I'm okay. If you don't mind, let's keep this between us."

The boy sounded entirely unconvincing, and he avoided looking at Matt. In fact, the whole situation troubled Matt. Nevertheless, he grudgingly decided against pressing the issue. While he sensed this was no ordinary scuffle between boys, Matt also believed Luke had his reasons for wanting to keep quiet about the argument. He wanted to give his son the opportunity to think for himself, to begin making the decisions that would turn the boy into a man. If Luke needed guidance, Matt hoped he would seek it.

"What happened here stays between us, son," he promised. "As long as you want it to."

"Thanks, Daddy," Luke said with a relieved smile. "Come on. Let's get the water."

The fact that he lied to his father troubled Luke almost as much as the bizarre run-in with Bobby and Wayne. Matt and Caroline had instilled in their children the virtues of honesty, compassion, courage, patience and perseverance. Except for falling short where his schoolwork was concerned, Luke had lived up to their expectations.

In the aftermath of the fight, Luke's values worked against him, especially his parents' teaching to respect his elders. While he had privately questioned the motives and smarts of some grown-ups, Luke had never openly challenged the merits of anyone he considered an adult. So even though he suspected Bobby Taylor had a few loose screws in his character, Luke felt enough trepidation to withhold a full accounting of the events between the Taylors and himself.

Luke truly believed Bobby was a tad crazy, and he thought people should know. Unfortunately, his own reputation lacked credibility, forcing Luke to give serious consideration to Bobby's prophecy that people would question the boy's motives if he dared to claim harassment by a respected man whom the county had almost twice elected sheriff. Indeed, the entire episode seemed farfetched enough that even Luke wondered if perhaps he was overreacting and misjudging the situation.

In his confusion, Luke tried to forget the strange affair. First, he focused on the jagged gash in his back. Somehow, his blood-soaked clothes escaped everyone's attention. He threw away the soiled clothes and tried unsuccessfully to doctor himself before finally seeking Bonnie's assistance.

Resorting to another lie, he told Bonnie that he had fallen on a piece of farm equipment and wanted to hide the injury from their parents, fearing they might deem him too young for the job. It was the perfect excuse for his little sister, who complained constantly that she was too young for anything.

Still, Bonnie could not help Luke cope with the unease he felt regarding Bobby Taylor. He wanted to tell his father, almost did once. But then a new fear entered his mind, a suspicion that if he revealed the truth, he would succeed only in creating more problems for Matt. Luke understood the drought's devastation on his family's livelihood. He had watched the worried look in his father's eyes at the beginning of summer glaze over with despair as the rains held off. Matt continued to work doggedly in hopes of salvaging a small portion of success, even as one neighbor after another plowed up their pitiful crops, but Luke knew they were ruined. And with his father already burdened, Luke refused to trouble him further, especially with something so seemingly inconsequential.

Only it was not inconsequential, and as much as Luke wanted to forget the situation, his better judgment refused to put the matter out of mind. The pressure became more than he could handle. First, he felt as if he had betrayed his father and family. Soon, however, he began to resent Matt and everyone else for putting him into the situation in the first place. He became moody, sniping at his brothers and sisters and uncharacteristically defying his mother when she gave him a chore to do. For the disobedience, Matt whipped him, letting Luke know that he was "not too big for his britches, yet."

The punishment embittered Luke. He had taken great pains to spare his father more headaches, and Matt had rewarded his good intentions with ten hard licks with the belt, leaving welts on the boy's backside.

The stress and strain finally became more than Luke could take. After an exhausting day in the tobacco field, he became physically ill. The day had been dreary for everyone but disastrous for Luke. Beginning before dawn when he accidentally snagged a tractor on the barn, ripping the door off its hinges, everything he touched fell apart, including the harvester, which refused to crank after Luke choked it down at mid-morning.

He spent the rest of the day trudging through the field with his brothers and Tom, cropping the tobacco on foot and piling it onto sleds, which his father and grandfather pulled from the field with tractors. At noon, they ate in the field—bologna sandwiches on stale bread, seasoned with their tar-stained hands. The afternoon brought more sleds, and supper was a repeat of dinner. They worked until eleven that Friday night, hanging the last tobacco stick in the barn by the glow of a small floodlight.

Luke collapsed in bed shortly after midnight. He woke less than an hour later, vomited on clean sheets and spent the remainder of the night with his head hung over the commode, while his mother kept a close watch on his fever.

The next evening, Luke realized he had to unburden his troubles. This conclusion came as he lay in bed, recuperating from his sickness under the watchful eyes of Caroline and Rachel.

After supper, he slipped out of bed and went to see Joe. "Where you goen tonight?" he asked after entering the closed room without warning.

"Can't you knock before you barge in a room?" Joe shot back, not even bothering to look his brother's way.

Luke waited while Joe pulled on his blue jeans, tucked in his shirt and began combing his hair. "Sorry to bother you," he said finally, when Joe showed no interest in talking to him. "I was aimen to talk to you about somethen, but it can wait."

The doleful tone of Luke's voice reminded Joe of some melancholy time in his own past. He laid down the comb, giving his full attention to the boy. "Hey, little brother," he said, "I didn't mean to sound so princely. You know you don't have to knock on my door. It's always open. What's on your mind?"

"See this," Luke answered, turning his back to Joe and lifting his T-shirt to display the crooked slash on his back.

"Good Lord, Luke!" Joe exclaimed.

The wound, which had turned flaming red on the sides, oozed puss and held a lousy scab.

"What in tarnation happened?" Joe asked.

"I got in a fight," Luke replied.

"Another fight, Luke?" Joe groaned. "You should have told somebody, and you should have seen a doctor. I bet you needed stitches, and I know your back's infected."

"Daddy knows about the fight—but not about my back," Luke revealed. "We decided to keep the fight between us. Bonnie knows about my back—but not the fight. She's been doctoren me."

"Remind me to tell her not to consider nursen as a career," Joe muttered. "What in the world has she been usen to doctor you?"

"She used Merthiolate at first," Luke answered. "But that hurt worse than the cut itself. Since then, she's been putten new bandages on it for me. I was hopen it would get better by itself."

Joe rolled his eyes. "Not one of your better thoughts," he said. "Take off your shirt and lie down on my bed. I'll be back in a second."

Joe left the room, returning quickly with a bottle of peroxide, gauze, tape and a tube of salve. Using his fingers, he pressed against the inflamed sides of the wound to drain the festering puss, wiping away the yellow fluid with gauze.

"Is that gonna burn?" Luke asked as his brother prepared to pour peroxide on the wound.

"It may tickle, but it won't burn," Joe promised. "Peroxide kills the germs. It boils out the infection."

After the peroxide bubbled for several minutes, Joe wiped away the liquid, put salve on the infected area and covered the cut with a large bandage. "Well, I don't know if Dr. Pittman would approve, but that's better than nothen," he said, putting the last piece of tape in place. "We'll check it tomorrow. If it's still bad come Monday, though, you'll have to see the doctor."

"It sure beats Merthiolate," Luke muttered as he came to a standing position.

"Now I want answers," Joe said abruptly, purposefully, crossing his arms. "Why so secretive about a fight, Luke? Who did you fight? And how did that happen to your back?"

"It was with Wayne Taylor," Luke answered.

Joe grabbed his brother by the shoulders. "Wayne Taylor! He did this to you?"

"I don't think he meant to hurt my back," Luke replied. "He pushed me, and I landed against that jagged edge on the water trailer."

"Wayne Taylor is two, no, three times your size, Luke," Joe said forcefully. "Daddy knew you were in a fight with him. What did he say about all this?"

"He came up after everything was over and done with," Luke answered. "He and Bobby Taylor had words over it. There's no love lost between them. I didn't want any more trouble, so I decided to keep quiet about my back."

"This sounds awfully strange, Luke," Joe remarked. "What started it?"

Like some gossipmonger who had held his tongue too long, Luke spewed forth the details of his beating at the hands of Wayne Taylor and his father. In the middle of his confession, the boy's broken spirit crumbled, and Joe understood the despair and humiliation of his brother. Against his will, Luke cried, a stream of low, anguished sobs that built in crescendo until Joe wrapped the boy in a protective embrace and buried Luke's head against his chest. Soon, the tears dissolved to hiccupping sobs, then disappeared altogether.

When he felt Luke nod against his chest, Joe released his brother and gestured him to sit on the bed.

"Feel better?" he asked, dragging his desk chair in front of Luke and taking a backward seat in it.

Luke nodded his head. "I cried in front of Bobby and Wayne, too," he admitted. "Bobby told me to be quiet. He said only sissies cry."

"Hogwash," Joe shrugged.

"I know that," Luke replied. "Bobby also said that while he doesn't think much of Baker men in general, he doesn't think of any of us as sissies."

"Somehow, that doesn't make me feel any better about any of this," Joe said. "Finish tellen me what happened, Luke."

His fears vanished, his anxieties purged, Luke rushed through the remaining details of the assault. Joe listened with keen interest, concealing his shock, yet finding the story so freakishly truthful that none of it could be discounted to his brother's imagination. Joe had always considered Bobby a bigoted huckster who managed to disguise his ghoulish ways with clever tricks. This black-hearted side of Bobby was a new revelation. The man's obsession with the color bar had caused him to cross the wrong side of the so-called thin line between sanity and insanity.

Still, like his youngest brother, Joe had few dealings with crazy men to help him put the situation into its proper context. Despite their faults, most people were decent at the core, and Joe refused to rush his declaration of Bobby Taylor as deranged. Had there been no history of ill feelings between the Bakers and the Taylors, Joe would have gone straightaway to his father for a discussion. The past, however, persuaded him to resist his first impulse in favor of some rational thought about the problem.

"Do you ever wish that Daddy and Lucas weren't such good friends?" Luke asked suddenly, breaking Joe's train of thought.

"What?" he asked, frowning at his little brother.

"Maybe we *are* nigger lovers," Luke said. "The Taylors aren't the only people who think that way. I've heard other people say almost the same thing, maybe not in those words, but the meaning was there. Daddy does tend to be all high and mighty about treaten colored people fair and all."

Joe chose his response carefully, understanding Luke's confusion, yet wanting to impress upon the boy the importance of the matter. "Frankly, Luke, I've never thought of Daddy as acten high and mighty about anything," he said. "Our father is simply a good, honest man who believes in treaten everyone he meets fairly and squarely. He doesn't like to see anyone mistreated, and he'll stick up for anyone he thinks is getten a raw deal. Daddy's a true friend, Luke. I try to be just like him in my dealens with people. I've always thought you were that way, too."

Joe eyed his brother closely, receiving a nod of understanding in response. Then he continued. "I would hope that erases any doubts you have about your daddy or your family, Luke, but I'll also say one more thing. If we are nigger lovers, then we're a poor excuse for them. When you get right down to it, Lucas is the only black friend Daddy has—unless you count Beauty and the children."

"What about Choopie, Red and Miss Reba?" Luke asked. "They're always out here asken if they can fish."

"I guess you could call them friends," Joe replied. "To tell you the truth, though, they were mainly hired hands back in the days when Daddy and Grandpa needed help gatheren tobacco. Whatever, they're good people, Luke. That's what matters most. Don't begrudge them a few fish."

"I don't," Luke replied. "And I'm glad Daddy's friends with Lucas. I'm glad I'm friends with Lucas. When you get right down to it, he's almost like family. I can't remember a time when he wasn't around here in one way or another."

Joe smiled, remembering just such a time.

Luke shrugged. "Why are people prejudiced?" he asked.

"I couldn't begin to answer that one, Luker," Joe responded sincerely. "I think everybody's prejudiced in one way or another. It's human nature. Prejudice is about a lot of things, Luke—things you don't understand yet, things I don't understand, things Daddy doesn't even understand. I don't think there'll ever be a solid line between right and wrong on this subject, but the heart of the matter is whether you believe people deserve a fair shake in life."

"Not everyone gets that," Luke supposed.

"No, they don't," Joe said. "For a number of reasons—not all of them bad, I think. Some people are mistreated plain and simple. Some people lose out to circumstances. Some people just waste their opportunity."

"You're pretty smart, Joe," Luke remarked abruptly.

Joe laughed heartily. "Hardly," he replied. "Maybe I've thought about this longer than you have, but mostly, I'm maken it up as I go. Sometimes, I think that's all you can do."

"Did you ever get beat up because of what you believe?" Luke inquired.

"Not particularly," Joe answered. "But I've had a few disagreements in my time. I'll probably have a few more."

"Was it the right thing to do—not tellen Daddy everything about the fight?" Luke asked.

"I hope so, I think so," Joe said. "In his frame of mind, Daddy might just have turned that into an opportunity to get rid of his frustration. If he knew what that man did to you, Luke, Daddy would kick Bobby Taylor from here to yonder. And that's the last thing we need to happen around here."

"It's helped talken to you about it," Luke replied. "Just getten all of this out of my system makes me feel a whole heap better, although I ain't none too happy about getten the starch beat out of me."

"A little humility never hurt anyone," Joe said lightly.

"You sound like Granny," Luke commented.

"I'll take that as a compliment," Joe responded. "In any case, let's watch that back closely. I'll leave the salve and everything else in here, and we can doctor the cut some more tomorrow."

"Thanks, Joe. It's good to know you can talk to someone and know everything will stay between you and them."

"Right here in this room," Joe smiled, abruptly changing his grin to a mischievous glower. "Now get out of here. I have to finish getten ready, so I can go rescue damsels in distress. If I get lucky, one of them might relieve some of mine."

———

The Tip-Toe Inn was a genuine honky tonk. Set in the middle of nowhere on the road between Cookville and Tifton, the tavern had a notorious reputation as an abode for drunken husbands, worldly women and other lost souls.

To accommodate their varied patrons, the owners, Butch and Cassie Griffin, offered a broad mix of music, pool tables, beer and booze. Sometimes, the Tip-Toe Inn featured a live band, but the regulars preferred to pop nickels into an old jukebox. Names like Hank Williams, Patsy Cline and Skeeter Davis dominated the playlist, but some surprising selections made the cut as well. Songs like *Poor Side of Town* by Johnny Rivers, *When a Man Loves a Woman* by Percy Sledge and *House of the Rising Sun* by the Animals occupied slots in the music box because they touched the right emotions at the right time of night, when the distinction between country and rock and roll could not be made and nobody cared.

The chrome music machine was an oddity in an otherwise dreary establishment, with dark corners, pale lights and dusty wooden floors. The sprawling, ramshackle roadhouse had evolved from a one-room block building that the Griffins had built in 1960, the year the county legalized beer, wine and liquor sales.

Plunked right on the county line, the liquor store and tavern provided a profitable living for the Griffins. Over the years, Butch and Cassie had expanded the business to take advantage of the increasing trade from neighboring Tift County, which was bone dry but had some very thirsty residents who beat a steady path along Highway 125.

The couple operated their establishment with only one ironclad rule: Absolutely no fighting was allowed inside the building, and the owners had a diehard reputation for calling on the sheriff's office to enforce the rule when necessary. As for what happened outside, they cared little. The policy had served them well over the years, except on two occasions, once when a man was found stabbed to death outside the joint and another time when a drunken woman had stumbled into the path of an oncoming tractor-trailer.

Joe had begun frequenting the Tip-Toe Inn in the last few months before he turned twenty-one. On the first occasion, he had downed a few beers with friends, dropped a nickel into the jukebox to hear Patsy Cline sing and left with no intentions of ever returning. A few weeks later, however, some college buddies had persuaded him to join them for another outing, and he had fallen into the routine of dropping by on weekend nights for lighthearted fun, drinking beer, shooting pool and chasing women.

On this night, however, Joe came to the Tip-Toe Inn with rage festering in his heart, an anger that he stoked with beer and whiskey, oblivious to the evening's party atmosphere. Despite his assurances to the contrary when he advised Luke earlier in the evening, Joe believed his little brother had received an undeserved lesson in humility at the hands of Bobby Taylor and his overgrown son. He was eager to mete out the payback.

As usual, Bobby intended to drink a single beer, then leave. While he counted Butch and Cassie Griffin among his friends, Bobby preferred to avoid being seen at the Tip-Toe Inn. He never knew how his supporters, even the diehard tag-tails, would react to news that he frequented a bawdy roadhouse. Although he had no political aspirations or any other intentions at the moment, Bobby was never sure when a motive would arise.

With country music blaring in his ears, Bobby pushed his way through the crowd and found an empty seat at the end of the bar. "Busy night," he noted for Cassie when she brought him a beer.

"My cash registers are jinglen," she replied before moving off to slake someone else's thirst.

Bobby exchanged pleasantries with Butch, then huddled over his beer trying to keep a low profile.

At half after ten, Joe had glued his eyes to the tavern door, finally admitting he had come to the Tip-Toe Inn for one reason. On numerous occasions, he had observed Bobby sneak into the joint, drink a beer or two and then leave unnoticed. As soon as Bobby walked through the door, with his head down as usual, Joe spotted the man. Without bothering to watch Bobby complete his barroom routine, Joe turned away, killing the last half of his bottle of beer.

When sufficient time had passed for Bobby to feel at ease, Joe skulked his way through the throng of bodies until he stood behind the man. Squeezing against the wall, Joe gripped the man's left shoulder, while leaning down on the right side of the bar.

Bobby reacted with clockwork predictability, looking toward the hand on his shoulder, then jerking his head around to find Joe in his face. His eyes widened, panicky with instant awareness that Joe knew everything about the incident with Luke.

"Hi, Bob," Joe said caustically, his firm grip on the large tendon of Bobby's shoulder tightening into an uncomfortable hold. "Saw you drinken all by your lonesome and just couldn't stop myself from comen over to see what's new with you. How the heck are you, Bobby?"

Bobby rotated his shoulder, trying unsuccessfully to break the younger man's painful grip. "Get out of here, Joe," he advised. "You're drunk as a skunk."

"You betcha, Bob," Joe said, his face frozen with a feral grin. "For once in your miserable life, Bobby, you are right about somethen. I'm drunk—roaren drunk—and I'm ticked off, too."

He hesitated, frightening Bobby with his cold regard as well as sheer command of voice, his tone alternating between false cordiality and real menace. "Do you know why I'm ticked off, Bobby?" he asked.

"I have a pretty good idea," Bobby replied with forced casualness, "but your pa and I settled our disagreement the other day."

Joe groaned with disbelieving delight, then laughed scornfully at Bobby's feeble attempt to avoid the issue. "Maybe you did, maybe you didn't," he said, his tone again falsely cordial. "My daddy can take care of himself, and I'd never be presumptuous enough to fight his battles. That said, you'd better guess again."

"Listen, Joe," Bobby reasoned. "Maybe you think you got reason to be mad at me. Right now, though, you're drunk, and you're not thinken straight. Come see me when you sober up."

"Spare me!" Joe growled, his tone turning deadly cold. "Pretend ignorance. I know it comes naturally. But while you're at it, Bobby, I'll go ahead and tell you why I'm not thinken straight tonight.

"Somethen happened to my little brother, Bobby," he continued, leaning closer, almost eyeball to eyeball. "Seems like he ran afoul of one crazy man and his dimwitted son. They nearly broke his arm. His back has a four-inch gash in it from where somebody shoved him against a piece of jagged steel."

Joe hesitated again, narrowed his eyes, becoming even more ominous. "Bad stuff for a kid to face," he declared. "But you know what upsets me most, Bobby?" He waited, then answered: "They messed with my baby brother's mind. I'm not pleased about that. Someone is gonna pay."

"You're talken like a crazy man, Joe Baker," Bobby said defensively, his voice quivering slightly. "I don't know the first thing about any of this."

"Come outside, and I'll do a much better job explainen myself," Joe vowed.

"Leave me alone, Joe!" Bobby pleaded. "I'm just sitten here minden my own business, and I don't want no trouble. You got no cause to bother me."

"You and your son should have thought about that when you went after my brother," Joe warned. "You can either come outside, Bobby, or we can take care of business right here."

"Listen, Joe," Bobby tried again, still believing he could reason with the man.

Joe cut him off. "That's all I care to hear from you," he said.

Joe grabbed Bobby by the nape of his hair, twice pounding the man's face into the bar in quick succession. The first blow shattered Bobby's nose; the second split his lip.

Oblivious to the splatter of blood on his shirt, Joe picked Bobby off the stool, slammed him against the wall and buried his shoulder against the man's chest. The impact knocked the breath from Bobby. Joe followed with three rapid jabs in the pit of his stomach, then back-handed his victim across the face, once for good measure, then straight up for Luke.

As far as Joe was concerned, his mission was completed. Bobby was limp, dangling at the end of Joe's fingers, supported only by the firm press of his head against the wall.

Unable to read his mind, however, nearby onlookers interpreted Joe's position as a sign of more violence to come. Two men quickly grabbed Joe, pulling him from Bobby. With no one to hold him up, the unconscious man buckled at the knees and tumbled to the floor.

"My god! Why'd you go and do a thing like that," Cassie Griffin yelled at Joe.

As soon as Joe had bashed Bobby's head against the bar, Cassie had yelled for Butch to call the sheriff. She had leapt over the bar and was kneeling beside Bobby.

"Just settlen business," Joe replied.

"He's out cold," she determined, examining the battered man. "I think his nose is broken. Blood's getten all over the floor. Somebody bring me towels!"

Joe shrugged off the two men, walked over to the bar and asked a waitress to bring him a beer.

"No more beer for you!" Cassie screamed. "You'll be talken to the sheriff as soon as he gets here. I expect you'll be spenden the night in jail, mister. If there's one thing Butch and I don't tolerate, it's fighten in our establishment. You've been comen here long enough, Joe, to know that."

Cassie's disclosure about the sheriff's pending involvement brought the first tinge of regret to Joe. His remorse was short-lived, however, smothered by conviction that he had given Bobby Taylor his just rewards.

Joe believed matters had been settled between the Taylors and Luke. And he took real satisfaction in having slapped the arrogance out of Bobby. He decided to enjoy the moment while it lasted—understanding full well there would be hell to pay later.

————————

By the time the flashing blue lights of the law arrived at the Tip-Toe Inn, Bobby had regained consciousness and ridded himself of the grogginess. He held a bloodied towel against his broken nose, while maintaining a watchful eye on Joe and weighing his options. His contemptuousness urged Bobby to make Joe pay dearly for his actions. The smarts in him advised to pretend nothing had happened and forget the matter. His savvy suggested to wait and see before making a final decision.

Bobby watched gleefully as one of Paul Berrien's deputies handcuffed Joe behind the back, pushed him to the patrol car and shoved him into the rear seat. Joe's head smacked the car roof as the deputy pushed him, and he nearly buckled from the force of the blow. Bobby almost laughed with delight as Joe staggered into the car, clearly with the surliness knocked from him.

When Joe was locked in the car, the deputy questioned Bobby and offered him a ride to the hospital to have his nose examined. Bobby was patient with the questions and gracious in accepting Cassie's assistance to the patrol car.

The deputy was a big, beefy man named Mack, with large hands and elephant-like facial features. He was also a stickler for rules and regulations, refusing to allow Bobby to ride beside him in the front seat, insisting he sit in back with Joe.

"But he just tried to kill me!" Bobby protested.

"He can't do anything to you now because I got him handcuffed," Mack explained. "I got regulations to follow, Bobby. You either sit in the backseat or find another way to the hospital."

"I oughtta go to Tifton instead of Cookville," Bobby muttered.

"Makes no difference to me," Mack replied sourly. "But if you go with me, you gotta ride in the backseat."

"I don't think you need to worry about him anymore," Cassie assured Bobby, her soothing voice failing to conceal an impatience to return to business as usual.

Disgruntled, Bobby climbed into the backseat and found himself locked in the car with Joe. "You'll be sorry for this, Joe Baker," he vowed, pressing a fresh handkerchief against his bleeding nose. "You're goen to jail—maybe to prison."

"I don't think so, Bobby," Joe replied, his tone full of unsettling aloofness.

"Well you oughtta think so," Bobby challenged. "I intend to see that every charge in the books is thrown at you."

"The way I see it, Bobby," Joe interrupted, "if you press charges, then the whole ugly story will come out—every last stinken detail. And if it does, I don't think there's a person in the county who would begrudge me for one minute."

"Y'all hush up back there," the deputy ordered as he entered the car.

He pointed a long, fat finger at Joe through the rearview mirror. "You can count on facen charges," he said. "Cassie and Butch already said they want 'em filed."

Mack cast an imposing impression, despite his stiff-necked approach to the situation. He wore a large brown hat, a permanent scowl and a resounding aura of authority. Joe obeyed his order, still confident he could force Bobby to persuade the Griffins to drop all charges, assuming he had an opportunity alone with his foe. The opportunity came at the hospital, where Mack needed several seconds to walk around the car and open Bobby's door.

"Bobby, you listen to me and listen good," Joe demanded, speaking quickly as soon as Mack exited the car. "You or no one else better file any charges against me. If my daddy finds out what you did to Luke, he'll beat you a whole lot worse than I did. And I wouldn't doubt there'd be a long line of other fellows right behind him—waiten for a turn of their own."

The back door opened, and the deputy ordered Bobby from the car before he responded to Joe. Still, Joe was confident of having made his point.

Bobby realized his dilemma, too. He never should have entangled himself in the skirmish between Wayne and Luke in the first place. Had he left well enough alone, Wayne would have pulverized the boy, and the matter would have been settled. But Bobby's ego had craved more than mere defeat for the Baker boy. He had wanted Luke to experience feelings of failure and worthlessness, to know the disappointed heart of a loser. In the final outcome, he had gotten what he wanted, however painful the ending was. While correctly assuming Luke would keep the secret safe from Matt, Bobby had failed to consider the possibility the boy would confide in his older brother. He could not afford an even bigger mistake by risking the episode to public exposure, simply to see Joe suffer.

"Come on and get out of the car," the deputy growled, impatient with Bobby's slow exit.

Joe and Bobby glowered at one another, like two gladiators who had just fought a battle rigged for only one outcome. Bobby knew he had been licked in the arena as well as in the back room, so he accepted defeat. He would have another opportunity to play the game, and the next outcome might be predicated on terms dictated by himself. Leaving Joe with a sneer, he stepped from the patrol car.

"Deputy," he said without even glancing at the lawman. "Is there a phone around here I could use before see'en the doctor? It's important."

"No problem," Mack grunted. "They'll fix you up inside."

"By the way," Bobby added, "I won't be pressen charges."

Those were the last words Joe heard before the door slammed shut.

———

Paul Berrien ran a tidy county. The Cookville jail rarely held prisoners, excepting the occasional drunkard, wife beater and men involved in disputes similar to the one between Joe and Bobby. It was a narrow, three-story, red-brick building, with a hanging gallows on the top floor. No one had swung from the gallows since the turn of the century, but the swing door still worked. Knotted oak trees shaded the jail by day, cloaked the building in darkness at night and fanned a few nightmares among prisoners in the dreary cells.

By the time the patrol car reached the jailhouse, Joe had sobered considerably and was trying to figure out how he could return to his car. The hour was late, and he hoped to avoid entangling his family in the situation.

Deputy Mack accompanied him into the front room, ordered Joe to sit and disappeared into an official-looking office. The deputy apparently forgot the handcuffs, which were biting into Joe's wrists. Joe sat on a worn office couch, waiting for his release.

In a few minutes, an inner office door opened, and the dispatcher emerged. Joe recognized the skinny young man with thick black glasses as Donald Peavy, a lifelong resident of Cookville, who had been a year behind Joe in school. Donald Peavy personified the pompous, self-centered, overbearing ways of the small-town people who looked down on country folk like Joe. Even worse, Donald tended to be patronizing with his sentiments. While he had never condescended to Joe, Donald had once dismissed the Carter's Mercantile as a "country-bumpkin operation with an awful and gaudy glass display of what's supposed to be fine treasures."

Joe had been glad that Tom had not overheard the remark, and he had crossed Donald Peavy off a mental list of people to pity because they wanted so desperately to be popular. Joe reserved the list for people with good hearts and good intentions, who needed their confidence boosted, not their egos stroked.

"By George, it is the Joe Baker I know," Donald remarked. "It just goes to show: Once a rooster, always a rooster." He winked at Joe. "I always thought you were too smart to get yourself into this kind of trouble," he added.

Joe kept mum.

"Oh, well, don't worry too much," Donald advised. "Cassie Griffin called a few minutes ago. Said she and her husband talked it over and decided not to press charges."

"Cassie called and said what!" Mack asked as he emerged from the office with fingerprinting equipment and a small camera.

"She said to let him go with a warnen this time around—and to tell him to keep away from their place," Donald explained. "You're a lucky one, Joe. I don't ever recall the Griffins deciden not to press charges."

Mack eyed Joe suspiciously, hating to waste good paperwork. "Somethen's fishy," he declared. "Cassie was hell-bent on assault and destruction of property when I was out there."

Pausing, he followed his reasoning with a direct question to Joe. "What were you and Bobby talken about in the car? What made you so cocky about not facen charges?"

"Nothen of consequence," Joe replied. "If there are no charges against me, may I go?"

"I want to know what you were talken about," the deputy declared. "Seems strange to have that much talken between two people who were at each other's throats moments earlier."

"We were just haven words," Joe said. "It wasn't important."

Mack sighed heavily. "Peavy!" he said. "Give the sheriff a call. Tell him we have a situation and need his help to sort through it. All this sounds mighty peculiar to me."

Any leftover semblance of bravado disappeared in Joe. His heart swapped places with his stomach. He had hoped desperately to keep Paul Berrien out of the matter, dreading the embarrassment it would cause, fearing it would create a conflict of interest. To make matters worse, the deputy abruptly decided Joe should spend the next few minutes locked in a jell cell. The only worse possibility was the specter of his family discovering the events of this night.

As Donald Peavy led him to the cell, Joe had a terrible feeling of having lost control of his life. And he wondered briefly whether Luke would judge his big brother very smart if he could see him now.

———

"Can you take off the handcuffs?" Joe asked when the cell door swung open.

"I don't have a key, but I'll tell Mack to come back and get them off you," Donald said, motioning his prisoner inside the steel bars. "Sorry about this, Joe," he added, sounding anything but.

Ignoring the gloat in the jailer's voice, Joe strode into the cell, trying to feign indifference as the steel door slammed behind him. He inspected the temporary arrangements wordlessly, waiting for Donald to exit, grateful that none of the other three cells were occupied. The cell had a sink and a commode, along with two stationary single beds, which contained thin rubber mattresses. He tested the mattress, then took to pacing in the tiny cage.

Joe supposed he should have used the opportunity to reflect on his motives, questioning whether he had erred in judgment. His mind was clear, however, and he had no regrets. Bobby Taylor had received everything he deserved. On second thought, the only thing he would have done differently was to have dragged Bobby to the parking lot before pounding the man.

The outer door opened again, and Donald came through it. He snapped his fingers. "I keep forgetten about those handcuffs, Joe," he said. "I'll get Mack. First, I wanted to let you know that I called your folks. I didn't want them worried about you."

"You didn't," Joe said in disbelief, gripping the cell door, pressing his face against the bars.

"Sure, I did," Donald said, grinning. "There's no tellen how long you're gonna be here. They needed to know."

Joe tightened his grip on the bars. "How considerate of you," he remarked flatly. "Thanks for your concern."

"You're welcome," Donald replied on his way out the door.

Joe checked his watch. It was well after midnight. The call would have woken up the whole house.

He plopped down on the couch, imagining the jangled nerves that would have taken flight with the late telephone call. Springing from their beds, their first fears would have been that Summer or he had been in a car wreck. Then, realizing that Summer had been home for almost two hours, they would prepare themselves for the worst—that Joe was dead or dying.

The one thing Joe could not imagine was his family's reaction to the news that he was in jail. He shook his head and waited.

Paul Berrien arrived at the jail a short time later. He listened to Mack explain the situation, then chastised the deputy for failing to release Joe. "When all the principles have agreed not to file charges, Mack, we don't have the right to hold somebody in jail just because you think somethen is fishy. You should have let him go. Since I'm here, though, I'll talk to him."

Paul found Joe slumped over on the cot. Joe had dozed off, sleep coming as the aftermath of too much beer and the lateness of the hour. He looked a mess, with bright bloodstains on his shirt and dark circles under his eyes. He smelled even worse, like a stale brewery.

A sympathetic pain tugged at Paul. As much as possible, Paul and his sisters doted on the Baker offspring, having realized many years earlier that the sons and daughters of Matt and Caroline were the closest they would come to caring for children of their own. In a way, Paul considered this moment an opportunity to have an important father-son talk with Joe

"Now this is a surprise," he began, opening the cell.

Joe's eyes popped open, clearly confused for a moment before focusing on Paul. He roused to an upright position on the cot, feeling the humiliation of his predicament like a balloon in the pit of his stomach, yet finding courage in the unassuming eyes of his father's best friend.

"I can't begin to tell you how embarrassed I am about all this," he replied.

"We all have moments we try to forget," Paul suggested.

"I don't think I'll ever be able to forget this one," Joe said miserably. "Your dispatcher called the house and let everyone know I was locked up down here."

Paul grimaced. "Now I really don't envy you," he said, mustering up a smile, then a frown at the handcuffs. "Sorry about the handcuffs. Mack gets carried away sometimes, but he's my best deputy. And Donald's very efficient with the office work."

He walked out of the cell to the hall door. "Mack!" he shouted. "Come back here and take off these handcuffs."

"Can't say I won't be glad to see them go," Joe muttered as Paul re-entered the cell.

Paul gave his young friend a warm smile, then pressed for details about the situation. "Joe, there's nothen in the law books that says you have to tell me what happened tonight or why you did what you did to Bobby," he began. "But I am mighty curious. This is unlike you, son. I have to figure you must've had a powerful reason to go after the man."

"Paul, I respect you enormously, and the truth is I'd like to tell you why," Joe replied. "In a way, I think it's somethen you should know, and maybe I'm maken a mistake keepen it to myself. But I have my reasons for stayen silent. My instincts tell me that's the best course for everybody concerned, at least for the time be'en."

"I can respect your reasons for wanten privacy, so I won't press you any further," the sheriff replied. "If you ever decide we need to talk, though ...."

"I won't hesitate to come see you," Joe finished the sentence for him. "In this particular case, you'd probably be the first person I'd go to, Paul. Honestly, though, I think it's a moot point at this time, so let's just leave it at that."

Paul gave the young man an obliging look of acceptance, admiring Joe's frankness. Few people had the wherewithal to be less than candid, without distorting the truth in the process. Still, he wanted to impress the seriousness of the situation.

"We'll do that," he said. "But Joe, I will say this: You need to understand that this whole mess could have blown up in your face. If somebody had pressed charges, you'd be in deep trouble. Next time you're in a similar situation, give it careful consideration before you act on an impulse."

"There was nothen impulsive about what I did, Paul," Joe replied honestly. "I did exactly what I meant to do to Bobby, and I won't apologize for that. Nevertheless, your point's well taken, and I appreciate the concern."

"You do have me curious about what inspired all this," Paul said with a smile, firmly patting Joe's shoulder to show the matter was settled as far as he was concerned.

At that moment, the hall door opened, and Mack entered the cellblock followed by Matt.

Although Matt appeared unperturbed, his calm demeanor failed to conceal the fury in his nearly black eyes. In moments of sheer anger, Matt's used his eyes to convey his feelings. He narrowed them slightly, ascertaining his position, then penetrating to the core like a drill.

As he came into the cellblock, Matt scanned the area, narrowed his focus to Joe's cell, then zeroed in on his son before casting a long glance at the handcuffs.

Unable to bear the scrutiny, Joe climbed to his feet, looking downward while the deputy removed the restraints.

No one said anything until Mack left the area and the door closed behind them. Finally, Joe forced himself to face his father, bracing for the inevitable first question by cracking his knuckles.

The popping joints infuriated Matt, who ground his teeth to keep from lashing out at his son.

"I hope you have a good excuse," Matt said finally, his voice even and straightforward. "But first, I want to know exactly what happened. Who did you fight?"

Joe hesitated, then answered, "Bobby Taylor."

"Bobby Taylor!" Matt muttered with disgust. "What on earth for?"

"Luke told me about the fight between Wayne and him," Joe explained. "I thought the odds were uneven, and I figured Bobby was the real culprit one way or another."

Matt already had revealed the details of the previous week's incident to Paul, so the revelation came as no surprise to the sheriff. He had guessed the fight triggered Joe. Still, many unanswered questions remained as to why Joe had taken it upon himself to jump into the middle of a dispute between two boys, even if one of them was the equal of a man in strength, while the other was pint-sized.

"There's got be more to it than that," Matt coaxed his son. "Tell me the rest."

"Nothen else to tell, Daddy," Joe replied. "Wayne Taylor pounded Luke pretty good, and Bobby didn't do anything to stop it. I thought he deserved to know firsthand what it's like when the fight's not fair."

"I think he got the message," Paul interjected.

Joe smiled briefly, then became serious again because his father was not amused by Paul's attempt to lighten the situation.

"I didn't mean for it to go this far, Daddy," he said, "and I'm sorry for embarrassen the family."

"Save the apologies for when you get home," Matt instructed, regarding his son with a quizzical stare.

"Yes, sir."

"Son, you didn't do any of this on my account, did you?" Matt asked.

"No, sir," Joe answered firmly. "I know you can fight your own battles."

"But you're not tellen me everything, are you?" Matt asked abruptly.

"Everything that matters," Joe said.

Matt glanced at Paul, who shrugged, suggesting the situation did not warrant further inquiry. Reluctantly, Matt agreed.

"I would have preferred the full story, Joe," he said, "but I'll trust your judgment."

Turning to Paul, he asked, "Is he free to go?"

"He's a free man," the sheriff replied. "He should have been released as soon as he was brought in. I apologize for the mistake in
procedure, Joe."

"I'm just sorry you got dragged out of the house for all of this,
Paul," Matt said before Joe could respond. "Maybe we can all go home
and get a good night's sleep."

"Sounds good to me," Paul replied as he led them from the cell.
"I'll see the two of y'all tomorrow—maybe at church in the
mornen."

"This one needs to be there," Matt said, gesturing to Joe, "but he
may not need a sermon by the time his mama and granny get through
with him."

The two older men laughed, but Joe failed to see the humor in the
situation.

A father did not punish his adult son, and Matt never considered such
a thing. He still remembered the search for good times in his own
youth, drinking too much and doing things he later regretted. As a
young man, Matt had been far from upright. As a soldier and later as
a young father, he had strayed even farther from proper behavior.

Liquor had tested Matt in his younger days, especially after the war
ended and Joe was born. Fortunately, Caroline had put her foot down,
issued an ultimatum and Matt had seen the light in time to spare his
family heartache. The transformation had not come overnight, of
course. For a long while, he had continued to drink beer from time to
time, even took a swig of whiskey on certain occasions. Long before
Bonnie was born, however, Matt came to the realization that he was
one of those men who should avoid alcohol.

Now, the thought crossed his mind that he should share the benefit
of his experience with his oldest son on their drive home. The words
failed Matt, however, as did his courage. A perfect father might have
offered good advice, but Matt was the first to admit he had paternal
flaws.

Besides, Matt also knew that any advice he offered would play second fiddle to Joe's own form of self-discipline. No one was harder on
the boy than himself.

With other people's shortcomings, Joe showed great tolerance, re-
sponding with patience, understanding and help when and where it
was needed. He gave encouragement instead of pity, offered advice

instead of answers, expected progress instead of perfection. With regards to himself, however, Joe eliminated some of the key elements of his tolerance. He expected himself to do the right thing, and he set exacting standards. If he failed to measure up to his or anyone else's expectations, Joe made amends where possible, then wrote his own prescription for comeuppance and took the medicine.

Matt attributed his quirky behavior to Caroline's influence. Caroline strove for perfection and fretted when she fell short of the mark. Over the years, however, his wife had come to an important understanding with herself. Some things mattered more than others, and Caroline had drawn the fine line between perfection and pickiness. She crossed that line rarely, only when the situation warranted an extra step.

Joe was still finding his way, aided immensely by his propensity for taking the reasonable route whenever possible. Still, when his way was difficult, the distinction between high self-expectations and impossible self-demands blurred. Sometimes, Joe got hung up on his mistakes. Usually, he made all the right moves.

Matt sensed this was one of those occasions when his son would right himself, take his punishment and move on without too much hesitation.

As it was, Matt was in a forgiving and understanding mood. Bobby Taylor boiled his blood, too. Still, Matt expected complete honesty from his children. While guilty himself of resorting to them on occasion, half-truths bothered Matt. He acknowledged that the search for the truth sometimes required compromise, but Joe had failed to demonstrate a compelling need for any concessions.

Matt believed his son was withholding a critical piece of information in this business with the Taylors and Luke.

Like Joe tonight, Luke had been nearly as evasive in his description of the altercation between the Taylors and himself. Obviously, the boy had been more forthcoming with his oldest brother. What had Luke shared with Joe that he refused to tell his father? Perhaps this missing piece of information explained Luke's bratty, bumbling behavior over the past few days.

Recalling his conversation with Luke in the schoolyard, Matt remembered feeling as if he should have pressed for more details. Sensing the boy's reluctance, Matt had settled for something less than a full explanation of the incident. Maybe he should have asked the one question that had been on his mind but remained unspoken: Had Bobby Taylor hurt his son in any way?

He fleetingly considered asking that question of Joe, dismissing the idea at once. The question would be unfair to Joe, to Luke, to the values Matt and Caroline had tried to instill in their children.

As a father, though, Matt had the responsibility to protect his children. If they were in danger, he wanted, needed and expected to know the full situation when at all possible.

He lit a cigarette, then told Joe, "The day Luke and Wayne fought, I had a feelen that somethen else happened, somethen Luke felt he couldn't tell me. Now I'm thinken you know what that is, Joe. I won't ask you to tell me everything that happened, or to break any promise you made to your brother. But, son, I am goen to ask you to let me know if I have any more cause for concern—if for nothen else than to ease my mind on this matter."

It was a loaded question, and Joe delayed his answer, lighting a cigarette as he developed a response. Joe believed the matter was settled for the moment. While he had some serious doubts about Bobby's mental stability, Joe also believed Luke faced no further danger.

"It's over and done with, Daddy," he replied finally, "or at least it's finished as much as anything is ever finished with Bobby Taylor. Rest easy. Don't worry about Luke."

Matt bit his lip. "If you say so," he said at length. "I'll trust your judgment."

As Matt and Joe bumped along the last stretch of dirt road in the pickup, the security light in front of their house came into view. Normally, the lamp's glow shone brighter, but a full moon had stolen some of its luster tonight. Joe felt kind of like that light, although it was impossible to blame his paled image on any natural occurrence.

As Granny often said when severe mistakes had been made, he had made his bed of roses. Now he would have to lie in it. Or as Grandpa said—when his mood was sincere and there was no trace of humor in his thoughts—the time had come for Joe to face the music and march into the cannon fire.

Joe dreaded the prospect of facing his family. He could explain the fight with Bobby Taylor. He could even persuade them to see the funny side of having been thrown in jail. But nothing he might ever say or do would make Caroline and Rachel understand about the Tip-Toe Inn.

Had he merely gone out and gotten himself into trouble while drinking alcohol, his mother and grandmother would have expressed grave disappointment and reprimanded him sharply. They also would have accepted his mistake, however, and Joe would have found forgiveness in their hearts.

To Caroline and Rachel, however, the Tip-Toe Inn represented a little bit of Sodom and Gomorrah right in the midst of their community. They despised the place. If misfortune befell a person in the Tip-Toe Inn, it was tit for tat. The two women had little sympathy for people who danced in the devil's den itself. They would make no exceptions for one of their own.

The sight of his mother pacing on the front porch confirmed Joe's worst fears as the pickup rolled to a stop in the yard. He sat in the truck for a minute, trying to find either a brave face or the true courage to accept her disappointment. Finally, his father mumbled something, the truck door opened and he prepared to face the inevitable.

Exiting the truck, he followed Matt up the concrete walkway, finding some consolation in the dark windows. At the worst, he would have to explain his actions only to Caroline, at least as far as this night was concerned. A good night's sleep, he decided, would allow him to function better when he faced everyone else.

Coming to the top porch step, Joe finally looked at his mother, honoring her with his most shamed expression. Her reaction was exactly as he anticipated. If Matt unknowingly revealed anger through his eyes, Caroline betrayed her rage with her mouth and nose. Her lips pursed, and her nostrils flared. Sometimes, she also tapped one foot nervously. At the moment, she seemed like a cow ready to charge.

The only saving grace was when Caroline twirled her wedding ring, a sign that his mother would reserve final judgment until she had heard all the facts. Currently, the golden band was whirling at double-time RPMs, giving Joe one last glimmer of hope.

He decided then for an aggressive approach to the situation. He would run into the battle instead of wait for the slaughter.

The up-front, free admission from Joe that there was no excuse for his behavior doused some of the fire in Caroline. His quick confession that tonight was not the first time he had frequented the roadhouse becalmed red-hot embers. His sincere apology left only the smoldering smell of smoke.

Caroline did not expect perfection of her children. Furthermore, she believed only imbeciles would hope for such a thing. The last years between youth and adulthood were fraught with seduction. Few people managed to avoid all of the temptations. Boys were particularly susceptible to wild ways, especially the sons of Matt Baker.

Caroline figured marriage had helped her avoid flirtation with the wilder whims of youth. Matt had found the path more treacherous to negotiate, and Joe was finding some seductions hard to resist, too. Caroline was not overly worried. If Joe followed his father's footsteps, he would become a good man. Still, the time had come for a course correction.

For some months now, Caroline had known Joe drank beer and maybe even whiskey. She first suspected the drinking late one night when he fumbled with the door. On another occasion, he had tripped coming up the porch steps, cursing and burping almost simultaneously. Caroline had started to nudge Matt from a deep sleep so he could check on their son, then changed her mind. Joe had carried around a hangover the next day, which he blamed on a bad headache. Later, she had smelled beer on his clothes when washing them.

Even as the evidence of drinking mounted against Joe, Caroline had held her reprimands. She understood he had to discover the allure of the world for himself. However, she also expected some sense of morality and decency to govern his actions along the way. Judging by his tawdry behavior, Joe obviously needed a stern reminder of these expectations. Caroline was ready to give it to him.

"It goes without sayen, Joe, that I'm extremely disappointed in you," she began when her son had given a complete explanation of his behavior and answered all of her questions. "I never once suspected you were goen into a common roadhouse and doen Lord knows what.

"None of us lead perfect lives, son," she continued. "It's impossible, especially when you sow some wild oats along the way. But there's a limit on the excesses to be taken from common decency. And, Joe, you have exceeded that limit tonight and every other night you've walked out of this house, gone to that tavern and come back with beer and whiskey in you. Your daddy and I will not tolerate that kind of behavior, or embarrassment and disgrace to our family."

Here, Caroline paused to give her boy an opportunity to consider the situation. Respect showed in his eyes. She had his full attention.

"You're a grown man, son," she continued, "and a good man, too—a few nights notwithstanden. It's up to you to choose the kind of life you will lead, Joe. But your daddy and I are still raisen children in this house, and I will not have them exposed to vulgar behavior. As long as you live in this house, you are expected to live by the morals and values your daddy, your grandparents and I have set for this family. If the time ever comes when you don't feel you can do that, then pack your bags and leave."

The finality stunned Joe as well as Matt. Caroline could tell her husband especially was irked with her. Still, she wanted Joe to understand her dim view of tonight's situation and his past extremes. In Caroline's opinion, mere disapproval lasted only until the next great temptation arrived. She wanted Joe to think more than twice the next time he considered a stunt like this one.

Joe scratched his ear, looked down at his feet and waited to see what else his mother had to say.

"Do we have an understanden?" Caroline asked.

"Yes, Mama," Joe said, smiling slightly.

"Good," she replied. "Now, I'm goen to bed. It's late, and tomorrow's a church Sunday. I'll expect you to be there with us."

"Yes, ma'am."

———

Joe picked his way through his brothers' dark room, nearly tripping on a pair of jeans and sneakers that had been left on the floor. Walking between the two beds, which flanked the entrance to his own niche in the house, Joe groped for the doorknob, found it and escaped into the privacy of his room. Shutting the door, he crossed over to his desk, flipped on a lamp and discovered all of his siblings piled on the single bed.

He groaned and turned around to empty his pockets on the desk. "Good news sure does travel fast," he muttered.

"Were you really in jail?" Bonnie asked, her voice full of disbelief, yet tinged with excitement.

"I was," Joe replied.

"What the heck happened?" Summer asked.

Joe sighed, wishing they would leave, knowing he had to offer an explanation. "The short version," he said. "I went to the Tip-Toe Inn tonight and had a little run-in with somebody. We argued. I hit him, and someone called a deputy who hauled me off to Cookville and put me in jail. Fortunately, no charges were filed, so I'm a free man. Now, if you please, I'd appreciate it if you guys would get the heck off my bed and let me go to sleep. It's late, and we have church tomorrow."

"Sounds like you'd better pay close attention to the sermon," Carrie teased.

"You're right, Carrie," Joe shot back. "I'd better pay close attention. Now get out!"

No one moved.

"Who'd you hit?" John asked.

Joe sat down in his chair and untied his shoes.

"Bobby Taylor," he answered at last, kicking off first one shoe, then the other.

His siblings were sufficiently shocked into silence.

"How on earth did you get mixed up with him?" Summer asked finally.

Joe saw Luke tense around the shoulders. "It was just one of those things," he said. "I'm not goen to explain it."

Everyone took him at his word.

"Were you drinken?" John asked a moment later.

"I've already covered that with Mama and Daddy," he replied.

"Well, were you?" John persisted.

"I had a few beers," Joe confessed.

"I think you've been doen too much of that lately," John observed.

Joe eyed Summer with suspicion.

"I haven't said anything to anybody," she said defensively. "Face it, Joe. You should be more careful with your wine and women."

Turning back to John, Joe said, "As I said, I've already covered that subject with Mama and Daddy." He took off his socks, then asked no one in particular, "Do Granny and Grandpa know anything about this?"

"The phone woke up everybody," Bonnie informed him.

"Granny's fit to be tied, but Grandpa told her she'd survive the scandal," Carrie explained.

"You know Grandpa with his, 'This, too, shall pass,'" Summer added.

"What did you mean by that crack about wine and women," John suddenly asked his oldest sister.

"Hey!" Joe said crossly. "This is not the time to pick apart my life."

"Has Tom ever gone with you to that place," Summer inquired, narrowing her eyes.

"Ask Tom!" Joe said, taking off the white shirt, now carrying dried bloodstains. "Get out of here, will you?"

"I *will* ask him," Summer said sharply. "Do you want me to soak that shirt in cold water for you?"

"No, I do not want you to soak it in cold water," Joe replied, exasperated by the conversation. "I'm gonna throw it away."

"Well, that's just plain ridiculous," Summer retorted. "A little cold water will take those stains right out of there. It'll be good as new."

Joe threw the shirt at his sister. "Then take it and soak it in cold water," he said slowly. "What is it with you people tonight? Can't you take a hint? I want y'all to leave. I want to go to bed."

"This is excitin stuff, Joe," Summer said. "It's not every day that a member of the family gets himself arrested and carted off to jail. We're in the middle of a full-fledged scandal, and you don't seem to have any interest in it at all. Do you realize all the gossip this will generate?"

Joe laughed, rubbing his face.

"I suppose you'll have a hangover tomorrow," Bonnie remarked.

"Of course not," Summer replied for Joe. "He'll simply have a *bad headache.*"

Joe gave up any hopes of persuading them to abide by his wishes, half wondering whether he had stepped into the twilight zone. He slipped off his blue jeans, then unceremoniously dumped enough siblings from his bed to make room for himself. "Get off my sheet, Bonnie!" he commanded crossly.

"Do you have a thing about taken off your pants in front of everybody?" Carrie asked.

"Just in front of girls, I think," Summer said innocently, rekindling John's interest in the conversation.

"I still want to know about the women, Joe," he said. "What gives?"

"Gee whiz, John!" Summer shot back. "Can't you make those hormones of yours pipe down?"

"I'm just curious," John said.

"I know what you're curious about, little brother," Summer replied sharply. "You men are all alike."

Tired as he was, even Joe could not resist the temptation to seek further clarification on that remark. "How's that, Summer?" he asked.

Summer crossed her arms, thought a moment, then answered, "You all want to have your cake, and you want to eat it to."

"What does cake have to do with it?" John prodded with a hint of mischief in his eyes.

"Do I have to spell it out for you, brainless wonders?" Summer replied, growing testy.

"Spell it out," John challenged.

"Yeah," Joe agreed. "Please do."

"Okay!" Summer said loudly. "Men want everything—the perfect girl, sex before marriage, a virgin in their wedden bed. Half of them want to charm the pants off every girl they meet, and the other half just wants the pants off without wasten any time on the charm."

"That's disgusten, Summer!" Carrie remarked.

"I agree," Bonnie said, still with obvious wonder. Then, without realizing it, she asked, "Is Tom that way?"

"Tom is perfect," Summer replied.

"Sounds like the voice of experience speaken," John suggested.

"You wouldn't know *experience* if it slapped you in the face, John," Summer said.

"Enough!" Joe interrupted. "No more of this," he ordered. "If Mama and Daddy hear a single word of this, they'll think I've corrupted the whole bunch of you. I mean this now: Once and for all, get out of here."

"But you still haven't told us about the Tip-Toe Inn," John protested.

"And I'm not goen to," Joe said. "Out!"

"We're just interested because we love you, Joe," Summer remarked airily. "We're concerned about your well-be'en."

"Then you most certainly understand why my sleep is so important," Joe said, pointing to the door. "Goodnight everyone."

Grumbling, they acquiesced to his will, filing out one by one until only Luke was left. "What really happened, Joe?" he asked, obviously worried about the situation.

"Everything is fine," Joe responded, giving the boy a gruff smile and tousling his hair. "Go to sleep, little brother. Forget about Bobby Taylor and his son. They won't be messen with you anymore."

Luke nodded, rising from the bed at last. At the door, he stopped, turned and asked, "Was it much of a fight?"

"What do you think?" Joe asked with a smile.

Luke grinned. "I bet you beat him good."

Joe nodded. "I had a good incentive," he replied.

Luke returned the nod. "Sleep well, Joe."

"Goodnight, Luke."

CHAPTER 5

AUGUST ARRIVED WITH NOTHING to distinguish it, except a new page on the calendar, soon stained with sweat and grime. By then, the land was burned, like a fine piece of meat cooked until nothing was left but grit. Still, for an empty stomach, that charred residue was as bitterly satisfying as it was tough—sustenance until proper nourishment was available.

For two weeks, Bobby Taylor spent the days on his rickety front porch swing, dumping the care of his useless fields on his wife and sons. Not much work was required, so Bobby had no qualms about putting undue hardship on his family. He went into a silent retreat, swilling beer, contemplating the unfairness of life, resenting the heat and plotting his revenge on anyone and everyone who had wronged him over the years. Mostly, however, he looked for new opportunities.

All his life, Bobby had fought for acceptance among the larger society. As a youngster, he had sought the admiration of other young boys. Becoming a young man, he had desired girls to think him handsome and charming. As an adult, he had wanted to lead others with his ideas. No matter which way he turned, however, Bobby found only grudging acceptance of his ways and attitudes. His best laid plans fell by the wayside, repeatedly foiled by smart alecks like Paul Berrien, Matt Baker and, now, even Joe Baker.

Some of this, Bobby had begun to realize when he lost the sheriff's election to Paul in 1964. But as he recuperated from the beating administered by the respectable Joe Baker, Bobby came to full grips with the fact that he would never win the respect he deserved—at least not from the larger elements of society. He understood at last that he would have to thrive among a smaller, more cliquish group of people.

Bobby considered himself smart, his aptitude tarnished only by a penchant for sudden, irrational decisions—primarily because he often misjudged people. Over the years, he had come across too many people who claimed to feel one way, yet failed to follow through on their promises when the moment of truth arrived. Overall, people obviously were confused as well as reluctant to declare their true allegiances and interests, which explained why Bobby continually misconstrued their feelings. If he could work within the framework of people who felt exactly as he did, Bobby reasoned he could feel the winds of success.

When he woke one morning to find his shattered nose had returned to its normal size, Bobby moved to put his plan into action.

The Ku Klux Klan had sparked fervent imagination in Bobby on numerous occasions. Yet, while he curried favor with its members, Bobby never considered joining the organization. He heard strange things about KKK members. And quite honestly, he felt uncomfortable with the Klan's ceremonial crap. The whole idea of grown men parading around in bed sheets was ludicrous.

In addition to his private misgivings about the organization, Klan membership also would have destroyed Bobby's hopes of winning full-fledged public support. Now that he had given up on the public, however, Bobby looked forward to becoming a Klansman. He envisioned himself rising quickly through the ranks of leadership, becoming a most reverend imperial grand dragon wizard and commanding the undying devotion of a whole army of hooded warriors who shared his passions and beliefs.

At seven o'clock on a Monday morning, Bobby placed a long-distance telephone call to the wizard of the closest klavern. Adjusting the story to suit his needs, Bobby wove an outlandish tale of rebellious niggers and white nigger lovers running amok in his beloved county. He began with the details of Wayne's run-in with Lucas Bartholomew, briefly mentioned his son's skirmish with Luke Baker and ended with Joe's vicious attack on himself. At times, he made vague references to Martin Luther King Jr., Mississippi, the Voting Rights Act, the NAACP, the ACLU, communists, Selma and recent race riots in New Jersey and Detroit. Bobby's knowledge of these things was sketchy, but the mere mention of them commanded Wizard Ralph Johnson's utmost attention. In a matter of minutes, the Klan leader was convinced that Cookville was primed for agitation and recruitment.

By Tuesday afternoon, Ralph Johnson had organized a parade through Cookville followed by a rally at the house of the Klan's newest recruit, Bobby. Ralph swore the event would become the focal point of the Klan's late summer activities. He predicted the state's most influential Klansman, the imperial grand wizard himself, would attend the festivities in Cookville.

"We'll burn a cross, maybe even scare a few coons," Ralph Johnson vowed. "You don't know what fun is, Bobby, until you've spent a few hours with a few good Klansmen. We're just a bunch of good-ole boys who love a good time."

When Bobby hung up the telephone, his head was swimming with anticipation.

Word of the impending KKK appearance spread quickly through the community. Bobby worked the county like a politician, drumming up support among friends, calling in all favors and putting ideas into the heads of those who stood on the edge of the fence.

Winds of success swirled, blowing a cool breeze in Bobby's direction, despite the heat of the moment.

————

Paul Berrien spent the week prior to the Saturday Klan rally trying to assuage the rising fears of the colored community. The Klan had never been active in their county, so most people had no experience to reflect upon in their consideration of the upcoming spectacle. But they were familiar with the Klan's legacy of intimidation and violence. For every true story told about the Klan, a dozen others swirled.

Exaggeration was not needed. The truth was frightening enough. The Klan lynched people, beat them beyond recognition, tarred and feathered them on occasion. Many innocent people had been whipped by the Klan, others blown apart by their bombs.

"Desperate, Dreadful, Desolate, Doleful, Dismal, Deadly and Dark," read a pamphlet circulated through the colored section of town. "Those are the seven days of the Klan Kalendar. On which day will they call for you?"

As soon as he read the pamphlet, Paul began preparing for the worst.

————

Saturday arrived, dawning hotter than usual and pushing the thermometer past the century mark shortly after the sun stood straight up in the cloudless sky. The heat came in waves, each hotter than the last. People drank gallons of iced tea, found a shady spot and attempted to keep their wits about them. The Cookville hospital treated two people for sunstroke, and an eighty-eight-year-old woman died from heat exhaustion.

"She had a fan runnen in her house, but all it did was churn hot air," Paul told his sisters when he came home for a bite to eat in the early afternoon. "The poor old lady literally cooked to death."

It was the hottest day of the year, and Paul hoped the heat would make people too lazy to care about the Klan. But he watched with keen anticipation and preparation, fearing the heat wave was an omen of an ill wind to come, which would bring out the worst in good people.

"Things could be worse," he told his best deputy, Mack, shortly before the rally was scheduled to begin. "At least we don't have a full moon to contend with tonight. Even sane people act crazy on a full moon."

"Unfortunately, we're not dealen with sane people today," Mack replied.

The rally was planned for late in the day to catch the many shoppers who filled the town on Saturday afternoons. As the final hour approached, Cookville took on a carnival atmosphere, with curious onlookers and willing participants shuffling about, anticipating the thrill of adventure or at least a welcome change from their humdrum days.

Even the black community failed to resist the temptation to see things for themselves. Ignoring the advice of Paul Berrien, who had personally visited every home, shanty and shack in the colored section of town, they swamped one corner of the town square.

Shortly after five o'clock, the distant sounds of automobile horns reached the courthouse square, and the town came to a standstill. The blaring horns grew louder, reaching a crescendo when all at once, a white pickup truck decked out in the Stars and Bars of the Confederacy rounded the northwest corner. The truck began a swift sweep through the streets, reckless, wanton and defiant. A dozen more trucks and cars joined the caravan, packed with about forty men, women and children, many wearing the Klan's official regalia, white robes and cone-shaped hats. The Klansmen waved their flags, blew their automobile horns, cheered and jeered the gathering of blacks on the northeast corner of the square.

All decked out in his new Klan costume, Bobby Taylor rode in the bed of the lead pickup truck. He smiled broadly, waving to family and friends, swelling with self-importance. On either side of him were Ralph Johnson and Larry Lester, the imperial grand wizard of the Invisible Knights of the Ku Klux Klan in Georgia. Bobby reckoned this was the most important day of his life, the beginning of a tremendous future that would lead him to glory.

The vast majority of the crowd failed to share Bobby's enthusiasm for this invasion of their town. As quickly as the first truck hurdled into their vision, most everyone's curiosity was chilled by the specter of these robed warriors coming together to share their hate. Their nearness to this fraternity of hatemongers with a mob mentality haunted some of Cookville's finest citizens. Many walked away from the freakish disgrace, berating themselves for having come in the first place. Most people, however, simply marveled at the abomination of it all, keeping their place, unable to escape the charms of their ghoulish voyeurism. Sheer boredom kept a few people there as well, while several onlookers howled approval as the cavalcade of Klansmen paraded around the square.

"Not too much rattles me in this world," Paul Berrien told his best deputy as they watched the parading Klansmen. "But this—this must have been what it was like on Calvary when they crucified Christ."

"It's disgusten, ain't it?" Mack replied. "I admit to haven my own prejudices from time to time. But these people are pathetic—the worst of the whole lot."

The procession circled three times around the square before the trucks ground to a halt beneath a sprawling live oak tree on the courthouse lawn. Klansmen leapt from the trucks and spilled out of the cars, scattering through the crowd, handing out leaflets and pumping handshakes.

In the bed of the head truck, Imperial Grand Dragon Larry Lester offered one final piece of advice to Bobby before giving him the megaphone. "Show them you care and are concerned about what's happenen in your community," he encouraged. "Tell them that's why you invited us here today. Speak clearly, but keep your voice low enough so everyone has to strain a little to hear you. People pay more attention when they have to work hard to hear what they want. And whatever you do, Klansmen Taylor, don't mention the bloody niggers. I'll handle that part of the program."

The imperial grand wizard handed Bobby the megaphone, nodded encouragement and pushed his newest recruit onto the back of a dog cage that was serving as a raised podium. For an awful moment as he faced friends and neighbors, Bobby smelled failure. His throat was dry, and he feared he was too nervous to speak.

He glanced again at Larry Lester, who only minutes ago had hailed Bobby as a "prized recruit," promising him a charter for a new klavern in the Cookville community.

"You can go far," the imperial grand wizard told Bobby. "You're a natural leader. One day, people will heed your every word, but you need the proper trainen first. Watch me, learn and you will prosper. Mark my words. Today is only the beginnen."

Bobby breathed deeply, refusing to squander his last opportunity for greatness. He gazed thoughtfully at the crowd around him, waited for the people to quiet down and began to speak.

To everyone who knew him, Bobby somehow seemed a changed man. He was unusually subdued. His voice quivered with sincerity, and his message was noteworthy for its brevity.

"Friends, neighbors," he began. "I've asked these good people here today because I'm concerned and I care about our way of life. Our rights are slowly be'en stole from us, and too many people seem to believe if they ignore all that's wrong, then the problems will simply disappear. I do not believe the problems will go away, and neither do the people who have joined us for today's rally. Folks, these men refuse to ignore the problem. They confront the issues. They are concerned, and they care about our way of life. I beg you, and I plead with you— listen to them. Thank you."

A smattering of applause rose from the crowd as Bobby returned the megaphone to the imperial grand wizard.

"Thank you, Klansman Taylor," Larry Lester said, climbing to the podium. "Thank you for inviten us here and for caren about what is happenen in your community and mine, our state and our country."

In contrast to Bobby's lack of fervor, the imperial grand wizard boomed with enthusiasm as he spoke.

"Ladies and gentleman," he said, "I will keep my remarks brief and straightforward because the day is hot and I've never trusted long-winded speakers. First, let me tell you why we are NOT here today. We are not here to start trouble with the colored community in Cookville. That is not our intentions. Now don't be confused. We haven't become fond of the Negroes. We just have other dogs to beat today."

A few people laughed, especially the robed Klansmen. Larry Lester waited for silence.

"A lot of what you've heard about the Klan is true," he continued. "We do believe Negroes are partly to blame for the bad things ailen our nation today. But they are not the only ones at fault by a long shot. In fact, the Negroes really are just enjoyen the advantages given over to them by a president, congressmen, bureaucrats and judges in Washington—people who cater to the whims and fancies of those who believe in ideas contrary to the American way. These people who we elected and appointed to high places have betrayed us. They have decreed that the majority of hard-worken Americans must give up their hard-earned money to support a small minority unwillen to do for themselves. They tell us where our children must go to school and who with—even though it's our tax dollars used to carry out their plans."

The imperial grand wizard paused for a growing round of applause, then moved toward the conclusion of his remarks.

"Day after day, our leaders in Washington impose their wills on us—wills that are dictated by smart-alecky niggers and their white liberal sympathizers," he said. "All you have to do is look around to see what's happenen. The wheels are comen off our way of life. In this county alone, I've been told that a grown black man nearly beat a young white boy to death earlier this month. Only a few weeks ago, some young white nigger lover staged an unprovoked attack on our good friend Bobby here—jumped him from behind, broke his nose and probably would have killed him if other people had not intervened."

Rumors had swirled about the altercation between Joe and Bobby, but this was the first official acknowledgment of the incident. Murmurs rippled through the crowd, and Larry Lester seized on the confusion.

"Yes, people," he bellowed. "This stuff happened right here in Cookville. And mark my word: Things will get worse before they get better. The time is just around the corner when the government and the judges come callen on Cookville, tellen y'all what you can and cannot do, demanden you run your schools their way or no way. It's happenen every day and in every place, and too many people are caught unprepared. It happened in my county. The rally cry was, 'Everyone deserves an equal education.' Now niggers and white children attend the same schools. They mix; they mingle. They become boyfriend and girlfriend. It sickens me. When your time comes, Cookville, I hope y'all will be better prepared to deal with it than we were.

"Once again, folks, you have my word that the Klan is not here to mess with anyone. Some of us might holler at them on our way out of town, remind everyone that a nigger is a nigger. Don't begrudge us a little fun. We have a reputation to uphold after all. When we leave here today, we're headen for Bobby Taylor's farm in the northwest part of the county. We're gonna do some socializen and have fun. You're welcome to join us."

The imperial grand wizard paused, glancing over the crowd.

"That's all I have to say, folks, except maybe for thank you. We just wanted an opportunity to tell our side of the story, to remind you good people that the overwhelmen majority of Americans are white people, and their rights are just as important as the rights of niggers. Our government is supposed to be based on majority rule, not the whims of minorities. If you don't do anything else, take that thought with you when you leave here today. Thank you."

His speech completed, Larry Lester threw up his hands in a victory gesture and was rewarded with a hearty round of applause. About a dozen men of all ages stepped forward to claim brochures, and Klansmen milled through the crowd in search of more recruits. A few minutes later, the white-robed warriors returned to their vehicles, paraded once more around the courthouse and drove out of town.

Even as he remained on guard for problems, Paul Berrien marveled at the ease with which this first hurdle was cleared. He had expected problems, but the event had gone off without a hitch. He followed the KKK procession in his patrol car as the group headed toward Bobby's farm. Since the Klan's social gathering would be held on private property, Paul was limited in his ability to respond. He planned to monitor the function from a distance. His goal was simple—keep the peace.

———

As the Klan caravan moved down Highway 125, the day turned into early evening, with the sun setting blood red in the sky. The procession had swollen to more than two dozen vehicles as the group headed toward Bobby's farm. At the general mercantile, the caravan slowed, then made the right-hand turn onto the dusty dirt road.

Matt never planned to make any defiant gesture toward the Klan. He had spent the hot afternoon with his sons and Lucas, setting up the new irrigation system in a field of late-season soybeans on the Berrien place. Lucas had plowed up the field's original crop of withered corn and replanted in hopes of salvaging a meager profit. It was a gamble, wagered in hopes of making the Berriens amenable to the idea of allowing Lucas to tend the land again next year. When Lucas had come to Matt for advice, the white man had offered his friend free use of the irrigation equipment.

"It's not doen me a dab of good," Matt told Lucas. "There's not a drop of water on my place, but the river's a short piece from that field,

Lucas. Somebody might as well get some good use out of that irrigation system. If my place was close enough to the river, I'd be maken use of it."

So it was by coincidence that Matt, his sons, his father and Lucas were standing in the front yard when the KKK procession began winding its way along the dirt road toward the Baker place. Having just spent five hours under a blazing sun to get the irrigation flowing, the men now discussed the irony of the weatherman's latest forecast. A hurricane was churning in the Gulf of Mexico, threatening to dump a downpour over drought-stricken South Georgia sometime in the next few days. Now, however, without a trace of cloud in the sky and the sting of sun blistered on their faces, everyone adopted a wait-and-see attitude to the forecast.

Luke was the first among them to spot the approaching cavalcade of cars and trucks. "Company's comen," he alerted them, his eyes full of fiery wrath.

"Uh-oh," Lucas remarked. "You want me to step around the corner, Matt?"

While Matt had ordered his family to ignore the Klan, he refused to allow his sons and Lucas to surrender their pride. "I don't see any reason why you should do that, Lucas," he replied, crossing his arms in a show of stubborn commitment to his own beliefs. "I intend to stay right here."

"Me, too," added Luke, assuming his father's position as every other Baker man quickly followed precedent.

Lucas shook out a small laugh of amazement and appreciation from deep within himself, then crossed his arms and waited with his friends.

It was more a show of solidarity, but the act enraged the Klansmen, who saw the stand as outright defiance by the enemy. The vehicles slowed to a crawl, with horns blowing incessantly and angry Klansmen hurling insults at their adversaries.

Through it all, however, Matt, his family and their friend remained impassive, staunch in their convictions and solid in their resistance to the threat. When the final truck passed, accelerating with a roar and one last insult yelled at them, the men were still standing there with crossed arms—feet firmly planted on the ground, with a whole skin and new strength in the security of their beliefs.

The Klansmen turned Martha Taylor's backyard into a picnic place, cavorting in the river, swilling beer and setting up portable grills to cook hamburgers and hotdogs.

Inside her home, Martha sat in a straight-backed chair, staring at the grimy mirror above the couch while trying to sort through her mixed feelings. She was furious with Bobby for bringing these intruders to their house. But she also considered the occasion a stroke of luck since no one expected her to cook and clean after them, and the children were out from underfoot as well.

Martha shared her husband's sentiments toward colored people. She had even less use, however, for the white men and women who were dressed up in bedclothes and floppy hoods, parading through her backyard. Grown people should have known better.

Unlike her husband, Martha harbored only a passive hatred for niggers. Once, when she was young and resentful of the whole world, she had shared Bobby's zeal for the fight. But the fight itself had become an insatiable quest for Bobby, and Martha had grown weary of the endless tide of losing battles. If she had her druthers, Martha would have kept her family isolated on their back-road farm. Since Martha rarely got what she wanted, she was content with simply keeping the outside world from invading her domain.

A roar from the crowd gathered outside her house provided Martha a sudden reminder of yet another failure. The world was beating on her doorsteps, and she had no place else to escape.

A long time ago, Martha had tried to convince herself that she loved Bobby Taylor. When she tugged on her heartstrings these days, however, she realized her only feelings for the man were those of undying gratitude.

Bobby had rescued her from a sordid, squalid existence in Opelika, Alabama. Coming to Cookville, Martha had felt as if she was Cinderella going to the ball, only she was leaving behind something worse than a mean stepmother and ugly stepsisters. When she escaped from Alabama, Martha was fleeing from an abusive father, who assaulted his wife and children on a whim, forcing sex on his daughters as well as his sons.

Bobby Taylor had been Martha's knight in shining armor, freeing her from a damnable life. While life with her husband had been loathsome at times, nothing bad enough had ever happened to make her regret the flight from Alabama.

Even though she had never loved Bobby, Martha still felt as if she had found her lucky star on the day he married her. The hard years since had dimmed her girlish ideas, but she still remembered the way he charmed her when they first met. While not exactly handsome, Bobby had the attitude and appearances to attract second glances from most women who passed him on the street. To a plain woman like Martha, he had seemed like a god.

Bobby had exaggerated facial features. His face was too wide, his nose too flared, his mouth too thin and his eyes too far apart. Somehow, however, his sky-blue eyes and beguiling charisma transcended his flaws, turning the man into a magnet with dirty dishwater blond hair, a sensual smile and flashy style.

Martha had been easy pickings for him when they were young, and Bobby had been trapped into marriage with her. Over the years, however, she had realized that no one woman would satisfy her husband. Early in their marriage, Bobby had covered up his indiscretions with other women. Now, however, he flaunted his affairs. Tonight, for instance, he was wooing some thirtyish-looking buxom blonde—in full view of their sons no less.

In one of her frequent trips to the kitchen window, which afforded a view of the goings-on outside the house, Martha had observed the flirting between her husband and the woman. The woman had dyed hair and wore black boots, skintight jeans and a white blouse that revealed much of her ample cleavage. Bobby had kissed the woman, and they were rubbing up against each other like dogs in heat. Martha half expected Bobby to bring the woman inside the house for a romp in the sack.

The idea saddened Martha, making her realize that she stayed married to Bobby because she had nothing else to do and nowhere else to go. As strange as it seemed, her gratitude to Bobby remained intact. Lately, however, Martha was beginning to feel she deserved better. She had borne her husband three sons, cooked and cleaned for him and done everything else he asked for nearly twenty-five years. Yet, nothing she ever did satisfied Bobby. He always insisted on something else, always demanded more.

And what Bobby wanted, Bobby got.

Nothing reminded Martha more of her husband's domineering control than the tarnished mirror hanging on the dingy living room wall. The mirror had been Bobby's Christmas present to her several years ago. The gift had come with orders to hang the mirror over the couch in their newly painted living room.

Martha hated mirrors, and the last place she wanted one was in the living room of her house, where the reflection would provide a constant reminder of her homeliness every time she passed it. She had shared none of these thoughts with Bobby. Instead, she had mustered up her most pleasant voice, informing her husband the mirror would look out of place in the living room and professing to want it hung in their bedroom.

"That way I can use it when I get dressed," she explained.

"Nope," Bobby declared firmly. He had been in a particularly happy mood, examining the various toys he had bought for the boys. "It belongs in this room. A mirror like that is too pretty to hide away in the bedroom."

Martha should have accepted his decision, but an unusual stubborn streak had caused her to press the matter, intent on having her way. Their peaceful Christmas morning had dissolved quickly into a shouting match, ending with one of Bobby's rare beatings of his wife. Later in the day, while a battered Martha applied the finishing touches to Christmas dinner, Bobby and the boys had hung the mirror on the living room wall.

Rising from her chair, Martha walked over to the mirror and gazed into the glass. The reflection showed a woman who looked closer to fifty than forty. The oversized nose was hawkish, while the deep-set gray eyes were lifeless and spread too far apart on her face. Her ears appeared ready to fly off Martha's head at any moment, and her pencil thin mouth had a permanent downward curve from too many years of frowning. Her face was a sad oval, with the pasty skin tightly drawn like a bad face-lift.

Martha pushed a graying strand of dull hair back into place and sighed at the sad sight staring back at her. All her life, she had heard about the gaunt little girls who grew into striking women as they aged. Obviously, she was not to become one of them. Age was making Martha even uglier.

Turning from the mirror, she recrossed the living room floor to the kitchen window to inspect the curious crowd. Bobby had disappeared, and the blonde floozy was flirting with another man. Wayne was talking to a group of teenage boys, his posture suggesting a bragging mood. Near the river's edge, she spotted Billy, sitting with his back against a tree with Carl cradled between his legs.

Her youngest son was obviously asleep. Glancing at the wall clock, she saw the hour hand had sailed well past ten. The four-year-old Carl should have been in bed instead of sleeping on the ground, but Martha had allowed the time to get away from her. It was not the first time. Nor would it likely be the last because Martha often failed in her motherly duties.

She wanted to be a good mother to her sons, but somehow, the magic of raising children eluded Martha. The boys were complete mysteries to her, and she tended to think of her sons as another chore that needed tending. Occasionally, when the children did something special, Martha experienced a pain of regret because the sense of a mother's love had never filled her. The feelings were fleeting, however, always swept away by an awareness that she had never loved anyone or anything. Facts were facts, and Martha saw no reason to pretend for her own sake.

From time to time, though, Martha wished she understood her sons. While watching her stories on television, she would vow to take more time with boys. By the time a suitable opportunity arrived, however, she usually lost interest or had something better to do.

As it stood now, Martha was not even certain she liked Wayne. Her oldest son was brash like his father and dimwitted like his mother. Sometimes, the boy scared Martha. He carried around a mean streak like a belligerent rattlesnake ready to strike.

Billy was the sensitive one of the bunch. He was always helpful and considerate, running here and there trying to please everyone. Yet, even he drove Martha batty with his consuming passion for basketball. He spent hours outside, dribbling and shooting, faking and driving, counting backward from five. The basketball rarely strayed far from his side. Even in the house, he twirled the ball on his fingers and practiced whipping it back and forth between his legs. He was a whir of motion, and Martha tired of his busyness.

As for Carl, Martha had no idea what to make of him. He was the silent one. More than anything, she was glad the boy had finally ceased wetting the bed he shared with Billy.

Prone to rash decisions, Martha suddenly made up her mind to leave Bobby. With only slightly more consideration, she decided to leave the children with him.

Abandoning her lookout at the window, she strode through the dark house to the bedroom and pulled her suitcase from the closet shelf. Bobby had bought the piece of luggage as a wedding gift for her. As she packed her things, Martha thought it odd that after all the years gone by, she could still fit her essential belongings into the suitcase.

Pushing away the thought and ignoring the new roar of noise coming from outside the house, she finished her packing.

———————

A few minutes later, Imperial Grand Wizard Larry Lester, Wizard Ralph Johnson and new Klansman Bobby Taylor tossed lighted matches onto three large crosses set on the edge of New River. Already doused with kerosene, the wooden timbers burst into flames as the hooded army of hatemongers gave their final shout of the long day.

Inside the living room, Martha sat in the straight-backed chair with the suitcase by her side.

The burning crosses cast a pale shadow across the room, but she disregarded the shenanigans. She wanted these intruders to pile into their vehicles and drive away, so that she could get on with her business. Her feet tapped against the floor in anticipation.

The front door opened, and Billy entered the house with his sleeping brother draped across his shoulder. Without even glancing at his mother, Billy passed through the room and carried Carl to bed.

Martha had debated whether to leave in secret or to tell Bobby and the children about her plans. She would have preferred to leave without fanfare but decided the boys were owed an explanation.

In their room, Carl protested the covers, and Billy insisted on a top sheet. Martha smiled, grateful for the protective instinct Billy felt toward his little brother. The knowledge comforted her, made her rest easy about this decision to abandon the children.

A short time later, Billy plodded back into the living room and dropped his slight frame on the couch. Then, he saw Martha's suitcase.

"What's with the suitcase, Ma?" he asked.

"I am goen away, Billy," Martha replied boldly. "You take care of yourself and Carl, too."

Billy sat up straight on the couch, a touch of worry flying into his eyes. "What do you mean you're goen away?" he asked. "Where will you go?"

"As far away from here as I can get," Martha answered, resisting the urge to walk over and pat the boy on the head one last time. "I'll write and let you boys know where I wind up."

Billy leaned forward. "What does Pa say about this?" he asked with increasing doubt.

"I'm fixen to tell him, so we'll see," Martha explained patiently. "I doubt he'll mind too much. He can replace me with that fake blonde he was flirten with tonight."

"Ma, you're maken a big mistake," Billy pleaded, coming to his feet. "Just please put up that suitcase quick, and forget about any of this."

Hearing footsteps on the porch, Martha rose from the chair. "I've made up my mind, Billy," she said firmly. "I am leaven."

Bobby heard this last remark as he opened the screen door and entered the house. His eyes scanned the dark room, going from Billy to Martha before landing on the suitcase. Behind him, Wayne allowed the door to slam shut and flipped on the light switch.

"What's goen on?" Bobby asked at length, after everyone adjusted to the flood of light.

"I'm leaven you, Bobby," Martha announced confidently.

Bobby scratched his nose, staring first at the suitcase, then at his wife. "Why you wanna go and do a thing like that?"

"Because I can't stand it here anymore," Martha replied. "I have to get away while I can still make a life for myself. The boys are old enough to take care of themselves, and you sure don't need or want me around here."

Bobby nodded slightly as if agreeing with the suggestion. "This is some bombshell to drop on us just short of midnight, Martha," he remarked, a hint of mean amusement creeping into his voice. "But tell me, sweetheart. Where do you plan to go tonight, and how on earth are you gonna get there?"

Details had always bothered Martha, even the simplest ones. Last year, for instance, she had fretted over wrapping paper for Christmas presents. The multiple choices of brightly colored paper had befuddled her to the point that she had wound up handing out the few presents without first wrapping them. Now, her confidence wavered.

"I don't exactly know," she said to the sea of strange faces staring back at her. "I figure I'll start walken, and somebody'll pick me up along the way. Maybe I'll go to Tifton—or maybe all the way to Atlanta."

Bobby began to laugh and even Wayne chuckled at the ludicrousness of her plans. Martha looked to Billy for reassurance, but he bowed his head, unable to look her in the eyes.

"You've got it all figured out, don't you Martha?" Bobby said, the voice of controlled rage replacing his laughter. He glared at her. "I know you're crazy as a bat, but this just takes the cake. Who do you think in their right mind would pick up a wretch like you walken alongside the road? And even if you managed to find your way to Tifton or all the way to Atlanta, how would you take care of yourself, Martha? What in the world would you do?"

Her hand flew to the side of her face, tapping nervously against her neck as Martha tried to decide what to do. Every thought failed her.

"I know what a cross it is to bear—believe me, I know—but the best place for you, Martha, is right where you are," Bobby continued when it became obvious his wife was confused. "You ain't goen anywhere—not now, not ever. Get on back to the bedroom, woman. Unpack that suitcase, and we'll forget any of this ever happened."

Desperation surged through Martha. She wanted to run from the house. Instead, she dabbed away the tears streaming down her face, bent to retrieve the suitcase and carried it back to her room without further protest.

CHAPTER 6

THE KLAN STARTED THE fire, unintentionally, when someone tossed a cigarette from the back of a pickup truck as the departing caravan paraded past the Baker farm sometime after midnight. The cigarette landed in a thick patch of dry grass, smoldered for a moment and finally flickered to a tiny flame. Fire quickly consumed the plot of beaten blades, then lagged along a narrow line of almost barren earth until the flame found a new source of dried turf and weeds.

Fueled by the tender clumps of brown grass, the flames flared into a bonfire, scorched the bottom of a dogwood tree and crawled through the fence. Within minutes, the blaze was licking at the parched cornfield. Now stoked and fanned by a gentle breeze, the fire roared into conflagration, incinerating stalk after stalk of the withered corn.

The flames cut a wide swath through the field, ever expanding and rolling a plume of smoke high across the nighttime sky. On the far side of the field, the fire burned through another fence, claiming its first taste of timber from a section of hardwoods on the Berrien estate. A smaller sheet of flames swept along the edge of the field closer to home, devoured a row of dogwood trees and began nipping the shingled sides of the first of the two tobacco barns.

Up to this point, the breeze had pushed the flames and smoke away from the house, which explained the failure of anyone to detect the fire. But—made prankish by the hurricane that churned in the balmy waters of the Gulf of Mexico, heading toward the Florida Panhandle and Alabama shoreline—the wind suddenly shifted, pushing flames in a new direction and wafting the first cloud of smoke toward open windows. Even before the stifling smell arrived, however, the hissing roar of the fire began to nudge awake the sleeping family.

By now, a pale yellow and orange glow lit the field, and red flames flagged from the tops of trees in the distance.

At last, the fire ate through an edge of the shingled barn side, then curled along the hot dry wood within and found the cooked tobacco hanging from the rafters. The barn became a torch within minutes, hissing and spewing red-hot embers onto the second tobacco barn.

Deep in the field, having gorged itself on dried corn and still licking at the leftovers, the blaze crossed the fencerow, found a fresh appetite for the opening bolls of stunted cotton and headed toward the towering piney wood.

The popping and cracking of barn timbers rousted Joe from sleep. Opening his eyes, he noticed the illuminated night outside his window with groggy curiosity. Immediately, however, he detected the smoky odor, coming to full sensibility as apprehension lifted him from bed and propelled him to the window. He discovered the world on fire, nearly ready to burn down around his family.

Joe yelled the initial warning, rushing to pull on clothes and shoes, even as everybody else in the house made the terrible discovery for themselves.

Everyone crowded onto the front porch to observe the raging fire, some of them hastily dressed, others still in their bedclothes or underwear. As they watched in horror, the tobacco barn farthest from the house shuddered and gave up the ghost, collapsing in a loud heap. Seconds later, flames shot through the roof of the second barn, licking at their chops, angry for having been denied too long the opportunity to feast.

Disbelief paralyzed the family. Then, the trickish wind launched a snarling wall of fire directly toward the house, and they could ill afford to stand still any longer.

"My God!" Matt exclaimed. "The whole place could go up. Go call for help, Caroline."

Even before he made the suggestion, she was headed for the telephone.

In a split second with no time to think, Matt shouted orders for his family, and everyone reacted with their instinct for survival.

Sam and Rachel rushed to the shed behind the house, grabbing shovels, rakes and anything else they figured could be used to fight a fire with scarcely a drop of water on the place. The girls, all wearing nightshirts, scattered to the corncrib, the barn and the loft in search of course tobacco sheets that could be used to beat back the flames.

Joe was ordered to cut a fire line alongside the house, an impossible task without their best tractor, which was parked in a back field along with the harrow needed for the job. He ran for the pickup, while his brothers ran to their room for clothes.

"Meet me at the orchard gate," he yelled to John, whose help was needed to hitch the harrow to the tractor.

Unless they hurried, perhaps even if they did, the flames would reach the house before there was time to cut a fire line.

———————

As her husband commanded, Martha began unpacking her suitcase. When she had put away several items, she came across her nightgown and decided she was too sleepy to finish the task. She shut the suitcase, shoved it under the bed and put on the flimsy nightgown.

Turning off the light, she climbed into bed and was ready to doze off when Bobby entered the room. Over the years, she had learned to read his mind through his movements. When he wanted her body, Bobby was deliberate and watchful with his movements about the room.

Sensing his intent, Martha shut her eyes tightly while Bobby undressed. When he was naked, her husband lay beside Martha, leaned over and nuzzled her face. He reeked of stale beer and sweat. Nausea filled her throat, and Martha lay deadly still, hoping to discourage him by pretending sleep. Her shallow breaths betrayed her. When Martha was asleep, even catnapping, she snored.

"Let's do it," Bobby urged when his tender side failed to arouse his wife. "I know you ain't asleep."

Knowing it was useless to resist his advances, Martha raised her nightgown, took off her panties and allowed Bobby to mount her without a single word passing between them. She simply wanted the act finished, and if her cooperation would hasten a fast end, then she would oblige her husband.

Bobby was close to climax when their bedroom door burst open, and the overhead light beamed on them. Wayne entered the room, claiming to have important news.

Rather than embarrassment, Martha felt relief at her son's intrusion. Her naked husband rolled off her, cursing as he withdrew, shouting at Wayne while Martha closed her legs and pulled a sheet over her.

"Damn it, Wayne!" Bobby hollered. "How many times do I have to tell you not to come runnen in here when you know we're busy?"

"Sorry, Pa," Wayne lied.

Just for fun, he occasionally interrupted his parents during sex. Since Bobby huffed, puffed and moaned loudly enough to keep anyone from sleeping through the act, Wayne considered it a right of pleasure to disturb their copulation. Tonight, however, Wayne had a genuine reason for barging into their bedroom.

"Turn off the light and get out of here so we can finish what we're doen," Bobby yelled when Wayne made no move to leave the room.

"Somethen's on fire down the road," Wayne explained, flipping off the light switch. "I think it's the Baker place, Pa, the whole place. The sky's lit up like the Fourth of July."

"Wouldn't that be a wonder?" Bobby muttered. "Okay, okay, I'll be there in two shakes of a stick. Get Billy out of bed for me, and y'all go wait in the truck."

Without replying, Wayne closed the door and went to wake Billy.

Bobby returned to the business at hand and finished it quickly. As he dressed, he suggested that Martha show a little more interest the next time he approached her. Then he opened the door and went out to see for himself what Wayne was yakking about. In her bed, Martha heard him whoop with delight a few moments later. He came back into the house, yelling at Billy who was grumbling about being woken up for something that did not concern him.

"This could be a great moment for your old man, boy, and you need to be a part of it," Bobby yelled, silencing Billy's protests. "After the day I've had, I can't think of a better enden than watchen Matt Baker's house burn to the ground—unless maybe if Matt and those sons of his burned right along with it."

Matt scanned the approaching fire once more, then decided the most pressing demand was to save the tractor parked beneath the shelter of the still standing tobacco barn. It was an old tractor but still in good condition, except for a faulty starter and a sticky choke.

They needed that tractor, so Matt called for Luke's help, and the boy came bounding out of the house, pulling on his shirt, buttoning his jeans. Side by side, they sprinted the football field distance between the house and the burning barn.

By the time they reached the blazing building, flames were licking at the shelter above the tractor as well as the machine's single front tire. Matt beat out the flames on the tire, while Luke climbed onto the hot tractor seat.

While Luke pressed the starter button, Matt pumped the choke. The tractor engine coughed, sputtered and turned over once, then fizzled. They worked frantically, trying to crank the tractor, but the engine refused to budge.

The barn's tin siding was white-hot now, throwing off blistering heat. Suddenly, flames burned through the barn door. The heavy wood-facing fell off the hinges, striking Matt on the back, burning the calf of his leg. He shook off the burning wood, stomped out the fire, then beat back another blaze licking at the rear tractor tire closest to the barn.

Once more, Matt fiddled with the choke, and Luke tried to crank the tractor. The engine was dead, however, and Matt realized the tractor was a goner.

"Let's get out of here!" he yelled to Luke.

As Luke climbed off the tractor, a familiar clicking came from inside the barn, where hundreds of dollars of tobacco burned out of control. Matt's face twisted with disbelief as he realized the timer on the barn cooker was signaling for an injection of gas into the furnace. Luke heard the noise, too, looking at his father for confirmation of his fear. For a flickering second, they stared blankly at one another. Then they broke into a run, their feet pounding furiously as they fled for safety.

Behind them, another ominous rumbling rattled the barn, followed by a screaming zip and a loud pop. Seconds later, the gas tank exploded, arcing a single, flaming yellow torch heavenward and peppering the sky with tiny pieces of hot steel. A second, smaller explosion followed almost instantly.

The booming blasts resonated across the countryside, shattering windows, rattling walls, piercing eardrums and jarring the entire community.

Like the trumpet of the Lord Himself, Rachel thought, and Jesus coming back to claim his flock at a most opportune time. She staggered against Sam as the force of explosion rocked them. A prized bottle fell off a shelf in the smokehouse, glancing off Sam's head before landing unharmed on the soft dirt floor. In the adjoining syrup house, a shelf collapsed, and bottles shattered.

The concussion of the exploding forces was violent, flinging Matt and Luke head over heels, airborne for several seconds before sprawling landings disoriented their faculties.

Stunned by the force, Matt needed time to pick himself off the ground after crashing. The smoke was thick around him. He shook his head, unable to get his bearings for a moment, then started on a dazed trot toward an uncertain destination.

Luke was not as fortunate. A single piece of white-hot steel landed on his shoulder, melted through his undershirt and branded him with a mark the size of a silver dime. Seared and screaming, Luke slung the steel from his body and staggered toward the house, fearful he would pass out before he could escape the burning field.

Caroline heard the explosion, the impact knocking the telephone receiver from her hand.

Summer saw the yellow flame streak across the sky as well as the tiny red, white and yellow pieces of shredded steel from the exploding gas tank, cascading like fireworks.

Both women had the same reaction, their protective instincts hurrying them toward the burning field in search of Matt and Luke. For one dizzying moment, Caroline wondered whether they had been blown to pieces. Summer's moment of terror arrived in the form of a single thought about her father and brother burning to death.

Their fears vanished instantly into the more important need for action, and they rushed toward the burning field, Caroline coming from the house, Summer from the corncrib across the road. They ran past each other into the rolling smoke, calling for Matt and Luke. In the distance, Luke screamed, and Summer ran toward his cry. Farther away, Caroline saw Matt trip over a bank of dirt and fall.

Moments later, the two women were leading Matt and Luke from the field to the porch.

Matt made a quick recovery with Caroline's help, resting less than a minute on the ground before his sense of duty took over, thrusting him back into the fight to save the house as well as everything else his family owned.

Luke was ravaged with burning pain. While Summer and Bonnie calmed him, Rachel applied the sap of her aloe plant to the deep burn. The natural ointment cooled the burn, enough to renew Luke's fierce determination to fight the fire. He took a deep breath, allowed Rachel to cover the burn with gauze and then ran to the field, beating at the advancing flames with a tobacco sheet.

The explosion had scattered embers across the parched field, igniting small blazes that soon burned into each other. Minutes later, a long line of flames danced furiously less than thirty yards from the house and the pecan orchard.

"If it gets into the orchard, we'll lose everything," Matt exhorted his family. "Fight it with all you've got."

Everyone answered the challenge, throwing themselves at the flames and fighting for their livelihood if not their lives. They beat at the fire with tobacco sheets, shoveled dirt on burning corn stalks and stomped at the flames with their shoes. Gradually, they lost the battle, retreating backward as the fire spread relentlessly toward the house.

At some point, Paul Berrien and Tom Carter joined the fight. Even with reinforcements, however, the sheet of fire stretched across a line too long to defend.

Blistered and exhausted, they doubled their efforts as well as hoped and prayed for a miracle. Still, the fire crept closer—until flames had pushed their backs against the fencerow no more than fifteen yards from the house.

Then, in the distance, they heard the strained whine of a tractor engine coming toward them as hard and fast as it would go.

———

A short time after Bobby and Wayne left the house in high spirits with Billy grumbling in their wake, Martha heard the shotgun blast of the ages. The loud explosion rattled the windows in her house and put a notion in Martha's cluttered head.

Rolling out of bed, she kneeled on the floor and pulled her suitcase from beneath the bed. She opened it and took out her prettiest dress, a cranberry colored imitation wool frock that had never fit properly. Pushing the suitcase off the other side of the bed, she spread the dress across the rumpled sheets and ironed out the wrinkles with her hands.

Next, Martha ran a hot bath, dumping into the water the remainder of an old box of bubble bath, which had never performed as advertised.

When she finished bathing, Martha coated her body with talcum powder, combed her hair and put on the cranberry dress. As an afterthought, she rummaged through a drawer, found an old bottle of cologne and doused herself with the sweet-smelling liquid.

Now finished dressing, she went into the living room, checked herself in the mirror and saw something missing. Returning to the bedroom, she searched through a bureau drawer and found a pair of earrings that almost matched her dress. She clipped the small nuggets on her ears, then walked back into the living room for another inspection.

This time, Martha was pleased. She was still not beautiful, but she was satisfied with the way she looked. After one final self-appraisal, she crossed the room and pulled a shotgun from the heavy rack of weapons.

Martha had given the gun to Bobby as a Christmas present in the same year he had given her the mirror. There was no reason to check whether the gun was loaded because that was the only kind of gun Bobby allowed in his house. Nevertheless, she opened a heavy desk drawer near the gun rack and found the box of cartridges. She took a handful of the shells and dropped them in her pocket.

Until now, Martha had never considered suicide. But with her mind made up on the matter and no one to question her about motives and details, she wanted to get it over and done with as soon as possible.

Martha talked aloud as she carried the shotgun around the house, checking to make sure the place was clean enough to leave for Bobby and the boys. In the kitchen, she rinsed two dirty cups and set them to dry in the dish rack.

Coming to the smallest bedroom, where Carl was sleeping in the double bed he shared with Billy, she paused, considering whether to take him with her, before concluding her youngest son should be allowed to make his own decision about these things. She considered giving him a goodbye kiss, rejecting the idea with a wave of her hand.

Finally, Martha returned to the living room. She picked a hat off the floor, placed it on the television and decided everything was in order. Returning to the sofa, she lifted the shotgun to her shoulder, aimed at the wall and blew the mirror to pieces. The shot gouged a hole in the wall, and shards of glass flew everywhere.

"I could kill myself for not thinken of this earlier," she said aloud, loading a second cartridge into the gun.

Martha laughed slightly and agreed with her husband's earlier suggestion: She was crazy as a bat. Closing her eyes, she stuck the barrel of the gun into her mouth and pulled the trigger.

––––––––––

The third explosion brought Carl Taylor fully awake. The night was popping like a firecracker around him, and he wondered if Pa and the boys were shooting deer outside the house. Realizing that Billy was not lying next to him, Carl decided to investigate the noise.

He eased out of bed, crossed the room and peeked out the door. The house was dark, except for the living room light, so he walked that way. Peering around the corner of the door, he saw his mother's brains and blood splattered around the room.

Carl promptly vomited, violently on the floor. When he was able, careful to keep his eyes closed, the boy turned away, pattered back to his room and returned to bed. Sleep eluded him as he wondered who would clean up the mess.

Sometime later, Bobby and his two oldest sons returned to the house and made the gruesome discovery for themselves. As it had done to Carl, the grisly scene and sickly sweet smell of perfume made Bobby and the boys violently ill.

Hearing the sounds of their retching, Carl felt certain he would not have to clean up the mess. He turned over on his stomach and went to sleep.

Joe resisted his brother's suggestion to turn back toward the house as the exploding gas tanks rocked the countryside. He calculated the tractor was needed more than ever to cut a fire line, especially if the streak of fire across the sky had carried flames any closer to the house. He drove the pickup as fast as he dared, treating the field lane as if it was a highway and bouncing John and himself around the cab like empty drink bottles.

Coming to the far end of the back field, Joe brought the truck to a sliding halt, both doors flying open before the truck came to a full stop. He raced for the tractor seat, while John ran toward the harrow.

The three-year-old tractor, a John Deere 1020, cranked on the first try, and Joe guided it to the harrow, backing the machine into a perfect position. With quick skill, John hooked the heavy frame of cutting disks to the tractor. He signaled Joe to go, jumped back from the harrow as his brother roared away, and ran for the truck.

Moments later, the fast-moving truck passed the tractor. By the time Joe got the tractor close enough to see how far the fire had come toward the house, his brother had parked the truck out of harm's way across the road and was beating frantically at the flames with nothing but his shirt.

The ferocity of the fire stunned Joe, who slowed the tractor only slightly to gauge the raging perimeters of the blaze. His family was stretched along the fencerow, with flames licking only a few feet from them. Matt and Sam fought desperately to keep the fire out of a large cedar tree, which was tender enough to burn in a flash and likely would toss embers onto the nearby house.

Already, the flames had scorched the roses and other flowers planted along the fencerow. Luke, Summer and Bonnie were waging a losing battle to keep flames from reaching the low branches of the pecan orchard.

Realizing the odds were against them, Joe guided the tractor through the pecan orchard, along the fence on the opposite side of the wall of flames. He felt the heat as the tractor raced past the weary firefighters, heard his daddy yelling at the top of his lungs. But Joe refused to heed Matt's frantic warning.

At the open fence gate, he braked the right wheel of the tractor and swung the equipment into the field. Revving the engine to full throttle, he lowered the harrow to the ground, shielded his face with an arm, eased off the clutch and drove straight into the cauldron.

The tractor moved through the flames as if guided by a daredevil pilot on the most important mission of his life.

Joe drove blindly along a straight line, willing himself to ignore the intense heat that singed his hair and blistered his face, arms and hands. In his wake, the harrow cut the burning stalks into the ground, turning the blaze into a faint version of its former self and making the flames manageable.

He was in the worst of the fire for no more than thirty seconds. But to his family and friends watching in terror, the ride seemed like an eternity in Hell. When the tractor burst through the far edge of the flames, Joe was coughing and sucking for air to clear the choking smoke from his lungs.

Slowing only to catch his breath, Joe continued to harrow down the edge of the field, putting a border of safety between the burning field and the larger field directly behind the house.

When he reached the stand of pine trees at the lower end of the field, Joe swung the tractor in a wide left-hand turn and cut a swath across the bottom section until another raging fire forced him to stop near the cotton patch. He halted the tractor to absorb the scope of flames, then turned around and traced over his original path, reinforcing the makeshift firebreak and cooling off lingering hot spots by harrowing the burning corn deeper into the ground.

A few minutes later, Joe reached his family as they extinguished the last of the flames closest to the house. Someone had cut a limb from one of the pecan trees to keep the fire out of the orchard, while one side of the cedar tree was charred on its lower branches. Fence poles still smoldered, and a patch of charred grass ran all the way to the side of the house.

Driving up beside his family and friends, Joe shut off the tractor and gave everyone a worried grin.

"That's one heck of a straight line you cut there, Joe," Sam praised. "I know your daddy taught you well, but I think—just this once—he would have cut you some slack had the row been a little crooked."

"It's a fact, son," Matt agreed. "You probably saved us from total ruin. The fire would have got the house, the orchard and a lot of other stuff if you hadn't plowed under those flames. I appreciate it. I'm not sure if I could have done it myself."

"Yeah, you would have, Daddy," Joe said lightly, uncomfortable with the praise.

"Face it, Matt," Caroline said, coming to her husband's side. "Among other things, we gave our children courage." She regarded Joe with a warm smile, then looked lovingly at her other children. "Joe and Summer are liven proof of that," she continued, "and so are John, Carrie, Luke and Bonnie."

Casting her gaze on Sam and Rachel, Caroline said, "You don't have to look far to see the secret of our success. Or that we've had plenty of support along the way," she added, glancing at Paul and Tom, and, finally, heavenward.

"Amen to that," Sam remarked.

"I know there's still work to do," Rachel agreed, "but I think the Lord's due a word of thanks."

No one disputed her claim, and they bowed their heads in a silent, prayerful moment of gratitude for their blessings.

When their eyes opened, everyone looked at each other, satisfaction etched on their faces along with the black soot. The moment was short-lived, however, and Joe provided the necessary closure.

"Daddy, we've got big problems back there," he said, gesturing to the flames raging in the distance. "There's fire in the cotton and in the woods closest to the bog. From what I can tell, it's burnen strong on your place, too, Paul. It's hot back there, with nothen to stop those flames without some help."

"There is the railroad," Paul remarked, an ominous warning that hundreds, perhaps even a thousand acres of timber, could burn along with everything else lost on this night.

Amid the flashing lights of heavy equipment and the blaring sirens on emergency vehicles, no one noticed the lone ambulance screaming past the Baker place on its way to answer another call for help in the community. In fact, the Bakers did not hear of Martha Taylor's suicide until morning, long after the fire had done its damage.

As Paul Berrien had warned, the rocky terrain of the railroad right of way was indeed the deciding factor in halting the fire's progress. Fortunately, the damage proved less severe than he or anyone else expected.

Flames blackened hundreds of acres on the Berrien estate, scorching the bottom trunks and exposed roots of hardwoods and pines. Few trees burned from top to bottom, however, and fewer still suffered any mortal harm because the blaze burned quickly and moved swiftly across the land.

"If you had struck the match yourself and started the fire, the results would have been pretty much the same," a young forest ranger informed Matt. "This could be a blessen in disguise for you, Sheriff Berrien. The fire thinned out a lot of scraggly oaks and underbrush that slows forest growth. It probably took care of some rattlesnakes, too."

While Paul and Tom helped the Bakers fight the fire, the Berrien sisters had joined Dan and Amelia Carter in guarding Benevolence Missionary Baptist Church from the flames. The fire curled along the edge of the church property, nipping at the cemetery and burning one of the long wooden tables where dinner was spread on Big Meeting Sundays. But the two aging sisters and the storekeepers never swerved in their dedication to keep the flames from lapping at the foundation of the little white church. Long after the real threat of danger had passed, the Berrien sisters and the Carters maintained their vigil, taking the initiative to rake and clean up the charred debris.

Arriving at the church at daybreak, on his way to offer moral support to the Bakers, Preacher Adam Cook found renewed faith in his congregants' unfaltering devotion to the church. He promptly changed the text of his upcoming sermon. Instead of dwelling on the fire and brimstone of Hell, a tactic he wielded effectively on rare occasions, the preacher would deliver a stirring sermon about unselfish service to the Lord.

One frightening consequence of the fire occurred just before daylight broke as two passersby collided in the thick smoke along a stretch of Highway 125 only moments before the State Patrol closed the road. A young woman drove her car into the smoke, which stretched a solid mile along the road, slowing the vehicle to a crawl as she attempted to navigate her way through the blinding conditions. An older man came behind her, traveling too fast for the conditions, and plowed his Volkswagen into the rear of the woman's car.

The woman cracked her head against the front window, suffering a concussion. The man broke his leg and required surgery to repair a ruptured spleen after the car's steering column crushed his chest.

Both victims were fortunate that a state trooper heard the crash as he erected a sign closing the road. Within a minute, he arrived at the crash site and rescued the woman and man from the choking smoke.

Without a doubt, the Baker place bore the brunt of damage. The fire destroyed the bulk of the front field of corn as well as the adjoining cotton patch.

Matt was unconcerned about the cotton. The dry weather had destroyed the crop long before the first flames licked it. All along, he had figured running a combine over the field would cost more than it was worth. Now the prospect of any waste whatsoever had vanished, and the field was primed for an early planting of winter grains.

While Matt also had never intended to run the combine through the corn, he had counted on the withered stalks to provide food and fodder for the hogs and cows over winter. Come fall, he had planned to graze the stock in those fields. As it stood now, he would have to sell more of his livestock. There was certainly no money to buy the feed necessary to carry the animals through the cold months—until the land could furnish enough nourishment for them.

Just as surely, he would not have to worry about the two cows that succumbed to heavy smoke. Matt needed to burn their carcasses, but he could not bring himself to start another fire. In fact, he was skittish of fire of any kind. Even the prospect of lighting a cigarette disturbed him.

Not everything about the fire was dismal, but Matt had to look hard around the blackened earth to find the bright spots. As he had explained to Paul Berrien, the forester also informed Matt that the fire would recharge his timber growth. Matt merely thanked the young man for his well-intentioned advice, refusing to point out that Sam intentionally burned the woods every few years for that very reason.

Apart from the bonus of rejuvenated timber, most of the farm had been spared the wrath of the flames. The farm's northern half, distinguished from the southern end by the dirt lane that bisected the land, escaped damage, except for one small section of corn—what else—planted in the field directly behind the house and the pecan orchard.

Fire had spread into that section of the farm when an exploding treetop rained down flaming debris on the field. Once again, Joe had come to the rescue, hemming around the fire with the harrow and containing the flames within a two-acre circle. And because his son had saved a third field from burning out of control, Matt still had crops of cantaloupes, corn, peanuts, soybeans and sweet potatoes to gather from his fields. He also had the last of the tobacco to strip from the stalks, even if there was no barn to cook it.

It seemed strange counting those crops as blessings. Of course, Matt realized some of the crops were worthless. He would not even waste the gas necessary to run the combine over the soybeans, while the cantaloupes were too thin—and the prices for them too low—to make the crop worth the picking time. Still, the cows could eat the beans, and Matt had never seen a hog—or cow either—who walked away from a cantaloupe, fresh or rotten.

Matt also knew he would not lose his shirt entirely on his peanuts, and the sweet potatoes were moneymakers despite the dry weather. And there again, his crops on the Castleberry place had fared better in the heat, benefiting from timely irrigation from the rented farm's gigantic pond.

So, yes, there were blessings to count on this early Sunday morning, which was exactly what his father tried to help Matt understand as they walked beside the rubble of their fallen tobacco barns.

"This, too, shall pass," Sam said as they surveyed the burnt timbers, which they had measured, cut and hammered with their own hands—not so long ago it seemed to both men.

"Where have I heard that before?" Matt muttered, trying to sound strong as his father offered a comforting pat on his shoulder.

In reality, Matt wanted to cry, to bury his head against his father's big shoulder and bawl like a baby. But no grown son of Sam Baker was going to act like a baby. On the contrary, he would take stock of the situation and meet the challenge as best he could. Sam understood that, even if Matt had his doubts.

"Be of good courage and play the man for your people," Sam remarked suddenly.

"Sir?" Matt replied.

"It's in the Bible," Sam explained. "That's what Joab—the commander of King David's army—told his troops one time when they fought the Syrians. Be of good courage, son. And play the man for your family."

"I'll do my best, Pa," Matt vowed, storing away that nugget of wisdom for another day when he would sorely need the inspiration.

From the rubble of ruined barns, the two men cast their gaze westward to where the bog boiled and bubbled like a witch's brew. The fire still simmered beneath that part of the earth, consuming the decayed plants and humus, which had belonged to some ancient swamp thousands of years ago and remained as a constant reminder that life rolled on without fail—in some form or another.

"I hope the black bears and bobcats and everything else in the bog fared as well as we did last night," Sam said.

Which was precisely what Sam should have said because he cared about the well-being of the animals, the plants and the trees. Suddenly, Matt realized he shared his father's concern for the living things.

"I hope so, too, Pa," he replied. "I also hope we didn't lose too many trees back there."

"Oh, we don't have to worry about the trees," Sam said. "They'll bounce back better than ever. Of course, we probably won't find much fat lighter in those woods over the next few years. But there's plenty of it elsewhere on the place. Maybe I'll go looken for some this afternoon; take John with me if he wants. Winter will be here before we know it."

It was an excuse for his father to see how the precious lay of the land had been altered by a single night of hell, which would matter as much to John as it did to Sam.

"Y'all watch out for the hot spots if you go," Matt cautioned. "There's still some out there."

"We'll be careful," Sam said, taking two steps forward, then turning to scan the distance behind Matt.

"It's a promisen sunrise we're blessed with this mornen," he observed, gesturing to where the sun rose on the horizon like a sheet of polished gold.

Matt turned and looked at the sunrise, wanting desperately to believe his father, who always watched the horizons for signs and usually saw only good things, coming and going.

Glancing again at his father, he nodded, and Sam started to leave. He took several steps westward, then whirled around to say one last thing to Matt.

"Remember one thing for me, son," Sam said with strong conviction. "There's plenty of everything we need still here on this farm—

even money. We can sell timber or do whatever else we might need to get by. So rest your mind. Things'll be better next year. You wait and see."

"I know, Pa," Matt said, regarding carefully this man with the black patch over his eye, seeing from a different side how much a father loved his son.

In nearly fifty years as the principal caretaker of this place, Sam had counted virtually every tree taken from the farm. During the worst of his financial struggles to keep the farm afloat, he had sold a few acres of hardwoods near the bog. With that lone exception, every other tree harvested from the place had been cut to clear new fields or to meet some need on the farm.

Sam believed trees should grow strong and tall for as long as possible—forever, if possible. The proof towered in the distance, near the bog where he had replanted the hardwoods with the pine trees, which were recently rejuvenated by the fire but still tall and proud despite being slightly scorched.

Without giving his son an opportunity to comment on the suggestion, Sam turned away once more and moved off through the field, leaving Matt to ponder dollars and cents.

From a purely financial point of view, the fire had done the most serious harm during the first hours, with the destruction of the tobacco barns, their cookers and the tractor. The buildings and equipment would have to be replaced before Matt could raise another crop, and he would bear the full cost. Out of necessity, Matt had risked the year without insurance. He had lost that gamble, and—as surely as the summer had been dry—the cost of replacing everything lost would exceed the little bit of change Matt had in the Farmers and Citizens Bank. His family also would need money to buy the necessities of life. Even before the fire, he had worried about making ends meet over the winter, through another spring and summer, until he could harvest a decent crop next fall.

Matt supposed he would have to get another loan from the bank, but he decided to dwell on the business problems tomorrow. Just this moment, he wanted to reflect some more on his blessings. It was Sunday after all, and they had not made it to church. How long since that had happened? Matt wondered as Caroline came toward him, wearing a sleeveless, everyday summer dress that was white, worn and one of Matt's favorites.

His wife was a beautiful woman, ripe with an understanding of and a passion for Matt. Caroline came to Matt, kissed him fully on the lips, not worrying that someone on their way to church might see them standing there like that in the field. She told her husband how thankful she was that Matt and their youngest son had survived the explosion— how her heart had raced and her stomach knotted when the thunder roared and the house shook on its foundations.

It was a blessing misplaced by Matt but now remembered. Luke or he could have been dead this morning—maybe both of them killed in the blast. By the grace of God, they were alive and well, able to reflect on their blessings and ponder the future.

"I love you, Matt," Caroline said.

"I love you, too, honey," he replied.

She was gone then, to tend some other troubled spirit. Caroline knew her husband well, understood that Matt was just beginning to soak up all that had happened, trying to comprehend the meaning. The full impact would hit him hardest a few days later, and he would need his wife especially then—her courage, her understanding, her reassurance and her touch. In this way, Matt and Caroline were alike, although neither one fully realized how their respective needs played into each other's strengths. By helping Matt cope, Caroline would draw strength from his courage, his understanding, his reassurance and his touch.

Joe came next, and Matt almost dreaded to face him. How could he tell his oldest son—who had risked his life for the family's livelihood, put his dreams on hold for his father's dream and never asked for anything in return—that more sacrifices were needed?

"Listen, Daddy," Joe said at length in their discussion. "I have somethen I'd like to tell you, and I want you to hear me out before you say anything."

"Sure, son."

"I don't intend to go back to school this year—at least not right away," he announced. "I only have two quarters left before I graduate. That's hardly any time at all. I can finish college next year or whenever it's more convenient. Right now, I want to help out around here— rebuilden the tobacco barns, getten grain planted for the winter or maybe even finden a job off the farm to bring some money into the house—whatever we need most to get by until next year."

Matt shuffled his feet, looked across the blackened field and wondered when his oldest son had grown such a large, comfortable shoulder. Once again, he wanted to bury his head and cry. Instead, he forced himself to look Joe in the eye and said, "You keep gallopen to the rescue, son. Keep doen it, and you'll wind up as my right-hand man."

"I can't be your right-hand man, Daddy," Joe replied sincerely, "but I do want to be in your corner—now and always."

Matt smiled and nodded. "You're a good man to have in anybody's corner," he said. "And thank you, son. I appreciate you comen to me like this."

It was a deep appreciation, the kind that made his heart ache, and the gratitude grew in Matt as the day progressed. One by one, his family came to him—in their own way and in their own time—offering and seeking reassurances as well as anything else that was needed to make life a bit easier, a little simpler.

Their outpouring of concern was not limited to Matt by any means. They sought each other out as well—not just the odd one but everyone. Earlier in the morning when the house had been saved, they had shared an important moment as a family, a collective of themselves. Now they needed private moments, to find the right words or expressions or touch that conveyed how much they meant to each other. In various ways, they showed one another what was in their hearts, which was love.

Summer tried to persuade Joe to use her scholarship money to pay his college tuition. She had observed her brother talking earnestly to Matt earlier in the day and guessed the content of their conversation.

Joe politely rejected her offer, kissed her on the cheek and steered the conversation to Tom. "He's my best friend in the world, and you've stolen him from me, little sister," he teased. "Please be gentle with him."

Summer had a surprise herself, which was news of her impending engagement to Tom. She shared that secret with Carrie because her sister was an incurable romantic at heart and—even in the midst of these bad times—would share the feeling of elation that surged within Summer's heart.

Carrie joined John on a walk through the woods because she understood his need to see how the flames had affected the place. She knew—but never mentioned—that John had walked a similar course with Grandpa earlier in the day.

John helped Bonnie pick butterbeans in the garden on the Castleberry place, even though it was Sunday and Caroline and Rachel frowned at working on the Sabbath. John frowned over work on Sundays, too, but his sister found comfort in gardens, and he believed God would not begrudge them a few butterbeans.

Bonnie put a new bandage on Luke's branded shoulder because

her brother seemed to keep getting hurt badly this summer and apparently appreciated the way his baby sister tended to his wounds.

On and on, the commiserating continued until the circle was complete, except for one tangent.

In the late evening, under another blood-red sky with the smell of smoke heavy and black drifts still rising from the burned earth, Tom Carter came to see Matt. Half-guessing what the young man had on his mind, Matt offered Tom a glass of iced tea, which Summer poured, and made the boy wait at the table while he ate fresh butterbeans.

When supper was finished, Tom walked his mentor into the pecan orchard and handed Matt a check worth three weeks of his salary.

"I realize I could have picked a better time to do this, Matt, but you know I only have one week left to work with you before I report to Fort Benning," Tom explained. "I was hopen you could keep this money for me as well as next week's check—kind of in trust until I come home in December. That way, I can be sure that I'll have enough saved to buy Summer an engagement ring.

"What do you say to that?" the young man asked.

Matt wanted to say he that he thought his daughter had found a man with a very large shoulder. Instead, he replied, "You've always been a part of this family, son. I'll be right pleased to see it become official."

He extended his handshake, then added, "I don't know of a better man for my daughter to marry than you, Tom."

Matt also started to tell Tom that while he would keep the check, he would not cash it. Then, he changed his mind. Sometimes, help came from unexpected places, and Matt did not like to kick a gift horse in the mouth—especially when the benefaction came out of respect for him and love for his daughter.

They wound up making small talk about the clouds gathering on the horizon.

CHAPTER 7

ON TUESDAY MORNING, EVERYONE overslept, fooled by an overcast sky into thinking they had time to linger in bed and just plain worn out from the strain of the last few days. No one emerged from beneath their cool sheets until Tom knocked on the door ready to begin another day of work. And Tom himself was more than an hour late, having turned off his own alarm clock, rolled over in bed and gone back to sleep on this dreary morning.

At the breakfast table with cold cereal and milk before them, the mood was sullen, dark and silent—except for the radio. As he had predicted incorrectly for two straight days now, the weatherman once again promised the first thunderstorm of the summer. With the hurricane lobbing warm moist air over South Georgia and poised to strike the Florida panhandle before noon, it was inconceivable that rain would not arrive sometime this day. He droned on, explaining why his forecasts had been wrong on Sunday and Monday, then laughed obnoxiously.

"Listen, folks," he bellowed. "If it don't rain today, we're never gonna get it."

Believing only half of what they heard, everyone marched from the house to the waiting work.

Sam, the girls and Tom spent the morning unstringing tobacco in the packhouse. Piled from floor to ceiling in stacks alongside the two long walls, the sticks of golden-brown leaf cramped the small room. With the limited floor space needed to spread out the burlap sheets on which Sam packed the tobacco in perfectly rounded mounds, Summer and Tom set up horses underneath the canopy of oak trees, which fronted the shed, while Carrie and Bonnie balanced their sticks in notches along the wall of the sagging front porch. There was a rhythm to their work as they pulled bunches of tobacco from the string that had been used to tie the leaves to the sticks.

The tobacco was in perfect *order*, which meant the leaves were not so heavy with moisture that they refused to yield the string or so dry that they crumbled at the slightest touch. Everyone worked methodically, and by dinnertime, only a few layers remained between the ceiling and the wooden floor beneath one of the two stacks.

Rachel and Caroline spent the morning in the summer garden, which just about had yielded its limit of vegetables for the year. With the pickings slim, their experienced hands flew across the bushes of beans and peas, dropping the bounty into bushel baskets without missing a beat. Their only break in routine occurred when the women wiped sweat from their brows or paused to anticipate the coming-in of the fall vegetables, which Matt had planted on the Castleberry place. The late garden had benefited from irrigation. With a little rain over the next few days, the garden would produce enough vegetables to fill the family's freezer and stock the pantry. If nothing else, Rachel and Caroline knew, their family would have food to eat during the hard winter ahead.

The task of clearing the rubble from the burned barns fell to Joe, John and Luke. They hustled through the morning. Joe lugged the charred rafters from the ruins, John stacked the smutty tin and Luke pulled melted pipes and burners from the debris. They worked in virtual silence, acknowledging one another when a particular effort demanded a helping hand, which was offered without being asked. Together, they dragged the crushed and twisted furnaces from beneath the ashes.

When dinnertime came, they were tired, streaked with black grime and satisfied with their progress. In the afternoon, they would tackle the job of removing the burned tractor.

Dinner was dismal, conspicuously noticeable for its sharp contrast to the hot meals Rachel had served virtually every day all summer long. With no apologies, Caroline and Rachel set packaged lunch meat on the table, except for one piece of leftover ham, which Luke grabbed from the refrigerator before anyone else remembered it was there.

Either Luke failed to see the envious glances cast his way, or he chose to ignore the disgusted expressions on the faces of his brothers and sisters. Regardless, he enjoyed his ham sandwich, which was more than could be said for those who slapped a piece of baloney between two slices of bread.

Only Sam and Joe dared to complain aloud about the victuals, declaring they could not stomach a baloney sandwich.

"Suit yourself," Rachel replied.

"It's a long time between now and supper," Caroline added, "and you may get more of the same."

Not intending to go hungry, Joe suited himself. He sliced a couple of mellow bananas, spread mayonnaise on four pieces of bread and offered one of the sandwiches to his grandfather.

The whole bunch of them was bored, listless and thirsty for something other than iced tea. And it was Carrie—the most silent one of them all, who could talk a blue streak when she put her mind to it, yet rarely ventured an unsought opinion—who pinpointed the cause of their malaise.

"I'd trade all the baloney in the world for just one raindrop on my face," she said.

Her declaration came as she sat hunched over the table, dreamily propped on an elbow, with a hand cupping her chin. Aimed at no one in particular, the off-handed remark startled everyone, especially Carrie. She took a long moment to comprehend the biting tone in her admission, then seemed almost embarrassed as drawn faces peered back at her with expressions of sympathy, disbelief and understanding.

"Amen to that, honey," said Matt, who had entered the house unnoticed and was standing at the kitchen door when Carrie voiced the thought on everyone's mind.

Matt had spent the morning hauling water and scouring the community for two empty barns that he could fill with the strippings of the tobacco. His appearance spared Carrie any further explanation. But her wish lingered over the table like an unfulfilled promise of dessert. And it breathed down their necks as they labored under a sweltering afternoon sun.

The skies held an almost undeniable promise of rain early in the day. Then, something strange, yet all too familiar, happened. The gray clouds scattered and disappeared. By noon, the sun shone like every other day that summer, which explained the staleness of the family's dinner far better than the idea of eating baloney sandwiches.

Everyone was fed up and tired of having their spirits dampened by the teasing, indecisive force of nature.

Restless with waiting, they stepped up the pace of their labor in the afternoon, as if the bustle would hurry the weather. But the exertion only tired them. They took a break from the work, drank cold drinks, ate moon pies and waited with the anticipation of an audience attending the grand premiere of the season.

At long last, when the day reached its hottest point—with the air as stagnant as it had ever been—the skies made up their mind. A plain of puffy white clouds galloped onto the southwestern horizon, riding a balmy breeze blown by some hurricane whose name no one could remember. The fresh scent of a coming rain cleared the air, and heat lightning rolled lazily—far off in the distance before cresting closer on waves of darkening cumulus. When the bellies of the clouds were girdled in black and the air strangely cool, the lightning found its thunder.

The first rolling clap idled the last industrious thoughts on the farm and chased the workers to the front porch of the house, where they trained their eyes on the blackened sky in search of anything remotely wet. Time made them wait still longer—until the dark clouds tricked the outside security light into thinking it was nighttime and the wind whipped the air with angry impatience. Finally, the heavy sky relinquished the first drops from a tear in its liner. The water fell hard against the dusty ground, followed by another heave that seemed to have been sloshed from the top of a full barrel. Seconds later, the clouds ripped apart and the heavens pounded the dry earth with rain.

The storm spent its pent-up fury swiftly, then settled into a steady summer shower. It was cleansing for the soul, sweet to the touch and refreshment for the spirit.

———————

No one made the mistake of recognizing the rain as any kind of panacea for their troubles. Especially Matt.

The smashing enormity of everything came crashing down on him as Matt watched the storm from the cab of the pickup truck. There was no way to rationalize the situation—just the cold comprehension of a hot summer filled with withered crops and dry fortunes.

Matt wanted to blank away the last few months, to remember the good feeling he had carried into the new year. But he could not push away the nagging aftermath of things unplanned and plans gone awry. He had to face the consequences.

He swallowed hard, his throat constricted as he wondered whether the promise of next year was enough to carry his family through the tough times ahead of them. So much was lost. Matt knew what it was like to take three steps forward, then fall back two.

But this was the first time he had felt as if he was losing at least three steps for every two he made. Now, when there was so much that needed doing, he wondered whether his shoulders would bear the burden.

Above everything else, though, Matt ached for the sacrifices his family would have to make in the coming year. Their faith and trust in him—their willingness to do whatever was necessary—had always given Matt a sense of pride unlike any other constant in his life. Right now, however, their unabridged devotion depressed him.

Matt did not grieve alone.

Caroline had sensed the rain would bring her husband a heavy heart. She shared his sorrow. She understood her family had suffered a loss far greater than the damage done by some ordinary blight on their fields. If the next year brought little else to this family, it would give them succinct understanding of what hardship really was. But goaded by the same instincts that now burdened her husband, Caroline found courage to face the future.

Peering through the glass window of the living room, she watched Matt slump against the truck door, knowing he needed her beside him. If for nothing else, then he craved the reassurance of her presence. Without waiting for the storm to slacken, Caroline went to her husband, ignoring the curious looks and calls from the children as she stepped off the porch and ran into the driving rain.

Matt barely acknowledged her arrival, staying slouched against the door and tight-lipped. Even so, he arched his eyebrows in the thoughtful, worried look she had grown accustomed to when they faced difficult times. Her husband's concern was all the encouragement Caroline needed. She slipped close to him, resting her head on his shoulder. As the hard rain settled into a steady tap against the truck, husband and wife engaged in a quiet give-and-take that buoyed their spirits.

In a while, Caroline felt the strength surging from her husband. Then, she straightened next to him, stroked his hair and helped Matt to understand what really mattered.

"If it's true what they say about hard times maken people appreciate the good times, then we oughtta be one more appreciative family come this time next year," she said. "But, Matt, I don't necessarily believe that's a matter of fact. For the most part, this family has settled for getten by year after year. With the good Lord's help, we've done fairly well for ourselves. As for this year, well, I can appreciate it just as much as those years when we've gotten by a little better than usual.

As long as we're doen it together—you and me, Ma and Pa, our children—then every ounce of sweat, every heartache and every happy moment is worthwhile. Because after all, Matt, we have so much—don't we?"

Without waiting for his answer, she added blithely, "We've faced hard times before, sweetheart. We'll get through this, too."

For a long moment, Matt stared into the summer shower. Finally, he put his arm around Caroline, and they leaned against each other.

"We will at that," he said simply.

QUESTIONS FOR DISCUSSION

Warning: Questions contain spoilers

1. Book Two begins with twelve-year-old Summer Baker complaining about having to do "women's work." Given that almost sixty years have passed since the setting of this scene, how do you identify today with her angst about her lot in life.

2. In the episode "Angels Sing," Rachel wrestles with self-doubt and self-worth as she recovers from her illness. At one point, Rachel feels as if she's spent her entire life preparing a feast, yet forgotten to set a place for herself at the banquet table. Do her struggles remind you of anyone you know? Do you think her feelings are common in older people?

3. Faith plays an important role in *Plowed Fields*, sometimes in very obvious ways such as Matt's struggle to come to terms with it and Caroline and Rachel's steady reliance on it. What faith moment stuck most with you in this story? Did the story ever cause you to consider your own faith in light of what happened to the characters in the book?

4. The farming life played a pivotal role throughout this story. What impressions most intrigued you about farm life?

5. Every job, every profession, has its ups and downs, no doubt, but farmers definitely face factors beyond their control in terms of weather and market prices among other things. Did the story make you feel sympathetic to the plight of farmers? How would, or do, you deal with forces beyond your control in the workplace? How do those forces affect you on a day-to-day basis?

6. In terms of language, *Plowed Fields* was true to the time of its setting. Given the day and age we live in, how did the liberal use of the N-word throughout the book make you feel? Could the author have found a better way to characterize the prejudice? Or was the actual approach—harsh as it is—the better choice?

PLOWED FIELDS
TRILOGY EDITION

Book One – The White Christmas and The Train
1960-1962

It's December 1960, and a cold wind is blowing a rare white Christmas toward the Baker farm in South Georgia. Joe Baker, an intense young man hell-bent on achievement and responsibility, finds himself torn between his own desire and ambition and his loyalty and responsibility to his family. Joe can't shake the notion that he is destined to remain solid and will never soar as long as he remains on the family farm.

Thus begins Book One of the *Plowed Fields* trilogy, setting the stage for a conflict that will nag at Joe for the next decade as he tries to reconcile his own desire and ambition with loyalty and responsibility to his family.

"The White Christmas" sets the stage, introducing Joe and his family, along with a host of friends and acquaintances who will shape their fates during the next decade. They include Lucas Bartholomew, a black farm laborer, and Bobby Taylor, the spitting image of a civil rights-minded Yankees' vision of a racist. Tensions erupt between the Bakers and the Taylors, sparked by a senseless act and fueled by Bobby campaigns for the sheriff's job against Matt Baker's best friend, the aristocratic and troubled Paul Berrien.

In "The Train," Joe confronts racial prejudice in his school and community and feels the strain of taking an unpopular stand. A girl claims his heart and a heroic deed plants a seed of hate that will fester as the decade unfolds.

Book Two – Angels Sing, The Garden, Faith and Grace, and The Fire
1963-1967

As the decade progresses, Joe Baker and his family see their fortunes rise and fall, beginning with an illness that shakes the family at its very core. Prosperity comes calling when it's least expected, but a harrowing ordeal forces a reckoning with faith that nearly shatters the family.

Book Two of the *Plowed Fields* trilogy offers an intimate portrayal of the farming life. The Bakers also encounter more unexpected turmoil with their friends and neighbors, including Lucas Bartholomew, Bobby Taylor and Sheriff Paul Berrien, stoking the conflict that will bring the family face-to-face with fire and famine, war and peace, good and evil.

Amid a severe drought, Book Two of *Plowed Fields* builds to an exciting climax as one violent act leads Joe to mete out his own vicious brand of retribution. Ultimately, the Bakers need an act of daring and courage to save them from utter ruin.

The family's journey—from innocence to sin, from good to evil, from despair to triumph—sets the stage for the riveting conclusion of the *Plowed Fields* saga.

Book Three – The War, The Dream, Horn of Plenty
1968-1970

When we first met Joe Baker and his family, it was December 1960, and a rare white Christmas was blowing toward their farm in South Georgia. As the decade unfolded, they faced fire and famine, war and peace, good and evil. But those weighty issues served only as the backdrop for hardships encountered by a large farming family more concerned with making ends meet than saving the world.

In Book Three, the Bakers and their friends and neighbors move from the tobacco field to the battlefield, from main street to city lights, from the church door to the gates of Hell.

Tom Carter, Joe's best friend and his sister's fiancé, finds himself slogging through the muck and mud in Vietnam, while an old flame entices Joe to participate in an antiwar demonstration. The resulting firestorm consumes the community, their friends and the Bakers themselves.

As the tumultuous year of 1968 gives way to the final year of the Sixties, Joe fulfills his dream of becoming a newspaper reporter and immerses himself in the South's last stand against school integration. The ensuing battle pits old adversaries like Lucas Bartholomew and Bobby Taylor, as long-simmering animosity unleashes the unthinkable and wields devastating consequences.

PLOWED FIELDS
TRILOGY EDITION

Get a head start on the final book in the
Plowed Fields Trilogy:

BOOK THREE
THE WAR

JOE BAKER STARED IN wide-eyed disbelief at the melee playing out in real life. Beneath the Hilton Hotel sign, police and National Guardsmen clubbed antiwar demonstrators senseless, smashing heads, limbs and crotches with reckless disregard of their victims. A store window shattered somewhere, and the cops intensified their assault until blood flowed in the streets of Chicago. Paddy wagons lined the avenues, waiting to cart away those who were arrested.

"Lousy pigs," someone muttered behind Joe.

For seventeen agonizing minutes, the violence raged, with the crowd of demonstrators chanting ominously, "The whole world is watching."

Joe was part of the whole world on this last Wednesday night of August 1968. He had been camped in a folding chair in front of the television for three straight hours. His bladder urged him to find a bathroom, but Joe stayed in his seat, mesmerized by the savagery on the television screen.

He was among a crowd of college students who had piled into the tiny living room of Elliot Frankel's apartment. Elliot enjoyed the well-earned reputation as the unofficial leader of a fledgling student movement at Valdosta State College. He was a novelty among the conservative collegians, most of whom adhered to values more American than apple pie itself. Besides his authentic Brooklyn accent, which was an oddity in itself on the campus, Elliot made a conscientious effort to distinguish himself from the crowd. His jet-black hair flowed in long locks down his back. His diamond-studded earring sparkled too loudly to go unnoticed by anyone within eye-shot. He typically wore an odd assortment of rag-tag clothes, love beads and sandals unless the occasion required conservative attire.

Then, he dressed in well-worn blue jeans, T-shirts and sneakers. On more than one occasion, he had inspired the question, "Is it a man or a woman?"

Despite his peculiarities and shenanigans, Elliot believed substance mattered more than style. He was no ordinary goof ball and refused treatment as such, though several professors had tried without success. He had migrated to the South Georgia college from New York University, hoping to discover firsthand the truth about race relations in the Deep South. He came across as sincere, dedicated to his convictions and resolute in his commitments. When he picked a fight with administrators, professors or fellow students, Elliot argued with passion and persuasiveness.

Joe and Elliot had become friends in the spring of 1967 during an American history class, unexpectedly brought together by their mutual praise for Martin Luther King Jr. In the face of bitter feelings among their classmates, they had defended the Nobel Peace Prize winner as a genuine American hero for his war on injustice and bigotry. Out of their battle scars, a genuine camaraderie had emerged even though they sat on opposite sides of the classroom and appeared socially at odds with each other. When the class ended, Elliot had invited Joe to join him for a bite to eat at the local Woolworth's lunch counter.

As Joe nursed a Coke and Elliot sipped coffee with the day's blue plate special—fried beef liver—the young men had spoken frankly of their misconceptions about each other. Elliot decided Joe was an unabashed square, committed to progress as long as it did not interfere too much with the way things were. Joe believed Elliot was a misguided revolutionary, whose freewheeling ways alienated the very people he hoped to change.

"You talk like McCarthy and Kennedy, but you're Buckley and Nixon in sheep's clothing," Elliot declared. "You believe change will occur simply for the sake of change, and you assume it will be change for the better. But while you're waiting and hoping for the best, very little gets accomplished, Joe. It takes men of action to bring about change. You prefer to sit back, watch and then make observations that more often than not come across as smug complicity rather than constructive feedback. Honestly, Joe, I question your commitment to change, to a great many of the things you profess to believe. With you, everything is a simple question of right and wrong. In my book, that's a selfish way to look at things. It's a set-up for a hard and fast fall. I suppose if you want to change the world—and probably you do—

then you are one of those people who believe it can be done one person at a time. Assuming you're right for the sake of argument, then there's a great deal of suffering to be done while we're waiting on your piecemeal change. I'm not much for suffering, Joe."

"You act too much like a hippie for my tastes," Joe responded in equally plain tones, "and you tend to go overboard with your beliefs. Deep down, you champion essentially sound principles. No one should fault you for your commitment to civil rights, and everyone probably should pay attention to your misgivens about Vietnam. But despite your best effort, Elliot, there's no way you can make me believe that Americans should see Fidel Castro as any kind of hero. Nor does this country need a social revolution. People make mistakes—me, you, the president, Congress, everybody. But good values never go out of style, and I think most people have good values. You, on the other hand, don't always advocate good values, Elliot. You want to live in a world where anything goes: Drink this, smoke that, free love, free sex, screw anything that walks and screw the consequences. You're so danged intent on tearen everything and everybody down that you can't separate what's good from what needs to be done."

"I'll take that under consideration next time I plan a revolution," Elliot said.

"Likewise," Joe agreed. "If I ever get around to it."

Eventually, they had decided their observations about each other probably were as much accurate as flawed and as astute as they were ignorant. But they had walked away from the dime store restaurant with a grudging respect for each other's way of thinking.

Their newfound friendship had languished soon after the spring-quarter history class ended, and they had lost touch completely when Joe left college to help his father after the fire. But on the evening of April fourth earlier this year, Elliot had telephoned long-distance to inform Joe of MLK's assassination at the Lorraine Motel in Memphis, Tennessee. A few days later, against his family's wishes, Joe had accompanied Elliot to Atlanta, where they attended the fallen civil rights leader's funeral. Months later, they had repeated the ritual when Robert Kennedy was cut down by Sirhan Sirhan.

In between the tragedies, Elliot had mentioned casually that Joe might enjoy attending one of the weekly meetings he hosted for "freethinkers" like himself. "There's nothing official about it or anything like that," Elliot explained. "It's a bunch of students and sometimes a professor or two who're feeling especially brave or oppressed. We sit around, listen to the music, drink coffee, wine, beer, booze or whatever your pleasure—maybe smoke a joint every now and then, and talk about whatever's groovy or hip."

"I probably wouldn't fit in," Joe surmised.

"You would well enough," Elliot replied. "Almost everyone who comes is more like you than me and the rest of the hard-core nuts."

"Who are the hard-core nuts?" Joe asked.

"We represent every stereotype you could want," Elliot said. "Darris Palmer is black and can't decide whether he wants to follow MLK or Malcolm X. I keep telling him they're both dead, so it doesn't matter. Cecil Bradley is light in the shoes if you catch my drift, but he can argue passionately about why the United States does not belong in Vietnam. Kevin Reid worked in Mississippi during Freedom Summer, then spent two years in 'Nam. He's generally confused about everything. Then there's Karen Baxter. She's a hodgepodge of every stereotype in our little group and then some.

"Do any of those names ring a bell?" Elliot asked.

"I went to high school with Karen," Joe answered. "She always was a freethinker, I suppose."

"Yes, indeed," Elliot sighed. "Karen has a style all her own. What she can do for peace remains to be seen. As a piece, however, the woman's not bad at all. You come to one or two of our meetings, and you're likely to learn for yourself."

"The meeten sounds interesten, but I think I'll pass on Karen and whatever she might offer," Joe said somewhat tersely.

Elliot laughed aloud, amused by the serious tone of Joe's voice. "A caustic comment that begs questioning," he teased. "But I'll be a gentleman for once and keep them to myself. Let's just say, shall we, that Karen makes sure the group's physical needs—at least those of the male persuasion—are attended to so that our minds might be at their brilliant best to satisfy her lusty liberal leanings."

"Say whatever you want about her," Joe said. "I couldn't care less."

A few days later, he had attended his first meeting. For the most part, he drank beer while everyone else analyzed a Simon and Garfunkel song. At subsequent meetings, they discussed Vietnam, the Great Society, the upcoming election and how America's youth was changing the country's way of thinking. Whether he agreed or disagreed with his new friends, Joe enjoyed the debate, as well as the companionship.

Appropriately enough, he had smoked marijuana for the first time while the group discussed the merits of legalized drugs, an idea Joe found ridiculous and flawed. But he had consumed far too much beer on that night to argue effectively against the notion, so he kept quiet and took a toke on a marijuana cigarette circulating around the room. Even in his alcoholic haze, Joe felt uneasy about smoking pot. But when the drug seemed to have no apparent effect on his behavior, he found it easier to accept the marijuana on the next occasion it was offered.

On this August night, Joe felt no remorse at all when Elliot offered him the remnants of a rolled joint. He inhaled deeply, took another drag for good measure and passed the joint to a girl waiting beside him with a roach clip. Almost instantly, his total awareness dulled as his attention zeroed in on the television screen.

As Joe saw it, the savagery in Chicago was a fitting climax to the carnage that would be remembered as 1968. He thought the violence in Chicago was hardly unexpected.

Although only a spectator to the Democratic National Convention, Joe had sensed the mounting tension and frustration that triggered this final clash between antiwar demonstrators and cops. For three days, he had watched television and read newspaper accounts of how students trashed police cars with rocks and bottles while baiting officers with taunts and threats. From the moment the cops first fired their guns into the air as a warning several days earlier, he had anticipated a frenzied climax to the madness. But even so, he watched the television in dismay. He was stunned by the show of force as the cops carried out their vicious attack. But his sympathies were tempered by the inclination that the mob of demonstrators deserved a few bruises for their own outrageous behavior.

He was wondering why both sides were not behaving more rationally when Karen Baxter interrupted his thoughts.

"This is mind-bogglen," Karen said to Joe. "It's a national disgrace and just goes to prove what we've been sayen all along. What about the right to peaceful protest?"

"I haven't seen anything peaceful about any of the whole sorry mess," Joe replied without taking his eyes off the television. "But you're right about one thing: It is a disgrace."

Karen backed away from Joe, biting her tongue to conceal the anger boiling within her. Once again, Joe had her on edge. She tried to decipher his remark about the bloodbath playing on television. Was there a hidden meaning in his flippant response to her observations, one she failed to understand? Had he intended to ridicule her?

Too often these days, she found herself floundering in Joe's presence. When Joe was among her circle of companions, she maintained a constant vigil on every word and thought. She felt threatened by Joe, as if he were a secret agent waiting to expose her as an intellectual and New Left fraud. The man's mere presence frayed her nerves, his smug complacency rankled her demeanor and his casual disregard preyed on her worst fears. Karen resented his intrusion into her elite group of radicals and revolutionaries. Worst of all, she despised having to hide her contempt for Joe.

Still, discretion was an annoying necessity. Karen needed every clever trick to keep these bouts of paranoia from revealing herself as a vain woman instead of the free-spirited intellectual she wanted to be.

She had orchestrated her image as a choreographer creates dance. Each step was planned with precision and flow, embracing every idea that smacked of rebellion. She maintained impeccable grades, yet flaunted her disregard for archaic institutions of learning. She denounced Vietnam, railed against prejudice, applauded Eugene McCarthy and was leading efforts to establish a chapter of Students for a Democratic Society on the VSC campus. She believed in black power, flower power, feminism and free love. She was ready to tune in, turn on and drop out. She was devoted to the ideas of rebellion and repression, revolution and resistance.

More than embracing any particular ideology, Karen adored all things extreme. On a given day, she was a devoted flower child, strolling on air as she sang *Are You Going to San Francisco*, even while she dreamed of standing side by side with the Black Panthers and making fast and furious love with Eldridge Cleaver. She deplored violence, yet licked her lips in fascination as scores died and flames burned throughout Watts, Newark and Detroit in urban rioting. She encouraged young men to burn their draft cards and flee to Canada, yet was enthralled by the sheer numbers coming out of Vietnam: half a million American soldiers there, fifteen thousand dead, almost two million acres defoliated in a single year. She had believed passionately in Robert Kennedy and Martin Luther King Jr., but found the men's violent deaths more inspiring than their principles. Now, she supported no one in the race to succeed Lyndon Johnson unless it was Eugene McCarthy. Even so, she hoped George Wallace would run a good campaign simply for the sake of a divisive election.

Her motives had been sincere at some point. She had come to college in search of liberation and ended up with a carefully cultivated reputation as a radical. She had become the embodiment of the New

Left, a radical whose reputation was surpassed only by the antics and maleness of Elliot Frankel. Earning her reputation had been pure bliss. Maintaining it was complicated. As queen of the revolution, she was expected to say all the right things, wear all the right clothes and think all the right thoughts. Often, Karen felt as if she were campaigning to become the next homecoming queen.

She owed her revolutionary status to Elliot. He was one of the few men who had seduced Karen rather than been seduced by her. From the moment she first laid eyes on the man, Karen had decided to sleep with Elliot on their second occasion together. Less than two hours later, she was underneath him, on the mattress laid across the living room floor in his tiny apartment. Men with long hair and earrings attracted Karen in the first place. Once Elliot had uttered his first words of liberal propaganda, she had become putty in his hands.

Karen had discovered the sexual revolution years before it became vogue. Sex made her heady with power and importance. She kept a running list of her sexual partners and the tab numbered more than a hundred. She had slept with schoolboys, collegians, professors, construction workers, a vacuum cleaner salesman and one black man. She advocated legalized abortion and free birth control pills for everyone. She understood the power of seduction, and she used it with great success. On a whim, she would turn a man into a sexual magnet, full of cock and swagger in his prowess. Or she might exploit every inch of vulnerability. On three occasions, she had extorted comfortable sums of money from the ignorant, telling them cash was needed to pay for an abortion. The claim had been true only once.

Karen was indeed queen of the revolution, and she enjoyed her favored status. But the mere presence of Joe Baker tarnished the luster of her crown. He evoked memories of the girl who had longed to be a hell-raiser while cast amid a sea of fuddy-duddies; a closet revolutionary who wanted to shake America at its roots while her peers thrived in their contentment; the siren who satisfied her restlessness by bringing to life the vivid fantasies of youthful lovers. Joe's presence was a direct link to the perky cheerleader, the Sunday school sweetheart, the bouffanted prom queen—all roles Karen had played at one time or another. But those were feelings that any of her high school classmates could have dredged to the surface, the cool and the popular ones, the jocks and the brains, the weirdoes and the wallflowers, even those who barely counted.

She felt ill at ease around Joe. She was jealous of his poise and unwavering self-assurance. His presence undermined her self-control, and his seeming indifference provoked her pettiness. He jeopardized her status, leaving Karen one slip of the tongue away from losing her credibility with the group.

On the first night Joe had attended one of Elliot's gatherings, Karen had picked the topic of discussion—an analysis of her favorite song, *Dangling Conversation,* by Simon and Garfunkel. The discussion had been probing, a free-spirited consideration of life's values and a welcomed relief from the endless dialectic over war, politics and violence. The lone dark spot had been Joe, who sat in his chair looking as if he deigned the entire exercise a waste of time. Irked by his silence, Karen had made a blunder. She had challenged Joe to contribute to the conversation, hoping to expose him as shallow and unable to grasp the subtle elements of the song. If she had thought first, she would have remembered Joe was a sponge, always aware of everything and willing to meet a challenge. But Karen had forgotten.

"You haven't said a word all evenen, Joe," she commented during a lull in the discussion. "Are we boren you? Or does the song have no meanen for you?"

"I like the poetry of Robert Frost," Joe answered with a shrug of his shoulders. "But I don't care much for Emily Dickinson. I don't understand her—maybe because I can't or don't want to identify with her."

When it became apparent Joe would say nothing else, Karen had pressed the issue. "You're missen the complexities of the song, Joe," she said with the slightest touch of condescension. "I don't think poetry has much to do with the message. It's about how superficial people are."

Joe considered the suggestion for a long moment. "Perhaps," he shrugged finally. "I tend to think it's up to each person to decide for themselves what is and isn't superficial. It's certainly not my place to make that decision for them."

"Right on!" said Darris Palmer, pumping his fist and winking at Joe.

"I agree," Elliot added quickly before his eyes turned lethal and his tone lecturing. "Besides Karen," he said. "Since when are we keeping score on who contributes what to the discussion?"

"I wasn't keepen score," Karen replied calmly, mustering a warm smile for Joe. "I happen to know Joe from way back when. I was hopen—maybe even expecten—somethen more profound from him."

Then, she had laughed easily. "No harm meant, Joe," she added, diffusing the tension. "You know how obsessive I get about things important to me. Didn't you once call me a bulldog?"

"I don't recall," Joe had said, shrugging off the incident as if there were no need for an apology.

From that point on, Karen had focused on making Joe feel accepted. She had smiled at him until her jaws ached and tried to draw him into conversation. But nothing she did commanded his attention. And although she had a strong inkling why he avoided her, Karen seethed over his rejection. Animosity festered within her like an infected sore, threatening to burst in an ugly spray of malice and envy.

Suddenly, a warm breath ran down her neck and across her throat. "I'd like to be inside that pretty head of yours now to see what wheels are turning," Elliot said. "What has Joe Baker done to inspire this gaze of fierce intensity?"

Karen tipped her head back and smiled through gritted teeth, allowing Elliot to muzzle her cheek with his day-old beard. "Was I staren," she asked. "I didn't realize."

"I didn't think so," Elliot laughed. "Nor do I really care." He pulled her against him. "Suppose you stick around tonight after everybody leaves," he leered. "We could stage some violence of our own, compromise each other and then make peace."

The suggestion appealed to Karen, and she knew suddenly what needed doing. She would bed a man tonight, but not Elliot Frankel.

"I don't think so, Elliot," she replied at length, slipping from his embrace. "Some other time. Tonight, I'm taken care of unfinished business."

Willowy arms wrapped around Joe's shoulders, breaking his concentration on the televised spectacle that would go down in infamy as the 1968 Democratic National Convention in Chicago. One hand caressed his chest, while another brought a taste of hard liquor to his lips. The hardened nipples of firm breasts pressed against his spine, and moist breath whispered in his ear. Joe knew Karen Baxter was seducing him. He decided to play along with her for a while, admiring her moxie if little else.

"Vodka on ice," she said. "That is your preference, Joe?"

"It is," Joe answered as she nibbled on his ear.

Karen was oblivious to the long-lived effects of her passionate dalliance with Joe years earlier. In his twenty-two years, she was the only woman who had come remotely close to claiming his heart. Joe counted his former feelings for her as nothing more than puppy love, and he regarded the lost relationship with casual detachment. Still, Karen intrigued him. And although he knew better, Joe was still captivated by what he saw as a delicate quality to the woman. More than once recently, he had caught himself fantasizing about making love to her, wondering about the passion they could create if they took the time to appreciate each other.

These thoughts were ridiculous, he knew, a complete waste of time. His infatuation with Karen was irrational, though less now that he was older and wiser. Joe harbored few illusions about her. He knew people who piled puppies and rocks in burlap bags, then tossed the bundle off the nearest bridge, and they had more heart than Karen. Furthermore, he suspected she was the reason he approached any relationship with a woman like a skilled bank robber, making his moves only when he was certain of the getaway.

Maybe that explained why he was willing to play along with her seduction. She was skilled at the art, a mixture of coy, cunning and straightforwardness in her quest to bed him. Above all, she was relentless, charming Joe with the fickle spells of enchantment and whim that had first attracted him years earlier. On this night, he was of mind to wait and see whatever sleight of hand Karen would play.

Hours later, Karen snuggled into the crook of his arm as Joe smoked a cigarette. She sighed contentedly, watching Joe blow smoke rings. They were sweaty, exhausted and satisfied.

"This beats the backseat of the family car, huh?" she giggled.

"Yeah," Joe said.

"Can you French-inhale?" she asked.

"I haven't done that in years," Joe answered, exhaling a straight line of smoke. "I pretty much stick to the basics."

"Do it for me," Karen said.

Joe drew on the cigarette, opened his mouth and breathed slowly, rotating the smoke in a circle between his nose and mouth. Karen giggled, pushing closer to him, resting her palm flat against his stomach.

Joe quickly exhaled the smoke and pulled away from her, pushing away the sheet as he sat up on the edge of the bed. "What time is it?" he asked, searching around the one-room apartment for a clock.

Karen rolled on her side and retrieved a clock from the floor. "It's three-thirty," she informed him. "Come back to bed. Let's sleep late and see if we can stage a repeat performance when we wake up."

"I have to get home," Joe replied. "We're diggen sweet potatoes today, and Daddy wants to get an early start. If I leave now, I can catch a little sleep before it's time to get up."

"You're leaven me?" she asked, disbelieving.

Joe stood unsteadily, found his clothes and put on his underwear and jeans. "It was fun, Karen, but I have to go," he said a moment later, his tone far more casual than his feelings about this encounter. "I guess we chalk this up as one for old time's sake."

"Beats the backseat of the family car," she said softly as Joe buttoned his shirt, stuffed socks into pants pockets and sat down beside her to tie his tennis shoes.

Joe looked at Karen for a long moment, appraising her petite figure, her milky white skin and soft brown hair. He wondered if a goodbye kiss was in order.

Karen sensed his mixed emotions. "Don't forget the protest," she reminded him. "We'll start the fall quarter off with a bang."

Joe shrugged. "I'm not sure I'll be there," he replied.

"You have to be there, Joe," she cried. "You promised."

Joe tried without success to remember the promise. "Believen the war is wrong is one thing, Karen," he said. "Protesten against it is somethen else again. I'm a veteran for gosh sake. I'm not sure I'd feel right about doen that. Those things have a way of getten blown out of proportion. A person ought to be damn sure about what—and whom—he's protesten against."

"We're sure, Joe," she argued. "We're demonstraten to stop the war in Vietnam, clear and simple."

"It's not clear and simple, Karen, and if you believe that, then you're sellen yourself a bill of goods," Joe fought back. "My best friend in the world is over there right now, right this moment. Guys you and I went to school with have been and are there now. Remember Scotty Dean. He went over there and came back without a leg, Karen. How do you think Scotty's gonna feel when he sees his friends protesten against the very thing that cost him such a high price?"

"That's why we have to protest," she pleaded. "So not one more person comes back maimed or worse. You know what we're up against, Joe. Those of us who oppose this war have to demonstrate our opposition. We have to show people the war is wrong."

"I'll think about it," Joe said. "That's the best I can do."

Karen exhaled an angry breath, sat up in bed and pulled the sheet against her. "Same old, Joe," she scoffed. "You're never able to come through when the chips are down, are you?"

"Exactly what does that mean?" Joe interrupted.

"It means you have the most half-assed convictions of anybody I've ever known," Karen said scathingly. "You start things, but you never finish them. It's one of the things that always bugged me about you."

"If it's somethen I believe in strongly enough, Karen, I'll see it through to the end," Joe said. "But I won't be pressured into doen somethen I disagree with or don't fully understand."

"What exactly do you believe in?" she asked scornfully.

Unexpectedly, surprising himself, Joe touched her face. Karen glanced up, and he saw her discontent.

"A long time ago," he said, "I believed I loved you."

She shook her head in disagreement. "Nothen but an infatuation," she replied without emotion.

"Maybe," Joe agreed, withdrawing his hand.

"Besides, Joe," she added. "I told you once: You and I aren't cut out for love."

"I'm not sure I believe that," he said. "What makes you so sure?"

"Because we're not willen to invest that much of ourselves," she snapped back. "You're just like me, Joe; you want to run away from everything that's familiar—from Cookville, from your home, from your family. We're gonna spend our whole lives runnen away and breaken ties."

Joe regarded her carefully. "That's a harsh life sentence to hang yourself with, Karen," he replied at last. "I don't buy it, at least not for myself. When and if I leave Cookville, you can be assured I'll be runnen *to* somethen. Maybe that's the difference between us. There's nothen or no one here that I'd ever want to run away from. It all means too much to me."

She shook her head to break the moment. "Just go, Joe," she urged softly, looking away and drawing up her knees. "Get out of here and go home."

He stood and left the room quickly, with a polite goodbye and without even looking back at her.

In the middle of September, Joe found himself standing on the edge of a group of students who intended to stage the first antiwar protest on the Valdosta State College campus. He was a dubious participant, reluctant to settle a battle of mind-sets that pitted his sense of loyalty against the growing notion that America had no business waging war in Vietnam. His final decision to participate was calculated, based on the facts as he saw them. His indecision arose from a belief that feelings as fierce and passionate as loyalty—whether to one's friends, family, country or brothers in arms—defied logic.

The call had been close, but Joe had gone with his head, because his heart told him the war was a mistake. No one back home knew of his decision to demonstrate against the war. Until a few minutes ago when he arrived on campus for the rally, his intentions had been declared to only one person, his best friend, who risked his life daily in the jungles of Vietnam.

In his frequent letters to Tom Carter—his best friend and his oldest sister Summer's fiancé—Joe had mentioned his concerns about the war, always careful to conceal any blatant antiwar sentiments. In writing to Tom several days earlier, Joe had chosen the words carefully to tell his friend about the upcoming protest. But he had not minced the truth about his decision to join the demonstration and his opposition to the war.

"I suppose I could keep everything a secret, Tom. I could simply attend the protest and never speak of it. But I don't want to lie to you. I'd rather lose your friendship to honesty than betray you with deception. The truth is that I think this war is a mistake.

"For years, I've watched the civil rights struggles and wanted to join in the fight. Maybe, too, I have in a small way. But I wish I could have done more to fight for something I believe in. Now I have an opportunity to make my voice heard. Although my opposition to the war in Vietnam is a murky issue compared with my belief in simple human dignity, I feel compelled this one time to join the front line of the battle rather than offer quiet support from the distance. Of course, once I get there, I might beat a hasty retreat. I wish you had that luxury.

"I have one last thing to say on the matter, and then I'll be quiet. Please don't consider my opposition to the war any reason to believe you have less than my full support for the job you're doing and the cause you're fighting for. I suppose that's an easy sentiment to lay claim to. Perhaps, too, it sounds like a coward's way out or nothing more than a feeble attempt to salve my conscience. I wouldn't blame you for feeling that way, Tom, or for feeling I've betrayed you in some way. But know this: I think about you every day over there, and I wish you were home, making babies with my sister and tending fields beside my daddy or on your own place. You belong here, Tom. Of that, I am certain."

Reflecting on the letter, Joe muttered a quick prayer for his friend and pushed aside his earlier doubts about joining the protest. His conscience was clear, and he was a willing soldier, at least for today, in this war against the War.

A group of nearly one hundred had massed beneath a grove of ancient live oak trees, draped with Spanish moss. Most were collegians, but the crowd also contained several professors and a smattering of local high school students. By far the most notable personalities gathered among the group, however, were three women whose sons had died in Vietnam. Elliot Frankel had persuaded these Gold Star mothers to share their grief, as well as their rage against the war. Their presence alone had guaranteed news coverage of the event by local newspapers, radio and television stations.

Fifteen minutes past the three o'clock starting time, the rally began officially. As Elliot stood on a flimsy wooden podium welcoming the group, Joe scouted the crowd. Several faces surprised him, belonging to people he would not have suspected to have strong sentiments against the war. About half the group carried signs and placards with antiwar messages. But generally, the protesters appeared hesitant and uncertain, almost as if they lacked the will or backbone to carry forth their cause. They shuffled their feet restlessly as Elliot outlined the itinerary and introduced the speakers, including the three bereaved mothers.

Astute as always, Elliot had asked the newest addition to the Gold Star club to deliver the first speech. The ploy seemed like shameless exploitation to Joe, who had heard Elliot predict the woman would break into tears almost at the onset. His assumption proved correct. Speaking just two weeks after burying her son, the woman lasted less than a minute at the speaker's stand before dissolving into sobs. She was ushered to the side to regain her composure as Elliot made a public offering of condolence. Still, the deed was done. The mother's loss was fresh, and it struck a sympathetic chord with the crowd.

The next Gold Star mother's speech was equally brief and soft-spoken, but she made an impression on the protesters. "His name was Mike," she said, holding aloft an eight-by-ten photograph of a young man with blond hair. "He was my son, and he was killed last year in Vietnam. I miss him terribly. I always will. I do not believe he should have died over there. I wish there had never been a war in the first place. But most of all, I wish it would end."

People hung on those words, and the number of demonstrators was rising steadily as the third Gold Star mother took the podium. She appeared frail, but her voice was strong, and the woman delivered a resounding denouncement of the war. She tugged at heartstrings with fond reminiscing about her nineteen-year-old son and chilling details about his death. He had died on a routine mission in a village beside the Mekong River, she said. Viet Cong sympathizers had ambushed the patrol, killing three American soldiers, including her young son. The woman was crying softly as she finished her story.

"I came here today against the wishes of my husband," she concluded, taking a deep breath to control her tears. "He believes that I am betrayen the legacy of our son. But I felt it was important to add my voice to those who are callen for an end to this dreadful war." She paused, then added, "If for no other reason, then because I wish with all my heart that not one more mother would have to hear the awful news that her son has died in Vietnam."

Murmurs of sympathy rose from the crowd, which had quickly swelled to around two hundred fifty people. Soon, the hushed whispers turned to shouts of outrage as the protesters found their voice. Elliot Frankel grabbed the megaphone, chanting the first of several antiwar messages. Immediately, others joined him, their voices clamoring underneath the afternoon sun. With Elliot and the three Gold Star mothers leading the way, the crowd surged from beneath the shady canopy of moss-laden oaks, committed to their goal of occupying the college's white-stucco administration building.

Traffic halted as the throng of protesters crossed the major thoroughfare that paralleled the college grounds, picking up recruits by the dozens as they invaded the campus. They marched past the gymnasium, moving along a winding road that cut through the heart of the campus, singing *We Shall Overcome* as they neared the administration building. By now, some three hundred people were active demonstrators, with half as many standing on the sidelines. Some of the onlookers were simply curious; others derided the protesters.

"I'm glad you came," a voice whispered behind Joe as he trudged along the road.

Turning around, he found Karen Baxter beside him, holding a heavy, painted placard. She lowered the sign and pressed against him as the crowd ground to a stop near the administration building.

"What about you, Joe?" Karen asked. "Are you glad you came?"

"No, Karen," he answered, wishing the woman was somewhere else, wondering how she had managed to find him in the crowd. "I can't say I'm glad to be here, or that I'm particularly proud of it. But I believe it's the right thing to do."

"Always a rebel with a cause," Karen smiled at him. "One day, Joe,

I'll probably regret giving you the big brush-off. Maybe you were right after all. We might have been good together."

"No, Karen," Joe said with a benign smile to mask his utter contempt for the woman. "I was dead wrong. Just slow to see it."

Her face was crestfallen as Joe turned away to survey the situation. A line of police officers, sheriff's deputies and state troopers had blocked the protesters' path to the administration building. Dressed like storm troopers, armed with billy clubs, rifles and tear gas canisters, wearing hideous gas masks, the lawmen had marshaled their forces about fifteen yards in front of the demonstrators' target.

Joe was wondering what would happen next when someone pushed against his back and someone else yelled in his direction. Catching his balance before stumbling, he whipped his head around to see who was causing the commotion and found himself staring into a photographer's camera lens. He glanced away almost immediately, though not before the shutter exploded several times.

Seconds later, Elliot Frankel leapt atop the front hood of a blue Pontiac parked on the street and raised the megaphone above his head in a wordless demand for silence. The crowd quieted almost at once, with only the occasional sound of static from the police radios piercing the quietness. When he commanded the group's full attention, Elliot lifted the megaphone to speak.

"In the scheme of things," he began, "what we are doing here today may not matter much to many. But it is important. There have been bigger and better-organized peace marches, and there will be more. Thousands already have marched on our nation's capital to criticize this immoral war. Doves are on the march in cities and towns all across our country. Students are rising up on university and college campuses with reputations far exceeding that of VSC. Still, our protest is equally important. The powers-that-be cannot dismiss our actions as any less important than those who march on Washington. We are a part of the groundswell of voices against the war rising up in this nation. We are just as committed to the cause of peace as those we see on TV. We are just as committed as those who protested for peace on the bloody streets of Chicago several weeks ago. Our voices count."

A smattering of applause greeted his message, and Elliot seized the moment like a seasoned politician. "You and I," he said, before pausing until the noise died. "You and I," he declared, "are here today because we believe the American government is waging an unjust and unnecessary war on the people of Vietnam and on the people of the United

States. Our government is sending thousands of young men—our friends, sons and brothers—to perpetuate unspeakable acts of violence in that little corner of Southeast Asia. The politicians tell us America is fighting in Vietnam because the Vietnamese people want us, because our presence is necessary to stop the spread of communism. They are noble intentions, perhaps. But when the very people who supposedly want them there kill our troops, I'm not convinced America is welcomed in Vietnam. And I'm not convinced the threat of communism in Vietnam or any other country in Southeast Asia merits enough concern to warrant the loss of thousands of American lives.

"I am Jewish, and I still shudder today at the atrocities committed against my people in another war not so long ago. I was not born when Hitler and the Nazis tried to exterminate Jews. But my relatives were there. Some died in those horrible gas chambers at Auschwitz. Others starved in Dachau. My parents were fortunate. They fled from Germany to the United States. They saw this country as a beacon of hope, and they believed in its greatness.

"That's one of the reasons I'm ashamed today—ashamed to see the government of the United States of America committing similar atrocities on the people of Vietnam. Maybe six million Vietnamese people have not yet died in the five years we've been fighting over there, but plenty have. Even more have suffered unimaginable pain from weapons that are every bit as vile as Hitler's gas chambers, weapons that never should have been invented, much less used on fellow human beings.

"My generation grew up fearful of the Bomb, that awesome weapon of destruction that obliterated two cities and thousands of people in a matter of seconds. The Bomb is frightening, but I wonder whether the Bomb is as gruesome as napalm.

"Do you folks know what napalm is?" Elliot asked, pausing like a teacher waiting for an answer.

"Napalm," he continued at length. "Napalm is a chemical weapon used by our military in Vietnam. Jet fighters fly over the lucky village of the hour, and they drop napalm bombs. There's no distinction between the good guys and the bad guys. Napalm sticks to the flesh of mothers, fathers and children, grandmothers, aunts and uncles. And it literally melts their flesh."

His tone, which had been thunderous at times, slowed as Elliot allowed every word to sink in deep and strike close to home among the crowd.

Without warning, he drew a cigarette lighter from the front pocket of his tie-dyed T-shirt and lit it. Everyone—protesters, police and by-standers—watched with rapt attention. With his eyes fixed solidly on the crowd, Elliot raised his arm and moved the lighter beneath one of his hairy wrists. The flame incinerated the black hairs, sending a wisp of smoke rising in the air and sparking an audible gasp of horror among the crowd.

"Napalm hurts," he said in carefully measured words. "It burns. The pain is excruciating. And children in Vietnam, and their parents, too, wish the pain would stop.

"Just like this." He snapped the lighter shut, flinching as the flame died. "But friends, if you're in Vietnam and you've been napalmed, the pain doesn't stop. It just goes on and on and on."

Elliot studied the crowd, almost as if he were searching their eyes for signs of commitment. Everyone regarded him with awe, the respectful silence broken only by the weeping of the three Gold Star mothers in the audience and occasional muffled sobs in the crowd. Joe, too, was mesmerized by the moment. His earlier reluctance to join the protest waned in the depths of Elliot's commitment to the antiwar cause. He felt as if he had witnessed history, a moment as memorable as Lincoln's address at Gettysburg or Franklin Delano Roosevelt's declaration of war in 1941.

Elliot cleared his throat at last, then raised the megaphone once more to his mouth. Speaking in measured words once again, he resumed the indictment of U.S. involvement in Vietnam. "I do not want my government committing acts of savagery in my name, and I know many of you share that point of view," he declared. "I love America. I want my country to be great. But today, I am ashamed of America.

"In ordinary times, I would not advocate defiance of authority," he continued, the tempo of his words slowly increasing. "But these are not ordinary times. It's 1968, and the world is a frightening place. For many of us, it's hard to see what's wrong, especially when we're gathered on this sun-splashed day enjoying our freedom and the right to exercise it. But ten thousand miles from here in another world—a hellish place of war—people like you and me are in pain, and they are dying. Some are Vietnamese children with napalm melting their skin. Others are American soldiers with shrapnel in their guts. Their conditions are most unordinary, and we must let our voices of protest be heard, so that the suffering does not continue."

Elliot paused to catch his breath, baiting the crowd with his silence as they willed him to continue. A long moment later, he obliged them.

"Many of us—and I've counted myself among them—can sit

snugly over here and ignore the war because it's a long way from home," he said. "Some of us, too, have the luxury of student deferrals because we attend college. But the deferrals are ending my friends. I know that personally because I got a notice from the local draft board in Jamaica, New York, last week, telling me to report for a physical. They say I'm headed for boot camp; I'm not convinced."

Murmurs rippled through the crowd at this revelation, and Elliot seized the opportunity for a moment of dramatic silence before declaring, "This is not a war I intend to fight."

Again, he paused, allowing the onlookers to ponder the intent of those last words. "To end this war," he continued in quickened tones, "it will take acts of defiance and disobedience, and that is precisely what I intend to do. I need your help, too. And I would like to have your promise to act peacefully, whatever course of action you may choose. But I do hope you will heed your conscience and act."

Pausing, giving people time to wonder what he would ask of them, Elliot made a careful sweep of the crowd, seeming to make eye contact with each of the protestors. Finally, he raised the megaphone once more to speak. "When I give the signal, calmly march past these officers and try to make your way into the administration building," Elliot continued after giving the protesters a short moment to consider his request. "It will be a small act of defiance; but it will be one of the ripples of discontent spreading across this nation, sending a signal loud and clear to our leaders in Washington; a strong message that Americans will no longer tolerate a war that is immoral and unjustified."

With the crowd almost breathlessly quiet, Elliot lowered the megaphone, placed it upright on the blue car hood and reached inside his shirt pocket, pulling out his draft card, holding it aloft for everyone to see. In a surreal second, the cigarette lighter appeared almost magically from the pocket of his ragged blue jeans. A flame of brazen glory arced, and Elliot Frankel blazed his way into the annals of local folk history.

The ensuing silence was deafening, the moment reverent like a candlelight vigil, until another young man standing near the forefront of protesters incinerated his draft card, too.

For a moment, the cops seemed confused by the two men's actions. But only a moment.

In rapid-fire order, they regrouped, rushing to quell the illegal act. Someone yelled and pandemonium erupted. The crowd surged forward, then broke apart as the police officers advanced. Some swarmed toward the administration building, others engaged in hand-to-hand combat with the lawmen. Two more young men burned their draft cards in open rebellion.

In the state of confusion, the Gold Star mothers were the only people who had a clear purpose in mind. Ignored and alone in the midst of the commotion, the three women marched into the administration building and quietly occupied the office of the dean of academic affairs. Once seated in comfortable chairs, they sipped coffee served to them by the dean himself and discussed the tragedy of their sons' deaths.

Joe held his ground until he heard the first thud of wood crunching against bone and saw two beefy police officers tackle Elliot Frankel. The officers pummeled Elliot, cracking his skull with billy clubs, punching him and kicking him with booted feet. In a matter of seconds, Elliot lay sprawled on the ground, unconscious with blood seeping from his cracked skull. The police left him there to take aim at other protesters.

The sight of blood prodded Joe into action. He shook off his confusion over the mad turn of events, taking the first few cautious steps toward Elliot, coming suddenly face-to-face with a scrawny young man probably younger than himself. But the man wore the blue uniform of a police officer. They eyed each other quickly, testily, before the officer made a feeble attempt to lash Joe with a billy club. Joe dodged the blow, wrestled the club from the cop and hurled the man into the middle of a boisterous group of high school students. It was obvious these boys cared little about the war in Vietnam. But they loved a good fight, and Joe eyed the officer with a pang of sympathy as the roughhousers pounced on the man. The concern was short-lived, however, as Joe fixed his attention on Elliot's limp form.

Elliot lay still as death, oblivious to the surrounding turmoil he had caused. The brash New Yorker had paid a price for burning his draft card. Joe wondered whether the cost was worth it. And then he wondered whether Elliot still owed a balance due.

Joe faced a bitter decision. He fought the urge to walk away, to disavow this demonstration and Elliot. With one foolish act, Elliot had destroyed the moment. When people remembered this day, they would see Elliot perched on the car, with his draft card thrust skyward, curling under flames. Few would recall the man's stirring words or the disturbing image of burning flesh. Joe resented the theatrics. But more than that, he was offended.

He would have abandoned Elliot, except for an intruding sense that his criticism contained a self-righteous and sanctimonious tone. He had chosen his side the moment he joined the crowd of protesters, and he refused to be a fair-weather follower. And, too, Joe felt a sense of loyalty to Elliot. They had never seen eye-to-eye. They had come together as friends out of common interests. But it was their differences—or at least a healthy respect for each other and a willingness to listen to the other point of view—that had sealed their friendship. His mind made up, Joe bolted pell-mell into the jumbled mass of agitated men and women. He moved stealthily through the maze of arms and legs, finding the path to Elliot remarkably clear.

Five feet away from his fallen friend, something hard and cold struck Joe squarely in the chest. The collision reeled Joe, halting his progress. He was stunned by the unexpected more than any pain. Metal clanked against the pavement below him; muffled explosions popped all around him. Joe peered downward and caught the first whiff of tear gas.

The noxious fumes sucked away his breath. He gasped for fresh air but managed only to gulp his lungs full of the poisonous gas. His windpipe convulsed, his chest heaved and his eyes burned like fire.

Joe staggered forward, moving blindly, propelled by nothing more than disorientation. He tripped over Elliot's legs, crashed to the ground and buried his face against the pavement, searching for one breath of untainted air. Gagging, convinced the makers of this particular batch of tear gas had miscalculated the ingredients, concocting a lethal dose in the process, Joe feared he was losing consciousness.

Then, instinct took over. He cupped his hands, found a cleansing breath and took his bearings.

Pandemonium reigned around him. The tear gas had felled only a few demonstrators. Several women screamed and a few men moaned, all the victims of billy clubs. Most people were running wildly, trying to escape the expanding gas, with the cops in full pursuit.

In a moment, Joe decided what to do. Although the gas fumes were still overpowering, he pulled himself to his knees and scanned the grounds. He had a clear path to escape.

Using the chaos as cover, Joe hoisted Elliot over his shoulder and calmly stole away unnoticed by the police. Ignoring the curious eyes of passersby, he willed himself strength and strode across campus. Upon reaching his Volkswagen, he allowed himself a furtive backward glance and found the trail still clear. Assured, he opened the car door, pushed Elliot into the passenger side and drove quickly away.